THE
DIVINITIES

Parker Bilal is the author of the Makana Investigations series, the third of which, *The Ghost Runner*, was longlisted for the Theakston's Old Peculier Crime Novel of the Year Award. *The Divinities*, the first in his Crane & Drake London crime series, was published in 2019. Parker Bilal is the pseudonym of Jamal Mahjoub, the critically acclaimed literary novelist. Born in London, he has lived in a number of places, including the UK, Denmark, Spain and, currently, the Netherlands.

@Parker_Bilal | jamalmahjoub.com

Also by Parker Bilal

The Heights
The Trenches
Whitehavens

THE DIVINITIES

PARKER BILAL

CANONGATE

The streets that Balboa walked were his own private ocean,

and Balboa was drowning.

August Wilson
'The Best Blues Singer in the World'

This paperback edition first published in Great Britain,
the USA and Canada in 2021 by Canongate Books Ltd,
14 High Street, Edinburgh EH1 1TE

Distributed in the USA by Publishers Group West
and in Canada by Publishers Group Canada

First published in 2019 by The Indigo Press,
50 Albemarle Street, London, W1S 4BD

canongate.co.uk

1

British Library Cataloguing-in-Publication Data
A catalogue record for this book is available on request from the British Library

ISBN 978 1 83885 514 7

Typeset by Palimpsest Book Production Ltd, Falkirk, Stirlingshire, Scotland
Printed and bound in Great Britain by Clays Ltd, Elcograf S.p.A.

CHAPTER 1

Cal Drake swayed, struggling a little to control the stream of piss that he was aiming at the dark, shadowy corner, while resting a hand on the wall to steady himself. His head buzzed and his stomach fizzed with acidic burn. It was gone four in the morning after a long night's boozing.

When he had finished he shook himself and zipped up before stepping back towards the car, an old BMW 3 Series, and the cup of coffee he had carefully placed on the roof. The Styrofoam had an evil chemical smell to it, the contents watery. Still, at this moment in time it was better than anything he'd ever tasted. He tossed his woollen hat through the open window onto the front seat, set the cup carefully back on the roof and took a bite out of his burger. The grease had seeped through the paper like glue. Swimming in fried onions and melted orange cheese, it was the kind of sustenance you didn't want to think too hard about. He took a deep breath and began to chew. A choice meal at a poncey restaurant in Park Lane couldn't have tasted better.

Not that he had much chance of ever making that particular comparison.

The sleet had eased off finally, leaving the streets slick with a wet, icy sheen. His breath came out in gushes of steam. Poker night. The Thursday night game was a regular fixture organized by an old army mate. He squinted at his watch, trying to focus. Where was he actually? Somewhere off the High Road in Balham. It was hardly worth going home. He might as well drive back to Raven Hill and get an hour's sleep on the backseat before the day began. The prospect of what lay ahead of him only made his spirits sink further and he took another bite out of his burger, swilling it down with the scalding hot coffee.

The shout came from behind him. Over his shoulder, Drake saw a woman standing in the middle of the brightly lit forecourt of the Texaco station, alongside a silver Audi A3. Nice. She wasn't too bad herself. Classy. She seemed to glow in the cold, artificial light. What she was doing around here at this time of the morning was anybody's guess. The car and the clothes said businesswoman, estate agent, maybe, on her way down to an early meeting. Failing that, a high-end working girl on her way home from a wealthy client.

All of this flashed through Drake's mind in a split second. His chewing slowed as his eyes settled on the scooter racing towards him. The kid clutching the handlebars wore a balaclava pulled tight over his face. Despite the fact that it was still dark, the one riding pillion had on Ray-Bans, probably knock-offs by the way they sat lopsided on his nose. It was this one who was holding the woman's phone. As the scooter came off the forecourt the rider had a choice. Left or right. He made the wrong call.

A tall, green wheelie bin with its flap down was parked on the kerb. Stepping into the road, Drake lifted as he swung, turning the way a dancer might spin his partner into the air, the bin gaining momentum before he launched it hard along the road.

The bin torpedoed straight into the front wheel of the scooter, knocking it sideways and sending bike and passengers skidding along the road. The engine gave a high-pitched whine in protest. Drake walked into the middle of the road. He could see now that they were just kids in their teens. Ray-Ban lay face up, gasping for air. He watched as Drake stepped over him to retrieve the phone, struggling to right himself.

'Stay,' said Drake. The kid stayed.

The driver had hurt his arm. He was on his knees swearing, clutching his elbow. When he saw Drake he tried to get up, managing to rise onto one knee. A flick-knife appeared from inside the bomber jacket. It snapped open with a sharp mechanical click to expose a short, nasty blade.

'You don't want to do that.'

With a growl the boy got his feet under him and charged.

Drake wasn't in the same shape he had been in the army. Soft living and poor diet had contributed to the decline, but he still had the moves. He turned into the charge, deflecting the half-hearted thrust and using the boy's own momentum to flip him over. He landed heavily on his back, the wind knocked out of his lungs. He was still holding onto the knife. Drake planted his boot on his wrist and the boy squealed. The knife clattered along the ground as Drake kicked it away.

'It's against the law to attack an officer of the law.'

'You wot? That's police brutality!'

'Get a life,' muttered Drake.

He turned as the woman came rushing over. At close quarters it became clear that she was older than she had first appeared. Clearly she'd made an effort some hours ago to look younger, but with dawn fast approaching the magic was wearing off.

'Oh my god, how can I thank you?' She was going through her bag. 'Please, take this.' Drake glanced at the fifty pound note she was holding out. His first instinct was to turn it down. But there was something about her, the way she looked at him. Not a call girl. She was more scared of him than of the kids who had just tried to rob her. The way she was standing just out of reach, as if he might be contagious or something. He plucked the note from her outstretched fingers and turned away. The kids were scrambling to their feet, trying to get the scooter up, pushing it along to get the thing started again.

'Shouldn't we call the police or something?'

'Waste of time,' said Drake. 'Nothing that would ever stick.'

She was looking at him in a strange way, watching him tuck the note into his pocket as if she was considering asking for it back.

'Have a nice day,' he said, over his shoulder.

The coffee had cooled down to the point where it tasted like washing-up liquid. He drank it all the same. His head was still buzzing. The burger had congealed into an indescribable mass. He wrapped it up again and looked for somewhere to throw it.

The sound of a helicopter closing in overhead made him freeze involuntarily. He looked up as the searchlight drew near. He could hear the high whoop of sirens approaching as the phone in his pocket began to buzz.

CHAPTER 2

Drake had no idea what Magnolia Quays was, let alone where. It turned out to be a development tucked into a bend on the river off the York Road in Battersea, just north of Wandsworth Bridge. As he drew closer he could see that the area had succumbed to the same wave of change that seemed to be transforming every nook and cranny of this city. Where there used to be old warehouses and storage facilities now there was plywood fencing. Cranes, scaffolding and the muddy tracks of large vehicles fishtailing across the road.

It was warm for the time of year. The sky was smeared with a greasy layer of low cloud that sealed the town in. People dreamed of clear, cold nights, pure white flakes of snow tumbling from a starry sky. Something that might turn back the clocks to a time when fairy tales were still believable. Back to an age when black and white was a description of your television set.

Drake had known this river all his life. It had grace if not beauty. Dirty and tired, shuffling along as best it could, like everyone else. People spoke of rivers as timeless, as if they were eternal, but this one was constantly changing. Every day, every minute. The movement of the water, the flow, the height, the slow shifting sediment surging beneath its surface. It carried time like a bad memory. A river was about change, but it was also about the things you could never forget.

DC Kelly Marsh was sheltering by the entrance to the building site. A lanky, awkward-looking figure with jet-black hair cut in a punky, aggressive style. She greeted Drake with a sniff. 'You look worse than I feel.'

'And good morning to you, too. Seen Milo?' he asked.

'He's around somewhere.'

Drake felt the rain running down his neck and pulled up the hood of his parka. 'So what have we got?'

'The usual. Looks like a couple of kids got in overnight and managed to bury themselves alive.' Kelly pointed across the open space of the building site.

Drake glanced back the way he had come. 'How easy is it to get in?'

'Well, it's not Fort Knox, that much I can tell you.'

Drake ran an eye along the perimeter fence. It wasn't as hard as it looked. Nothing kids like more than a challenge. There was always a spot that had been overlooked. A lamp post that could be climbed, a weakness in the fence.

'Did you take a look?' he asked.

'Negative. Thought I'd wait for you.'

'Okay, let's give it a whirl.'

They wandered from the entrance towards the centre of the site where a deep square hole had been excavated.

'What is that?'

Kelly shrugged. 'My guess is a car park, or maybe one of those underground pools everyone is crazy about?'

He stared at her. 'People do that?'

'You wouldn't believe the things people are willing to pay for.'

'I'll take your word for it.'

On the rim of the hole a dumper truck was parked, its loader bed cranked all the way up on a gleaming hydraulic shaft. The cab door hung open. Drake peered inside. The upholstery was slick with rain. The green paintwork and the interior of the cab were all shiny, which would do a nice job of messing up the forensic work. So far this looked like a case of accidental death. Nothing more sinister than a couple of kids getting into more trouble than they bargained for.

They walked to the edge and looked down into the pit. It was about thirty metres across and five or six deep. A muddy hole, pooling with iridescent water. The glints of colour seemed out of place against all that grey. Right now the centrepiece of this montage was an untidy pyramid of grey rock, industrial gravel, small limestone chips used for mixing into cement or laying on forecourts. Again, nothing out of place on a construction site.

'What's wrong with this picture?' Drake muttered.

For starters, there was the hand sticking up out of the mound of rock as if reaching for the sky. The hand was attached to a grey figure, buried up to its chest. One of two. They faced each other and appeared to be clinging to one another.

'I thought you said they were kids.'

Kelly tilted her head. 'That's what the uniforms said.'

Drake led the way down the muddy ramp, trying not to slip. 'Never repeat what they tell you unless you're sure.'

'Aye, aye, sir.'

Drake would have looked to see if she was taking the piss, but he didn't want to risk slipping, so kept his eyes glued to the ground in front of him. When they reached the bottom it was possible to get the measure of what it must have been like. Looking up at the battered steel slide perched on the rim above, it wasn't hard to imagine the horror of seeing that rock falling. A weird game that had gone wrong?

Drake was beginning to get a bad feeling about this. The hand didn't look like a child's. And there was something about the shape of the victims' heads. It was hard to be sure from this angle. He circled around the base of the mound. The heads were covered in a layer of rock dust that had been turned to the same grey mass by the rain. He put a foot up and felt the rock start to slide beneath him.

'You sure you want to do that, sir?'

Drake paused to look at her, then lifted his other boot. Stones scattered left and right and he felt himself slide back. Maybe she had a point. He waited for it to stop.

'We should really call this in.'

'We're not calling it in till we know what it is.' Drake tried another step and felt himself sliding again as the mountain shifted beneath him. Kelly took a step back.

'Forensics are not going to thank you for contaminating it.'

'Thank you, DC Marsh.' Drake took two more steps quickly and prayed he didn't lose his balance. 'We're assessing the situation.'

'Right, sir.' She sounded unconvinced.

He stopped for a break halfway up. 'What do you see here, DC Marsh?'

'A lot of stones, sir.'

'Opportunity, is the answer to that one.'

'Right.' But there was now an element of interest in her voice. 'You think they'll let us keep it?'

'First on the scene counts for a lot.'

'Yes, but . . .' Kelly left the rest of it unsaid. She didn't have to spell it out.

'Let's live in hope.'

'Right.'

Drake didn't need reminding of what was at stake. He knew how easy it would be to fuck it up. But he could feel something here.

Something like his old self. He wanted to hold on to that. If it all went pear-shaped then they would be put back on liaison work, talking to teachers, community leaders and shopkeepers whose windows had been kicked in, trying to persuade kids that there was some purpose to life. The way he looked at it, he had nothing to lose.

Now that he was level with the top of the mound, Drake could see that the victims' heads were covered. Hoodies, he had thought when looking down from above, but up close he could see where the cloth had been torn away by the force of the rockfall. Not kids in sweatshirts. Rough canvas hoods. A man and a woman. Both had been badly battered by the rockfall. Coated in grey dust, they might have been carved out of stone. The man looked as though he was toiling at sea, caught in a wave, trying to rise up, to get free. But he wasn't going anywhere.

'We're calling it,' said Drake, without looking up.

'Sure?'

He was staring at what looked like a scrap of duct tape hanging from the man's wrist. 'Something here doesn't feel right.' Drake straightened up, fished his phone out of his jacket pocket and called Wheeler. The superintendent sounded as though he might have been asleep. He listened while Drake explained the situation.

'So, what are you saying. That they were tortured?' Wheeler asked.

'It's hard to say at this point.'

'Why are you on this and not Major Crimes?'

'It was called as a break in.' It was starting to rain again and Drake pulled his hood up. What worried him was that Wheeler didn't sound convinced. 'The caretaker who found the bodies thought some kids had got onto the site and had an accident.'

By rights the case should have been handed to Homicide and Major Crimes Command.

'So that makes you first officer on the scene.' There was a long silence. Drake cleared his voice.

'I'm qualified to handle it, sir. You know I am.'

'Are you sure about this, Cal?' asked Wheeler.

'It's been nearly two years, guv.' Drake took a deep breath. Two years of dealing with drunks and derelicts, kids stabbing one another, husbands battering wives and enough overdoses to fill the stands at Stamford Bridge. 'I'm ready.'

'I'll have to go out on a limb for you.'

'I know that, sir.'

There was a long silence down the line. Wheeler was chewing it over. 'HMCC is snowed under with work. That much I do know. They would be happy to pass on this one. But it means we have to bring it in, and fast.'

''Preciate it, guv.'

'Our reputation's on the line, Cal. If this goes belly up they're going to hang us out to dry.'

'Understood, sir.' Drake surveyed the mound of stone, the muddy site. The heavy drops spattering into the watery pools.

'Forty-eight hours, Cal. After that I'll have DCI Pryce breathing down my neck asking why his lot didn't get the case.'

'Got it.'

'Okay, you know the drill. Call in forensics and set up a crime scene.'

'As good as done, sir.'

'Don't make me regret this, Cal.'

'No, sir, I won't.'

'So?' Kelly was holding her hands up for an answer. 'What'd he say?'

'Forty-eight hours, then it's going to be taken away.'

'Shit! Well, at least that's something.'

'Call it in to forensics. Ask for Archie Narayan at the Coroner's Office.'

'Gotcha.'

Drake squatted down to get a better look. Drops fell onto the battered faces. There was something undeniably, painfully human about the suffering conveyed in these two figures. The rain was clearing the man's face. He was not young. Perhaps in his late fifties, maybe older. Oriental features. Before he tucked his phone away, Drake took a couple of pictures.

'Does he look Oriental to you?'

'Oriental? Is that acceptable nowadays?'

'You know what I mean.'

Kelly shook her head. 'Japanese. I used to go out with one.'

Drake looked over at her. 'Real Japanese, or one parent or something?'

'Real Japanese.'

'Not adopted?' Drake went back to studying the victims' positions.

'Not adopted. Kosher.'

'Kosher Japanese, that's a new one. How did that work out for you?'

Kelly shrugged. 'He had issues.'

'I'll bet.' Drake was only half listening, his mind filtering out what was relevant to the current situation. 'Okay, let's go with Japanese for the moment. So, I'm guessing not a labourer. Could he be working on the project as an engineer of some kind?'

'How about prospective buyer?' Kelly nodded. 'Don't look like they come cheap.'

Drake followed her gaze. A billboard alongside the gate displayed a computer-simulated image of the finished product. Slick and clean. Happy couples pushing strollers. Men in suits. Young women on telephones. Everybody smiling. The tagline ran along the bottom: LUXURY APARTMENTS WITH A TIMELESS VIEW. It made it sound as if you were paying for a slice of eternity.

The shoulders and torsos of the victims looked as though they had been stamped on by a herd of wild animals. Shards of bone protruded, trapped in dark patches of blood. The couple were lying almost on top of one another, wrapped in each other's embrace. Out of fear, terror, love?

Their upper bodies were twisted as if they had been trying to wrestle free from the weight of rubble. How long had they been aware of what was going to happen to them? They had been wrapped in canvas shrouds and bound with duct tape. The hand reaching upwards was evidence that the man had managed to tear one arm free. He was clearly scrabbling to get loose at the moment of death. The woman's face was a picture of torment, her mouth open in a permanent scream.

Had the killer been working alone? If so he would have had to walk back up the ramp to operate the truck.

'Let's see if we can find something to protect them from the elements.' The rain risked dissolving everything into a grey, muddy mass. Kelly disappeared and came back with a tarpaulin.

'You sure this is a good idea?' She looked up at him as he began dragging it up over the bodies. 'I mean, from a forensic standpoint?'

'It's either this or watching valuable evidence getting washed away. We can't take that chance.'

'You're the boss.'

There was something about these grey figures that jolted him, took him straight back to Iraq. The dusty brutality of it. Something ancient, medieval.

In Iraq, people would often talk about home; what they missed. Something that had never bothered him. He'd joined up to get away from this place, this life, himself. If the circumstances had allowed it he might have stayed there. There was nothing to go back to. A missing father, a mother with a drink problem, and a country he wasn't sure he belonged in. In Iraq, dusty, broken down and alien as it was, he had felt at ease, perhaps for the first time in his life.

'What's the name of that place in Italy,' Kelly asked, breaking into his thoughts. 'You know, where everyone was buried in ash from the nearby volcano?'

'Pompeii.'

'That's the one.'

They walked back up the ramp to wait for the forensics team to arrive. DC Milo Kowalski had appeared. He was wearing a bright red anorak that was slick with rain, and he was smiling.

'Looks like an excavation.'

'A what?'

'You know, like a dig.'

Kelly was scowling. 'Do me a favour, Milo, don't go getting religious on me.'

'No, not religious. Palaeontology. It's in the clay.' Drake looked back down, wondering if he'd missed something. Milo continued. 'London Clay. The city's built on it. Everything. It was formed in the days when dinosaurs still walked the earth.'

'You make this stuff up, right?'

Kelly laughed. 'You know he doesn't.' She was right, of course. This was Milo's speciality, knowing things. His glasses were speckled with rain. He pushed them back up his nose.

'The whole city is a massive burial ground. Didn't you know that?'

'No, Milo, we didn't know.' Kelly rolled her eyes.

'We have forty-eight hours, Milo,' said Drake. 'So we need to move fast.'

'Gotcha, chief.'

Drake shivered. The wind off the river cut through his damp parka.

'Let's go over what we have so far. Who found them?'

'Feller who opens the place up in the mornings.' Kelly flipped through her notebook. 'A Mr . . . Cataract.' She muttered a curse at the rain-spattered page flapping in the wind. 'Christ, I can't even read my own handwriting.'

Drake looked up at the concrete frame of the building that curved around them in an arch. He imagined this might be what it felt like to be in the middle of a stage.

'It's almost as if he wanted the world to see this, to see how they suffered.'

'Come again?' Kelly pushed wet hair out of her eyes.

'I mean, why here?'

'Sorry?'

Through the gap between the two sides of the building's skeleton the river was visible. The rain was picking up, spitting thick lashes of it into the air, pitting the surface like a thousand invisible dancing demons.

'Why this particular spot?'

'Maybe he liked the view?' shrugged Milo. 'In medieval times they threw women into this river. For witchcraft, you know? Only the ones with magical powers floated.'

'So the innocent drowned? Nice logic,' Kelly muttered. 'Damned if you do and damned if you don't.'

The view. To define what had changed about London you could begin here. Luxury waterfront developments now cluttered the riverside, north, but mostly south. Everyone wanted a piece of the timeless river. The legend. The lore. Plain old romanticism. It wasn't just the river, of course, that was an added benefit. It was all part and parcel of the mechanism that was summoning the super-rich to this city like vampires to a bloodfest. They didn't so much live in the city as float high above it, dropping by on the circuit of their global empires. They were fast turning the city into a dead zone in which mere mortals had no place. And there was no sign of it letting up any time soon.

'Let's talk to the caretaker, the one who found them.'

'Mr Cricket?' Kelly stared off towards a stack of Portakabins by the perimeter fence. 'Not much of a talker.'

'How's his English?'

Kelly waggled a hand. 'Touch and go.'

'That bad?'

'The uniforms say they can't even tell what language he's speaking.'

'He's not putting it on?'

'No, he seems keen to cooperate. We just can't understand fuck all of what he's saying.'

Kelly hailed from the west coast of Scotland somewhere. When she swore, which was fairly frequently, it sounded almost exotic to Drake, like you might feel hearing someone swear in Italian, or Greek.

Overhead a jet airliner screeched down the flight path towards Heathrow. In the grand scheme of things two dead people on a construction site in South London didn't amount to much. The world rolled on.

CHAPTER 3

Sunlight broke through the cloud cover, throwing a sudden flourish of colour over the scene. It put Drake in mind of a school visit to the National Portrait Gallery. How old was he then? Eleven, twelve? He'd been in care at the time. One of his mother's bad moments. No space for him while she was battling her demons. His father was off too, on one of his regular jaunts. You never knew where he went, or when he would be back, if at all.

The visit came as a distraction, but also as a revelation. He remembered the solid building. The sense of calm, of history being firmly held in place by heavy stones. And he remembered the paintings of the old masters. He'd never seen anything like it, would never have dreamed of going in there on his own. He didn't understand art then, couldn't really claim to now. At one point the teacher said something that had stuck with him. She said, think of each painting as a window into the mind of someone who once walked the earth hundreds of years ago. That hit him. The idea of cutting across time, that this frame was a doorway that allowed him to look back, to see the world the way some painter who was now a pile of bones in the ground had seen things centuries ago. He was just this dumb kid. He knew he was looking at his own death; one day he too would be gone and there would be nothing, not even a scrap of canvas to remember him by.

Over by the gates, the forensics team had arrived and was getting suited up. Between the blue jumpsuits Drake spotted Archie Narayan, everyone trying to give him a wide berth. Drake took one last look back at the crime scene. In a moment it would be sealed off and swamped by a layer of scientific professionals, protective tents, forensics officers, suited and booted. He wanted to remember it as it was, raw, the way the killer would have seen it as he walked away.

Drake didn't know much about the construction business, but someone had dreamed up a fancy name for this one. Magnolia Quays. A fantasy handle to fit the delirious price tag. Right now it was just a muddy hole in the ground, pitched up against the river, fenced off from the road by high siding decked with Klieg lights, warnings about guard dogs and security sweeps. As if that ever helped. Drake spotted a number of smaller logos on the advertising hoarding.

'Do we have a note of those?'

'Already done, chief.' Kelly held up her iPhone to show him the picture she had taken. 'Don't go getting any ideas. Prices start at three million.'

'All good things come to those who wait, isn't that what they say?'

'You're asking the wrong person,' she shrugged. 'Uh oh.'

Drake followed her eye. In his tweed jacket and wellington boots, the chief pathologist was striding towards them. A dinosaur wading towards its own extinction.

'Let's give the honourable doctor some space.'

'Right you are, chief.'

Every time she called him that, it reminded him that he had been demoted from Inspector back to Detective Sergeant. There was no reason for him to make that connection, he just did; the fact that his career, to all intents and purposes, had stalled.

Drake nodded in the direction of the crowd that was gathering by the gate. Casual labourers turning up in the hope of work.

'Let's make sure we have a record of everyone who's been in and out of this place in the last few months.'

The construction business was like the collision of two alien worlds. On the one hand, there were the clients paying astronomical sums for their little slice of heaven. A chance to fence themselves off from the masses. Qataris, Kuwaitis, Russians, along with all manner of wealthy globetrotters. Money-laden moguls from around the world eager to plough their cash into London Clay, hoping to spin it into gold. On the flip side of that coin were the wary-looking workers who now stood in cheap, sodden jackets huddling from the rain just beyond the crime-scene tape. It put Drake in mind of a picture his mother used to have hanging on her wall. A black-and-white photo of Mohawks balancing along girders high above New York City. The Native Americans who built the first skyscrapers on land their ancestors had inhabited for generations. It wasn't quite the same here. These people came from all over the shop, Eastern Europe, South Asia, Africa, the Far East, you name it. They toiled on muddy building sites, picking up irregular wages while constructing little palaces for the super-rich. They lived in crowded rooms, flats and terraced houses converted into flimsy barracks, dirty, overcrowded, submerged from contact with officialdom of any kind.

'This is their Klondike,' Cal said, hardly aware that he was speaking aloud.

'Sorry, chief?'

'We need to round them up before they vanish into the woodwork. Gently does it, Kelly. We don't want to spook anyone. We just need to talk to them. And we need to speak to the site manager.'

'Gotcha.'

As she walked off to speak to a couple of uniforms Drake turned his attention back to Archie Narayan who was fast approaching.

'Surprised to see you here.' Drops of rain pooled at the ends of his silvery hair like pearls. His eyebrows were bushy shoots of grey bobbing in the air like insect feelers.

'It was called in as a couple of kids trespassing.'

'And they handed it to you?' The eyebrows lifted.

'Thanks for the vote of confidence.'

'You know what I mean.' The coroner was gazing down at the bodies. 'Looks like someone's been scrambling all over there. Who put that tarp up?'

'I was trying to protect the evidence.'

'I might have guessed. Who uncovered them?'

'Caretaker. Saw a hand and started digging.'

'Christ!' the coroner wailed. 'It's a free-for-all. Why didn't he just call the police?'

'He thought he could save someone. Also, and I'm going to stick my neck out here, I'd say that where he comes from, the police are not their friends.'

'That sounds about right.' Archie Narayan's sharp eyes studied Drake. 'How long is it since you handled a real murder investigation?'

'It's like riding a bike, doc.'

'I wouldn't bet on it.'

'Until they take it away, I'm the one you're working with, so, what can you tell me?'

'Aren't you going to let me at least take a closer look?'

'First impressions. They were buried alive, right?'

'I wouldn't know, I forgot to bring my crystal ball.' Archie sighed. 'I'll give you a simple answer. Wait for my report.' In the old days the coroner had been a svelte figure, half-a-dozen sizes smaller. Now he was Falstaff.

'Morning, sir.' Predictably, Kelly's cheerful greeting drew a scowl from the coroner.

'And you are?'

'DC Marsh, sir.'

'Of course you are.' The scowl soured into an acid smile.

'Any ideas why anyone would dump a ton of stone on a living person?'

He gave her a withering look. 'Perhaps the perpetrator doesn't like getting his hands dirty.'

'Is he always that cheerful?' Kelly asked as they watched Narayan walk away.

'Archie is an acquired taste.'

'What was wrong with my question?'

'It's not personal. He treats everyone the same way.'

'You're saying I should take it because I'm a woman?'

'Not exactly what I meant.' Drake glanced at his watch. 'Let's focus on the location. Either our killer has some connection to this place, or he's trying to send a message.'

'Might be easier if he wrote us a bloody letter.'

Trying to second-guess someone capable of killing in cold blood was a mug's game. Kelly rubbed her chin with the tip of her biro before scribbling in her notebook.

'What's Klondike?'

'Charlie Chaplin?' He glanced sideways at her.

The name meant something to her, but not enough.

'A place in the Yukon, Canada,' he went on. 'Famous gold deposits. People rushed out there by the thousand. It was a stampede. The classic example of a town being swamped by desperate workers.' Drake nodded at the crowd by the gates. 'Klondike.'

'You're a regular walking Wiki-fiend. Worse than Milo.'

'Do we have the site manager?'

'On the way. He had to drop his kids off at school.'

'At least someone's got his priorities straight. We need a list of anyone that has been sacked recently, anyone with a grudge.'

'You really think that's what this is?'

'More often than not, the best answer is the one staring you in the face. Forty-eight hours, Kelly, then it's out of our hands.'

'I hear you.'

'Find out who hasn't shown up for work this morning.'

Kelly pointed. 'One thing, there's a car parked out there.'

Drake followed her finger towards a mauve Porsche Cayenne visible through the open gates. It was already ringed by crime-scene tape. They walked out to take a look. When they got there Drake was careful not to touch anything, peering instead through the windows and seeing nothing out of the ordinary. A pile of papers on the back seat. Magazines, brochures of some kind. A cable to charge a telephone was attached to the dashboard panel.

'Did anyone run the plates?' Drake asked over his shoulder.

'It's registered to one Marsha Thwaite.'

'Thwaite? Where have I seen that name?'

Kelly was jerking a thumb over her shoulder. Drake looked up. Running across the bottom of the billboard behind her was the name Thwaite Property Group.

'Okay, well, that's going to change things.' Drake turned back to the car with renewed interest. It was parked under a street lamp. The kind of spot you might leave your car if you parked around here late at night. Perhaps there was a perfectly reasonable explanation. A glance up and down the deserted street told Drake that was unlikely.

The car was unlocked. The keys were still in the ignition. Kelly pulled on a pair of latex gloves and went round to the other side. A handbag had been pushed under the passenger seat. Inside was a driving licence. She held it out for him to look at.

'You think that could be her?' she asked.

'Could be.' Drake tried to match the picture to the image in his mind of the female victim he had just seen. A grey, petrified version of this face.

'Let's assume that it is her, until we can prove otherwise. Get onto the development company. Speak to an assistant, someone who knows Mr and Mrs Thwaite.'

'I'm on it.'

'And get forensics to run a full check. Where's Milo?'

'He's over by the site office.' Kelly turned away to use her phone. As they walked back towards the entrance to the site she looked up. 'Someone is going to call you. An assistant to the director, Mr Howard Thwaite.'

'If they haven't called in ten minutes we call them back.'

They found Milo sheltering from the rain in the lee of the site office. Drake tapped him on the shoulder.

'Try and find out if there is any CCTV on the approach road, or failing that, the closest in the vicinity.'

Milo pulled a tablet out from under his jacket and went to it. Drake pressed his back against the side of the shelter. The rain was coming down hard now, puddles danced on the glistening mud. He squinted through the rain at a couple of technicians in overalls dusting the lorry cab for prints. Forensics would carry on sifting patiently through every chip of stone in the hope that it might yield a clue. It was all time, the one thing they didn't have enough of. Drake suspected that when Wheeler discovered that the abandoned car of the property developer's wife had been found at the site, this case would take on another level of importance. Forty-eight hours would look like wishful thinking.

He turned his attention back to the crime scene. Water was dripping down his neck and he stamped his feet to keep the blood flowing.

Procedure was a waste of time, until it wasn't. There was always a chance the killer had been surprised, that he'd left the flatbed up and the door open because he'd departed in a hurry. Somehow, Drake knew that didn't chime with someone who had gone to all the trouble of setting this up. Choosing this location. The stone chips. Instinct told him this wasn't the type to leave fingerprints behind. Still, if criminals never made mistakes most of them would never be caught.

Kelly Marsh came back over. She was pointing to her phone.

'I've got Howard Thwaite's PR person.'

'Ask her to confirm who the car belongs to, and tell them we will be coming over to speak to Mr Thwaite. Make sure he stays where he is.'

Kelly nodded and turned away. She shook her head as she finished the call.

'Thwaite is waiting for us at his home. You really fancy him for this?'

'I'm trying not to jump to conclusions. Get the uniforms to sit on Thwaite until we get there. I mean, in the same room. We don't want him trying anything stupid.'

'Roger that.' As she turned away Kelly nodded towards the gate. 'Looks like things are about to get interesting.'

A sleek black saloon car was bumping over the uneven ground onto the site. When it came to a halt a uniformed driver leapt out, nearly losing his footing on the wet ground. The tall, awkward figure of Division Superintendent Dryden Wheeler unfolded itself from the rear. With a quick glance around him he strode towards Drake. Kelly made herself scarce.

'Didn't expect to see you here, sir.'

'You didn't tell me whose site this was.'

'You know Mr Thwaite, sir?'

'Howard Thwaite, yes, as a matter of fact, I do.' Wheeler's thick eyebrows knit themselves firmly together. 'Frankly, this complicates matters. Thwaite has a lot of friends in the House of Lords.'

'Always good to know, if I happen to be passing that way.'

The Yorkshireman was a good head taller than Cal. He glowered over him. 'This is going to draw the media in like flies to a shitstorm.'

'I still have forty-eight hours, right?'

Wheeler gave Drake a withering gaze. 'If this goes the way I think it might, you'll be wishing you'd never heard of this place.'

'I'm willing to take my chances.'

'Fair enough. On the positive side, my feeling is that Pryce is going to be wary of walking into this now.'

Wheeler was a politician first and a policeman second. Drake knew that much. Clearance rates, crime statistics, a clean sheet. It wasn't so much about policing at that level as management. When the Police Commissioners started calling you needed to have your house in order. Wheeler was a specialist in keeping his nose clean. He'd back you just so long as it was convenient. Right now he was calculating the fallout risk against possible gains. If Thwaite was to become prime suspect then every step they took would be under scrutiny. And the officer in charge of the case could find himself at the wrong end of an inquiry, which was the last thing Drake needed.

'What have we got so far?'

'Two victims. Female and male. Both look to be in their fifties or thereabouts. Hard to tell before the coroner gets to work.' Drake took a deep breath. 'We haven't ruled out the possibility that the female victim might be Thwaite's wife.'

'Bugger!' It wasn't clear if Wheeler was referring to the case, or the mud he was trying to scrape off his polished shoes without much success. 'We need to let him know.'

'I thought it might be best to do it in person.'

'I should bloody well hope so!' Wheeler broke off from worrying about his shoes. 'This is not your way of telling me you think Thwaite was involved?'

'At this point I'm not telling anyone anything.'

'Good, because to make an accusation like that you need to have brass bollocks the size of King Kong's.' Wheeler stared out over the killing ground. The rain had stopped for a time and the icy wind blew hard and cold across the muddy clay. Crows fluttered overhead like tattered flags. 'He's got a bloody knighthood,' he muttered. 'I'd better tag along with you.' Wheeler saw Drake's objection and waved it down before he could speak. 'You have no choice in the matter. We'll take your car. Mine can follow behind.'

Drake took a moment to fill Kelly in. 'He insists on coming along.'

'I don't like the way this is shaping up.'

'It might work in our favour.'

'Careful, chief, that sounded almost like optimism.'

'Let me know the moment the coroner mutters a word. However trivial it might seem.'

'Not sure he sees me as worthy of his time.'

'Just use your charms.'

'Not sure I like the sound of that.'

On the way over to Fulham, Drake had to listen to Wheeler laying down the guidelines.

'I'm taking a chance on you, Cal, so I want this run by the book. No fanciful leaps, no cutting corners. You have to keep me in the loop. Do I make myself clear?'

'Crystal.'

'No going off-script. Everything must be accountable. There will be a lot of eyes on this one. Don't make me regret giving you the case.'

'I'll do my best, sir.'

'Okay, so tell me: if we put aside this absurd notion that Howard Thwaite killed his own wife, what does your instinct tell you?'

Cal was silent for a moment. In his mind's eye he saw the crime scene once more. The barren, open stretch of ground, the lorry, the heap of rock chips.

'I don't know. There's something almost medieval about it.'

'Medieval?'

'The hoods . . . It's almost like the enactment of a ritual.'

'Interesting,' murmured Wheeler. His expression changed. 'What the hell is that smell?'

Drake had been wondering the same thing for days. Judging by the way Wheeler was looking at the car, it was worse than he had been telling himself.

'It's like something died in here. You shouldn't be using a personal vehicle for public service.'

'Our motor pool is down to just one car, and nobody ever seems to know who has it.'

'That can't be right.'

'It's fine, I just need to take it in for a service.'

'Don't bother, man. Just drive it to the dump and have done with it. Christ! How do you stand it?'

CHAPTER 4

Howard Thwaite owned a townhouse overlooking a leafy private square off the Fulham Road. Drake wondered vaguely how much it might have cost and then told himself he was wasting his time. A squad car was parked outside. Two uniforms stood shaking the rain off their hi-vis jackets as a brief ray of sunshine cut through the dense cloud.

'Anyone spoken to him?'

'Our orders were to leave it to you,' said the first one.

He had the sullen attitude of a man unhappy with his lot. Drake couldn't place him, though he recognized the distrust. It often felt as though he was walking in the shadow of his own ghost.

The front door swung open before they had reached the top of the front steps. A WPC was standing there, adjusting her hat in the mirror.

'We'll take it from here, constable,' Wheeler said, marching straight past her.

'Thank you, sir.'

The tiled floor was spotless. A staircase led upwards. Another, tucked behind it, led down to the basement. Cut flowers stood wilting in a vase under a coat stand. A muffled voice from below told them somebody was finishing a phone call. A moment later they heard him coming up the stairs and Howard Thwaite arrived in the room.

He was a spry figure in his early sixties. Dressed in a black polo neck and jeans, his greying hair shaven close to the skull.

Seeing Wheeler, his face fell. 'Dryden? Now I know something bad has happened.'

'Howard, I wish the circumstances could have been better.'

'What is this all about? They won't tell me anything. Is it to do with Marsha?'

Wheeler straighted up to full height. 'I'm afraid it's too early to say,' he said awkwardly, glancing at Drake before going on. 'This is Detective Sergeant Drake. He'll be in charge of the investigation.'

'I see.' Thwaite looked Drake over as if seeing him for the first time. 'We'd better go in here.'

He gestured towards a drawing room to the right. Drake waited for Wheeler to go first, then Thwaite walked right in front of him and took up a position by the ornamental fireplace. The room was crammed with heavy furniture and thick carpets. Built-in bookcases took up one side, while the other walls were crammed with expensive-looking paintings and framed photographs. To Drake it looked almost like a trophy room.

'Now, will one of you please tell me what the hell is going on?'

Drake cleared his throat. 'Might I ask when you last saw your wife, sir?'

'Yesterday morning. I was working at home. I have a studio downstairs. She was off to the theatre that evening. She said she wouldn't be returning from work.'

'Where does she work?'

'She runs a gallery, the Arcadia, in Beauchamp Place.'

'And that's normal, for you not to see each other?'

'It's fairly common.' Thwaite cocked a beady eye. 'We both work a great deal. During the week there are often days when we don't have much chance of meeting up until the evening.'

'Did you realize she had not come home?'

'Well, we sometimes sleep in separate rooms. I work late into the night and it's usually me who takes the spare room.' Thwaite broke off. 'This is really intolerable! What have you found? Is she hurt?'

With a glance at Wheeler, Drake went on. 'Two bodies were discovered early this morning on a building site in Battersea run by your company.'

'Two bodies?' Thwaite shook his head as if to clear it. 'And you think one of them is Marsha?'

'Your wife's car was found close to Magnolia Quays. It appears to have been parked there last night.'

There was a long silence. Drake carried on.

'Was there any reason Mrs Thwaite might have been visiting the place late in the evening?'

'No, of course not. None at all. She had nothing to do with the construction.'

Wheeler had installed himself on one of the sofas in the middle of the room, his hat perched on his knee. 'I know how distressing this must be, Howard, but any details you can give us might be vital.'

Thwaite didn't even register Wheeler's words. He put out a hand and gently eased himself into an armchair.

'You said there were two bodies.'

'That is correct, sir. The second victim is a male of about fifty to sixty years old. Also unidentified at this time.'

Thwaite stared lifelessly at the polished wooden floor. 'I assumed she had come in late. She went to the theatre. Usually she goes on afterwards to eat something.'

'Was she going with somebody?'

'A friend.' Thwaite's gaze came to rest on Drake. 'I don't have much patience with contemporary theatre. Something to do with my age, no doubt. I like the classics, Greek, Shakespeare, that kind of thing.'

'I'm sure,' said Drake, as if the state of contemporary theatre kept him awake at night. 'Do you happen to know the name of this friend?'

'I'm sorry. Mary? Diana?' Howard Thwaite shook his head. 'She told me, but I don't recall.'

'I'm sure you're not the first husband to be guilty of that,' Wheeler chuckled. Old pals, Drake recalled. The remark failed to draw a smile from Thwaite.

'How did they die?'

Drake closed the cover of his notebook. 'It's important to remember that we still have not identified Mrs Thwaite as being one of the victims.'

'You wouldn't be here if you didn't think there was a high probability it is her.'

'Until we have confirmation from the coroner's office we can't be sure.'

Thwaite glanced at Wheeler. 'Was it that bad?'

'As DS Drake has indicated, we'll know more when the forensic investigators have done their work.'

'I'm not asking for a detailed analysis. Just tell me how they died. Please.'

Drake hesitated. 'They appear to have been crushed by stone.'

'What?' Thwaite leaned forwards, his fingers white where they dug into the chair's arms.

There was a long silence. Thwaite's voice trembled as he spoke. 'They were alive at the time?'

'We don't know for sure.' Drake recalled the anguished

expressions on the faces protruding from the rock pile. 'But that seems likely.'

'My god.' Howard Thwaite glanced at Wheeler. 'I appreciate this, Dryden. Coming to me like this. It can't have been easy.' He fell silent.

'Is there someone we could call, Howard? A friend or relative?'

Thwaite didn't seem to hear. Drake took a moment to look around him. The paintings on the walls were a mix of old and new. In one, hunters gathered in a dark green landscape alongside horses slung with dead pheasants. Opposite this was what looked like a female Christ being crucified on Golgotha.

Between the French windows hung a number of framed photographs. These showed a smiling Thwaite, sometimes with his wife. They were in glamorous company. In one it was the Duke of Edinburgh, in the next someone who might have been Elton John. All dressed up as if attending a gala of some kind. Several were of people Drake did not recognize. Politicians, some of them. Thwaite's friends in Whitehall. Another set showed foreign locations. A villa in what might have been Spain or Greece. Others showed him wearing a hard hat in what appeared to be China.

'What can you tell us about Magnolia Quays?'

Thwaite stirred, coming back to the present. 'It's a luxury complex. Penthouse flats. First-class fittings. Excellent view.' He spoke as if reciting from memory.

'So, it's a major project, for you and your development firm?'

'Of course. This kind of thing is the future, and it's happening now. London is a global reference point and if you're not in the game you'll be sidelined by the competition.'

'You own the Thwaite Property Group?'

'I hold a majority of shares, along with Marsha, my wife.' The mention of her name gave him pause. 'Are you suggesting this might have been aimed at me in some way?'

'You're a big man, Mr Thwaite. People in your position have enemies.'

'Why would they hurt my wife?'

'Sometimes, to hurt someone you go after the things that matter to them.' Thwaite made no attempt to reply, so Drake continued. 'May I ask what were you doing last night, sir?'

'What?' Thwaite blinked in disbelief. 'You're asking me?'

'It's a formality. I have to ask. If you would just answer the question.'

'I was here. Working in my studio downstairs.'

'Alone?'

'I'm afraid so.' Thwaite glanced at Wheeler, who studied his hat.

'You said you worked late,' said Drake.

'Oh, I often lose track of time. It was after midnight. As you can imagine we're incredibly busy right now. Magnolia Quays is a big project. We have ongoing constructions all over the world, but this is London, our stomping ground, if you like.'

'Is there any reason that you can think of why your wife might have visited the site late last night?'

'None at all. Especially at that time. It makes no sense.'

'Could she have been showing the place to a potential buyer?'

'Absolutely not.' Thwaite frowned. 'I don't really understand where this is going.'

'That's all right, sir. I think that's all I need to know at this point. We'll need a full statement from you eventually.'

'Of course, anything.'

'And we may need you to identify the body formally at some point, if it turns out to be –'

'Are you sure there's nobody we can call?' Wheeler said.

'No, I . . .' Thwaite relented. 'Of course, there are people I should . . .'

Drake waited in the hall while Wheeler said his goodbyes. The door was not quite closed and he could hear Thwaite's urgent whispering.

'All I'm saying is that you might have found someone more senior.'

Outside, Wheeler stopped halfway to his car.

'You should have handled that a little better. At least you could have tried to go gently on him.'

'I thought I did.'

'You need to be discreet, Cal. A man like Howard Thwaite will automatically draw interest, from the press as well as anything else.'

Drake watched him climb into the Mercedes, the driver standing to attention to close the door shut before running round to the front. As the car pulled away, his eye caught the uniforms across the street. They stopped talking and looked away. Drake walked back to his car. The smell hadn't improved.

CHAPTER 5

Kelly Marsh led the way across to an ambulance where a small, wizened man with a grey beard was shrouded in a blanket and sipping tea. Mr Cricket. Not quite.

'Mr Karattack?' Kelly double-checked the name she had scribbled down in her notebook.

'Kardax, Kardax.' The man nodded vigorously, tapping his chest. 'Ali Kardax.'

'I understand you found them?' Kelly pointed over his shoulder. The man followed her hand. 'The bodies, right?'

This sparked a stream of words, some of which might have been in English, all of which were unintelligible. London was like a complex puzzle that you were forever trying to figure out. Kelly appealed to Drake.

'You see what I mean?'

'Slow down there,' he said.

'I'll make a call, maybe we can get an interpreter. I don't even know what language he's speaking.'

'Kurdish,' said Drake. 'It's Kurdish.'

'Right . . .'

'Kurmanji, I think. The common dialect in the Kurdish area.'

'Which you just happen to speak?' Kelly raised her eyebrows.

'I picked up a few words when I was stationed there. It's related to Persian.'

'If you say so, chief.'

'If he says what?'

They both turned to see Milo's lanky figure ambling towards them, coffee in hand.

'Here he is,' beamed Kelly. 'The boy wonder himself.'

Drake squatted down beside Mr Kardax. His face was lined and his eyes were deep and expressive. He seemed amused and nodded towards Milo.

'See if you can fetch a coffee for him,' Drake translated.

The witness smiled, nodding his appreciation. Clearly, he understood some English. Drake spoke, using the few words he could remember from his time in Kurdish Iraq.

'He comes every day at the same time. Every morning he opens the gates to let the workers in. There is no trouble here. Never trouble. Until today.'

It was all about tempo. Kardax was trying to speak English, but Drake suspected that Kelly had been going too quickly for him, and not listening carefully enough. Milo returned with the coffee. The gatekeeper grew more agitated and his speech became faster and less coherent until Drake finally had to give up. He turned aside, shaking his head.

'We need to make some calls and get a proper interpreter down here.'

'Aye, aye, boss.'

Inside the site offices the workers were gathered around the site supervisor, an overweight figure in a hi-vis jacket, a safety hat wobbling on his head. Clearly, not a happy man.

'You've got nothing to worry about,' he was saying, raising his voice to calm the storm. The men didn't look convinced. They pushed roughly past Drake on their way out.

'And you are?' the man called to Drake as he approached him.

Drake waved his badge. The man removed his hard hat, wiped the back of his hand across a sweaty forehead.

'We're thirty days behind schedule. If we don't finish on time we get penalized. You want to explain that to my boss?' He sounded Welsh and out of his depth. The room was small and cramped.

'Your first time out as supervisor?'

'No.' He glanced around the room as if wondering what had given him away. 'Second.'

'Okay, so,' Drake leaned forward to squint at the tag around his neck, 'Steven, you're going to call everyone and tell them that everything is on hold until we finish our work here.'

'Everyone?'

'Meaning: head office, suppliers, technicians, specialists, deliveries. The whole schedule is going to be put back.'

'You're not serious?'

'You've got two bodies lying out there in the rain, pal. This is not your average weekday.'

'Right.' Steven stared dumbly back at Drake, as if he'd said something offensive.

'Good. Then I need a list of all your employees, and I mean official and unofficial.' Drake held up a hand to stem the protests even before he had finished speaking.

The site supervisor screwed up his face scornfully. 'We don't even know half their names.'

'Then perhaps it's about time you did.'

He was younger than he had first appeared. Just a kid really, who'd no doubt been told to keep his head down and cut as many corners as he could. He was also probably terrified of most of the people in his charge.

'We don't want to scare anyone off, okay? Remind them we're not from Immigration Enforcement. We're after whoever did this. That's all. Whether they are here legally is not our concern. All I want is their cooperation.'

'They're not going to believe you. They don't trust any officials.'

'They trust you, right? Do it in person. They still want to work when this is over. All they have to do is answer some questions. Also, I'm interested in no-shows. Anyone who didn't turn up this morning, understand?'

His eyes darted left and right. He ran a hand over his mouth. 'I can't believe this is happening.'

Drake stepped closer. 'Are you on something?'

He stepped back clumsily, bumping into a wall. 'I have a condition.'

'Great. Well, try to keep it together.'

Outside, the workers were huddled by the fence. They had separated into small groups. Brits on one side, Europeans on another, with Asians, Arabs and all parts further afield making up a third faction. The one thing they shared was the worried look on their faces.

'We need to be quick,' Drake said. 'They are about ready to bolt.'

'Not a happy man,' Kelly observed as they watched the supervisor approaching his workers.

'He'll survive.'

In the distance, the SOCOs or crime-scene officers could be seen packing away their equipment to head back to the lab. Another group was still going over the truck, dusting doors, the interior, the buttons of the control box. The name on the side was Dobson Creek. Drake took in the whole scene. The hole in the ground, the tomb, as Milo would have it, and the backdrop of the cement skeleton and the river beyond. Somebody had gone to a lot of trouble to set up this killing ground. The question was why.

CHAPTER 6

Raven Hill was something of a lost outpost that had long been neglected. There were always rumours of a facelift in the offing, something involving paint and knocking through some plasterboard. Until that little miracle happened they would be stuck with cramped offices, nicotine-yellow walls and boxy corridors, along with tea-stained carpets and peeling wallpaper that almost gave it a retro 1980s look. Almost.

Coming back here six months ago, Drake had discovered that the police station had pretty much remained unchanged since he was sent north nearly two years ago. Anything that might be described as improvement was mostly superficial; new ceiling panels, a splash of colour here and there, a few posters encouraging officers to be creative in their approach, to apply 'blue sky thinking', whatever that was. The Murder Room, as it had always been known, remained essentially the same. True, they kept changing the name, which was clearly somebody's idea of progress. For a time it was the Violent Crime Unit, then it became Homicide and Serious

Crimes Command. It didn't change the nature of what they were dealing with, which was probably why everyone still called it the Murder Room.

Every other station Drake happened to visit seemed to be inhabited by eager young officers devoted to online abuse, cyber-stalking, physical stalking, bullying, along with a hit list of other twenty-first-century offences. They had open-plan workspaces, up-to-date computers, modern filing systems. Raven Hill seemed to be stuck in the dark ages. It wasn't that Drake longed for modernization. Far from it. He shuddered at the thought of those grey workspaces where people hunched silently over their keyboards, swiping their smart phones, and whispering to themselves.

Wheeler had been tasked with salvaging Raven Hill, although Drake often wondered if he was really there to oversee the station's dismantling and demise. Everything was moving towards centralizing the force around the Curtis Green building now known as New Scotland Yard.

Drake spotted Milo at his desk as he came in. He had boxed himself into a corner of the Murder Room using filing cabinets and flimsy walls. Less of an office and more of a fortress. His workspace was dominated by two oversized flat screens, along with countless other gadgets, all sewn together with cables.

'Any luck with the CCTV?'

'There are two cameras around the entrance to the site. One right overhead the Porsche we found. Problem is that both of them appear to be out of commission.'

'Coincidence or enemy action?'

'I've been on to the outfit that runs security. They promised to look into it.'

'Keep on at them, Milo. We're on a countdown. Time is not our friend.'

'Right, boss.'

Kelly appeared carrying bags of sandwiches and a tray of coffee. She went around the room delivering the orders, ending with Milo. Drake wound up empty handed.

'Sorry, chief, you weren't on the list.'

'I won't take it personally, but if I drink the stuff that comes out of the machine and it kills me, you'll only have yourself to blame.'

'We'll go into mourning. It's not personal.'

'It never is,' murmured Drake.

Someone had helpfully rolled a large notice board in to fence off one side. A large map of the city covered half of this. Drake stared at Magnolia Quays, wondering if the geographic location might have some significance. He ran a finger along the narrow cut that led away from the site to where it met the York Road. To the north and south of the site were warehouses.

'Did we check these?'

Kelly looked up from the croissant she was eating. 'There's nothing there. Converted or disused warehouses. An antique store, used furniture, that sort of thing, all awaiting extinction.'

He knew what she meant. In a couple of years they would be gone. Ripped down to make way for new properties.

'Get uniforms to pay them a visit. We need to keep track of all of it.'

'I'm on it.' Dropping the half-finished croissant, Kelly dusted her hands off. 'What's that?'

Drake's finger had carried on the line south-east from the site across the York Road and into Battersea to arrive at a complex of low housing blocks set around an open square.

'The Freetown estate.'

'More like Troubleville,' Kelly snorted.

'Ever been there?'

'I've been through it a few times at high speed, if that counts.'

'I lived there for a time.'

'Interesting. Well, whatever it was, it's not the same. Believe you me. Nowadays it's more like Baghdad.'

'I heard some things had improved.'

'You know how it is. They throw some paint at it and like a magic cape all is solved. Emperor's New Clothes.'

Drake wandered out to the dreaded dispenser in the hallway. The coffee tasted like someone had washed their socks in it. He took a sip and grimaced. When he got back Milo was waving a preliminary forensics report confirming Marsha Thwaite as the female victim.

'Okay, so now we need to ask what she was doing out there that time of night.'

'The obvious?' Kelly suggested. 'Meeting her gentleman friend?'

'Have we identified him yet?'

Milo spoke without taking his eyes from the screens in front of him.

'Tei Hideo. He was carrying a French identity card. Japanese origin, French citizen. Resident in this country for three years.' Milo handed over a mauve Post-it. Milo Kowalski had his own system for everything. Drake had never seen anyone so organized.

'Tell me about him.'

Milo swung round in his chair eagerly. 'This guy is a real character. He made a name for himself back in the eighties as a mountaineer. He climbed all the big Himalayan peaks, solo. That's impressive. All for charity. He's also into birds, the feathered kind. If you ask me, he's trying to save the planet single-handedly.'

'What about family, have you spoken to anyone?'

'There's a daughter here in London. Works in Regent's Park.'

Drake turned to Kelly. 'We should speak to her today.'

'I'll set it up.' Kelly reached for her phone.

'Seems like an odd mix. Was he thinking of buying a flat?'

'An art collector?' Kelly speculated.

'Possible. We need to build up a picture of these two. Did they know each other? How did they meet? Generally and specifically, on that evening. Why were they killed together? Were they chosen at random, or is there some kind of meaning to this?'

The phone on the desk rang. It was Wheeler.

'Sir?'

'My office, asap.'

'On my way, sir.' Drake caught Kelly's eye.

'Big chief?'

'Sounds like he's onto something.'

'Never a good sign,' muttered Kelly.

'Did they get any prints off the car?'

'Forensics have logged dozens of prints. They're looking for matches now,' said Kelly.

'Milo, we need to run the CCTV footage to see how the truck arrived at the site. Maybe we'll get lucky.'

'I'm already on it, chief,' Milo called.

'Course you are.'

Drake took the stairs slowly, wondering what idea Wheeler had got into his head now. Generally speaking, such initiatives never boded well. The best response was to listen patiently, nod appreciatively, promise to do some digging and then go away and let time take care of the rest. Wheeler saw himself as a creative person, a man with a ready solution to everything. Drake suspected the superintendent had missed certain opportunities available to him. Wheeler saw himself as an agent of change in a system that thrived on hierarchy and chain of command. Most of the ideas he came up with were unworkable. It was just a matter of waiting until he saw what was plain to everyone else. As he walked into the office, Drake had no idea what awaited him, but he was pretty sure that whatever it was he wasn't going to like it.

'Come in, Cal, pull up a chair.' Wheeler was wearing the cheesy smile of a game-show host. The reason for the smile was standing over by the window. 'This is Doctor Crane.'

It wasn't hard to see why a woman like that would put a smile on his face. She was around Drake's height, her skin a shade lighter. She had narrow, almond-shaped green eyes and jet-black hair. The thick hair and high cheekbones suggested some Persian heritage, a parent from Iran. She carried herself with the loose confidence of someone who worked out regularly. Her handshake was firm. She was dressed in a charcoal business suit, and there was a flash of silver from a bracelet around her wrist as she took his hand, a wink of what might have been a diamond in one ear. Classy, yet understated. Somebody who had learned that good looks could draw the wrong kind of attention, especially if you were trying to get them to take you seriously.

'Detective Sergeant Drake has taken charge of the investigation.' Wheeler was still beaming like a sickly schoolboy trying to impress.

'What's this all about, sir?'

'Our conversation with Howard Thwaite set me thinking. Perhaps we should try something a little more creative?'

'I see.' Drake glanced in the direction of Doctor Crane. So far she hadn't said a word.

'No need to look so glum, Cal. It was your idea, after all.'

'My idea?'

'Rituals. Medieval. That's what you said. Instincts. Always go with your instincts.'

'Yes, sir.'

'As it happens, Doctor Crane has been brought on board by the Serious Crimes mob.'

'I'm not sure I follow.'

'Doctor Crane is a forensic psychologist. Highly qualified, it goes without saying. Done work for the MoD abroad. She recently took over from Julius Rosen.'

'I remember Doctor Rosen,' said Drake.

'Exactly, we all do. So, Doctor Crane has been seconded to us in an advisory capacity.' Drake had a feeling he knew what was coming. 'And I've asked her to join the investigation.'

'I see.'

There was an awkward pause. Wheeler sensed that he had overstepped the mark. Crane, for her part, looked equally ill at ease. 'It's a high-profile case, Cal, and we need to bring all our guns to bear.'

'I understand.'

'Good man. I suggest that you fill Doctor Crane in on the details. Where are you?'

'I was just about to head out to interview a couple of relatives. The daughter of the male victim and Mrs Thwaite's gallery assistant.'

'Perfect, you can take Doctor Crane with you.'

'Sir . . .'

Wheeler didn't seem to hear. A beaming smile filled his face.

'You'll be in safe hands, Doctor Crane. Cal is one of the finest detectives we have.'

CHAPTER 7

They walked in almost complete silence out of the building as Drake led the way round the corner to an old bus-station waiting room that had been recently converted into some kind of hipster café. The Java Junction wasn't his kind of place, but he was guessing it was probably more to Doctor Crane's taste than the greasy spoon he tended to frequent.

The bare brick was brightened by weird light sculptures and the floor was polished hardwood. It was almost deserted at that hour, which was handy. They sat in the far corner by a rusty iron table.

'So what do I call you, Doctor Crane?'

'Ray. People call me Ray.'

'Ray?'

'As in Rayhana.'

The waitress appeared. Drake ordered black coffee. Doctor Crane, Ray, asked for the same.

'Just to be clear, I think Superintendent Wheeler has managed to get a little ahead of himself.'

'I got the impression you weren't thrilled with the idea,' she nodded.

'It's nothing personal, but we have to move quickly on this one and I really don't have time to act as a chaperone.'

'Point taken, and for your information, I didn't ask for this.'

'Okay.' Drake waited for an explanation.

'I was taken on by Julius, Doctor Rosen, as his assistant. He was training me to take over his practice.'

'Then he died.'

'Which was inconvenient, to say the least.' She had a habit of tossing her hair when she spoke, which he found distracting. 'So, I was left with my own patients, who are still in treatment, along with the commitments he had made before he died.'

'You can't just cancel? He did die, after all.'

Crane sighed. 'Julius meant well, but he was terrible at arranging his finances. He left me saddled with debt. I have to take everything that comes my way.'

She broke off as the coffee arrived. For a moment there was silence.

'You don't need to tell me all this, you know.'

'I wanted to tell you.' She put down her mug. 'Look, the point I'm trying to make is that we're both stuck with it. I have a contract to fulfil and you're obliged to do what Wheeler tells you.'

Drake dipped his head. 'So far we're on the same page, at least.'

'Then maybe we should just play it loose. You let me tag along and if I see something I let you know. Win-win.'

'Sounds tremendous.'

She smiled at that.

'Tell me, you've helped on a lot of cases?'

'Some.'

'That's that they call a non-committal answer.'

Crane tapped a fingernail on the side of her mug. 'Ever

see pictures of hangings in Tehran in the early days of the Islamic revolution?'

Drake sat back and looked at her. 'We're not dealing with a hanging.'

'The point is that this is unusual in a number of ways, principally the setting.'

'Go on.'

'How much do you know about sharia law?' She waited a beat before going on. 'After 1979, the Islamic Revolution was in such a hurry they put an industrial slant into their punishment schedule. They used to hang people in the streets from construction cranes.'

'How about stoning?'

'That too. Ever hear of Muaz al-Kasasbeh?'

'The Jordanian pilot?'

She nodded. 'In 2015 his plane came down in Syria. Islamic State executed him. They burned him alive, then dumped a truck load of rubble on him.'

'That'll do it.'

'They were burying him in a manner that would be deemed undignified. At the same time following the tenets of sharia.'

'Stoning him alive. You think that's what this is?'

'I think it's a possibility worth considering.'

Drake wasn't convinced. 'Wheeler hinted you did some kind of work abroad.'

Crane smiled. 'I'm here as a consultant on a case. I'm not being cross-examined.'

'So, you don't want to talk about it, or you can't?'

'Does it make a difference?' She got to her feet. 'Shall we go?'

Drake wondered what she was holding back. He hung back and called the forensic medical examiner. Archie Narayan wasn't exactly happy to hear from him.

'Why are you bothering me? I told you, it's too early to have any proper results.'

'All I'm asking for is a breakdown.'

'No, Cal, what you are asking for is a miracle.'

'Listen, doc, you know the position I'm in, right?'

'You need to be patient. I understand you've got Wheeler breathing down your neck. But that's not how things work. We have protocols, methods, procedures.'

'Must be something wrong with the line. I can hear violins.'

'I've already speculated far more extensively than I should. Why bother making me go to all the trouble of carefully composing my words in a report if a rough breakdown, as you put it, would suffice?'

Archie Narayan was one of the most stubborn, uncooperative coroners Drake had ever encountered. He was also the best. Drake heard him rummaging around his desk.

'Let's see what we've got. Magnolia Quays. Limestone dust and micro-fragments found in the throat and nostrils of both victims indicating they were breathing when they were buried.'

'So he buried them alive.'

'It looks that way. I would think that they would have lost consciousness quickly, but still . . .'

'Not a pleasant way to go.'

Archie Narayan made a sound like a whale expelling air. 'Murderers are, in my view, not in the business of making their victims' departure from this world a pleasant experience.'

'Any sign the victims had engaged in sexual activity?'

'You mean in their lifetimes? As two adults, I would have thought that highly probable, although I couldn't give you any precise details.' He gave a loud sigh. 'If you mean with one another, prior to death, then initial examination would suggest not, but don't quote me on that.'

Through the window Drake could see Doctor Crane pulling a pair of sunglasses from her jacket.

'Let me ask you, did you ever have any dealings with a forensic psychologist by the name of Crane?'

'Yes, of course. Worked with my old friend Julius Rosen.'

'What can you tell me about her?'

'She can be very persuasive.'

'Meaning?'

'Just watch your step, she takes no prisoners.'

'You're doing wonders for my mood. One last question. Any signs this could have been part of a religious ritual?'

'What did you have in mind?'

'I don't know. Anything.'

Archie gave a cluck of impatience. 'You should listen to yourself some time. Talk about clutching at straws.'

CHAPTER 8

The reception desk at One Hyde Park was manned by a uniformed crew who were unhappy to see Drake's badge. Kelly let out a low whistle as they came into the lobby.

'Should have worn the Pradas.'

'Too late for that now.'

A young concierge with an accent that wavered between the East End and somewhere in the Balkans led them over to the lifts and used a card key to take them up.

'Miss Hideo is in some kind of trouble?' he sniffed.

'Whatever happened to discretion?' Kelly asked.

The man grunted but kept his mouth shut. He stared at the indicator panel above his head for the rest of the journey.

On the ninth floor the lift doors opened to reveal a marble-lined entrance hall and a Filipina maid. She ushered them into a large living room. It seemed to project into space, with glass walls on three sides, windows that stretched from floor to ceiling, offering a view over the park and the placid surface of the Serpentine.

'Try closing your mouth,' Drake murmured.

Before Kelly could respond a door on the right opened and a woman entered. He would have put her age at about thirty, with an angular face and round eyes. There was something informal and detached about her.

'Please,' she gestured for them to be seated with a slight bow. If her appearance was western, her manner was eastern. Drake remained standing while Kelly sat down opposite Miss Hideo, who was struggling to hold back tears. 'You've come about my father.'

'I believe you spoke to one of my colleagues?' Drake asked.

Yuko Hideo nodded. 'They said my father had been found on a building site?' She turned towards Kelly. 'How is that possible?'

'That's why we're here. We're trying to find out what he might have been doing there.'

Hideo spoke with a slight French accent. 'It makes no sense.'

'Do you know if your father was meeting someone last night?'

The young woman was clutching her hands together, opening and closing her fingers. 'We had reservations for dinner.'

'Was it a special occasion?' Kelly's voice was gentle.

Hideo nodded. 'My birthday. My father never missed my birthday.'

'You're a biologist, right?' Kelly asked.

'A zoologist. I specialize in marine mammals.'

'Marine mammals? Like seals?'

'Seals, dolphins, whales.'

'Nice.' Kelly leaned closer. 'If you don't mind my asking, where does all this come from?' She gestured at the room they were in, the view of the park. At first Yuko Hideo seemed not to understand, then she dipped her head.

'My mother inherited money. When she died, my father moved here to be near me.'

'Miss Hideo, I understand this is a difficult time for you,' said Drake. 'But we have to move quickly.'

'Of course.' Hideo's daughter tilted her head in a slight bow.

'In order to find out why your father was killed we need to establish his relationship to the other victim.'

'He was not alone?'

Drake shook his head. 'Does the name Marsha Thwaite mean anything to you?'

Hideo shook her head wordlessly.

'Was your father seeing anyone?' Kelly asked gently. 'A woman?'

'I tried to encourage him. After my mother died he basically lost interest. I told him he should go out more.'

'So, is it possible that he might have met Mrs Thwaite somewhere?'

'It's possible, but then I'm sure he would have mentioned it.'

Drake's eye was drawn to the pictures hanging on the walls. A few large photographs of landscapes, mountains. Sharp cut ridges and icy peaks. The sketches alongside looked traditional. Deft ink strokes on rice paper that looked almost like calligraphy. These were of birds.

'Did your father do these?' Drake asked.

Yuko Hideo stood up and came over. 'Yes. Birds were more than a job to him, they were his . . . passion. Birds and mountains.'

'Mrs Thwaite ran an art gallery in Knightsbridge, the Arcadia. Did you ever hear of it?'

'An art gallery? No.' She was silent for a moment, then cleared her throat. 'Now I remember he mentioned a Ukiyo-e print that was for sale.'

'Ukiyo-e?' said Kelly.

Hideo turned towards her. 'A traditional woodblock form. Very old. He was debating whether to buy it. My father hated spending money on himself. He was very tough that way.'

'I'm sorry,' interrupted Drake. 'What are we talking about?'

'Ukiyo-e means, Pictures of the Floating World. This was an eighteenth-century work by Jakucho, an undervalued artist. A painting of a white phoenix.'

'Right,' said Drake, none the wiser. 'So, how did he hear about this?'

'I don't remember.' Yuko looked down at her hands. 'He must have told me, but I wasn't paying attention. I encouraged him to buy it.'

When the interview was over, she walked them to the lift.

'He was a good man,' Yuko said. 'I find it hard to imagine anyone wanting to hurt him.'

'You need to give yourself time,' he said, shaking her hand.

'I really hate that.' Kelly slumped against the side of the lift as the doors closed. 'Somebody's life has just been shattered. It makes me feel like a vulture picking over a carcass.'

'So what ties a bird-lover to the wife of a construction developer?'

'I thought you were going to tell me.'

Drake was thinking of his conversation with Doctor Crane. After talking to Yuko Hideo the idea of a connection to some kind of radical Islamic action seemed even more unlikely.

'Milo found nothing on the phones to link them?'

'Nothing.'

Drake settled back behind the wheel, his mind going over the picture that was forming. The traffic was stalled. Ahead of them a stretch limousine was racked across the road trying to manoeuvre itself onto the forecourt of the big hotel across the street. It wasn't clear what the problem was, but people were already out of patience. The driver of the limousine clearly didn't know what he was doing. The long vehicle rolled backward off the ramp. As they all waited for him to work out what to do a yellow Lamborghini growled into view and, switching into the opposite lane, cut across the line of waiting traffic, drove straight past and onto the forecourt. Kelly laughed.

'That showed them.'

The limo was still lumbering about trying to straighten up. As the cars began to move again, Drake eased the BMW into gear. As they went by he watched a doorman in top hat and tails step out to open the door for the passengers of the Lamborghini.

'Ever get the feeling we missed out on something?' Kelly asked.

CHAPTER 9

It was a short ride down the Brompton Road to Beauchamp Place, but the traffic was slow, clogged with coaches and double deckers. Drake watched a pair of young mothers in hijabs and sportswear jogging along behind ergonomically designed pushchairs. Kelly used the time to do some digging on her phone.

'Married for nearly nine years. His second. Her first. No children. He has two from his first marriage.'

'Where are you getting all this?'

'*Hello!* magazine did a full spread on them a couple of years ago.' Kelly looked up from the screen. 'I know it doesn't sound reliable, but hey, they know their stuff.'

'Spoken like a true fan of celebrity gossip,' said Drake.

'Don't knock it till you've tried it.'

'Still, Thwaite doesn't strike me as the kind of man who would know how to operate a dump truck.'

'Ah, well, there you would be wrong. His grandfather, who

started the construction business, insisted that young Howard work his way up. I'm sure that doesn't mean he was mixing cement for ten years, but you get the idea. Don't you just hate it?'

'Hate what?' Drake glanced across.

'Success.'

'Everybody hates success.'

At the Arcadia Gallery they waited while Marsha Thwaite's assistant dealt with a client in a sharp blue suit and keffiyeh. The white walls were hung with art works, some contemporary and abstract, others more figurative, landscapes and portraits. Drake recalled the eclectic mix in the Thwaites' living room.

'What makes people decide what they are interested in?' he asked the assistant when she was free, as he squinted at a price tag that he wasn't quite sure he had read correctly.

'Oh, it's very subjective.' The woman made it sound like a mystery of the cosmos.

The business card she held out gave her name as Bianca Darca. On the home stretch of her forties. Made up to the eyeballs. Dyed blonde hair and glossy lipstick. The revealing cleavage was designed to take your eyes away from her features, which were layered with enough face paint to start a war. The string of gold baubles around her neck was so thick it could have choked a cat. She pursed her lips when she spoke.

'The appreciation of art is a very personal matter. People choose one piece over another because it touches them.'

'So, not just because they think it will match their furniture?' said Drake.

Ms Darca ran an eye over him and seemed to conclude that there was little to salvage.

Drake ignored the look. 'Can you tell us when you last saw Mrs Thwaite?'

'Marsha? Yesterday afternoon. I left early. I had a date.' She fluttered her eyes to hit the point home. 'She had plans to go to the theatre with a friend.'

'How did it go?'

'Sorry?' Bianca flapped her fake eyelashes at Kelly.

'The date. Just wondering if you had any luck.'

The question seemed to fluster Bianca. 'That is private and I hope you won't start pushing me for a description.' She examined her nails.

'Nobody is accusing you of anything,' Kelly assured her. Bianca didn't look so sure.

Drake tried to steer the conversation back. 'You left Mrs Thwaite here alone. As far as you know, she locked up and drove to the theatre to meet her friend.'

'Yes, that is what I told you.' She faltered then, as if the situation was just beginning to hit home. 'I can't believe she's really dead. It wasn't . . . I mean, she didn't kill herself, did she?'

'Was that something she talked about?' Kelly asked.

'No, not at all, I was just thinking.'

'It wasn't suicide,' said Drake.

'Someone killed her? Why? It makes no sense.'

'Did she ever receive threats of any kind? Something unusual perhaps? A letter or card. An email. Something that worried her?'

'No. Nothing like that.'

'Does the name Tei Hideo mean anything to you?' Drake asked.

Bianca asked him to repeat the name. When he did so she shook her head.

'I never heard that name.'

'He's not a client? Do you do any trade in Japanese wood carvings?'

'Ukiyo-e?' Kelly almost sounded as if she knew what she was talking about.

'We deal with contemporary art, as you can see.' Bianca gestured around her. Drake looked. If contemporary meant you had a hard time understanding it, then that was what they had.

'How long have you worked here?' Drake decided to change tack.

The question produced a sharp double take. 'You mean, in this country?'

'I mean in this job.'

'Two years, perhaps a little longer. Why you ask?' She was growing suspicious. 'Why do you ask such questions? Maybe I call Mr Thwaite?' Her English seemed to deteriorate as she grew more agitated.

'We're just trying to get a better picture of the situation.'

Bianca fidgeted uncomfortably. 'I really think I should check with Howard. I'm not happy about this questions.' She lifted her phone and began stabbing at the screen with a finger tipped with pink nail varnish. 'He is not answering. Poor Howard, he must be devastated!'

'I'm sure he is. One final question. Does this gallery belong to Mr Thwaite?'

'Why everybody always think it is man who is rich?' She gave a heavy sigh. 'Howard lose all his money. So unfair. Such a talented man!'

'He had financial problems?'

'Yes, yes.' Bianca hesitated before going on, realizing perhaps that she had said too much. 'Six years ago, he lose a lot of money. A lot. She save him really. A tragedy. I can't believe.'

'One last question, then we will truly leave you in peace.' Kelly smiled. 'How would you describe the state of their marriage?'

'Oh . . . you know.' Her gaze bobbed around the gallery. 'Like every couple. They had their ups and downs, I suppose. Sometimes they argue, but solid, very solid.'

'I'm just having a thought,' Kelly said when they were back in the car. 'Is there a chance her being coy about her date was because it was a married man by the name of Howard Thwaite?'

'You really have to stop reading those scandal rags.'

'I'm serious. We're looking for motive, right?'

'We need to dig deeper,' said Drake. 'We should take a look at Thwaite's finances.

'Right.' Kelly was looking out of the window. 'You didn't tell me what Wheeler wanted.'

'He wants to bring in a Doctor Rayhana Crane, forensic psychologist.'

'Good looking?'

Cal squinted at her. 'I'm not sure I see the relevance of that question.'

'Ah, cagey answer, which suggests you might be interested.'

'Can we try and stay with the investigation?'

'As you wish, but just remember what I said. What did she say?'

Drake drummed a finger on the wheel as they waited for the lights to change. 'She thinks we might be looking at a re-enactment of sharia punishment.'

'Great, so all aboard the crazy train.'

'Something like that,' murmured Drake.

CHAPTER 10

'So, Wheeler actually bought into this?' Kelly asked.

'You know what he's like. He wants to make sure he's covered all the angles. He wants to be able to say he's done everything he could.'

'And she seriously thinks the killings may be an Islamic ritual execution?'

'It's a theory. That's her job, to come up with creative solutions.'

'Creative being the operative word.'

Drake was sifting through the cupboards. 'How come we never have any cups?'

'Because this coffee is a health hazard.' Kelly reached under the sink and came up with a stack of plastic cups. Drake took one and placed it in the machine and listened while it whirred itself into action. Kelly folded her arms and leaned against the wall.

'So, what do we do with all this?'

'Nothing, for the moment. Let her run with it.' Drake bent

to peer into the delivery port. 'Did we get the interpreter for the caretaker?'

'Ah, yes, Mr Cricket. Turns out his English isn't so bad after all.' Kelly waggled a hand in the air. 'My feeling is he's up to something.'

'Too many favours for friends?'

'Nobody from east of the Med had a bad word to say about him, but the rest of them hate the man. Which made me wonder.'

'He's providing illegals, you mean?' Drake tapped the side of the machine.

'And taking a cut off their pay packets.'

He leapt back as, without warning, coffee shot from the spout, knocking the cup over and spilling scalding hot liquid all over the floor. Drake cursed and began mopping up the mess with paper towels.

'Interesting technique you have there, chief.'

'What about the no shows?' Drake asked, reaching for more towels.

'Ah, that's where it gets better. Mr Cricket had egg all over his face by the time he'd finished.' Kelly was chuckling. 'Three of them had done a runner in the past week. Every now and then someone decides to make an anonymous call to Border Force. Just for fun. According to our helpful site supervisor, Mr Cricket was about to be suspended.'

'For taking kickbacks?'

'It looks that way.'

'Speaking of our friendly supervisor, did you get the lists we asked for?'

'Ah, our Welsh boyo, the master of disaster.' Kelly Marsh rolled her eyes. 'He's up to his neck in problems, mostly of his own making, I should add. He's working another site for sure, maybe two. Small operations. The whole set-up is in free fall. Organized chaos. They are ninety days behind schedule, not thirty. If they go over again they get hit with hefty fines.'

'Most of the buyers are foreign?'

'It's the global economy, stupid. We cut Europe loose so we could sell everything we've got to the highest bidder. There's a logic in there somewhere but don't ask me to explain it.'

Drake snorted. 'Careful, you're beginning to sound like a socialist.'

'It comes with the territory.'

'Let's get back to the case in point.'

'The point is people come and go. Nobody has a clue what's really happening. Christ, most of them don't understand what the foreman is saying.'

'Which is where Mr Cricket comes in.'

'When he walked in there he thought it was just another cock-up. Someone dumping a load of gravel in the wrong place. Happens all the time apparently.'

'We should get him in.'

'Way ahead of you,' Kelly glanced at her watch. 'He should be waiting in the sweatbox.'

Drake dried off his hands. 'Then what are we standing about for?'

The 'sweatbox' or interview room was an airless room whose shadows were split by a couple of white neon strips in the ceiling. The refurbishment budget hadn't quite reached this far. Like an old gym, it reeked of vomit and stale perspiration, as if the walls had been painted with the stuff. You could squeeze three or four people in there, so long as they didn't breathe too deeply.

Kardax was slumped over the narrow table in an uncomfortable plastic chair. Beside him was a bald, bespectacled man wearing a corduroy suit that was tight around the shoulders and midriff. Hussein Shamshad, nicknamed 'The Shambles'. Drake recognized the particular combination of mothballs and Old Spice before he'd even stepped through the door. Shamshad was an experienced public defender who relished his role as an agitator. He started to speak before Kelly had time to do the honours with the audio recorder. She stopped him and got everyone to state their names clearly before letting him continue.

'Before we begin, I must protest in the strongest possible terms. My client has been deprived of his rights. He's been kept here for hours.'

'Duly noted,' said Drake. 'Your client has been a naughty boy and if he doesn't start cooperating I am going to be forced to call in IE.'

'Are you threatening my client?'

'Not at all,' beamed Drake. 'Just letting him know that we have an obligation to inform Immigration Enforcement of any infringements.'

Kardax leaned over to his lawyer and the two men consulted in whispers.

'Profiting from illegal aliens is a serious crime and he could find himself imprisoned or deported, maybe both if he's lucky.' Drake locked his fingers together on the table. 'Does Mr Kardax understand what I am saying or does he require the services of an interpreter?'

Kardax's eyes darted back and forth between Drake and Kelly before nodding.

'Is okay.'

'Good. The statement provided by your client is notable for what it leaves out and makes a convincing argument for perverting the course of justice. Is your client aware of the consequences of such a charge?'

Shamshad licked his lips. 'My client rejects any suggestion he had anything to do with these murders.'

'The only way the perpetrators could get in and out of the site without being noticed is if they had access to keys and the electronic passcode on the front gate.'

'That's pure speculation. We have no idea how the perpetrators entered or left the site. Either way, you can't prove that it was my client who provided access.'

'I don't need to. I need him to prove that he didn't. Otherwise, I'm charging him with being an accomplice.'

'What are you talking about?' Shamshad demanded. 'My client is a witness. He called the police.'

'I'd like to know why your client took so long to call the police.' Drake flipped through the pages of the cardboard folder in front of him. 'According to the site manager the caretaker arrives on site at 5.30 a.m. But he didn't call it in until nearly an hour later.'

'We've already been through this.'

'You know how this works. Ask him.'

'Okay, okay,' Shamshad huddled with his client, then began to speak. 'He saw a hand sticking out. He began digging, thinking there had been a terrible accident.'

Drake leaned forwards to tap the table in front of Kardax. 'Do us all a favour and speak for yourself. Your English is probably better than mine.'

The lawyer put a hand out to caution his client to remain silent, but Kardax pushed it aside wearily.

'I thought it was some of my boys.'

'Your boys? What exactly does that mean?'

Kardax took a deep breath. 'I owe money.'

'Okay, now we're getting somewhere. Who do you owe money to?'

'Some men.'

'What men?'

'I can't.' Kardax shook his head. 'Very dangerous.'

'You have no idea.' Drake tapped a finger on the table. 'This is dangerous. You want to be sent home, because believe me, it's easier than you think.'

'They bring me people, I find them work.'

'These men provide workers and in exchange you get a cut of their wages, is that it?'

Kardax glanced at his lawyer and then nodded.

'Mr Kardax has just nodded to indicate a yes,' Kelly said for the record.

Drake took over again. 'You pay a fee to the suppliers. So basically the workers get nothing, or next to nothing?'

Another nod. Drake sat back.

'Everyone goes home happy,' said Kelly. Kardax looked at her, but said nothing. 'And you're in a lot of trouble.'

'No, no,' pleaded Kardax. 'I want to help.'

'So, why didn't you call the police straight away?'

'In my country, police very bad.'

Drake leaned in again. 'You didn't call because you thought the victims were illegals. You were afraid it would get you into trouble.'

Kardax was silent, but the point had been made and he wasn't disputing it.

'I think perhaps we all need a break.' Shamshad flashed a packet of Silk Cut. Drake indicated for Kelly to do the honours with the tape machine. Leaving Kelly with Kardax, Drake led the way out of the room and down the corridor to a fire escape that led up to a corner of the roof littered with cigarette butts. Seagulls fluttered over the river and somewhere in the distance a helicopter buzzed an urgent line towards the City.

'You're a real piece of work, Drake,' said Shamshad as he lit up.

'Your client is complicit in people trafficking. He's making a profit from employing illegals, that's exploitative. On top of that we have two bodies crushed into hamburger meat.'

'You're threatening to deport him. That's cold.'

'He's playing games. He's protecting his suppliers and someone somewhere knows how the perpetrators got onto the site.'

'How do you live with yourself?'

'Don't get cute with me, Hussein. We both know how this works.'

'You know what I mean.' White smoke streamed from Shamshad's nostrils. 'Here you are, working for a racist organization, the token minority officer.'

Drake pushed his hands into his pockets and stared west towards the river. 'Save it for the rallies.'

'You're playing Tonto to their Lone Ranger.'

'I don't know what that's supposed to mean.'

'It means you're a sell out, to your own people.'

'Nice try,' Drake said. 'But I don't have people.'

'We all have people.' Shamshad held his stance. 'They demoted you, Cal, remember, dropped you from Inspector to Detective Sergeant. They fucked you and you still don't get it.'

'Have it your own way. You know who he's running these workers for?'

'He has an appeal ongoing. They turned him down for asylum. He loves this country, worships the Queen. He wants to bring his family here.'

'Who's he working for?'

Shamshad shrugged. 'All you have to do is put in a good word, a note describing him as a model citizen, cooperating fully with the police.'

'And you ask how I live with myself?'

'It's the way of the world, Cal. Don't pretend you're any different.'

Back in the sweatbox, Kelly looked relieved. Drake waited for Shamshad to explain the situation. Kardax sat back in his chair, his hands resting on the table. His eyes rested on Drake.

'I need names,' said Drake.

'I don't have names. I swear. They change all the time.'

'Then what do you have?'

'The man I speak to, they call him the king.'

'The king?' echoed Kelly.

'King,' Kardax nodded. 'He has a mark on his skin.' He raised his hand to the back of his neck. 'Here.'

CHAPTER 11

The clock in the Murder Room said it was closing on six-thirty. They were almost twelve hours in already and it felt like they were nowhere. Milo was still at it, working on the CCTV footage.

'Tell me you've got something.'

'I've been trying to track the lorry's movements backwards. It's registered with a firm based in Uxbridge.'

Milo tapped and clicked away until an image appeared on one of his screens. The right-hand side was covered in lines of code. He brought up a black-and-white shot taken at night of a parking area fenced by trees. Drake squinted at the grainy image.

'What are we looking at?'

'This is a service station just south of Uxbridge, around nine thirty-five the night before the bodies were found. The driver was assaulted, tied up and gagged. He wasn't found until the cleaners arrived this morning.'

Another click brought the image to life. A flare of light from the concourse of the petrol station covered the bottom left-hand corner with a white glow. Blurred grey shadows moved across the screen. Some were easily identifiable makes of cars, others less so. The images jerked unevenly.

'These cameras are not high-end but they serve the purpose.' Milo nodded. 'Here it comes.'

The lorry lumbered slowly into sight. The name Dobson Creek could be made out along the side. A tarpaulin was drawn over the back. The company had confirmed that one of their lorries had left Yarlton gravel pits in Oxfordshire that evening. A late delivery for a site in Pimlico.

'Now watch.'

A figure detached itself from the shadows and loped out behind the slow-moving lorry.

'There's our man,' said Drake, leaning into the screen. It was hard to see much. The quality of the image was not good. At that distance and in poor light, he could make out a tall, athletic figure wearing a hoodie. The brim of a baseball cap protruded from the sweatshirt.

'Can you get more detail?'

Milo cued the tape. The figure drew back into the shadows, then emerged again. The lorry reappeared, this time from a different angle. Hazard lights flashing, it looked as though it was stalled in the middle of the slip road. Headlights streamed by on the motorway to the right.

'Wait for it,' said Milo.

For a long time the lorry didn't move. It rolled a few metres, then stopped again. Then the passenger door opened and a man slipped down, hauling something, presumably the driver, and vanished into the shadows. A few moments later the man reappeared, readjusted his head and the hood of his sweatshirt, then stepped out of the trees.

'That's him.' Milo hit the space bar and the image froze. 'This is the best I could get.' Milo looked disappointed. He brought up a still image he had drawn up. It was blurry and not a lot of help. Drake stared at it. 'I could do better if I had more time maybe.'

There was something strange about the man's head.

'Is he wearing some kind of mask?'

'It's hard to tell in this light.'

'Go back. Play it again, the part where he first appears.'

Milo replayed the sequence. Then again, and again, until Drake was pretty sure he'd seen all there was to see. What interested him most was the way the man moved, with smooth confident steps, coolly and calmly in control of the situation. Acting alone, yet with complete physical ease. If he had to take a guess, he would have said the man was in his thirties, not much older.

Milo said he still had to work on the cameras leading away from Magnolia Quays to see if they could piece the time frame together. The images from the service station were from nine hours before the bodies were discovered, and twelve hours from when Marsha Thwaite left the Arcadia Gallery.

'There's a time gap. We need to fill it. How did the killer know about the delivery, what route they use? I mean, was he monitoring their emails, phones, what? How did he set this up?'

'We checked with Dobson's. The order came through their computer system. They're waiting to hear back from the client, but it looks as though someone hacked into the system.'

'Okay, we need to keep on at them until we have all the details.'

'Right, boss.'

'Oh, one other thing; how does this fit with the timing of when Marsha Thwaite went missing? Was there enough time for the perpetrator to get to that service station?'

'Perhaps there was more than one of them,' said Milo.

'Exactly. So we might be looking at at least two killers.'

Drake's eyes were still on the blurred image that filled one of Milo's screens. Who are you, he wondered. And what is it you want?

Kelly was pinning a list of names up on the board, striking through some, circling others, using her notebook to check the spellings: the workers who had been debriefed at the site.

'Most of them provided alibis for one another. A few of them gave the same address.' She was linking names with arrows and brackets as she went. 'These three were drinking together. These two were out with friends. This little piggy stayed at home, but he has a girlfriend, or so he claims. We'll be checking that.' She let the notebook drop to her side. 'To be honest, chief, I'm not sure any of them are reliable.'

'So far so normal. Who runs security on the site?'

'A company called Kronnos.' Milo had the details. 'A guard passes by two or three times a night, depending on how busy they are. No fixed times. They try to avoid fixed patterns, but the guard logs in with their central office using an app and that time is recorded.'

'And everything checks out?'

Milo nodded. 'Last guard went by at 1.47 a.m. Everything was in order and no sign of anything wrong.'

'Did he notice Mrs Thwaite's car parked there?'

'No mention of it. He probably wouldn't be looking at a parked car.'

'Do yourself a favour. Don't make assumptions. Check with him again.'

'Okay, boss.' Milo reached for the phone.

Drake stepped back to survey the whole board.

'So nobody sees anything until Kardax turns up?'

Kelly checked her notes. 'According to one of the Slovaks, who is not too happy about the situation, there are usually people hanging around outside the gates waiting for Cricket.'

'In the hope he can find them some work.'

'Exactly.'

'And they all vanished when the shit hit the fan.'

Kelly beamed. 'Couldn't have put it better myself, sir.'

'Okay, good work both of you. What do we have on Hideo's background?'

'He was a teacher at some kind of high school in France.' Kelly frowned at the page she was reading slowly. 'Ecole Superior des Sciences Lorraine.'

'It's a university.' Milo cleared his throat. 'École Supérior des Sciences.'

'Oh, excusez-moi.'

'Get in touch with them, Milo. Find out what they can tell us about Hideo. Anything at all, his background, his friends, etc.'

'Right, boss,' said Milo. He seemed to be waiting for something.

'What is it, Milo?'

'I promised to be somewhere . . .'

Drake glanced at Kelly, who shrugged. 'Prenatal classes. The boy wonder is going to become a father.'

'Sure, go ahead. We'll pick this up tomorrow.'

'Thanks, boss.' Milo looked visibly relieved.

'You too,' Drake said to Kelly.

'No prenatal classes for me, chief.'

'It doesn't matter. Just go home and get some rest. We can start again early tomorrow.'

When they had gone, Drake sat alone for a time in his chair, staring at the board. The map. The photographs from the crime scene. The victims. He needed a drink.

The BMW was cold and unresponsive. He swung round, unable to bring himself to go home just yet. The traffic coming out of town was heavy at this time and he found himself turning, left, right, any direction just so long as he could keep moving. People moved through this city with the same fluidity as the rain that was hitting the glass in front of him. They came from all across the face of the earth. They changed their clothes, their hair, their names, their faces. They remade themselves. It was in the nature of the city. People could lay claim to it, but it belonged to no one.

Drake had grown up all over South London. After the breakup, they had moved around constantly. For several years they had no fixed address. His mother in those days lived in fear that his father would find them. She jumped at shadows, peered around doors and through curtains before walking into the street. It was a form of paranoia that would later feed into her mental imbalance. Running became her default mode. Arriving breathlessly at yet another friend's house, her child wrapped up in her arms. They slept on floors, on sofas, in people's attics, in lock-ups, caravans and garden sheds. He was very small at the time, but it left him with the impression of the world as being in constant flux.

Orange sodium lights flitted by overhead. A bus swerved in front of him on Falcon Road. He slowed, catching sight of two men coming out of a shuttered Halal chicken-and-chips joint. They high-fived and sauntered off, tucking earphones into place. He drove on, past a succession of pizzerias, estate agents, mobile repair shops, more property agents, Kebabistan, a pharmacy, more mobile repairs, more estate agents, betting shops, a Travelodge, a wholefood store. On and on it went, the names like a mantra running through his head.

By fourteen, Drake had been in trouble with the law. Street life offered a welcome alternative to witnessing his mother in meltdown. Everything was always overshadowed by the looming threat of a return to the heaving wreck of it all; the inevitable bust up with friends and out again, wandering from place to place clutching their belongings, napping on the Tube, in hostels where they shared a room with the stench of other people's misery. His mother's instability hung over everything like a curse, even in the best of times.

All Drake could remember of his father were fragments. A tall, dark-skinned man with long, elegant fingers holding a cigarette. His mother cursed him for ruining her life, but then, paradoxically, cried for him to come back to her. Right up to the end she carried a dog-eared picture of him in her purse. It was as if everything, the beatings, the other women, could all be forgiven and put aside. She never really accepted that he wasn't stalking them, that he wasn't coming back for her. Then it was as if all the drugs, the string of casual boyfriends, was a weird way of trying to get him back. That was his memory. A skewed snapshot of his own childhood seen through the lens of a woman who was defined by her unhappiness. He learned that life was a mess. No fucking happy endings, no forever afters, only here and now.

CHAPTER 12

The coroner's office was housed in a large building off the Albert Embankment. It had a solid colonial weight to it. The interior had been refurbished, stripped right down to the brick and then modernized. A high doorway led past a deserted reception desk to a lobby with a metal staircase leading up to galleries that ran around the upper floors. On the first floor Archie Narayan's office was in a corner, with a view through the window of the river and the MI5 offices on Millbank. The room was lit only by a desk lamp, which cast a warm glow on the bottle of single malt whisky standing alongside it. Archie peered over the rim of his glass as Drake came in.

'Ah, our intrepid investigator,' he said, reaching behind him for another glass. Drake waved aside the offer of a drink as he sank down onto the leather sofa that ran along one wall. 'How are you coping?'

Drake rubbed a hand over his face. 'Wheeler's given me two days to reel this one in. After that it'll be taken off me.'

'At least he's giving you a shot.'

'I can't afford to fuck this one up, Archie.'

The coroner nodded. 'You're trying to climb out from under a mountain.'

'This is my last chance to put the Goran business behind me.'

'So, you've come asking for favours.' Archie raised his eyebrows as he rolled the whisky around his mouth.

'I need all the help I can get.'

'How are you getting on with the delectable Doctor Crane?'

'Don't say it like that, makes you sound like an old letch.'

'Call me old-fashioned, but there was a time when it was considered acceptable to pay a woman a compliment about her looks. Now we're all supposed to treat one another like automatons, humping one another without feelings or passions.'

'Your old-fashioned romanticism is getting rusty.'

'Call me what you like.' Archie returned to his chair and raised his glass. 'She looks like an Italian actress from the 1960s whose name escapes me. I used to have impure thoughts.'

'I'm not sure I need to hear this.'

'The one advantage of age is that you lose all inhibitions. You can say the most outlandish things without shame.'

'The point being that you do actually know her?'

'Oh, yes.' Archie nodded. 'Interesting. Highly intelligent, of course. Double first from Cambridge. She's made a couple of smart moves, got herself in with the MoD. Mother Iranian dissident, father eccentric English lord who denounced his heritage.'

Drake lifted a hand to stop him. 'Back up a moment. You seem to know a lot about her.'

'Ah, well, she was taken on by an old friend of mine, Julius Rosen. He never had children so when he passed away, she inherited the practice.'

'She's doing consultancy work for the Met.'

'A PR exercise.' Archie waved his glass. 'She got herself into hot water treating victims of police brutality. It got her onto the front pages of the tabloids for all the wrong reasons.'

A faint bell rang in the back of Drake's memory. He couldn't remember the details, but it had something to do with a foiled terror plot.

'Forensic psychology is a strange beast. Doctor Crane has made a name for herself, largely as a profiler.' Archie reached for the bottle again to refill his glass. He gave Drake a nod. 'Actually, you and she should have a lot in common.'

'How so?'

'Both outsiders, both struggling to convince the establishment that you are trustworthy.'

'You should stick to the dead,' Drake said. 'Tell me you've got something for me?'

'You're asking for miracles.' Archie gave a loud sigh. 'I get that you're worried. Come along, then.' Picking up the bottle, Archie led the way out of the office, down the stairs and through a locked door into a dark corridor. The smell of chemicals hit Drake's nostrils with a jolt. Familiar, like the sharp memory of something nasty he thought he'd forgotten. The autopsy room crackled with electric energy. Neon lights buzzed, refrigerators hummed, a gigantic extractor whirred overhead. In one corner a centrifuge spun in regular cycles, up to who knows what mischief. Two of the four examination tables in the centre of the room were occupied.

'Our Stone Cold Lovers, as I like to think of them.' Archie Narayan pulled away the sheet with a flourish.

'Very droll.'

The coroner seemed remarkably upbeat, considering. But then, for a man who spent most of his waking hours in the company of the dead, you might think that any contact with a living person would have been a plus. You'd have been wrong. Drake tried to recall how long he had known Narayan. Years, on and off. Didn't seem to make a difference. Nobody ever seemed to get close to Archie. It was hard to imagine anyone more rigid and unforgiving.

Now he pulled a rubberized black apron over his head. Cal swallowed hard and tried not to think of the greasy kebab he had wolfed down for lunch. Throwing up at this point would not help proceedings, nor improve his standing with the touchy medical examiner. Stretched out on the brushed steel tables, the bodies looked more out of place than when he had seen them early that morning. The coating of grey dust had been washed off and their injuries were more obvious. The heads crushed into pulpy masses, fingers and arms twisted into grotesque shapes.

'Music, maestro, please.'

Archie appeared to have acquired one of those sound systems that was activated by his voice. Handy, no doubt, when your hands were covered in all manner of organic material. The room was fitted with top of the range speakers. The string section of an orchestra began to slowly seep through, building gently. It felt as if they were standing right behind him.

'Mozart's "Requiem",' Archie murmured as he moved around the table.

'Whatever floats your boat, doc.' Drake didn't care what it was. He found the music a distraction. Fancy strings and harmonies were unwelcome intrusions. What he needed to focus on, what he needed to feel, was the pain that Marsha Thwaite had experienced. The body splayed out on the table in front of him was a brutal sight, and he wanted to feel the anger in a pure and unadulterated form.

She had been split up the middle from groin to thorax. Drake's eye found the tag on her left foot. A cocktail of rotting bodily gases and chemicals made his stomach lurch. He held his breath and waited for it to pass.

'They were buried alive, right?'

Archie glanced up over the rim of his spectacles. 'You could see that from their posture at the crime scene. They were struggling to get out.' The coroner moved around the table. 'On their knees. Immobilized. Hands tied behind their backs.' He indicated the specimen tray on one side where the cut-off plastic ties lay. 'They were hooded, bound and gagged. Then they were stoned to death. Literally.'

'How did they manage that? I mean, how were they subdued?'

'Ah, take a look here.' Archie indicated a series of parallel marks on Marsha Thwaite's neck. 'Those are burn marks, slight, with local tissue damage.'

'They were tasered?'

'The size looks about right.' Archie held a set of callipers against the burns.

Somewhere in the corridor behind them a door slammed. Footsteps moved slowly away. The music was still twittering on in the background but now Drake found it easier to filter it out. They moved to the next table where Archie had not really begun his work. Tei Hideo was still in one piece. His body looked in good shape for his age. Slim build. Firm muscle definition. A man who worked out regularly. No steroids and weights, but plenty of fresh air, exercise and a good diet. Drake thought about the daughter and how she was going to miss him. He thought about his own father. All kids grow up learning that one day their parents would be gone.

'We're still trying to establish the reason they were killed together. Anything about this to indicate it could be some kind of, I don't know, religious thing?'

'Religious thing?' Archie straightened up.

'Just something Doctor Crane mentioned.'

'You're thinking of Saudi Arabia? Places where they bury people upright in the sand and pelt them with stones?'

'Something like that. She was talking about Daesh, and Iran. People being hanged on cranes.' Drake surveyed the autopsy table.

'Stoning is for adulterers, isn't it?'

'There were no signs they were engaged in sexual activity at the time of death.'

'Sorry, no.'

'But that doesn't mean they weren't involved.'

'No, of course not.' Archie rested his hands on the steel table. 'I don't really see it. Why here? I mean it hardly makes sense.'

'Maybe that's the point.'

'Does anyone really believe that sharia law has a chance of being imposed in this country?'

'People generally believe what they want to believe.'

'Spoken like a wise man.' Archie raised his glass in salute. 'Sure you won't join me?'

'The spirit is willing but the stomach is weak.'

The coroner heaved a long sigh. 'Whatever they were up to, these people met a violent end for a reason.'

'Someone wanted them to suffer.' Drake was staring at one of the woman's wrists. It had been sliced almost all the way through, bone and all. The hand was hanging from a sliver of skin. It took effort not to reach over and put it back in place. He tried to imagine what it would have been like for them. To have been dragged, stunned, unconscious or semi-conscious, from the car, across the broken ground, down into the pit. To find themselves tied and gagged, looking up at a dump truck rising above them and a ton of rocks coming tumbling down on top of them.

During his time in the army, Drake had witnessed death. He'd grown used to the absurdity of it. People caught in mid-stride by a stray bullet. Laughing at a joke when an IED goes off and rips your body in two. He'd seen children die senselessly and over the course of two tours he had learned that in order to survive you had to grow a second skin, a layer of armour that could protect you from things that people should never have to experience.

That was part of what made him angry. He knew what this was. Instinctively, whatever idea the killer had built up in their heads, he knew what they were trying to do; to bring that madness here, to spin it out right here at the heart of his world. The killer or killers wanted people to know that they were not immune from this violence. Not here. Not anywhere. That made it personal. It made it about everything he had fought for. Not queen and country, but common sense, decency. The order of things. He knew it was his job to stop them.

He watched Archie pour himself another generous glass of malt whisky. He was about ready for a drink himself, but he needed this moment. This clarity. He needed to hold on to it, to understand why he was doing this, why he was going to catch whoever did this, no matter what.

'In the old days this building was used by resurrection men.' Archie smacked his lips and tilted his head back to gaze at the vaulted ceiling. Drake followed suit. 'They used to steal corpses and sell them to medical colleges. Education was opening up and more and more people wanted to become doctors, but there was a shortage of bodies for dissection purposes. By law you were only allowed to use the bodies of men who had been condemned to death. So, people being people, a lucrative trade sprang up. They kept the bodies down here.' Archie held his glass up to watch the light passing through the amber liquid. 'People forget that we are only custodians of this world. Millions passed before us, and millions will come after us, if we don't manage to destroy the planet beforehand.' He lifted his glass. 'Amen to all that.'

CHAPTER 13

Kostas and Eleni Markaris had been living in London for close on forty years, but to listen to them talk you might be forgiven for thinking they had arrived in the country a week ago. Kostas was a stooping, awkwardly shaped man with a head devoid of hair apart from his thick moustache and a thin band of grey wisps floating above his ears. He peered over the frames of his lopsided NHS spectacles as Drake came through the door, and gave a philosophical shrug.

'Ah, the wanderer returns. Elenitsa, we have a victim!' He winked as he leaned across the counter. 'Today, she made a giovetsi better than any I have eaten, better even than my mother, God rest her soul.' His eyes fluttered towards heaven.

'I'll take your word for it.'

Kostas tapped his protruding belly. 'I eat too much, always, but I will die a happy man.'

'Don't we all?'

The Ithaka was almost empty, but still Drake took his usual table at the back, generally reserved for staff. Kostas brought over a bowl of ice and a bottle of ouzo. He sat and poured without asking, his eyes searching Drake's face.

'You're good?'

'Busy.'

'On the news they say two people were found dead on a building site. No accident?'

'No accident.' Drake poured a splash of water into the glass and watched the liquid turn cloudy. He stared at it for a long while. 'Someone crushed them to death on purpose.'

Kostas winced. 'People are crazy. I've said that all my life, but you know what? Every day the world proves me right.'

'He's boring you? I can throw him out.' Eleni set a plate of roasted lamb and pasta in front of Drake. 'Kali órexi.' She stood with her hands wrapped over her apron, as she always did, waiting for his approval. 'He's a one man show. All he is lacking is some of that pink sugar on his head.'

'Candy floss?'

'Exactly.' She stroked her husband's bald pate. 'You like?'

'Delicious. I don't know why I eat anywhere else.'

'Ah, be careful, you make him jealous.'

The two of them disappeared into the kitchen. Drake was happy to be left to his own thoughts. From time to time he glanced up at the television screen on the wall. Magnolia Quays was front and centre. Two people crushed to death made for a juicy story. A shaky camera panned across the rain-swept building site. Long shots of the workers and uniformed officers standing around. They tried to speak to a couple of labourers, but they seemed reluctant, shaking their heads and ducking away. Drake stopped chewing, his eyes scanning the faces, the movements of people in the background. Perpetrators had been known to hang around the scene of a crime, just to get a glimpse of the investigation. He reached for his glass as the images turned to shots of ambulances and police vehicles, SOCOs wandering around in their Teletubby suits looking lost. As the news moved on, Drake went back over the crime scene in his head. Was there something he'd missed?

His train of thought was broken as the door opened and five men entered. At the head of the line was the unmistakable figure of Adonis 'Donny' Apostolis. A short, stocky brute of a man with a bronzed shaven head and a goatee that made him look rather like a deranged jazz musician. He wore so many rings on his fingers it was hard to imagine how he got anything done. He led the way to a table in the middle of the room where he threw himself down. His goons settled around him like plump crows. They all subscribed to the same fashion code. Knock-off replicas of designer-label T-shirts, Dolce this and Armani that, all in black, matched with elasticated tracksuit pants to accommodate expanding waistlines.

Donny was the head of the Apostolis family. There were nine brothers and sisters. Their main legitimate enterprise was the furniture business. They brought it in from the Far East, adding to the decimation of Indonesia's hard-wood forests in order to stock garden centres and furniture warehouses with crappy benches and lopsided tables. Who cares about the planet when there's a market to exploit? Global entrepreneurs. They ran kebab bars, chip shops, cafés, hotels, car washes, fitness centres and lap-dancing clubs. The other stuff – the drugs, the stolen cars, the money laundering and what have you – took place behind the curtain of the legit stuff. Donny had connections everywhere, from Surabaya to Saint Petersburg, by way of Chicago, Sicily and Sinaloa.

They had posted a guard outside. Donny had enough enemies to dictate that he never took chances. Another sat waiting behind the wheel of the Merc. Drake picked out the one they called King – Donny's closest bodyguard. Wherever Donny went, King went too. Small and compact, as mean as a circus dwarf on steroids, he had one glass eye, his real one lost in a fight back in the day. He also had a crown tattooed on the back of his neck. Drake couldn't think of a lot of people with a tattoo like that. He wondered if Kardax would be able to recognize him from a mugshot. Even if he did, Drake knew there was a good chance the foreman would be reluctant to identify King.

Kostas greeted Donny who then launched into a long monologue in Greek. Time to leave. Drake got to his feet, placing a note on the counter as he went by.

'Dibble Dibble. Who do I see?'

There was a gentle chorus of laughter from Donny's entourage. People around Donny tended to laugh when he did. Most of his musclemen had the IQ of a dumb-bell. They chortled now. Probably had no idea who Top Cat's policeman was. Donny waved him over, eyes and rings glinting in the harsh neon.

'Officer Dibble. You know, when I see you, I see a dead man walking.' In his right hand Donny carried a rosary. He was always flipping the prayer beads. Some kind of nod towards respectability. He saw himself as a responsible member of his community, but he still looked like a thug flipping a string of beads.

'What's happening, Donny?'

'You see?' He grinned like a shark, revealing a flash of gold from an eye tooth. 'We're like old friends. Our fates are tied together in a way that the ancients would understand.'

'You always had a lively imagination, Donny.'

Donny threw back his head and laughed like a hyena on speed. 'You see why I love this man? He has spirit. Not like the other malakias. In the old days I would have cut him into pieces and roasted him on the grill like lamb's kidneys. I'm kidding, eh? I'm just kidding. Come and have a drink.'

'Sorry, no drinking with the clients.'

Donny wagged a finger. 'Now you're being impolite.'

'Some other time.'

'Ah, you're busy chasing the little criminals.'

'Someone has to do it.'

'Keeping the world safe. Good for you.' Somewhere underneath that waxed glare lurked a very dangerous animal, one that could turn in a heartbeat.

'I'll be seeing you, Donny.' Drake reached for the door. He would have made it if one of the goons hadn't stepped in his way. King. Drake held his gaze.

'Just the man I was looking for. I hear you've been nosing around Magnolia Quays.'

King's face scrunched itself up into a scowl. For a second Drake thought he was going to take a swing at him. Instead, he looked over towards his boss. Donny got to his feet and clicked his fingers. King stepped aside. Donny leaned in close.

'You know, I liked you better in the old days, when you didn't take your work so seriously.'

'What can I tell you, Donny? We all have to move with the times. When did you take an interest in the construction business?'

'Who said I did? You know who you remind me of?' Donny snapped his fingers. 'That movie about the Indian who becomes a cowboy, then he becomes an Indian again?' He drew blank stares from his audience. *Finding Nemo* was more their style. 'Dustin Hoffman? I love that movie. No, I swear. I love it. Just like you, I'm never sure whose side you're on.'

'See you around, Donny.'

CHAPTER 14

Outside, Drake stood for a moment in the rain and took a deep breath to clear his head. Battersea Park Road was quiet. Too early for the gangbangers, too late for the commuters. He waited for a double-decker bus to hum by before crossing the street on foot, cutting through the car park and between the Neptune Chip Shop and the Hot Thai Take Away. There was the usual collection of smokers hanging on the stairs beneath the sign for the Anchor. Ducking through the shadows, Drake turned a corner towards the block where he lived.

The row of flats was originally built as council housing but most had been sold off over the years. Drake had been lucky. He came home at the right time. One good thing you could say about the war. Up on the top floor, Drake still enjoyed a view of the London skyline that was the envy of many an estate agent. How long it would last was anybody's guess. At the rate they were building round here he would soon be staring at another block of luxury lifestyle units, or whatever the current term was.

The hallway was dark. Nobody had managed to change the lightbulb yet. The lift clanked and creaked so much that Drake generally felt safer taking the stairs. On the floor below his he hesitated. He could hear music from the door on the right. Stan Getz and João Gilberto. 'The Girl From Ipanema'. Drake leaned a hand on the doorframe, debating whether to knock. As if by magic the door opened.

'You think you can just walk by my door and not stop?'

'It's late and I'm tired,' said Drake, but he was already addressing an empty space. He stepped inside, closing the door behind him.

The entrance was lit only by a faint red light that came from within a fusebox on the wall. Cal felt his way along until he could find the opening to the kitchen. Maritza was already fixing him a drink, pouring dark rum over ice and a slice of lime before sashaying through the bead curtain on the other side. Drake picked up the glass as he followed her through to the living room.

She threw herself down into an old leather armchair that seemed to have given up all hope of having a shape. He sank into the sofa opposite.

'Where's Joe?'

'Ah, my god!' She slapped a hand to her forehead. 'He's driving me crazy.'

Joe, or João, as he was properly named, was Maritza's seven-year-old boy.

'Always he's asking questions. How can a child's head be so full of ideas?'

Drake had to smile. He sipped his drink while she talked. About her boy, but also about her work. Canvasses were stacked four or five deep along the walls. It was a mystery to him, but Maritza somehow made a living from painting. She drew pictures of strange still lifes. He didn't know how else to describe them. Giant ravens spread out over stark forests. The paintings were haunting yet not scary.

They seemed to represent some kind of magical world. It always amazed him that they had all come from inside the head of one person.

The two of them had met a couple of months ago, when Cal had seen her struggling up the stairs with shopping bags in one hand and a child writhing about in the other. He hesitated, knowing that sometimes help was not welcomed, but by the time they had made it up another flight she relented. They looked at one another, and although they had never really exchanged anything more than a passing greeting, there was an immediate understanding. He reached out and she handed him the bags.

'Pride will only get you so far,' she muttered.

'You'd do the same for me, right?' he grinned.

'Right.'

In return she had cooked a meal for him, the first of many. On the second date they had slept together. Drake wasn't the most expressive person in the world. He knew that. He tended to push people away from him, afraid of getting too close. But in Maritza he had found someone who basically wanted the same. She had her life in place. She worked, earned enough to feed herself and her child.

'I'm not looking for some kind of sugar daddy,' she told him.

'That's good,' Drake laughed, 'because you're not looking at one.'

They finished their rum and then it was late. Drake watched her get to her feet and walk over towards the hallway. She turned around when she reached the doorway. Then she reached down to the hem of her dress and pulled it slowly up over her head.

'Are you coming?'

He woke in the early hours, shivering and bathed in sweat The sound of a helicopter drifting away over the rooftops. It always happened like this. The chop of rotors brought out a visceral reaction. It triggered something deep in his memory, brought him awake, no matter how deeply he had been sleeping. It was always there, waiting to be found again.

The sky tilted and through the open side of the Westland Lynx, the earth rushed up to meet them. They were east of Basra when they were hit by small-arms fire. An occupational hazard, but the bullets must have hit something vital. The aft rotor whined that it was out of action. Black smoke began streaming into the cabin. Alarms went off as they spun round in space losing height. The pilot did his best to right the machine as they went down. The strange keening sound of that helicopter as it went down was wired into his memory. Even in sleep, he felt it. His body tensing, getting ready to run or fight, getting ready to die.

Cal's leg was broken in three places when they struck the ground. Of the six people on board, only he and one other survived, Corporal Jamie Miller, whose spine was broken on impact. Drake managed to pull Miller from the machine, dragging both of them through the sand on his back with his one good leg. A bloody shard of bone protruded from the other. Flames were already licking around the interior. Sparks sputtered from the wiring. Miller was screaming. There was no way Drake could get anyone else out.

By the time they reached the shelter of a long mound of earth beside an irrigation ditch they were already under attack. Light automatic weapons coming from a line of date palms across a sodden field. Drake managed to return fire, holding off the insurgents until help arrived.

It was 3 a.m. as he climbed the stairs to his own flat. The layout was identical to Maritza's place, but unlike hers, his looked abandoned. There were cardboard storage boxes stacked by the door that for some reason he had never got round to unpacking. A pile of coats hung from a rack that was falling off the wall. Plates were stacked in the kitchen sink. He walked straight past them to stand by the window. Dawn was still some hours away, but the night sky was bright with the glow of artificial light. The four towers of Battersea power station stood out like the pillars of a shattered temple. The horizon was still dotted with angry red eyes; the warning lights on dozens of crane rigs that ranged across the skyline. He didn't bother undressing and going to bed. Instead he threw himself down on the sofa and lay there. Through the window he watched the sky unfolding, clouds sliding overhead, their colours shifting from purple to orange and black. After a while his eyes closed, and for a time he found peace.

CHAPTER 15

The early hours found Ray Crane still restless. The previous evening she had allowed herself to be talked into taking part in a discussion panel on Radio Four. One of those late-night programmes that nobody ever listens to. It didn't matter. She found herself facing a spokesman for the new populism. His line was that Britain was under siege. 'We are under attack. Our way of life is under threat,' he kept saying.

'Who is "we"?' she asked, several times. He sidestepped the question.

It wasn't that she lacked experience. She was more than adequate when it came to defending her position, and she was usually good at sniffing out set-ups. In this instance she had not seen it coming. Her opponent had been primed and the presenter had soft footed around him, allowing him to speak unimpeded, which left Ray to pick up the pieces. You never knew nowadays with broadcasters.

It was not the first time she had felt annoyed with herself following a media appearance. She hated the things, but she knew it was necessary. Nowadays if you weren't working on raising your profile you were basically busy sinking without trace.

She changed out of her clothes and went straight into a workout in the downstairs gym area. She warmed up with a skipping rope and then went at the heavy bag with punches and kicks until the sweat was pouring down her face. Then she took a shower and padded upstairs in a tracksuit to her office.

The practice was located in an extensive terraced house that lay on one of those little mews behind Paddington Station. The narrow street that dipped down from the main road was still covered in cobblestones from the days when these buildings were stables. There were people who would have killed for a place like this but Ray had simply inherited it all from her former employer, the late, rather eccentric Doctor Julius Rosen.

Five years ago, after her career hit an unexpected bump, Ray had opted out. She spent two years travelling the world. It would be fair to say she went off the rails. Things got pretty wild for a time. She just wanted to get away from it all, to lose herself in the world, and for a time she did. Berlin, Barcelona, Prague, Paris, then further afield; Beirut, Bamako, Nairobi, Marrakesh. A few months here, a few weeks there. She kept herself moving, refusing to put down roots or form lasting bonds.

In the end, standing on the sea front in Lamu she saw that she was coming to the end. Running out of funds and desperate for work, tired of the despair that comes from aimless wandering, she came home. She missed the discipline of being a professional, the intellectual challenge. She was tired of punishing herself. Julius Rosen took her in. He was, by any measure, one eccentric character. His partner had recently died, and he was trying to run the practice alone. Ray was young and hungry, and had enough of an offbeat streak to endear her to him. He took her on as a junior partner. They each had an office on either side of the staircase. The central area was a shared reception office, run by the dutiful Heather, who had worked there for years. At some point the ground-floor garage was converted into a communal living space that was now her home. Julius thought this only fair; she had been crashing there since she had first appeared on his doorstep after all.

Both of them needed the operation to work, and it did. To say they got along well would be an understatement. They understood one another to the point where they could finish each other's sentences. Julius Rosen realized that he had stumbled upon the perfect partner.

'If we were just a couple of decades closer in age I could have married you,' he once said. 'It would have been ideal.'

'Except for the fact that you're gay.'

'Well,' he shrugged, 'nobody's perfect.'

Perhaps not, but their partnership worked well enough for both of them. It was almost too good to be true. Then, nine months ago, Julius had been diagnosed with a brain tumour. Three months later he was dead. Ray was left to run the whole place by herself. She thought about finding a new partner to share the practice, and even interviewed a couple of people. But somehow it never felt quite right. It was as if bringing someone else in would be a betrayal of what she and Julius had had together. So everything had remained the way it was. Every morning, Heather would dutifully go through to his side and water all the plants, as if he was just away on holiday, and not dead at all. But along with the practice, Ray had also inherited a sizeable hole in his accounts. Apparently, Julius had been borrowing against the house, which left Ray with a choice; give up the property or try and pay off the money he owed. It wasn't a huge amount, but the payments along with general overheads meant she found herself struggling to decide which to pay and which to hold off.

Clicking the computer into life, Ray scanned the news outlets to see if there were any updates on Magnolia Quays. She had been a little disappointed that DS Drake had been less than enthusiastic about her presence. It was easy to see that he was under a lot of pressure, and that made her curious. She checked her email and found a couple of preliminary forensic reports, so at least Wheeler was making sure that she was in the loop.

A search on Drake turned up quite a bit. She went out to the kitchenette they had in the reception area and fed the fish in the aquarium while waiting for the kettle to boil. When she got back to her desk she began to go through the search results. Almost all of them related to investigation into organized crime and a certain Goran Malevich, the head of a Bosnian Serb gang.

According to what she could access online, Drake had been demoted after the death of Malevich. The circumstances were not clear. Drake had been transferred out of the Met to a unit of the South Yorkshire police. She sat back in her chair. They had sent him to somewhere called Matlock. She wondered how he had found that. Six months ago he had been transferred back to the Met. As far as she could make out, the gist of it was that Drake had been suspected of having been compromised in some way. A key witness had disappeared under his watch; he'd been the undercover officer who had recruited Esma Danin, a hostess at one of Malevich's clubs. She went by the name of Zelda and was to have been a key witness in the case. Then Zelda disappeared and the implication was that Drake had helped to get rid of her. In other words, he was playing both sides, taking money from Malevich while stringing along the Serious Crimes squad. The Crown Prosecution Service was adamant that their case against Goran Malevich had collapsed with the death of their star witness. Malevich had subsequently died, shot along with two of his bodyguards in what looked like a textbook gangland ambush. A car park in Brighton. CCTV deactivated. A hail of bullets from at least two AK47 assault rifles. The crime scene photos showed the bodies splayed out around a red Maserati that stood with its doors open.

The key figure in the case against Drake was DI Vernon Pryce, the man who had been leading the team. Drake had gone undercover while Pryce remained on the outside. Pryce had submitted three separate reports to the Professional Standards Department that Ray had managed to track down through her sources. Pryce put forward the same theory every time; that Drake had been turned and was on the payroll of Goran Malevich.

Ray's coffee was cold. She pushed her chair back away from the desk and stood up, turning to face the window. It was gone three in the morning and the city was as quiet as it ever gets. High above the rooftops clouds swirled in that strange colour that came off the street lighting. A solitary night bus grumbled by at the end of the road.

What she loved about this corner of London was the way it connected to the past. The sooty old buildings. The mud, blood and tides that had washed through here over the centuries. You could feel the brush of ghosts rumbling through the walls, rattling the chains of history.

Was Drake bent, or had he been railroaded? Until the Malevich business had come along he had been an exemplary officer. He qualified as an actual hero, having been awarded a medal in the Iraq war. He had risen through the ranks from police constable to detective and his arrest record was outstanding. Not exactly corruption material. Going after Malevich was a considerable step up from ordinary investigative work. There was a lot at stake for him personally. Working undercover in an organization like that would have put him at serious risk. If Malevich had learned his true identity he would have paid with his life. But if they had pulled it off and taken down Malevich's operation, it would have been a major coup for the squad and for him personally. So, had he lost faith? It was a question that intrigued her. She wanted to know more.

She sat back down again and composed an email to her contact in the intelligence services. Stewart Mason was somewhere in MI5 these days. It wasn't that she didn't trust Drake exactly, she just wanted to know what she was getting herself into.

CHAPTER 16

When he was fifteen Drake discovered the answers to all his troubles in a single book. Something of a miracle in itself. He'd been looking for a way out. His own get-out-of-jail-free card, a secret rabbit hole that would deliver him from the chaos that he was drowning in. Doctor Crane might have said it was the missing piece in his life that should have been filled by his father. Drake wasn't inclined towards self-analysis. Even back then he had been smart enough to realize that there was no simple set of answers to everything. What he did know was that if he didn't change course he was going to wind up dead, stabbed in some pointless clash with another gang.

So one day he walked into an East London mosque and felt something stir in his soul.

It was the summer of 1995. The headlines were filled with stories about Muslims being massacred in Bosnia, a place he couldn't have found on a map if you paid him. He'd never thought about any of this before, but suddenly it felt real. Here was history happening, not in a remote century, or in a book, but now, today. He felt as if he was the only witness. Nobody else seemed to care, as though it had nothing to do with them. He was starting to see the world for what it was.

They were living in a house in Bethnal Green, upstairs from his mother's new boyfriend, and his wife, who didn't know what was going on. Cal stayed out till all hours, carving out his own reputation. Running with the wild ones. The only thing he knew he could trust was a Stanley knife. He was set on course for a life that led straight through juvenile court to detention and a lifetime in and out of prison, with nothing but a string of tattoos to show for it. It didn't matter. Nothing mattered.

That afternoon he had sheltered in a doorway. He was cold and so he joined the crowd of men arriving for Friday prayers. People murmured greetings, they stepped out of his way, made a space for him to stand between them. He lingered, thinking there might be a few pockets to pick. People focused on communing with their god. When the sermon was over, tea was served and a small group of them sat around in a circle and listened to this bearded man who spoke with passion about injustice.

'Brothers, ask yourselves why it is the poorest people in this country who are in prison. Why are we at each other's throats, fighting one another instead of fighting the powers of oppression?'

It felt as though the imam was speaking directly to him.

'In the Holy Quran we are told, "Hold fast and be not divided among yourselves." Our enemies profit from our divisions.' He smiled around the group. 'Only in Islam can we find the unity that gives us strength.'

Here, for the first time, was a place he could belong. The following week he found himself going back, and the week after that, and so it went. He had no idea what he was supposed to do. In the beginning, he simply followed the others in their routine, washing before prayer, sitting on the carpet, bowing down, rising up, finding solace in the Arabic words.

But it was in the study classes after prayers that he found purpose. Here they spoke of injustice, of what was happening in the world. He found his anger reflected and chanelled, and he began to understand that he was not alone, and that there was a name to this need for revolt he felt, and it was called Islam. For a time, that became his life.

It was an odd course, but it was his. And it had led him here, eventually, to Raven Hill where Milo had something on his mind. He was fidgeting, wrapping rubber bands around his fingers until they twanged off across the room.

'Okay, Milo,' said Drake. 'What's eating you?'

'I've got something I think you should see.'

It was CCTV footage from the street leading past Magnolia Quays. Milo had it on fast forward. White lights cruised out of the darkness, flashing by, growing fewer as the hour ticked by on the counter, until it reached 22:47. Then the speed cut back to normal to reveal a Porsche Cayenne as it slowed to a halt before turning off onto the narrow access road.

'I've managed to enhance the image. If you look closely at the interior?' Milo clicked the mouse, bringing up a palette that allowed him to play with the light and zoom. 'There's only one person in there, a woman, presumably Marsha Thwaite. So where is Mr Hideo?'

'The mystery man,' said Kelly. 'Maybe he's one of those, what do you call it, ninjas?'

'Are you serious?' Milo looked up at her.

'She's not serious, Milo. Was he already on site?'

'The security cameras at Magnolia Quays were disabled, so we have nothing from the front gate or the interior. The mud on the tyres of the Porsche suggests it was driven inside.'

'So, Hideo might already have been inside the car?'

Milo sighed. 'It's possible.'

'How about identifying the driver?'

'That's the best I can get.' Milo shook his head in apology. Drake squinted at the blur of pixels for a time. Kelly leaned past him.

'Could be a man in a wig.'

'Let's face it, that could be Kermit the Frog.' Drake turned back to Milo. 'Can we trace the car backwards?'

'I tried.' Milo was disheartened. 'Too many on the road. Too many of the same model.'

Drake stared at the image. 'What if that's not Marsha Thwaite? We could be looking at the killer. That would mean he already had the victims in the car with him, restrained, tied up in some way, yeah?'

'Sure.' Milo bobbed his head. 'It's possible.'

'So who's driving the dumper truck?'

'There are two of them,' said Kelly. 'Oh, before I forget, the caretaker, Mr Carattack?'

'What about him?'

'He came back with a list of people who had not turned up for work.'

'And, anything interesting?'

'One, possibly.'

'One of his illegals?'

Kelly shrugged vaguely. 'He didn't like the look of him.'

'Do we have a name?'

'Wally.'

Drake squinted. 'Wally? That's it? No surname, nothing?'

Kelly shook her head. 'Says he can't remember. He's going back through the files to see if he can find it.'

'What was odd about him, then?'

Kelly shrugged. 'Apparently Mr Cricket just didn't like the look of him. Head not good.' She did a passable imitation of the Magnolia Quays' gatekeeper, complete with head wagging.

'Head not good. Just the kind of nuanced description we relish.'

'Thought you'd like it.'

'Get back to him. Talk to his lawyer. Tell him it's not good enough.'

'I'll try.'

Drake kicked his chair back from the desk and got to his feet. 'I'd better go up and have a word with the chief. Any sign of that shrink, by the way?'

'Doctor Crane, you mean?' Milo sounded defensive.

'Yes, Doctor Crane. No sign of her today?'

Milo shook his head.

'Must have something better to do with her time,' said Kelly.

'Great,' said Drake. 'One other thing. Hideo's daughter mentioned a picture.'

'Ukiyo-e,' supplied Kelly.

'Exactly.'

'Japanese woodblock painting?' asked Milo.

'Impressive,' whistled Kelly.

'Check his mails, text messages, see if there is any mention close to his disappearance.'

'I'm on it, chief.'

On his way upstairs Drake ran into DCI Pryce. A big man, putting on weight as he headed into middle age. A broadening gut along with a narrow jaw and straight hair cut so short it looked like iron filings stuck to his head. Vernon Pryce. Three years ago they had worked together on the Malevich case. It hadn't been a perfect partnership, and when it all went sour the blame fell on Drake's shoulders. Pryce had been smart enough to get out from underneath, partly by pointing the finger at Drake. He'd even managed to get himself promoted and was now in charge of some unit or other over at New Scotland Yard in Whitehall.

'Well, look who it is, the man of the hour.'

'Vernon. Still crawling your way up the ladder?'

'Enjoy your moment in the spotlight, Cal. You'll be off the case before you know it.'

'Nice seeing you, too.'

Pryce was already gone, bounding down the stairs trying to look athletic. Wheeler was in a foul mood.

'I've just had Pryce in here pressing to take over the case.'

'Can he do that?'

'If we give him a reason.' Wheeler lifted his chin. 'Tell me you're making progress.'

'Some, but it's slow going.'

'That's not good enough. We've got the whole world looking up our skirts on this one.'

'Right, sir.' Drake often wondered about the superintendent's metaphors, but perhaps this wasn't the moment.

'It's already getting traction in the press.' He passed a hand over the newspapers spread out before him on his desk. 'Did you give any more thought to bringing Doctor Crane in on this?'

'I still don't see the point of it.'

'She's good, Cal. Has a profile in the media. They know her. She'll give our case credence.'

'Sir, all due respect, but shouldn't we just be focusing on solving the case?'

Wheeler leaned back in the big leather chair and looked up at Drake.

'You begged me to give you the case, but I'm not sure you grasp the significance of it. If you don't clear this one fast, and I mean fast, you'll never get another chance.'

'I appreciate that, sir.'

'I hope so, for your sake. Get over your prejudice about shrinks and listen to what she has to say. What?' Wheeler had been swinging from side to side in his chair. The expression on Drake's face caused him to stop.

'Nothing. Just that she thinks we're dealing with some kind of Islamist revival.'

Wheeler frowned as though in pain. 'I don't know anything about that. I do know that she's highly qualified, speaks seven languages, all that kind of thing. Next to her, you're a Neanderthal. And that's not some kind of racial slur, by the way.'

'Never entered my head.'

'So, tell me where we are.'

'We're tracking Thwaite's car backwards to find out where the victims were picked up.'

'Forensics?'

'Nothing concrete as yet.'

'What we need, Cal, what you need, is a miracle. Do I make myself clear?'

'Sir?'

'Okay now, formally, I have promised Pryce you will keep him informed of your progress. That might keep him out of your hair for a bit.'

'Right, sir.'

Downstairs, Drake found himself staring at the notice board. His eye shifted to the map of the crime-scene area. Once again he traced the access road leading south east from Magnolia Quays.

'Freetown,' said Kelly, as she was passing. It sounded like the answer to a question.

CHAPTER 17

Drake punched the dashboard radio to summon up a rock station. Something hard and driving to blow away the blues that had descended. There was nothing. All of it sounded boring and predictable. He wound up leaving it on a phone-in show where a caller was berating the host on the subject of the world having gone to hell.

'This is a case of the hens coming home to roost, or however the saying goes, okay? I mean, for the last fifteen years we've been getting involved in other countries' problems overseas. Am I right? Now, you can't do that without some kind of blowback.'

The host wasn't having it. 'Sorry, John, but what exactly does that have to do with people being stoned to death on building sites in London?'

'It's obvious, innit?'

'Well, John, I'm actually saying it isn't all that obvious. Why don't you explain?'

'The level of sheer savagery around the world. That's what I'm saying. This kind of thing has been going on for years over there. Now it's come back here.'

'Right, John, well, I'm not sure we all agree with you, but if you have an opinion we'd love to hear from you, so call in on oh eight seven...'

Drake had stopped listening long before he reached for the switch to flip the radio off. Already he felt as though this case was dragging him back, asking him to question his past, things he thought he was done with.

His reasons for joining the army had always been confusing to him. On the one hand, he wasn't sure he believed in the logic of invading Iraq. If he'd had any doubts they were certainly cleared up when he saw the situation on the ground. By the time he arrived the country was on the verge of a sectarian war between Sunni and Shia.

From the age of fifteen he had believed that Islam offered him a place to belong. In time he began to see that what he was learning about had more to do with the egotistical needs of the people whose sermons he listened to than to any pure ideal.

Then 7/7 happened.

In July 2005, Cal woke up and realized that he could no longer defend his radicalization. Joining the army seemed a logical step, a way of reclaiming his birthright. What more proof could you ask for than laying your life on the line?

Some nights he still woke up with the stench of burning flesh in his nostrils. He saw things, heard the screams as his mates died. He remembered a young boy lying on the ground, mortally wounded by shrapnel, his guts raw and sprinkled with earth. There was no justice in war. A lie sold by dishonest men who had no honour to defend.

Pretty early on in his first tour in Iraq he began to pick up words – yallah, itharak along with sayings he already knew, like salaam aleikum – peace be with you; which now took on an ironic aspect since he was carrying an assault rifle when he said it. He found an Iraqi interpreter to give him lessons. None of this helped his position in the unit.

'You sure you know which side you're on, Drake?'

It became a standard joke. Send Drake in first. See if they want to make peace, and if the answer is no, we come in with guns blazing. There was an acid burn under all the jokes. He learned to carry himself carefully, to watch his back. Never walk into a situation that he couldn't get himself out of. And never, ever, fully trust anyone.

The feeling of the hot wind blowing in his face was a physical sensation rather than something he remembered. The people who came up to him in the streets on foot patrol. A young woman carrying a sick child, an old man in tears. They all zeroed in on the one soldier who looked like one of them. Holding out their hands, begging for help, for understanding, for reason.

Realizing that he was complicit in their suffering made him feel responsible. He had seen what happened to men when you put a weapon in their hands and sent them to a foreign land. It felt like a natural progression to apply for the Special Investigations Branch. Someone had to police their own side. So, in his second term, during the surge of 2007, he went back as a corporal in the Military Police.

It was his mother who had brought them to the Freetown estate. She had sorted herself out, found a job in the local library and stopped drinking. For a time they ate regular meals. For a time, this was his manor. It was still a grim sight. The dull grey buildings, covered runways and reinforced glass faced onto an open patch of scrubland that on somebody's drawing board had been intended as a playing field. A row of shops and a pub had been thrown in to create a sense of community. Most of them were shuttered now, scarred by graffiti, wrapped in iron grilles with doorways bricked in and glass replaced by hardboard sheets.

Drake had good memories and bad from when he used to run here. When dreams stretched no further than becoming hip hop stars, drinking Hennessey in sleazy nightclubs with a stripper on each knee; the So Solid Crew, NWA, Ice Cube; gangsta rap, carjacking and a piece of the drug action. Drake remembered some of the faces, a couple of the names. When he came back from Iraq and joined the force they sent him here. Straight out of Hendon academy. An exercise in what they called community policing. It didn't take long for him to see it for what it was, a career dead end. He took the first exit he could find and got off that gig for good.

A police van was parked at the entrance to the estate. A handful of sleepy uniforms dozing in the fug inside. Drake leaned out of his window and slapped a hand against the door to wake them up.

'Anything happening?'

'What does it look like?' came back the reply. He hadn't really expected a serious answer, he just wanted to show them his face.

The central area was prowled by kids who looked far younger than he remembered, all in their early to mid-teens. They spun round on BMX bikes. A mixed bag, all the races united by the same raggedy clothes and hard stares.

The name over the pub read Mad King George, but nobody ever called it that. Around here it was always known as the Alamo, as a hand-painted sign over the bar made clear. Leaning in the doorway was a familiar figure with greying dreadlocks tumbling down his shoulders. When he spotted Drake, Doc Wyatt folded his arms, watching him warily before turning and disappearing back inside.

One summer, when he was around nine, Drake's mother had taken up with a man named Hendricks. A tall, gentle figure of a man. His background was West Indian, but the startling blue eyes spoke of the passage of other blood lineages. While the summer lasted they often went over to Clapham Common to sit on the grass in the sunshine. His mother would make sandwiches and Hendricks would drink cider and tell stories. He was older than Drake's mother and had travelled the world. To hear him talk was to feel the world was close. Drake felt safe with him. His greying dreadlocks gave him the impression of wisdom, although the truth was that he had little in the way of formal education. Often he talked about abolitionists who used to live around the common and meet at the Holy Trinity Church.

'They came clean, you see?'

Drake could have listened to that slow, hypnotic drawl all day. He hated it when his mother broke in with her comments, usually pointless, and totally unconnected.

'The wealth of this country was built on a lie of the mind, a deception. The idea that slavery was not such a bad thing. You catch my drift? People wanted to believe that it brought wealth and prosperity to the whole world, when of course it only helped the people on this side of the water. Over there, wherever there might be, it brought only suffering and misery.'

It was Hendricks who first told him about the Clapham Saints. A small sect of progressives. Many of whom had, of course, made their money from the benefits of the slave trade.

'The Bible tells us that slavery is bad, and yet for centuries good Christian people in this country slept soundly in their beds at night, not thinking about the consequences of their actions.'

Drake dreamed only of stability. His mother's nervous disposition drove her frenetically on towards the next man; a ship forever bound for rocky shores.

According to Hendricks, the original Freetown was established as a colony for freed slaves in West Africa. William Wilberforce and a group of abolitionists launched the idea in 1792. The Clapham Saints, they were dubbed, a group of like-minded progressives who lived in the fine mansions around the common and gathered at the

Holy Trinity Church. The estate bearing the same name was built in the early 1960s, designed by a Hungarian named Goldfinger. The leading exponent of what became known as 'Brutalist Architecture'. A monument to affordable housing for the masses where the cement was displayed front and centre. When the oil crisis hit, bringing recession, these buildings were left as high and dry as a forgotten shipwreck. Like the dinosaurs and scaly beasts buried down in the London Clay below their feet, they weren't going anywhere soon.

A quick glance around the faces inside the pub told Drake that some things never changed. Bearded hipsters, Anatolian builders, Congolese hairstylists, along with a few older men with pale skin and rugged eyes, who stared through him as they sipped their beer. Drake rapped his knuckles on the counter until Wyatt gave up his pretence of not seeing him and slid down the bar.

'Well, well, look what the cat done drag in.' He spoke with an exaggerated West Indian lilt.

'Good to see you, too, Doc.'

'Sightseeing, or on business?'

'A bit of both.'

They had been friends once, a long time ago it felt now.

'Was it the fire over at the mosque?' Doc Wyatt had a large gap between his front teeth that some people thought made him look goofy, but Drake had seen him take on knives and bicycle chains and not break a sweat. He might look like a pacifist, but you wouldn't want to get on the wrong side of him.

'Yeah, when was that again?'

Doc Wyatt rolled his eyes. 'Seriously? What they pay you for up there? Oh, yes, now I recall. Somethin' to do with rattin' out your own people, right?'

That was how it had ended, when Drake came back wearing a uniform. Community policing and him just out of Hendon. He knew he had made mistakes, come down heavier than he needed to. Back in those days he had been trying to prove himself.

Drake nodded at the rows of bottles. 'You got any decent rum back there?'

'I might have.' Doc Wyatt swivelled a toothpick from one side of his mouth to the other without touching it. 'Serving a cop can do some serious damage to my reputation, you know.'

'Your reputation will be fine.'

'Always smooth with the talk, eh, Cal?' He still reached for a bottle.

'You're not so bad yourself.'

'Difference being, I not in the business of lockin' people up, innit?'

'Tell me about this fire.'

'Ah, it's just part and parcel of the situation round here. People say things is progressin', but ya aks me and I don' see a lot in that way roun' here.'

Drake recalled an incident report on the fire. He hadn't paid much attention to it, putting it down to the kind of vandalism that happened from time to time.

'Usual thing, innit? Nobody give a fuck about what happen. People mindin' they own business, sayin' they prayers.'

'You're saying there was no investigation?'

'Investigation? Now that's a big word. It's what people say when they busy doin' nuttin'. Sure, man, we investigatin'. Raas, man. Nothing changes.'

Doc Wyatt tilted his head towards the outside. 'Now we got the goon squad parked up out there every day, try to stir things up.'

'They succeed?'

'Sure, sooner or later the kids let down dey tyre or pop a bag of dog shit off dey windscreen and they come charging in like the Light Brigade, innit? Fall for it every time. So, you just slumming it, right?'

'I didn't say that.'

'You didn't say no different, neither.' Doc Wyatt leaned his elbows on the counter. 'If you're really here to help, then it's about time. People stopped caring about this place years ago. Them boys in blue just waitin' for a chance to send in de riot squad.' He hesitated for a moment.

'I was sorry to hear about your mum,' said Doc.

'She was a junkie.'

'Everybody was.'

Drake's mother had set her flat alight one night. An old paraffin heater, a burning cigarette and a bottle of White Horse. A recipe for disaster that summed up her entire life.

With that Doc Wyatt wiped his hands on a cloth and slid down the bar to serve an old guy holding an empty pint glass. Drake turned to survey the room. It was starting to get busy. The closed looks and deflected glances told him that word had already spread about who he was.

Through the archway that led to the Lounge Bar next door Drake spotted an odd collection of four men sitting together. Three of them were young, skinheads, wearing green bomber jackets. They were grinning and snarling at one another. The table in front of them was littered with pints of lager and torn packets of crisps. The fourth man was older, in his late thirties. The sides of his head were shaven and the hair that remained on top was combed over and back in a thick wave of oil. Some kind of Hitler Youth thing going for him. When Wyatt came back Drake asked if he knew who the man was. Wyatt's mouth wrinkled in disgust.

'That's Stephen Moss. You wanna steer clear of him. Nasty piece of work.'

'Interesting,' said Drake.

Outside, a group of kids on bikes circled round his car, their chains whirring like rattlesnakes. Someone had spray painted '5-Oh' on the side. The paint was still running. When they saw Drake, they took off, standing up as they peddled hard, flying away towards the shadows.

As he drove out of the estate, Drake pulled up by the TSG carrier and banged on the side again. He waited for the driver to wind down his window.

'Can you pull back a bit?'

'Back?'

'Off the estate. Give these people some space.'

The beefy sergeant scratched his ear. 'You need to take it up with DCI Pryce.'

'There will be trouble if you hang around here looking aggressive.'

'Like I said, you need to take that up with DCI Pryce.'

Drake thought he could hear laughter from inside the van as he pulled away.

CHAPTER 18

The Birch Lane mosque was, strictly speaking, not part of Freetown. It was down a narrow side street across from the main playing field at the centre of the estate. An old red-brick building that had once been a synagogue. There were places where you could strip away the wallpaper to find carved menorahs and stars of David in the woodwork. The imam had insisted they be covered up but not removed, out of respect for the Jews, who, as 'People of the Book', had to be respected. Drake knew this because back in the day he had prayed here. A million years ago, or so it felt now. It had been converted into a rectory. Then it was a music studio. Eventually it was reborn as a community centre and then cuts left it desolate until it came back to life as a mosque. And if the sign now planted in the front yard was genuine, it had just been acquired by Jerome Clapp Associates and was about to be converted into 'unique housing modules'. All enquiries to the number given.

The low garden wall still bore a smattering of swastikas and quips about towel-heads and camel fuckers. The community artists had been busy again. Drake called Kelly and asked for the details, then waited while she pulled the file.

'Three weeks ago, the fire started with a low-grade incendiary device being thrown through the front door.'

The stone arch around the entrance to the building was charred. The heavy wooden doors were blackened and split from the heat.

'The guy in charge of the place was hurt. Not badly. Some burns and smoke inhalation. Why the interest?' Kelly meant, why now?

'I'm not sure. It may be nothing. This damage looks like more than just a homemade fire bomb.'

'Take it up with forensics. They still haven't filed a full report.'

That meant nobody was taking it too seriously, which was what you might expect. Someone pours lighter fuel through a letter box and drops a match in after it. Happens all the time, mate.

Drake went around the side of the building and found another entrance. The door stood open. He stepped up into a kind of utility room. There was a washing machine and dryer. At the far end a door led into a toilet. Alongside were shelves of cleaning products, brooms, dusters and a large, industrial hoover.

'Hello?' Drake called out. There was no reply.

He was standing in the hallway that ran the length of the building. To his right he could see the entrance. The cracked door and crime-scene tape flapping outside. A chill breeze ran through. From here it was clear that the damage was far more extensive than was apparent from the outside. For one thing the fire had cut down the hallway, charring the walls and the ceiling which had been lined with false panelling. This had melted in places, accounting for the burnt plastic smell. From this side the fire seemed to be centred on a room just off the hallway, to the right of the front entrance.

'What are you doing here?'

Drake turned to see a woman dressed in black from head

to toe. The yellow rubber gloves on her hands added a weird touch of colour. He put her age at somewhere in her late forties. Her eyes and nose were red. Clearly she had been crying.

'Police,' he said, holding up his badge. She squinted at the name before turning away.

'You've come too late,' she said over her shoulder.

Drake followed her through a doorway into a prayer room. She went back to her work, cleaning the wood of the mihrab, the niche in the wall that indicated the direction of Mecca. Drake tried to shake off the feeling of discomfort he felt in that room. The woman seemed to notice. She looked at him.

'Have we met before?'

'I don't think so. Look, I'm a detective.' He produced his notebook and pen to try to look more convincing. 'Can I ask who you are?'

'I am Mrs Ahmad, the wife of the imam. This . . .' She made a conscious effort to control her anger. 'This is our home, or was.'

Drake looked round and nodded. 'I understand your husband was hurt in the attack.'

'Third-degree burns and smoke inhalation. They say he will never recover fully.'

'I'm sorry to hear that.'

Her expression said this was little comfort. 'What do you want here?'

'Like I said, I'm a detective.'

'I mean, why do you come now?'

'These things take time.'

She gave a dismissive snort. 'Nobody is interested. A mosque burns. It's a natural hazard.'

There was a touch of Eastern Europe to her accent.

'Where is your husband now?' Drake asked.

'We could not stay here. Too much damage. They put us in

a hotel.' Her eyes were flat, but her nose now wrinkled. 'Dirty place. Noisy. Full of dirty people.'

'Right.' Drake nodded at the gloves and the bucket of soapy water. 'So you're cleaning up.'

'We want our home back.'

'Can you tell me what happened?'

The woman heaved a sigh.

'I was in the kitchen, preparing breakfast, we do it every Friday, for the people, after prayers. The place was packed. It's a miracle more didn't die.'

The prayer room was a wide open space. Some walls had been knocked through. The floor was covered with carpet imprinted with a repeated motif: rows of arched doorways lined up in the same direction. The faithful would each stand on one of these doors to face Mecca.

'How many were here when the attack happened?'

Mrs Ahmad shrugged. 'Thirty, forty men? In the kitchen, maybe ten women, helping me.'

'They all gave statements?'

'No, of course not.'

Drake tapped the notebook against his side. People didn't hang around waiting for the cops to show up and start asking questions.

'Can you give me any names?'

The woman met his gaze levelly. 'It's a masjid, a mosque. A place of worship, people are free to come and go as they please. This is a free country.'

'Course it is. So, tell me, the imam was in the hallway when the attack happened?'

'No, no. The doorbell rang. Ahmad had just finished his tafsir. That is . . .'

'I know what tafsir is.'

'Of course.' She looked at him strangely before going on. 'I was in the kitchen. I hear the bell. I think it is strange. The door is open so that people can just walk in. I remember coming to stand in the doorway. I thought I will go answer it, but Ahmad waved for me not to bother, and he went himself.'

'What happened then?'

'I go back to kitchen. Suddenly, I hear loud noise, like someone is coughing. Very loud. I could feel it going through the building. I shout and run to the hallway, but it's impossible. The whole place is white, white with fire. Ya Allah! I've never seen anything like it. Ahmad, my poor Ahmad! He was in flames. I didn't know what to do. He was coming towards me. There was a coat lying on a chair in the hallway. He always complained when people did not use the coat stand by the front door, but lucky for him. I picked it up and threw it on him to put out the flames.'

'Good thinking.'

'Why do people hate us so much? We do not preach hatred. Ahmad, he . . .' She began to cry softly, burying her face in her hands for a second. There was a moment's awkward silence. Then she sniffed and looked up. 'Your badge says your name is Calil. You are Muslim?'

Drake hesitated, then nodded. 'I used to come here, a long time ago.'

'I knew it.' A knowing smile appeared. 'Faith is not a garment you put on and take off. Once a Muslim, always a Muslim.'

He let that one go and stepped back out. The hall looked as if it had been seared by a giant blowtorch; walls, floor, ceiling. A cheap chandelier had melted into twisted swirls of metal and fused glass.

'Can I ask, was there anyone else living here, apart from yourself and your husband when it happened?'

She glanced away from him, then shook her head.

'I'd like to talk to your husband, if that's all right with you.'

'Why, what is the point?'

'We might find out who did this.'

'Nobody cares who did this,' she said. 'You know why? They think we deserve it.'

He watched her walk back to her bucket and retrieve her sponge to begin dabbing at the walls. Rivulets of black water ran down the wall.

CHAPTER 19

Crane had always had a thing about motorcycles. Ever since she was a child. She was drawn to the kind of swagger that accompanied them. The feeling of the world rushing towards you as you twisted the grip. When she was thirteen she watched a film with Mickey Rourke. Motorcycle Boy. That was his name. She didn't remember what the film was called but she did remember that he rode a red Kawasaki GPZ. For a time she had owned a similar model. Years later she watched the film again, and hated it. A lot of macho posturing that hadn't aged well. But she still loved bikes.

The engine responded eagerly as she twisted the throttle, zipping between a van and a Mini that had stalled. Car horns sounded behind her, but she was already past it, looking ahead. That was the thing about riding a bike; you always had to be looking ahead. The danger came from every direction: a pothole in the road, a patch of diesel oil, other motorists. You soon learned that you couldn't trust anyone else on the road. Cars, buses, black cabs in particular, other bikes, reckless cyclists, and pedestrians, of course, who often seemed completely oblivious of moving vehicles.

The midnight blue Triumph Bonneville always gave her a sense of purpose. She zipped through the traffic, riding the white lines. A car in central London made about as much sense as a horse-drawn carriage and was statistically no faster. She often cycled about the city, but the Triumph was a little indulgence that she told herself also had practical benefits.

She spun down the Edgware Road and opened up the engine on Park Lane. She cut left through Mayfair, threading her way easily along the sidestreets until she arrived in Soho. The tarmac was still slick from a recent rain shower. The afternoon sun sliced down Frith Street, cutting the street into angles of shadow and light. She climbed off the bike and shook her hair free from the helmet as she hurried along the street, pulling her scarf up to protect her from another brief flurry.

There was nothing about the red door to indicate that it was anything more than an ordinary terraced house. Except that there wasn't much around here that could be described as ordinary. There weren't many people who could afford one of these places as a private residence these days, unless they'd hung on to it for decades. The only thing that appeared on the polished brass plaque beside the door were the numbers $33^{1/3}$. Not the street number. A reference perhaps to the fact that once upon a time the music industry used to be centred around this area. Maybe it still was, but Crane wasn't here to break into the music or any other business. She leaned a finger on the reception buzzer and stared straight into the glowing eye of the camera until the door clicked open. Inside, the entrance had been remodelled to retain as much as possible of its original form. Chequerboard tiles disappeared down a narrow hallway past a dinky little reception desk tucked under the staircase. The woman behind the desk wore an emerald-green satin dress and cherry-red lipstick. The smile congealed on her face. Crane didn't slow her pace. She knew what it was. The headscarf, which she decided there and then was staying put on her head.

'Doctor Rayhana Crane to meet Stewart Mason.' She even put a little bit of an accent on her voice. Just for fun.

'Of course.' To her credit the smile stayed in place as the hostess ran a finger carefully down the ledger in front of her looking for a mistake. There wasn't one. She pointed towards the stairs.

'I'll leave this here.'

Crane dumped her helmet on the counter alongside a silver ice bucket that contained a bottle of pink champagne. No offer of an aperitif. The receptionist seemed uncomfortable. She began wringing her hands, apparently unable to make up her mind. Through a doorway to the right Crane glimpsed a front room that had been turned into a lounge, with designer lighting and leather armchairs. Already she felt irritated by the place. Part old-fashioned men's club, part trendy watering hole for wannabe media types.

Ready to punch anyone who got in her way, Ray climbed the stairs to the first floor and entered a long, dark room. A backlit bar ran along the rear wall. Low windows with discreet drapes faced out onto a side street to the left. Apart from the man behind the bar the room was almost empty. There was a sofa along the right wall while the rest of the room was taken up with small tables. Two of them were by the windows. One of these was empty, the other occupied by a tall, bald man in an expensive, bespoke suit. Stewart Mason rolled his eyes as she entered.

'Ah,' he simpered. 'You came as the devout diva.'

'Save it,' Ray said, sitting down, shrugging off her leather jacket.

'I never know what to make of you. Biker moll or swinging sister.'

'You sound embarrassed, Stewart.'

'The point about this place is that nobody cares what you do or how you dress.'

'You can believe that if you want to.' She looked up as a waiter appeared. He wore a crushed velvet waistcoat. Very Marc Bolan. All he needed was a feather boa.

'What are you drinking?' Ray asked Mason.

'Bourbon, ginger ale and lime.' Mason held the glass up to the light. 'It's not bad.'

'I'll have the same.'

'The same?'

'Yes, only drop the ginger ale.'

The waiter seemed to falter a little before recovering and spinning on his heels and disappearing. A rather smug smile played on Mason's lips as Crane shrugged the scarf off her head.

'You like that, don't you, unsettling people?'

'Why am I here, Stewart?'

'I thought you'd like the place. It's discreet, not too exclusive, less formal than my club in St James.'

'Forgive me, but I see only a change in decór. Otherwise it's old men doing what they always do, building little fortresses to keep the riff-raff out.' She looked around. 'It's also way too fashionable for you.'

Mason seemed to enjoy being baited. 'You're too quick to judge. Give it a chance.'

'Why am I really here?'

'How's the practice going?'

'It's going.' Ray sat back in her chair as the waiter set her drink down. She put out a hand to grab his wrist. 'Wait.' She took a sip and shook her head. 'More bourbon, less ice.' He did a double take and then ducked away.

'You're being mean to him, just to change the subject.'

'Not at all. The ice dilutes the bourbon. Just like that sticky syrup you've got in there.'

Stewart leaned his elbows on the table. 'Okay, I'll get to the point. I want you to come and work for me.'

'We tried that, remember? Didn't work out too well, if you recall.'

'You're wasting your time soothing the egos of your few patients. We both know that.'

'Well, it beats working behind a bar.' She flashed the waiter an acid smile as he returned with her drink. This time it was better.

'I'm putting together a private company. Risk management. I could use someone like you.'

'I'll bet you could.'

'Come on. Don't tell me you've got something better going. I know you're on the brink of going under.'

'Actually, I'm on a new case.'

'Interesting.' Mason leaned back. 'Who called you in?'

'Superintendent Wheeler.'

'This is the double murder, on a building site?'

'Magnolia Quays.'

'We've become a nation obsessed with the macabre. Who's in charge?'

'DS Drake, out of Raven Hill.' She saw his expression change. 'You know him?'

'I know of him. There's a shadow hanging over him.'

'He was demoted, claims he was railroaded.'

'They all do. It's never their fault.' Ice rattled as Mason took a long sip of his drink. 'That's the problem with this country, nobody wants to take responsibility for anything.'

Ray looked around the room. They were playing some kind of mood music somewhere. A lounge version of an old Clash song. Heavy damask drapes covered the doors. A couple entered. The woman was young enough to be the man's daughter, but the way he had his hand around her waist made it clear that she wasn't. The longer she spent here the less Ray liked it.

'A key witness was killed. She was under his protection at the time.'

Mason nodded. 'I remember the case. Goran Malevich. Nasty piece of work. This Drake was supposedly in his pay.'

'He was working undercover, trying to infiltrate Malevich's organization.'

'That's right. Only he was working for Malevich all the time.'

'That was the claim.' Ray circled a finger round the rim of her glass. 'They couldn't prove anything.'

'If memory serves, the court case fell apart because he lost a witness.'

'She disappeared. The assumption was that Drake had helped to get her out of the way. He was demoted and transferred out of the Met for a time.'

'Malevich was killed in the end, wasn't he?'

'Gunned down in a car park.'

'Charming, and you say you're working with this guy?'

'I'm trying to. He's not so keen on the idea. Wants to solve it by himself and clear his name. Some such macho bullshit.'

'Right.' Mason studied her over his glass. 'I'm assuming you agreed to meet because you want something from me.'

'I need the same thing.'

'I didn't think macho bullshit was your line,' said Mason cattily.

'You have access to files. You know people. You know Howard Thwaite.'

'Only indirectly.'

Mason had a long career behind him in the intelligence services, moving around from one grey area to another. Over the years, Ray would never be sure exactly who he was working for, or on what. Counter-intelligence. Anti-terrorism. Special-Ops. Pysch-Ops.

Six years ago it was Stewart Mason who had come to her with an interesting proposition; a think tank, the Vesta Institute, had contacted him. They were developing a scheme to analyse radicalization. They proposed counselling civilians and former fighters who were returning from Syria and Iraq after going out to join ISIS. There was a problem with the optics, which was why it was being handled by a private foundation rather than a government institution. Public opinion was unlikely to accept the notion of giving returning jihadis a second chance. Certainly it would have been difficult to argue that it was possible to learn from them, to try and put their experience to work. The general view was that they were fanatics who had turned against their own country. They deserved to be stripped of their citizenship and thrown into a bottomless pit, at the very least.

Crane knew going in that it was a risky venture, but that was never something that caused her to shy away. On the contrary, she felt it was vital to try to understand what drove people to leave behind their jobs and families, to sacrifice the comfort they knew for the unknown, for an idea. Some of them went as fighters, others as doctors, nurses, hospital orderlies, teachers, computer scientists, housewives, men and women. Most were young, some still in their teens. There were women who had been enticed over chat rooms to come out and marry fighters, and men who had been in trouble with the law. What they had in common was their choosing an Islamic caliphate they knew nothing about over the country they had called home for most if not all of their lives.

Then, one morning a young man named Salim Anwar walked into a shopping mall in Leeds and tried to blow himself up. The device failed to detonate, but Anwar had been one of Crane's patients and someone had to take the fall. Mason had tried to help her. Not to the extent that he was willing to take responsibility, of course. He disappeared into the system to emerge, as always, higher up than he'd been before. So, Mason owed her and he knew that.

'I need to get ahead. I need an edge,' said Ray.

'And you think I can provide this? Let's order.'

'I'm not hungry.'

Mason pulled a face. 'Why do you reject my advances?'

'You're a married man, remember?'

'We're both consenting adults. Let me worry about that.'

Mason put out a hand to grab her wrist. She looked down at it, waited until he let go.

'At least consider my offer. Civilian life will bore you to death and you know it.'

'I'll think about it,' Ray promised. Finishing her drink she got to her feet. She looked around at their surroundings. 'The thing is,' she said. 'You can throw fancy wallpaper at it, but it doesn't get rid of the old stench.'

He watched her walk away.

CHAPTER 20

On the way back to Raven Hill, Drake gave Fast Eddie a call. As always, the forensic officer sounded half asleep.

'I was over in Freetown, looking at the fire there.'

'Interesting. I thought you were on the Magnolia Quays case.'

'I was just curious. What can you tell me?'

'I had the feeling it wasn't a priority.'

In person, Fast Eddie was a tall, lanky man in need of a haircut. He might have looked and sounded like a hippy, but in practice he was anything but.

'Humour me, okay?'

'Not a problem. Okay, well, first off, this is not your average juvenile delinquent special.'

'Meaning?'

'Somebody knew what they were doing.'

'It looked like there was a lot of damage close to the door.'

'Well, right, you know. That would be consistent with accelerant being introduced close to the entrance.'

'But?' The thing about Fast Eddie was that he didn't offer up information willingly, you had to ask nicely. Drake sensed he was holding something back.

'So, left of the main entrance is a spare room. We found the remains of a bed. Some belongings. It looked like someone was sleeping in there.'

'But no body, right?'

'No, that would have taken things to another level. The indications are that no one was in there at the time.'

'The attack took place in the middle of the day, so presumably the room was empty.'

Fast Eddie cleared his throat. 'You should really talk to Bishop.'

'DS Bishop?'

'He's the man.'

Drake's heart sank. Bishop was a hopeless case.

'I'll do that. In the meantime, give me a breakdown. What are we talking about? A can of paraffin for a stove?'

'That was my first thought. A camping stove or gas bottle exploding. But the pattern is all wrong. This was a little more intense.'

'Meaning?'

'Meaning, whatever it was, it was powerful enough to blow through the brickwork in places. We found cracks. I would put the temperature as up in the hundreds.'

'So, you're talking what, military grade?'

'That would do it.'

'But you found nothing. No casings or packaging?'

'Nothing like that. I sent some of the residue to the lab.'

'And?'

'It's too early to say for sure. And if I were to speculate, which I don't do as a rule...'

'Course you don't.'

'I'd say this was specialist stuff, for the connoisseur only. The way the burn pattern spread along the wall suggests a serious incendiary device. Ever come across Thermite in your time in the service?'

Drake had heard of it. It was the stuff they used in anti-tank rockets. An armour piercing shell would deliver a payload that could turn the interior into a furnace in seconds. 1600 degrees.

'So, not your average arsonist.'

'Doesn't look like it. We're trying to trace where it came from now.'

'How did it get in there?'

'Well, that's the thing. The two parts of the fire seem to have been separate, at least to begin with. So the initial damage to the front door and the hallway are different.'

'No entry point? No impact or detonation?'

'Our analysis of the fire pattern suggests the fire actually started inside the building.'

'You can see that?'

'We have models based on all kinds of scenarios. The second blast was like a wave that swept everything before it. Produces a very distinctive shape.'

'And that came from within?'

'It looks that way. Thermite is normally sealed into stable packages to stop accidental detonation.'

'So how do you explain that?'

'I can't,' said Fast Eddie. 'Unless someone had removed the material from its packaging.'

'And it was detonated by the lighter fuel . . .'

'That's about the size of it.'

Drake thanked him and rang off. At Raven Hill he found Milo and Kelly looking frantic.

'Where've you been, chief?' Kelly asked.

'I was over in the estate, taking a look around.'

'Someone decorated your car, I see.' She nodded out the window.

'Yeah, artists, what can I say?' Drake studied the notice board where nothing seemed to have changed. They were running out of time.

Kelly came to stand beside him. 'We were beginning to get worried.'

'I'm touched.'

'Seriously, Wheeler keeps popping in to find out how we're doing. Milo and me, we're crawling the walls. The fact of the matter is we don't have shit.'

'Language, DC Marsh.'

'Sorry,' muttered Kelly.

'What did you get on Thwaite's finances?'

'Oh.' Kelly ran a hand through her hair. 'It's a mess. He's up to his neck in debt. The bank are calling in their loans. According to one source he is willing to take money from anyone.'

'The woman at the gallery said that Thwaite lost a lot six years ago.'

'That's right.' Kelly leaned over to her desk to retrieve her notes. She flipped through the pages. 'So, this was a project somewhere in the Gulf. Doha?' She looked up.

'It's a place.'

'Right. That much I knew. Anyway, he was supposed to be building some kind of institution. A lot of money involved. And he got into trouble. They couldn't deliver on time and the contract was sold off at a loss.' She folded her notebook closed. 'That's all I've got.'

'Okay, maybe we can arrange to talk to him about that. Can you set up an appointment?'

'Sure, but . . .'

'But?'

Kelly cast around her. 'I don't know, boss. I'm just wondering if we're not getting off track. Time being what it is and all.'

Drake perched himself on the edge of Milo's desk. 'What's on your mind?'

'We're nowhere. We've got statements from workers, the ones we could track down, from possible witnesses around the site, even from Mr Cricket, who's now cooperating, but none of it leads anywhere.'

'Doesn't that make the case for spreading the net wider?'

'What if it's just a nut job, a one-man crazy band?'

'We know there are at least two of them,' corrected Milo.

Kelly gave him a long glare. 'Okay, so two crazies.'

'The point is,' Drake said. 'We have to keep shaking this tree from every angle, until something falls out.'

Kelly gave a long sigh. 'Truth be told, chief, I'm beginning to wonder if we're not out of our depth. I mean, we're into day two. We don't have that much time left.'

'What happened to never say die?'

Kelly shifted uncomfortably. Milo found a spot on one of his screens that needed cleaning.

'Let's get back to the facts,' Drake continued. 'Milo, how far did you get with tracing Mrs Thwaite's car?'

Milo reached for a notepad lying on his desk.

'I traced the Porsche SUV back from the site and picked it up in Vauxhall.' He cued up the images in a few clicks of his mouse. The black-and-white image rolled, showing the car sliding under lights. 'Then I lost it.'

Kelly pulled up her chair. 'Hideo left his house after receiving a text message. According to his daughter he became very agitated and then went out without explanation.'

'I pulled a text message off Hideo's Samsung that came from a number that matched with one on Mrs Thwaite's iPhone. It mentioned a name . . .' He frowned at the screen. 'Jakucho.'

'Wasn't that the woodblock artist the daughter mentioned?' Kelly asked. 'Ukiyo-e?'

'Could you trace the number?' asked Drake.

'Negative,' said Milo. 'No activity since then. It's pay as you go. No name. No address.'

'Okay,' said Drake. 'Let's look at the time.'

Kelly went over to the whiteboard where a timeline had been marked in. 'Marsha Thwaite was due at the theatre in Sloane Square at seven-thirty. She never arrived. Her assistant says she left her to close up the shop an hour before that.'

'Any cameras around the shop?'

'I'm ahead of you,' said Milo. 'There are security cameras inside the Arcadia gallery. One at the entrance shows Mrs Thwaite leaving at 18.43. She's late and she's in a hurry. That's the last we see of her. I couldn't find any trace of the car leaving the area until this.' Milo cued up more footage. 'This is from an ATM on the corner of the Brompton Road.'

The camera afforded them a downward angle. The grainy, grey images shunted along at speed, showing people approaching the machine, then walking away. It was there to deter people from being robbed as they withdrew cash. In the background the street was just visible. The wheels of vehicles passing by. The shops on the other side of the street. For a time there was nothing. Then a figure, male, wearing a light-coloured windcheater and chinos.

'Is that Hideo?' asked Drake.

'Looks like he's off to play golf,' said Kelly.

Hideo seemed to be waiting for something. He walked a few paces, then turned and walked back again.

'He's meeting someone,' said Drake.

'Here it comes,' murmured Milo.

The Porsche appeared in the foreground, rolling to a halt. Hideo stopped and turned towards the car. The window rolled down, but it was impossible to see into the interior. Then Hideo opened the door and climbed inside.

'It's like he went willingly,' said Kelly quietly.

'He was expecting to meet someone. He goes to the agreed spot and a car pulls up. He gets in.' Drake reached for one of Milo's rubber bands. 'We can't see if Mrs Thwaite is driving.' He waited for Milo to shake his head. 'What then?'

'I lost it. There's nothing until it turns onto the access road by Magnolia Quays.'

'How can that be?' asked Kelly.

Drake turned back to the map. Picking up a marker pen he traced a wide arc from Wandsworth Bridge around Clapham Junction and up to Battersea Bridge.

'We have nearly four hours to account for. Between the victims disappearing in the Knightsbridge, SW1 area and when the Porsche is seen entering the site area at . . .'

Milo consulted his screen. '22.47.'

'Okay, so where were they?' Drake ran a finger over the map. 'We have to assume they had to be close. They wouldn't move around in order to avoid traffic cameras. So let's look at industrial sites, abandoned warehouses, lock-ups, that kind of thing.'

'I'll get onto it,' said Kelly.

'Good,' said Drake. 'Time is running out and if we don't start making progress, Wheeler is going to throw this little bone to DCI Pryce, and we don't want that.'

'Speaking of which, Wheeler was looking for you.'

'Well, you didn't see me.' Drake reached for his coat.

'What do I tell him when he asks?'

'Tell him the truth, Kelly. Tell him I'm out there chasing down leads.'

'Of course you are. Oh, and our favourite psychic was looking for you. It sounded urgent.'

'Tell her I'll call back.' Drake started towards the door and then stopped. 'One other thing. Now we know this was not a case of random victims selected by chance. He wanted these two together. Why?'

'He's Japanese, she's Jewish,' Kelly quipped. 'It's a natural fit.'

'We need to know more about them both. Can we find out exactly what Hideo was doing for the UN?'

He snapped the rubber band back to Milo.

'Nice work, both of you. Now let's wrap this thing up.'

CHAPTER 21

A t Salon Zarif, Marouan sat reading a newspaper in one of the old flip-down cinema seats that were reserved for waiting customers. Above him hung a framed certificate that declared him a qualified graduate of the Eiffel Tour École de Coiffure. It sounded the way it looked, like it had fallen out of a packet of Frosties.

'Khalil. Long time no see.'

Marouan insisted on pronouncing Cal's name the Arabic way. Drake didn't mind. What he objected to was the way the other man seemed to assume this established some form of trust between them, as if they had known each other for a lifetime. Marouan put aside his copy of *Hello!* magazine and got slowly to his feet to come over.

Only one of the two big red chairs was occupied. Mimo, Marouan's young assistant, was drawing a pattern with a razor in the back of a young man's bristly head. Drake sat down in the other chair. In the mirror he watched the reverse image of the television screen high on the wall behind him. It was tuned to a religious channel that was playing a recital of a verse from the Quran. The slow rhythmic tones rose and fell in time with a bouncing ball that ran over the text running across the screen. It seemed incongruous, considering Marouan's inclinations. But this was just his way of trying to look respectable. The sound of the recital was familiar. It felt like an echo from a lifetime ago.

'What can I do for you?' Marouan stood behind him.

'Just run over it with the machine.' Drake glanced in the mirror at the man sitting next to him who, on closer inspection, must have been all of seventeen. 'Nothing fancy.'

'Nothing fancy,' chuckled Marouan. 'That'll be the day.' He snapped a nylon apron and placed it over Drake, tying it at the neck over a folded strip of tissue before going about preparing the electric trimmer. 'You're not the type to fuss over yourself.'

'Not exactly.'

Drake caught the look from the kid in the mirror. Not exactly disapproval, but it made having your hair cut and spliced in whatever weird form was in vogue into something more than a fashion statement. The look in the kid's eyes told him he knew Drake was police.

Settling into the big chair, Drake closed his eyes. The truth was that he did appreciate the attention that went into all of this. He wasn't sure about any school in Paris, but there was a degree of professionalism in Marouan's attitude. He watched the older man's eyes in the mirror.

'So, what brings you around here?' Marouan asked as he blew the blades clean.

'Do you still pray in the mosque over in Freetown?'

'That's why you're here, the fire?' Marouan lifted his shoulders. 'I thought that was all forgotten.'

'Nothing's forgotten. Things just take time these days.'

'Right,' said Marouan slowly. 'But you're on it now.' He blew at the head of the machine. 'Makes sense, I guess.'

'What's that supposed to mean?'

'Nothing. It's just what you expect, right? I mean, they're never going to respect you.' Marouan shook his head as he buzzed the trimmer into action. Drake put a hand up to stop him.

'Hold on a second.'

'It's just my opinion, right?' Marouan held up his hands defensively. 'Everybody is entitled to an opinion, right?'

Drake held the other man's gaze in the mirror. 'You were there that day.'

'It was a Friday, everyone was there.' Marouan clicked the trimmer on again and pushed Drake's head to one side.

'I'm not talking about everyone. I'm asking about you.'

Marouan was clearly annoyed. He didn't like being talked to this way in front of his employees and customers. He turned to his assistant.

'You nearly finished?' Marouan asked. Mimo looked up, surprised.

'Nah, still got this innit?'

'Finish up later, okay? On the house, all right mate?'

The kid in the chair wasn't happy. He ripped the smock from around his neck before Mimo could finish removing it and started towards the door.

'Boss?' protested Mimo, but Marouan aimed his thumb at the door. Mimo grabbed his coat from behind the door and followed his client out. Marouan looked at Drake in the mirror.

'So, what's this all about then? Why you come here accusing me?'

'I'm not accusing anyone. You got something on your conscience?'

'I don't know what you're talkin' about.'

'Everyone assumed that fire was a bunch of kids with swastika tattoos.'

Marouan rolled his fleshy shoulders. 'Who else is gonna do

something like that?' The trimmer buzzed back into life as he pushed Drake's head forward to work on the back of his neck.

'I used to know your father,' Marouan murmured. 'In the old days. He was a gentleman.'

'A gentleman? That's a new one.'

'You don't remember. You were young. But your father had class. He was good to everybody. In those days none of us had any money. We couldn't afford fine clothes or good food. The way you judged character was all about how you conducted yourself. And in that sense your father was royalty.'

'That's not how I remember him.'

Marouan shrugged. 'People change. When he left your mother it wasn't because of another woman, it was because he simply couldn't take it any longer. Living in this country is not easy. The defeats, the setbacks, the prejudice. It changed him. Back then it was difficult for all of us.'

'You're breaking my heart.'

Marouan stared at him in the mirror. 'He lost his soul.'

'What does that mean?'

'I mean, there is good and bad in all people. He started out good, but in the end it was the bad that took over.'

'You know where he is?'

Marouan resumed his work. 'I haven't seen him for years, and I don't want to see him.'

Drake thought about this for a moment. He hadn't come here looking for his father. That was a whole other story that would have to be addressed at some other time and place.

'Tell me about the fire.'

'What's to tell?' Marouan spread his hands wide. 'It was a fire.'

'You saw it happen?'

'I was in the room with everyone else.'

'The prayer room.'

'Right, the prayer room. There was a noise. Imam Ahmad went out to see what was happening. The next thing we heard screaming.'

'Who was screaming?'

'Everyone. The imam, his wife. He was in flames.' Marouan blew the air out of his lungs. 'That was scary. I mean, the man was on fire. We ran out and tried to save him.'

'What did you hear?'

'Hear?'

Drake held Marouan's eyes in the mirror. 'Was there one explosion, or two?'

'What difference does it make?' The big, fleshy face was a picture of indifference. Then he frowned. 'Okay, maybe it was two. One small, and then a bigger one.' He went back to his work.

'Do you know if anyone was staying there?'

'In the masjid?' Marouan stopped again, the trimmer still buzzing. 'Why do you ask?'

'You're an old regular. You know the imam.'

'Why don't you ask him?'

'I asked his wife, she seemed unsure.'

'Well, I don't know what to say. Maybe.'

'Look, it makes no difference to me. That's not what I'm after.' Drake waited. Marouan said nothing. He stared at the floor. 'So, what are we talking about, illegals?'

'Refugees,' Marouan shrugged.

'From where?'

'I don't know. Syrians, Yemenis, Sudanese.'

'And they slept in the masjid?'

'You didn't hear it from me.'

'I never said I did.' Drake watched him in the mirror as Marouan resumed his work. 'So they would stay in the front room, by the entrance, right?'

'Front room?' Marouan stopped. 'No, they just slept on the floor in the prayer room. They came and went.' He paused. 'No, you're thinking of Waleed's room.'

'Waleed?'

'The imam's son. He has . . . problems.' Marouan tapped his head. 'Breakdown. Very sad.'

'What kind of breakdown?'

'It's confusing for young people. This country, I mean. To stay true to your faith. Everyone wants you to go out drinking, chasing women.'

'And that led to a breakdown?'

Marouan lifted his shoulders. 'Some people can't handle it. Live one life at home, another outside. It confuses them.' He circled a finger around his temple. 'He was in hospital for a time. This all started years ago. He goes along fine for a time, but then he has another episode. They don't like to talk about it. They're ashamed, you know? Their son. It's painful. You understand that.'

For a time there was only the buzz of the machine.

'What happened to you?' Marouan asked after a while. 'I mean, you used to be one of us. You used to come to masjid. You were part of the study group. You was interested in politics.'

'That was a long time ago.'

'We all change, but joining the army? Going to fight in Iraq? We all know that it's a war against Muslims. And now this, the police?'

'Tell me about Waleed. How can I find him?'

The trimmer stopped its buzzing as Marouan clicked off the machine. Drake followed him with his eyes in the mirror.

'You used to be one of us. The moment you put that uniform on you became one of them.' Marouan was shaking his head. 'They will never accept you. One day, maybe you'll realize that.'

'I get it. You have a noble idea of the past. Islam, the old country, some sense of order. You look around and you see a world gone to hell. We all see it. The drink, the drugs, the crime. The money that goes flowing past. The prejudice, ignorance, the hatred. Well, I've seen all of that too.'

'They are using you. It makes them look good to have a brown person on their side.'

Drake got to his feet, pulling the apron from around his neck.

'If all you care about is saving yourself you've already lost.'

Marouan fiddled with the trimmer blades as he began to speak.

'People don't know what's going on. They don't see the drone strikes, the gas attacks, the dead babies. The violence that is being done in their name.'

'Isn't it written that we have no right to judge others? Allah will take care of that on the Day of Judgement.'

Marouan gave a thin smile. 'So you do remember something.'

'The world is in a mess,' said Drake. 'But you're not helping.' He swivelled round to face Marouan. 'Waleed may be out of his depth. You want to help, then tell me where he is.'

'What difference does it make?' Marouan sighed, sinking back into the chair by the wall where he had been sitting earlier, reaching for the tattered copy of Hello! 'The last I heard he had come out of hospital. But where he is now, your guess is as good as mine.'

Drake headed for the door, where he stopped to look back. 'Did he ever work as a labourer, on a building site, I mean?'

Marouan shrugged. 'I don't know. I know he worked for a time for that black gangster. The African. You know.'

'You mean, Papa Zemba?'

'That's the one. African.'

'Right.'

CHAPTER 22

Forty minutes later, Drake spun the BMW off Westbourne Terrace and dipped into the narrow mews behind Paddington Station. Immediately, he felt the wheels slip and juggle over wet cobblestones. When he climbed out of the car he looked around, wondering if he was in the right place. There was something rather sinister and removed about it. A dark, stony gully. The rain hissed down around him in sharp, icy nails, turning everything black. There weren't a lot of doors to choose from, so it didn't take long to find the right one. He pressed the intercom and squinted at the camera as a bright light beamed at him.

The door buzzed to admit him into what appeared to be a converted garage space. It had been cleaned up nicely and the floor was now tastefully covered with oiled oak flooring. Directly in front of him hung a heavy punchbag that didn't look as if it was there for decoration. It swayed back and forth gently. He gave it a playful shove as he went by only to discover that it was heavier than expected. On the wall hung a pair of battered nunchakus. He took them down and flipped them around for a bit, before hitting himself on the chin and putting them back.

In the shadows to his left a customized Triumph Bonneville motorcycle rested on its stand. Midnight blue. Rather classy. There were tool racks fixed to the wall that didn't look ornamental.

'Innerestin',' Drake murmured to himself.

The rear half of the room was given over to a living area with a long, heavy solid wooden table in the middle that would have seated ten or twelve. To the left of this was an open-plan kitchen. At the far end, French windows looked out onto an enclosed patio. Big wooden doors that could be slid open in the summer.

'Inspector?'

Drake turned to see Crane standing in a doorway to his right. She looked smaller, slimmer, and darker than he remembered. She was wearing sweat pants and a singlet. A towel loosely draped around her neck. She crossed in front of him to go behind the high counter into the kitchen.

'Nice of you to come over. What can I get you?'

'Oh, I'm fine.' This wasn't meant to be a social call.

'A beer?' She pulled open the refrigerator.

'Sure. So, what's the story here? You live here, work here, what?'

'Both.' She was piling chunks of kiwi, banana and carrot into a blender. Her arms were well defined and muscular, without being excessively so. The tightly cut singlet she wore was damp with sweat. He turned away so as not to be caught staring.

'Nice neighbourhood.'

'It's all right, considering.' Her voice was lost in the grind of the machine. 'I don't really know it,' she said when it had finished.

'So you didn't grow up round here.'

'Not exactly.'

'Where then, if you don't mind me asking.'

'Tehran.'

'Okay, so not local.'

'Not exactly.' She drank her smoothie directly from the jug. 'Any progress on the case?'

'I'd be lying if I said there was.' Drake sipped his beer. 'Not a lot to go on. You?'

'A couple of things. That's why I called.'

She led the way through the doorway she had come from. Drake took a last look around and followed through to what appeared to be the next house.

'Very nice,' said Drake, ducking his head to avoid a wooden beam.

'This is the business side of things.'

He followed her up a creaky narrow staircase. On the first floor there was an open reception area to the right that was dark and deserted. Light came from inside a large tank on the far wall. Bright tropical fish swam through ferns and floating green fronds.

At either end of the landing was a door. One was still marked Dr Rosen. Crane opened the other. The interior was furnished in rich dark colours: bookshelves along both side walls, with a leather sofa and armchair in the middle of the room around a rug that Drake guessed was Persian. At the far end, between two low windows, was a wide desk.

Crane was behind this, shuffling through the papers until she came up with the photograph she was looking for.

'This is what I wanted to show you.'

It was a high-angle photograph of the crime scene at Magnolia Quays. Drake looked up.

'Where did you get this?'

'Oh, sorry,' Crane flashed a tiny smile. 'Milo gave me a set of crime scene photos.'

'Is that right?'

'I hope that wasn't wrong of him.'

Drake waved the matter aside. 'What am I looking for?' He

placed his hands on the table and bowed over the photograph. Crane came round to lean over his shoulder. She gave off a warm smell, a combination of classy soap and shampoo laced with a light veneer of sweat. Not unpleasant.

'This was taken, I assume, from inside the building structure.' Crane pointed to the pattern traced in the mud. 'What does that look like?'

Drake reached for the desk lamp, twisting it to shed more light on the picture. From that angle the crime scene looked like a flat, bare stage. At the centre was the pit and the grey pyramid of rubble.

'I haven't seen this before.'

Crane shrugged. 'It was in the envelope Milo gave me.'

Drake thought about that, then he took another look. One of the forensics officers had taken the initiative to climb up into the frame of the unfinished building. The angle was not directly overhead, but still, it provided a view of the crime scene and its surroundings. The mound of rock in which the two victims were embedded stood more or less at the centre.

Crane reached over to point, her finger tracing a line in the mud.

'What do you see there?'

'What am I supposed to see?'

'A line, running through the middle. Doesn't that look familiar? The river.'

'The Thames?'

'You're saying someone set up the crime scene to resemble the river running through the city?'

'Does that sound crazy to you?'

Drake looked round at her. 'No more crazy than anything else.' He straightened up and watched her walk over to the armchair and sit down, legs crossed underneath her. He picked up his beer and settled himself in the sofa opposite her. 'The obvious question is why?'

'He's turned the crime scene into a map of London.'

Drake asked himself why he hadn't noticed this. He didn't recall seeing the photo before.

'But why, what is he trying to tell us?'

Crane shrugged. 'I can't say for sure, but if he is trying to draw our attention to the city, perhaps he has other things planned.'

'Other murders?'

'It's possible.' Crane moved over to the window to peer out. Rain was still hitting the glass. She spoke without turning. 'He sees his actions in a larger context, which adds importance to what he is doing.'

'How does this connect to your ideas about sharia executions?'

'I think he sees himself as morally superior. He's trying to teach us a lesson.'

'Morally superior,' Drake repeated, reaching for his beer. 'Maybe he didn't like Orientals.'

'Orientals?' She raised an eyebrow.

'Mr Hideo.' Drake paused. 'I'm sorry, is that . . . you know, not PC enough?'

Crane smiled. 'You're testing me? Trying to see if you can provoke me?'

'I just like to know who I'm dealing with.' Drake sipped his beer.

'Right. Look, I don't know what this means. Sometimes we read too much into things.'

'That's what you do, right? Help us to think outside the box?'

'Something like that.' Ray pushed herself off the wall and came over to tap the photo again. 'There's something else as well. I did some digging on Thwaite's wife. Before she married him she was kidnapped.'

'Kidnapped?'

'Kidnapped, held for ransom. This was in Iraq, in 2008. There was a big deal about it. Thwaite hired a private contractor.'

'They knew each other?'

'It looks that way.'

'He never mentioned it.'

'Not so strange,' Ray shrugged. 'It was a while ago.'

Cal, suddenly restless, got to his feet and moved about the room. His eye caught sight of a framed photograph on the wall that showed Crane standing in the middle of the desert somewhere. She was wearing cargo pants and a long khaki shirt with rolled up sleeves. Alongside her were four men, all muscular and bearded, wearing sunglasses and carrying automatic rifles.

'Security contractors.' Drake tapped the frame. 'Iraq? Afghanistan?'

'Northern Iraq. You were there too, right?'

Which meant she had been looking into his background. 'What were you doing there?'

'Counselling.'

He held her gaze, waiting for her to go on. 'Not something you can talk about?'

'Classified, I'm afraid.' Ray held his gaze. 'I was attached to military intelligence.'

'Right. How did that work out for you?'

'Like I said, it's classified.'

'I can imagine.' Cal nodded. 'Dealing with the spooks can be tricky.' He'd finished his beer. Ray reached into a cabinet and produced a bottle of tequila and two glasses. They sat down again as she poured.

'So, tell me, what's your story?'

'Ah, this is what you learned about interrogation.' He lifted his glass and drained it. She did the same before refilling both.

'I understand you lost a witness.'

'I'm sure you wouldn't be asking me this if you didn't already have the story.'

'I wanted to hear your version.'

'Things went sideways. I was in the wrong place at the wrong time.' He set down the empty glass and watched her refill it again. 'You seriously want to dig up my fall from grace?'

'Not if you're uncomfortable with talking about it.'

'Some other time, maybe.'

'This is why you have a conflict with DCI Pryce?'

'It's a long story.'

'The case fell through when she disappeared. What was her name?'

'Zelda. She called herself Zelda. A nickname.'

'Why does Pryce not trust you?'

'Because I didn't tell him everything.'

'You didn't trust him.'

'That's what they call an impasse, I think.'

'It's more than that, isn't it?' Crane folded her legs up and sat back in the big chair. 'It looks like he won't be happy until he's drummed you out of the police.'

'Where'd you hear that?'

'I think Wheeler mentioned something.'

Drake licked his lips. He still wasn't sure he could trust her, but there was something about Crane that he liked. He set down his glass and got to his feet.

'I'm working against the clock. I'd better get moving.'

Crane got to her feet. 'I want to help you. That's why I asked you to come over.'

Drake looked around the room. 'What's in it for you?'

'You may have heard – I have a cloud hanging over me.' She put her hands on her hips. 'I need to prove myself. It's a boys' club and they take a lot of convincing.'

'I'm open to suggestion,' he said, as he started for the door. 'Right now I can use all the help I can get.'

'So we're working together?'

Drake stopped to look back at her. Something about the angle of the light through her hair struck a match inside him somewhere. He nodded. 'Be careful what you wish for.'

CHAPTER 23

The big man perched on the bar stool at the Booty Parlour posed a serious challenge to gravity. He resembled a watermelon balanced on a toothpick. The striped green shirt added to the effect. Having said that, Papa Zemba didn't look overly worried about his situation. The round face broke into a gap-toothed grin when he caught sight of Drake.

'Who's my favourite bobby? Where you bin, mon frère?'

Drake leaned in for the obligatory handclasp and shoulder bump, catching a whiff of stale sweat heavily laced with an industrial dose of some overpowering and no doubt ridiculously expensive cologne that the big man had drenched himself in. It wasn't doing the trick. In the club's low lighting, Papa Zemba's fleshy, round face resembled a rubber ball of a mask. He went from happy to sad in a heartbeat. The story went that you didn't see his anger until the pain hit you. Legend had it that growing up on the streets of Brazzaville had made him immune to emotion. It wasn't true. Drake had witnessed how gentle he could be with his daughters. But there was no doubting the stories of savage beatings meted out to rivals, and of minions who were despatched in cruel and unforgiving fashion at the slightest hint of disloyalty. If rumour was to be believed, Papa Zemba was not averse to using a machete to remove fingers, and worse, in order to get what he wanted. Basically, you didn't want to get on the wrong side of him.

On the catwalk that stretched the length of the U-shaped bar a woman wearing a fluorescent thong and matching purple lipstick strutted her stuff to the sound of 50 Cent's 'Candy Shop'. As she went by Papa Zemba rubbed a hand over his shaved scalp and waggled his fingers for another Jack Daniels and one for Drake. Around his neck he wore a heavy gold chain. Silver rings competed for space on his hands.

'How's business?' Drake asked.

'You never hear me complain.' Papa waved over a bodyguard. There were never less than three of them around him somewhere. This one wore a black Armani T-shirt over steroid-swollen biceps. The Incredible Hulk's African cousin. 'Go see what's keeping Vanessa.'

The Hulk grunted something indecipherable and turned away.

'So, what brings you around here?' The big man rattled the ice in his glass.

'You know, a bit of this, a bit of that.'

'I don't know why you waste your time. Come and work for me.' Papa Zemba spoke with an accent that was part French African, part London, part West Coast rap. He just absorbed it all and threw it together in his own unique mix.

'Everyone seems to think I'm in the wrong game.'

'Maybe you should listen.' Papa frowned. 'You still hanging around that Greek psycho?'

'Donny? I don't work for him.'

'You need to stay away from him.'

'What makes you say that?'

'People talk, Cal. That's what they do. Sometimes they have something to say, other times they just make it up.'

'So what are they saying?' Drake reached for the glass that had appeared before him.

'That he has something on you. That it buys him a free pass.'

'You believe that?'

'Hey, din't you hear? Truth don't matter no more.' Papa Zemba chuckled quietly into his drink. 'You know what your problem is, right? You turned your back on God.'

'This sounds familiar.'

'Did I ever tell you that my father was a priest?'

'A couple of times.'

'You can say what you like about religion, but it provides a moral compass. What is right and what is wrong.'

'If you ever give up the bar business you should become one of those evangelists they have on television. You'll make a fortune.'

'I'm being serious. You thought you were doing the right thing by joining the army, but the fact is you ended up on a crusade.'

'If this is you trying to make me feel better, you're failing miserably.'

Papa Zemba rapped his knuckles on the counter and the bartender jumped into action, replacing their glasses with fresh ones.

'They pulled a fast one on you, mon frere.' The big head rocked from side to side. 'You swallowed their lies. Now we are all paying the price.'

Drake had long since accepted that Papa Zemba was more useful as an ally than an adversary. Their relationship was a delicate balance of trust. Papa's strength lay in the network of contacts that rippled outwards from here into places Drake would have been hard pressed to find, let alone access. As for the gambling rooms, the betting shops, the massage parlours, Drake relied on Papa Zemba to stay within an unwritten code of limits. There were certain areas that Drake knew the other man would not stray into. Drugs was one. The abuse of children was another.

'I hear they found a couple of bodies yesterday morning.'

'A building site over by the river. Do you know anything?'

'Not my area. We Africans don't do building. We live in huts, right?' The big head reared back as Papa Zemba roared at his own joke.

'What about this trade in illegals?'

'You know as well as I do: if there's an opportunity, someone's gonna step in for a cut.' Papa Zemba shrugged. 'You can order workers like you order take away. Day or night. You want someone to break down a wall, or rip out a bathroom? You want three men, four, forty? Two days work? Ten days? It's like going to the Job Centre, only these people aren't on their books.'

'The invisibles.'

'You see what I'm saying?' The big man pulled the shirt away from where it was sticking to his chest. He kept the air conditioning to a minimum. It saved on overheads and besides, hot people get thirsty. He broke off to turn and raise his voice. 'Hey, where did that fool get to now, eh? Aiiee, you can't find good help any more. I'm serious. Come and work for me, you'll earn good money.'

'Let me think about it.'

Papa Zemba sucked his teeth. 'Why you want to work for them?'

'It's what I do,' said Drake, swirling the ice around his glass.

Papa Zemba nudged his glass against Drake's. 'At least here you'll be among your own.'

'Let me ask you about something else.'

'Sure, what do you want to know?'

'The fire over in Freetown.'

'What's to tell? Nobody cares about a masjid burning down.

Now if it was a synagogue, you wait and see the trouble they would be raising.'

'The imam has a son, Waleed. You know him?'

'Ah! That boy is a headache.' He rubbed his shiny dome of a head as if to stress the point. 'I don't know what his problem is. I tried to help.'

'How?'

'I gave him a job, here, behind the bar. He didn't like that so I put him in the kitchen. His head is mixed up. I can't tell you how much I lost in breakages. Hold on a minute.' He held a finger up and turned away again. 'Hey, find out where that dumb fuck lost himself.' A second goon disappeared in search of the first. Papa snapped his fingers to wake the barman up.

'You let a man die of thirst, eh? And get Zazie out here.'

Zazie was one of Papa's string of daughters. It was impossible to keep track of his offspring. Every now and then another would turn up. They popped out of the woodwork on a regular basis. Zazie was one of the established family. She was in her thirties and worked for him in a number of capacities. The fact that he had no sons, so far, Papa took as a sign from the Almighty. But in terms of business acumen, it was hard to see how any boy would outdo Zazie. She appeared through a doorway, dressed in a sharp suit.

'Hey Cal,' she smiled.

'Zazie.'

'He's looking for that fool boy, the imam's son.'

Zazie's face grew sombre. 'Waleed. Why, what's he done now?'

'You know how it is. I'm looking into the fire.'

'Right.' Zazie looked as though she wasn't quite sure she believed him.

'I hear he was a lot of trouble.'

She sucked her teeth, doing a passable imitation of her father. 'He filled his head with all kinds of religious nonsense. You know,

Salafist stuff about this country being at war with Islam. When it got to the point where he refused to shake hands with any women I told him to go and sort himself out before he could work here.'

Papa Zemba chuckled. 'You don wan to mess with my girl, eh?'

'So you haven't seen him since then? You know where I could find him?'

Zazie leaned her elbows on the bar. 'You think he had something to do with the fire?'

'I just want to talk to him.'

She weighed this up. She was smart. Her clothes, hair, the gold rings in her ears, they stood in stark contrast to her father's loud shirts and neck chains. She seemed to make up her mind.

'He had another stint in hospital. It wasn't so bad this time. They moved him to a halfway house in Earls Court.' She gave him the address without looking it up. 'It's a dump. He should have been with his family, but because of the fire that wasn't an option.'

'Sounds like you've been looking out for him.'

'Somebody has to,' Zazie shrugged.

'Ah,' the big man purred. 'Here she is.'

Drake looked up to see a caramel-coloured woman twirling herself round the dance pole. Vanessa. She had pneumatic, surgically enhanced breasts and wore a thong so minimal you could count the pimples where she'd shaved. Papa sucked in air like a man drowning. Zazie rolled her eyes and disappeared back through the door she'd come from.

'She's heavenly, don't you think?'

'She's certainly something,' consented Drake.

'Don't go getting any ideas. This one's mine. Now get out of here, I'm working.' Papa rolled ice around his mouth, his eyes fixed on Vanessa's ass as she bent over to give him a better view. Drake left him to it.

CHAPTER 24

As Drake nudged his car up the kerb, close to the perimeter wall, it struck him that he wasn't quite sober. The access road was quiet now. Taking a deep breath, he clambered up onto the boot of the car and from there to the roof, feeling the soft metal flexing beneath his weight. Leaning one boot against the lamp post, the same one that Marsha Thwaite had parked under, he leaned over and grabbed the top of the wooden boundary fence. It wasn't graceful, but scrabbling about, slipping on the smooth surface, he managed to haul himself over. A splinter dug into his left hand and the pocket of his parka ripped on a nail. He landed heavily, cursing his own clumsiness. Pressing the sleeve of his coat over his bleeding hand, he limped off, past the Portakabins and out into the open area of the site.

No alarms went off. No guard dogs rushed him. Drake felt the old reckless spirit of his youth surging back. He breathed in deeply, feeling a strange, mystical kinship with this place. The mud and rust reeked of history, good and evil. Once upon a time on these wharfs sugar had been unloaded from the plantations across the sea, bringing with it a legacy of slavery and wealth.

As a teenager, he had spent time exploring its reaches. Different sections of the river corresponded to various periods of his life. A loner, always skiving off looking for something he could call his own. It was close to here that he smoked his first joint, drank whisky, had sex. His mother had been going through one of her good periods. She was off the booze and even holding down a job, at a florist's of all places. The house was always full of cut flowers. There was a steady boyfriend, Baz, a lost soul who had been an unsuccessful burglar, but since his last stretch had been holding down a job as a plumber's mate. For a time they ate well. Cal had new clothes that actually felt like his, rather than the usual ill-fitting cast-offs his mother nicked from Oxfam. She refused to pay for them on the grounds that somebody already paid for them once, so why should she pay a second time?

Death was there too, tucked into the riverbank. A dead woman lying undisturbed on the low tide flats, her skin as grey as the mud she rested on. She looked like she had sprung from one of the books he used to read on the long afternoons in the local library where his mother often left him while she went to the pub, with strict orders to stay put until they closed. He would wait for her outside on the steps, and sometimes he wouldn't.

That woman came to occupy his thoughts, waking and sleeping. He saw her in his dreams, rising from the mud, covered in slime, worms coming out of her eyes and mouth. He half believed she wasn't dead at all but had come up from below to take him down to the underworld. She wore the remains of a blue dress decorated with red roses. A pattern which, even now, never failed to make him shudder. Still, he remembered the details. The roots of her hair where the dye had grown out. The broken nails on her left hand. He was ten, too scared to tell anyone. Worried it was his fault, that he would be blamed. He felt a certain loyalty, a need to protect her, even though it was already too late for that. On the third afternoon he arrived to find the riverbank crawling with police. An old man in a tweed cap pointed and he took off running.

The river was quiet now. Through the skeleton of the unfinished building he glimpsed light reflecting back from the black surface. The water had a silken quality to it that gave it a special glow, like a river of ancient legend. The air was so cold it felt as though it might snow.

He passed the site office and walked out into the open space, passing the hole in the ground. It looked more like an open tomb in the moonlight. Crime-scene tape flapped agitatedly in the breeze around the spot where the bodies had been found. The completed part of Magnolia Quays was right up against the river. Future residents wanted nothing to obstruct their view. The site was narrow and the developers planned to use every available inch.

If anyone had asked him what he was doing here, he wasn't sure he could have explained. It was some kind of instinct that brought him back, the need to feel out the space, to inhabit the mind of the perpetrator, the person or persons who had carried out this crime. Through the shadows of the concrete frame he wandered, looking back at the burial site. Years from now people would live in these penthouses and duplexes, and they would in all likelihood be completely oblivious to the fact that two people had once been buried alive here. As he turned his head four shadows broke away from the pillars and began to run.

'Hey! Stop! Police!'

Drake took off after them. They were young, men he guessed, and they moved quickly. Lean black shadows cutting through the shadows of the concrete framework. He could hear their footsteps and their voices, calling to one another. Drake crashed into a light wooden trestle of some kind and tumbled to the ground. He swore as he picked himself up. The sound of their footsteps was already disappearing.

A bright light snapped on, blinding him. He held up a hand to shield his eyes.

'Don't move,' said a voice.

'I'm police,' said Drake, getting to his feet. 'Point that thing somewhere else, will you?'

The beam of light dipped, picking out a white spot on the ground. Drake fished his badge out of his pocket and held it up. The man holding the light stepped closer and studied it.

'Detective Sergeant Drake?'

'You'd better believe it.' Cal dusted himself off. 'Now tell me who you are.'

'Kronnos Security. We're patrolling the site.'

In the glow around the beam, Drake could make out a tall, bearded man. He was wearing a uniform and a baseball cap with a logo on it.

'You're bleeding,' he said, pointing to Drake's sleeve.

'It's just a scratch. You've got people dossing on the site.'

'Yeah, I know.' The light did a circle of the surrounding shadows. 'They get in from time to time. My feeling is the caretaker is in on it.'

'How do they get in?'

'Same way you did, I suppose.' The beam came back to find Drake. 'I wasn't told you were on site.'

'It's not official. I was just taking a look around.'

'Always better to let us know. We have dogs sometimes. You could have been hurt.'

'Let's not go making this into a drama.'

There was a long pause. 'Wait a second, you're leading the murder investigation, right?'

'That's me. Are you out here every night?'

'These last weeks I've had the honour of the graveyard shift.'

'So, you would have seen the victim's car parked out there three nights ago.'

'Yeah, that's right.'

'You didn't call it in.'

There was a laugh. 'Sounds like you're interrogating me.'

'Just curious.'

'Well, it's always a judgement call. Sometimes you see a car and it strikes you as off.' He pointed the torch off towards the gate. 'That your BMW out there?'

'Guilty as charged.'

'I was just about to call it in.'

'So, whether or not you report it depends on the make and model?'

The other man chuckled. 'Yeah, you could say that. It's nothing personal.'

It was hard to get a clear picture of him with the light from the fence behind him, and the flashlight he was holding. He was tall, and well built, that much Drake could see. He pulled a packet of cigarettes from his pocket. Drake shook his head at the offer.

'I'm still trying to quit.'

'Good for you. I'd better be going,' the man said, looking at his watch. They crossed the open ground towards the gates.

'They keep you busy then?'

'You could say that.'

The guard nodded towards the crime-scene tape. 'Nasty business.'

'Yeah, it is.' Drake would have put his age in the late thirties. Mountain-man beard. Close cropped hair. The name on the lapel of his uniform read M. Flinders. He unlocked the gates and locked them carefully behind them.

'Let me ask. You come through here around the same time every night?'

'We try to vary it, so as not to be too predictable. You're thinking of Sunday? I can check.' He reached into his pocket for his phone and flicked through with his finger. '01.47.' He looked up and grinned. 'Can't do anything these days without it being logged. Big Brother and all that.'

'Right.'

'I gave a statement to one of your officers, young feller. Tall, glasses?'

'That would be DC Kowalski.'

'That's the one.' They were standing by the bright lights on the gate. On the back of the hand holding the cigarette Drake could make out a tattoo of a black panther head.

'What's that, the Light Brigade?' Flinders' eyes flickered down to his hand. He nodded. 'So, where were you, Afghanistan, Iraq?'

'Iraq. Two tours. How about yourself?'

'Infantry and then the Special Investigation Branch.'

'Military Police.' Flinders smiled. 'That explains why you joined the Met.'

'In a way, yes. A bit like you, I suppose.' Drake nodded at the car. A large Volkswagen van. It was painted dark blue. A jagged red cardiogram ran along the side with the words KRONNOS SECURITY SERVICES on it.

'Plastic fantastic.' Flinders flicked the shiny badge on his shoulder. 'Toy soldiers in kiddie uniforms. It's not the same thing.'

'It's a job, right?'

'Sure. A lot of people came out worse.'

'Is there anything you can remember about that night, anything at all that might be useful?'

Flinders shook his head. 'Whoever did this must have some balls on them.'

The two of them turned to survey the site. It was quiet now, nothing moved.

'To drive in like that would require keys. They didn't break the lock.'

'You see all sorts in this game. Always someone trying to make a little on the side.' Flinders examined his cigarette. 'When a firm is struggling, they tend to be less picky about who they hire.'

'How long did you say you've been in this game?'

'I didn't,' Flinders said flatly. 'But it's coming on two years now.'

'And before that, where were you?'

'This is beginning to sound like an interview,' Flinders grinned.

'Sorry, comes with the territory.'

'I hear you. The fact is it took me a while to settle down again. I tried all manner of things.' Flinders shrugged. 'You do what you have to do to make ends meet, right?'

'Sure.'

Drake glanced off down the street. From where they were standing you could hardly see the main road. The killer would have been able to work unseen.

'Did you get anything off the cameras?' Flinders asked.

'Well, that's an interesting question. The cameras on the main road show the lorry arriving, but there's no indication of how our man left. That's one reason I came back.'

Flinders nodded as if this made sense. 'The fact is these cameras are not always as reliable as people think.'

'True, but I still don't see how he could disappear into thin air.'

Flinders nodded over his shoulder. 'There's always the river.'

'Possible, but with low tide it would have been difficult.'

'Sounds like you've considered all the possibilities.'

'Yeah,' agreed Drake. 'For all the good it's done.'

'I'm not trying to be funny or anything, but what if he never left the site?'

The idea had occurred to Drake. 'It would take a lot of nerve.'

'Sure, but might work. You know, staying on, and then mixing in with the workers when they arrived. That might explain how he got access.'

'Well, we're checking them all, so if that's the case we'll pick him up.'

'Right.' Flinders was nodding as he glanced at his watch. 'Well, that's me. I need to get on. Give me a shout if I can be of service.'

'I will.'

'Good luck with finding him. Nutter like that. The sooner you get him the sooner people can sleep easier in their beds.'

Amen to that, thought Drake as he watched the security van pull away.

CHAPTER 25

Maybe it was the river that had brought memories, or maybe it was revisiting Freetown, but Drake slept badly. He found himself remembering when his mother had died. He had just arrived back in Iraq, on his second tour, after retraining and joining the Special Investigation Branch of the Royal Military Police. After the accident he was offered the chance of a transfer. At the time it had felt a little absurd, like someone's crazy idea of a joke. Drake remembered half expecting someone to discover who he really was and throw him out. It never happened. Instead, Drake found life as an investigator was a little easier. Even the resentment that came with the job. Drake had been dealing with rejection of one sort or another all his life, so this was familiar territory. It was simply formalized into his uniform.

He was stationed in Kirkuk when Captain Madoc called him into his office and told him the bad news about his mother. For a long moment the two men stood staring at one another. Drake realized that Madoc was expecting some kind of reaction from him, something that he didn't feel. He came around the desk to rest a hand on Cal's shoulder.

'Sometimes these things can have a delayed impact.'

Drake didn't know how to explain that he simply didn't feel anything, expect maybe relief. His mother had been trying to get out of this world for as long as he could remember. Now, finally, she had managed it.

After that he found himself on a Hercules C130, swooping down at an unbelievably high angle into Baghdad. Then from there back to London. In less than twelve hours he found himself back in Freetown, standing in the rain, looking up at the gallery and the boarded-up door of the old flat. Burn marks stretched up the wall over the plywood sheets. Flecks of grey ash floated in the air like butterflies.

There had been a mix-up in the booking at the crematorium in Lambeth. Another family was already waiting for them to be finished. They stood under umbrellas outside in the rain, holding their flowers, watching him as he left.

As he was walking to the bus stop, beret in hand, a car slowed beside him. A Mazda, canary yellow with a sun roof. About as cheesy an excuse for a sports car as you could find. The man behind the wheel ticked all the boxes for a midlife crisis. Over the purple shirt hung a fistful of medallions and juju beads, cowries and shark's teeth. Drake recognized his father despite this transformation and the years since he had last seen him.

'You lost?'

'Came to pay my respects, didn't I?'

'A little late, don't you think?'

Drake had started walking again. Now his father pulled the car over to the kerb and jumped out. He had put on weight, a hefty belly pushing out the waistband of his shiny trousers. He blocked Drake's way.

'Don't be like that. Time like this, we should be together.'

His accent was not what he remembered. A jumble of North Africa meets South London, with a dash of West Indian thrown in for good measure. This was the only consistent aspect of his father that would never change; the ability to shapeshift, to turn himself into something new. Right now he was dressed like a pimp from an old 1970s blaxploitation film. The blonde in the passenger seat added to the effect. All he needed was a wide-brimmed hat, which Drake wouldn't have been surprised to find in the back seat.

'Come on, let's go get a drink. We should talk.'

'There's nothing to talk about,' said Drake.

'Denny?' the woman whined. She couldn't have been more than twenty. She was wearing a dress that revealed more than it covered up. She tossed her hair and pouted before drawing on the fat joint she was holding.

'She's hungry,' snickered his father. 'You know what I mean?'

'Denny!'

'It's what I'm calling meself these days. A lot of bad feeling towards us.' He sniffed. 'So what's all this I hear, you bein' in the army?'

'It's a job. Regular hours, roof over your head, money in your pocket.'

'Blood money,' nodded his father. His skin was darker than Drake recalled.

'I have to get going.' Drake moved to get by. His father stepped off the kerb, went back round to get into the car.

'Once you sell your soul to them there's no going back.'

A cloud of black exhaust coughed from the rear end as the car broke away with complete disregard for traffic. Horns sounded in its wake like a fanfare.

It felt like a relief to be back in the shuddering draughty interior of a transport plane, hemmed in between loaded pallets.

He'd requested an immediate return to duty and he was glad of that. It was a long, slow ride but he felt safe there, sleeping upright in his seat. The warm judder of the engines. Then the first gust of dusty air hit him in the face as he was coming down the ramp. A kind of homecoming.

The halfway house in Earls Court was steadily crumbling into little pieces. A rundown row of grey terraced houses that shuddered beneath the steady flow of heavy-goods vehicles and coaches rumbling past. The front yard was cluttered with junk; rusty bicycles, overturned rubbish bins and the skeletal remains of what looked like an upright piano that had fallen from a great height. The debris trailed up the front steps to a door that was patched over with a sheet of plywood. It swung open beneath his touch. A dark hallway had been stripped down to bare floorboards and hanging tails of tattered wallpaper. The smell of rot mixed with fresh paint coming from somewhere. A sign on the wall said the house was untended during daytime hours but a monitor could be reached in case of an emergency. A telephone number had been scratched out and written over so many times you couldn't make sense of it.

Drake walked down the hallway, following the stench of piss. Maybe cats, maybe just people who hadn't been housebroken. One step down from hospital. One step up from living on the streets.

At the end of the corridor a large common room awaited him, with high bay windows facing onto a backyard full of more junk. A century ago this house might have been occupied by a well-to-do family. Now it teetered on the brink of the abyss. A counter fenced off an open kitchen to the right of the door. Everything was cluttered with pans, dirty dishes and scattered cereal packets. A thin man was sifting through the grey water in the sink as if panning for gold. He looked up and stood there, his jawbone twitching from side to side.

'Waleed?'

In his fifties, dishevelled, the man resembled a scarecrow. All he needed was straw in his knotted hair. There was paint on his fingers and on his clothes. He stared Drake in the eye as he used the spoon he had found to shovel cereal into his mouth, milk dribbling around the corners.

'You a fucking copper?'

Drake repeated his question.

'What's a fucking copper doin' 'ere then?'

Drake moved on into the big room. A young man was seated over by the bay window in an armchair scarred by cigarette burns. His face was puffy. Close up he had the look of a lost soul. Like a teenager who'd fallen asleep at the wheel and was trying to wake up four decades later. Rip van fucking Winkle.

'Waleed? Are you Waleed Ahmad?'

'Who are you?' The figure in the chair looked up.

'He's a fucking copper is what he is,' growled the man from the doorway behind him. Drake ignored him. When he moved closer, the young man reared back slightly. His eyes were at half-mast and what you could see of them was dulled by medication. Drake wondered if perhaps it might have been an idea to bring Crane with him. At least she had some experience of this sort of thing. Brilliant, Drake. Always coming up with bright ideas when it's way too late.

'I'm DS Drake.'

'I know who you are,' nodded the boy. He had a weird smile on his face, like he knew something nobody else knew.

Drake moved slowly round to the window and leaned his weight against the frame.

'How are you doing, Waleed?'

'Don't talk to him. He's a copper. They lie!'

'Hey, do us a favour, will you, go and find some kitten to torture,' Drake called over. The man ducked out of sight into the kitchen.

'I didn't do anything wrong,' said Waleed. His voice was a twisted mumble.

'I never said you did. I just came to ask you some questions.'

'Questions? About what?'

'About the fire. Remember the fire?'

Waleed's eyes widened. 'I didn't start it.'

'Nobody said you did.' Drake held up his hands. 'Did I say that?'

Waleed stared at Drake for a moment and then, slowly, he shook his head. 'No.'

'No, exactly.' Drake nodded. 'So, do you remember where you were when the fire started?'

'I was here.'

'I can vouch for that,' said the scarecrow in the kitchen. 'I can vouch for anything he says.'

Drake ignored him. 'Tell me about the masjid.'

'What about it?' Waleed frowned. He began picking at the arm of the chair.

'You're an only child, aren't you?'

'Yes.' The swollen face cracked in a wonky smile. 'They took one look at me and decided never again.'

'When you stayed there you would stay in the little room by the front door?'

'It was easier. I didn't want to live upstairs with them. They . . . worry about me.'

Drake nodded. 'You need some distance, that makes sense.'

'Exactly.' The dull cloud seemed to lift from Waleed's eyes for a moment. 'Distance.'

'Tell me about Magnolia Quays, Waleed.'

'What about it?'

'I heard you had a job there.'

'What's that got to do with anything?' He was growing agitated, writhing about in the chair as if trying to get out of it. 'I mean, why are you asking me these questions?'

'They're just questions.'

'What does any of this have to do with the fire?'

'Hey!' The kitchen scarecrow was back, this time holding a big knife. Waleed squealed and jumped to his feet, hiding behind the chair.

'Careful with that thing,' said Drake.

'You can't come here, just come here asking questions.' Water dripped from the steel blade.

'You'll do yourself an injury.'

'Sure, that would suit you, right? Fucking copper!' He stepped forward. Waleed chose that moment to rush by and out of the room. Drake made to go after him but the scarecrow thrust the knife in his way. Drake sidestepped, blocked the man's wrist and then twisted it into a lock. The fingers splayed open and the knife clattered to the floor.

'You can't do that! That's assault!'

'Not even close.' Drake kept turning the man's wrist until he was kneeling on the floor. Then he let go and went after Waleed.

The front door stood open.

CHAPTER 26

When she stepped into the outer office Ray found Heather feeding the fish. She turned away from the tank, still sprinkling fish food on the surface of the water.

'He's here.'

'Who is?'

'Your nine o'clock. Richard Haynes?'

'I don't have a nine o'clock, Heather. I thought I made that clear. I don't want any private patients while we're on this case.'

'Sorry, but I understood you had arranged it yourself.' Heather stood clutching the pot of fish food. She lowered her voice. 'He's an old client of Doctor Rosen's.'

'Are you sure? I never arranged anything.' Ray exhaled slowly. 'You're saying he's in my office now?'

'I'm sorry, I just assumed . . .' Heather started to speak but Ray held up a hand.

'It's all right, but check with me first. No matter what the patient tells you.'

'Yes, but . . .'

'Heather.'

'Sorry!'

Richard Haynes was seated on the sofa leafing through a book of landscape photographs by Ansel Adams that Ray kept on the coffee table for patients to distract themselves with. He jumped to his feet as she came in.

'Mr Haynes, I'm sorry, there seems to have been some sort of misunderstanding.'

'Oh, dear, I feel like it's my fault.' He was still holding the book for some reason. 'My aunt, you see, Margot Haynes? She was a long-time patient of Doctor Rosen's. He was practically family to her. I simply assumed . . .'

Haynes resembled a would-be hipster on the verge of a breakdown. He was wearing a chequered shirt and tweed jacket. The glasses and scruffy hair gave him a rumpled look, as if he had just got out of bed.

'I have a history, you know, of substance abuse. I'm a recovering addict.'

'I'm sorry to hear that.' Ray moved around behind her desk. There were two folders lying there, put there by Heather. The first was marked with the name Margot Haynes, written in Julius's distinctive handwriting. The second one, thinner, bore the name Richard Haynes.

'I brought over my file from my former therapist. I know it's forward of me, but my aunt swore by Doctor Rosen, and I am rather desperate. When I heard he had passed away I just knew I had to try you.'

Ray sat down and began to go through the file. It was an awkward situation, but there were two factors which obliged her to at least show some modicum of interest. The first was financial, and the second was the debt she felt to Julius and his legacy. This was personal. She couldn't simply turn Haynes away.

It took her five minutes to glean the basic information from the file: Richard Haynes was forty-two years old and working through the impact of his wife's recent suicide. They had no children. He had been in counselling for three months and was also being treated for addiction to alcohol and cocaine.

'I'm sorry if this seems rushed, but you have rather sprung this on me and I do have a lot of work and . . .'

'I appreciate that. I wouldn't be here, except for the fact that I had an anxiety attack,' Haynes was quick to explain. He stared down at his hands. 'I simply couldn't deal with it. I was afraid, you understand, that I would go back to my old ways.'

'Don't you have a support group for that?'

'I do, or rather I did.' Haynes was silent again. 'I have trust issues.'

Crane studied him carefully. Automatically, Ray was doing what she always did, which was to listen. That was her job, listening. To the patient, to the crime scene, to the autopsy report. It was all there. All you had to do was pay attention. Patients often didn't even know what it was they were trying to tell themselves. They couldn't. They came in, sat down and started talking. They had something they wanted to get out. They just didn't know how to start, or where, in their confused range of emotions, the important stuff had got lost in the mix. Her job was to guide them through. To unravel the tangle. To help each patient to find what it was, where their particular pain was located. She sometimes liked to think of herself as a kind of exorcist. A person who drove the bad spirits away. We all have our inner demons. They gather, build up, accumulate over time.

Already she was beginning to sense that the problem with Richard Haynes was that he was not only intelligent, but also perceptive. You had to prove your sincerity. You couldn't feign interest. His nerves were so wound up he would be able to tell immediately.

'Look, since you're here, we may as well do this, but I can't promise that we can continue treatment.'

'I understand,' he said earnestly. 'I can only apologize again.'

Ray clicked on her recorder and took her place in the armchair opposite him.

'Okay, why don't you begin by just talking me through everything.'

'Well, the fact is, I feel guilty. I know I shouldn't. There's no reason for me to feel that way. It wasn't my fault that she died.'

'Suicide is often harder to come to terms with than other forms of death.'

'Other forms of death?'

'When we lose someone in an accident, or to an illness, there is a kind of logic that applies. We can understand that this was out of our hands. There was nothing we could do.' Ray spoke slowly, patiently, in an effort to convey the fact that she was trying to understand his pain. She was distracted partly by the fact that Haynes had a kind of halfway smile on his face as she spoke, which made her wonder. 'Suicide leaves us with questions about whether we could have done more. To be more understanding, more supportive, more sensitive to the other person's pain.'

'The thing is,' Haynes said after a long silence. 'And this is hard for me to talk about, but I was often filled with feelings of loathing. In some ways I wanted her to die.'

'You wanted her to die, rather than you wanted to end the marriage?'

Haynes grinned. 'I knew this was the right place to come. Already, I feel you are helping me to see my situation more clearly.'

Ray leaned back in her chair. Once in a while, a patient would turn up trying to challenge her in some kind of intellectual way. They saw themselves as superior. Some couldn't handle the idea of a woman knowing more about them than they did themselves. Listening to Haynes now, it almost sounded like listening to a scripted conversation. He seemed to have constructed his answers to elicit a particular response. The question was why.

'So which is it?' she said.

Haynes crouched forwards, resting his elbows on his knees. 'It wasn't about our relationship. No, I think I just wanted her to die. More than that, I wanted her to suffer.'

'That's quite a statement. Are you sure that's how you felt?'

'You mean am I chanelling my grief into some form of self-harm as a kind of punishment?'

'I mean, do you really think you would have been capable of hurting her, making her suffer?'

'It's strange, but I honestly think I was.'

'Okay, can you tell me why?'

'The thing is, I always felt we were not compatible. She lived such a superficial life, never questioning anything, never curious. You see?'

'If that was the case, why stay together? Why not separate?'

'That would have been impossible. She often said that if I left her she would kill herself.'

'Does that go some way towards explaining your feelings of guilt?'

'Oh, it's much worse than that.' The smile on Haynes' face was rigid, almost like a grimace of pain. 'You see, I suspect that I might have actually encouraged her.'

'Suspect, or know?'

'I'm not sure, that's why I'm here, isn't it?'

Ray set her notebook on the arm of the chair and locked her fingers together. 'Mr Haynes, I am beginning to wonder if perhaps you might be better off with another analyst.'

'Ah,' Haynes snorted. 'You don't have time for me. My case is not interesting enough.'

'It's not that. I feel that your case deserves more than I can offer at this time.' Crane got to her feet. 'I can get my assistant to draw up a list of colleagues. All of whom come highly recommended.' She held out her hand. 'And of course, there will be no charge for this session.'

Haynes remained seated. 'You think I'm intimidated by you?'

'I'm sorry?'

'It's true that I find it distracting that you are so attractive. Can I say that?'

'You can say it, but it only makes me more convinced that you would be better off with another analyst.'

'Sure, I get it,' Haynes nodded. 'You're uncomfortable with my case, with me.'

'This is not taking us anywhere.'

'It's all about trust, right? Mutual trust. But so far this has all been one way. I have to tell you about myself, but what about you? What about your secrets?'

'I think perhaps it's better you leave.'

She moved towards the door and opened it.

Haynes stood up slowly and came over to stand in front of her.

'You haven't talked about your feelings of guilt.'

'My feelings of guilt?' she repeated. Crane was dealing with somebody who was more dangerous than she had realized. She wasn't afraid of him, but she felt annoyed for having her time wasted.

'The only reason we're talking is because of your aunt's connection to Doctor Rosen.'

Haynes just smiled. 'Have you never questioned whether your so-called expertise could be part of the problem rather than the solution?'

'Goodbye, Mr Haynes.'

After he'd gone, Ray moved back slowly behind her desk and sat down. She swung the big chair round to face the window, staring at the reassuring brickwork and the slate roofs across the other side of the street. Haynes was a creep, but hopefully he would be someone else's problem from now on. She reached forward for the buzzer to summon Heather.

CHAPTER 27

Time was running out. Wheeler had been trying to call him all morning. Drake didn't pick up, suspecting that the superintendent was only going to remind him that his forty-eight hours were up and that he still had Pryce breathing down his neck. He also didn't know how to explain why he was so convinced that his best lead on the case so far was a mentally unstable young man who may or may not have been involved in an arson attack on a mosque. It wasn't hard to imagine how that would go down with his boss.

It took all of fifteen minutes to track Waleed to a café on Earls Court Road. One of those places that seemed to be trapped in a time warp. Beige Formica tables bolted to a tiled floor. It resembled a cheesy burger bar from the eighties.

The man behind the counter bore a faint resemblance to an Indian Buddy Holly. His hair was spiked with enough gel to choke a seal. Negotiations led to two black coffees in Styrofoam cups. Buddy Holly looked so happy that he might have just performed successful open-heart surgery.

When Drake set the coffees down Waleed didn't even look up. He had frozen when he caught sight of Drake coming through the door.

'You don't need to be afraid of me. I'm not here to hurt you.'

Waleed gave no indication that he had heard him. His eyes remained fixed on the table, which looked as if someone had taken a bite out of it.

'The thing is, I have the feeling you'd like to help.' Drake paused to sip his coffee, and instantly regretted it. 'Sometimes we try to do something good, and it turns out bad, right?'

Waleed sniffed loudly but said nothing.

'I spoke to your mother.'

'You spoke to her? What did she say?'

'Well, she was upset, as you can imagine. Your father was badly hurt.'

'I didn't think anyone would be hurt.'

'I believe you.'

Waleed spoke without looking up. 'People hate us. Our beliefs. It's because we are pure.'

'Sure, tell me something I don't know.' Drake leaned his elbows on the table. He gestured at the coffee which Waleed hadn't touched. 'You want something else? Are you hungry?'

Waleed twisted round to stare at the bright menu board. 'Maybe a cheeseburger.'

'Fries?'

Waleed nodded as Drake headed back to the counter. Buddy Holly was pleased to see him. As he waited for the order to be filled he kept one eye on Waleed, half expecting him to make a run for it. When he put the tray in front of him, Waleed blinked in confusion, then realized the food was for him.

'So, you were trying to help someone?'

Stuffing French fries into his mouth three at a time, Waleed nodded. 'Akky. He needed money. To do Allah's work.'

'Akky? This is who you let stay in your room at the masjid?'

'He's my brother. I had to help him.'

'Sure, I understand.' Drake watched Waleed bite into the cheeseburger and chew with slow satisfaction. 'So, this guy . . .'

'Akky?' Waleed squirmed in his chair.

'What is that short for, Akram? Akeel? Akeeb?'

'Akky is cool. He'll do good things.'

'I don't doubt it. Did he cover for you at the building site, too?'

'I never liked that work, man. I swear.' Waleed grinned, suddenly cheerful. 'One ring to rule them all.'

'What does that mean?' Drake frowned, afraid this was suddenly about to go sideways.

Across from them two young Asian women sat and compared images on their iPhones. Behind them sat a man who, in another context, might be described as a local character. He was hunched over. A career junkie. Drake recognized the type. Jaundiced skin the colour of leather, torn yellow anorak. Skinny frame. He was doing a bad job of pretending not to look at the rucksack the girls had obligingly left on the floor. The back of the bag had a picture on it of Viggo Mortensen as Aragorn. One ring.

'Tell me about this friend of yours.'

'He's not a bad person.'

'I know. A true believer.'

Waleed looked up, mouth buried in his burger.

'How did you get the job at Magnolia Quays?'

'This guy who comes to the masjid regularly. He's a bit funny, you know? Not that I'm like that. But he's a hairdresser, so what do you expect.' Waleed giggled to himself.

'Are you talking about Marouan?'

'You know him?'

Drake took another sip of coffee hoping it might have improved. It hadn't. Over Waleed's shoulder he watched the junkie as he stared at the ceiling, his long fingers snaking into the open rucksack. Drake leaned across.

'You want to give that a rest, mate.'

The junkie sat up, studied the wall and ran his hands through his greasy hair. The two tourists stared at Drake as if he was a lunatic. They gathered up their things and left.

'You know that Allah judges you by your deeds, by the purity of your heart, right?' Drake said. Waleed gave a guilty lurch that might have been a nod. 'Okay, so I am going to ask you again, because I know that in your heart you are good. You never meant your father to be hurt, right? You want to do the right thing.' Drake paused, trying not to overdo it, giving his words time to sink in. 'You were helping a brother in need. You let him stay and you let him take your job, yes?'

'He wanted to work there. Said we could share it.'

'He told you about Magnolia Quays?'

Waleed frowned. 'I think so, yeah. He'd tried to work there, or he had worked there. I can't remember. Anyway, he was cool. He'd even been to make jihad, to fight.'

'He told you that?'

'Yeah, you know, right?'

Drake glanced over at the junkie, who was rocking back and forth on his chair as if in pain. He got up and went over. 'Do yourself a favour and move on, before they call the cops.' He tucked a ten-pound note into the man's jacket. 'And get yourself something to eat, for god's sake.'

The man disappeared out of the door without another word. Drake returned to his seat.

'Okay, so listen to me carefully, Waleed. Did he tell you about the Thermite?'

'Thermite?' Waleed's jaw hung open, revealing a mouthful of half-chewed burger and yellow clumps of cheese. 'I don't even know what that is.'

'Okay, don't sweat it. You're doing well, Waleed. This is really helpful, but I need you to give me a little bit more. You see, I need to talk to your friend. You think he'd talk to me?'

Waleed squeezed his shoulders upwards. 'I don't know,' he murmured softly.

'Where is he now?'

'Wallahi, I don't know, I swear. If I did I would tell you.' He was starting to unravel. Nose running, sobbing gently. God knows what he was on, but emotionally Waleed was a mess.

'Okay, look, we're really close now. I just need a little more. After the fire, he went away. He would need to hide. Did he have somewhere to go? A friend maybe? Somewhere nobody could find him?'

'I think I'm going to be sick.' Waleed was hyperventilating. Over by the counter, Drake could see Buddy Holly looking worried.

'You're fine. You're doing really well.'

'A lock-up.'

'A lock-up?' Drake thought he might have misheard.

'Yeah, like a place they keep cars at night.'

'That's great, Waleed. Really helpful. Do you know where? Can you tell me that?'

Waleed rocked back and forth, eyes closed, his face scrunched up as if in pain. Like a man with a fever, the words came out of him in stuttering fits and starts.

'He gu . . . gets in at n . . . night. Nobody knows. The old m . . . man who runs the pl . . . is stupid and . . . old.'

'Where? I need a name.'

'Fenton. Used Cars. Over in Fulham somewhere.' Waleed clutched at Drake's parka as he stood. 'My father will kill me if he knew. That masjid is everything to him. You mustn't tell him. Swear you won't!'

'I won't. Oh, before I forget. You didn't tell me how you two met?'

'We were in Maudsley hospital together.' Waleed looked at his hands. 'He said there's a reason they lock up people like us.'

'I have one last question,' said Drake. 'Was he alone, or were there others?'

'Only one that I know of; his master, the murshid.'

'His guide? Like what, a spiritual guide?'

Waleed grinned, a pale ghostly smile.

'A guide to the eternal light of Allah.'

CHAPTER 28

Drake walked into the Murder Room to find the place buzzing. People were bustling about the corridors, blocking the stairs, bumping into him as they hurried past bearing stacks of files, photocopiers and monitors. The odd thing was that most of them were unfamiliar faces. An ominous sign had been taped to the glass wall of the conference room. It had only three letters on it: MIU. Drake shrugged off his coat and threw it over the back of his chair.

'What's going on?'

'It's Wheeler.' Kelly was sitting in her chair chewing a pencil. 'He's caved in to Pryce.'

'Why didn't I hear about this?'

'You're about to.' Kelly nodded over his shoulder and Drake turned to see the superintendent coming through the door. The expression on his face was a familiar grimace. Drake had seen that look before.

'Where the hell have you been?' Wheeler asked, leading Drake to one side.

'Phone.' Drake held up the offending item. 'Ran out of juice.'

'That's the best you can come up with?' Wheeler folded his arms. 'I warned you that I couldn't cover you indefinitely. This is not the time to go AWOL.'

'With respect, sir,' Drake began, breaking off as Wheeler's hand rose to stop him.

'DCI Pryce has accused you of interfering with a drug operation he's running.'

'I'm sorry?'

'The way he tells it you were over in the Freetown estate, sticking your nose in where it wasn't welcome.'

'I was following a lead.'

'What lead?'

'The fire at the Birch Lane mosque.'

Wheeler's face soured with disgust. 'That was weeks ago, man. Are you saying there's a connection between that and these murders?'

'Not exactly.'

'No, then what are you saying?'

'I think there is a link between a suspect working on the site and the imam's son.'

'What did DCI Pryce say?'

Drake looked at the floor. 'I haven't actually spoken to him about it yet.'

Wheeler cursed under his breath.

'I warned you about this, Cal. I told you that you were hanging onto this case by the skin of your teeth.' Wheeler winced. 'You disappear and then you turn up spouting all kinds of nonsense. I told you we needed results. I can't tell the commissioners that you are off chasing down fires.'

'No sir, I realize that.'

'Well, your time is up. Pryce is ranking officer and he will be taking direct charge.'

'Where does that leave us? I mean, ourselves and Doctor Crane?' Drake threw her name into the mix thinking it might help his cause. From the look on Wheeler's face it didn't have the desired effect.

'You'll carry on, but you'll coordinate with Pryce. They're setting up a logistics base in here.' Wheeler nodded over at the conference room. 'I know there's bad blood between the two of you, but at the end of the day he's the ranking officer. That means you report to him, and remember, Cal, you're part of a team now, so act like it.'

'Yes, sir.'

Wheeler was eager to move on. 'Sort out whatever problem you have with Pryce. I don't want your personal differences to affect the running of the case.' Drake watched him disappear into the conference room, his frown turning to a smile.

'So, we're working for Pryce now?' Milo sounded unhappy.

'You heard the man, we're part of the team.'

This was the way of things. Murder Investigation Units could be sent out when and where they were needed. It saved on keeping idle units staffed. It all made perfect sense, on paper.

'But we're still on the case, right?' Kelly asked.

'Uh huh.'

Kelly screwed up her nose. 'How fucked up is that?'

'We have no choice, Kelly.'

'Right, so it works both ways? I mean, they'll share what they have?'

'That's generally how it goes.'

'And people said pigs don't fly,' Kelly muttered.

'So, have we got anything new?'

Kelly scrabbled among the papers on her desk for a printed sheet.

'Thwaite's wife. Family name is Chaikin. Turns out they are originally from Belarus, somewhere over there.' She waved vaguely in the direction of the east. 'Her grandparents moved here to escape persecution.'

'Okay, so this might fit in with something Doctor Crane told me.' Drake sat back and put his feet on the desk.

'Sounds like the two of you are getting very chatty.' Kelly winked.

'According to Crane, Mrs Thwaite was kidnapped while in Iraq.'

Kelly let out a low whistle. 'Didn't see that one coming.'

'We should have picked up on it,' agreed Drake.

'When was this?' Milo asked.

'Ten years ago, before she became Mrs Thwaite.'

'Why didn't Thwaite mention it?'

Drake had been wondering about that. 'Maybe he thought it wasn't relevant. It was ten years ago. There was no reason to think there was a connection.'

'But . . .?' asked Kelly.

'But there's more. Three people were kidnapped and held for ransom.'

'Who were the others?'

Milo beat them to it. He had been busy working the keyboard of his computer and now sat back to reveal the screen.

'Tei Hideo.'

Drake and Kelly leaned down to take a look. The screen showed a page from a French newspaper. The picture in the centre of the article was an old black-and-white photograph of a younger Hideo waving as he came down the steps of a plane.

'We have our connection.'

'Well, that changes everything,' said Kelly. 'You said there were three?'

'The third hostage didn't make it,' said Milo. 'An American woman named Janet Avery.' He swung round to face the others. 'This gives us a connection to the Iraq war.'

'Correct. We need to also reconsider Doctor Crane's theory about a link to some kind of Islamist motive.'

'Sounds like she should be here,' said Kelly.

'She's going to join when we visit Thwaite.' Drake turned back to Milo. 'That's another thing. She showed me a photograph of the crime scene that I'm sure I haven't seen.'

Milo nodded. 'Yeah, she already emailed me about it.'

'And...?'

'I don't know, I can't explain it. I don't have that picture. I called over to forensics and they sent over another set.'

'Is this important?' Kelly sounded doubtful.

'Right now, any cracks need to be examined carefully.'

A loud crash came from the conference room. A projector had fallen onto the floor.

'Speaking of cracks. There goes the department budget,' muttered Kelly. 'Don't forget we have an appointment with Thwaite.' She tapped her watch. 'We should get a move on. Also, I found stuff about his finances.'

'What did you find?'

Kelly was shaking her head. 'It's a real mixed bag, chief. I mean there are companies, conglomerates, banks, foundations. And the money comes from all over. The Middle East, Russia, you name it.' She was flipping through her notebook as she spoke. Now she stopped. 'The upshot of it is that his shareholders are about to turn on him. I heard that these murders might just push him over the edge.'

'Meaning?'

'Meaning they will take control of the company if it looks as if they are about to take a hit.'

Milo handed him a large brown envelope. 'These are all the shots of the crime scene we got from forensics.'

'Thanks. One other thing, Milo. Last night, I met the security guard who was on the site. Can you get someone to do a background check on him? Flinders? Kronnos Security. He was with the Light Brigade in Iraq.'

Milo noted down the details. 'Any special reason?'

'Other than idle curiosity? None.'

'Okay, when I get a moment.'

'See if you can get hold of his military record.'

Kelly waved her pencil in the air. 'What's going on with this fire? You said something about the imam's son. Is he involved?'

Drake gave them a breakdown of the mosque fire and his conversation with Waleed.

'So, the arson attack triggered this Thermite stuff that was already there?'

'Thermite isn't something you just leave lying around. Someone had it there for a purpose. Waleed was covering for someone who was staying at the mosque. The same person who was covering for him at Magnolia Quays.'

'Did you get a name?' asked Milo.

'Waleed has a very fluid relationship with reality. Also, he was trying to protect him. I could only get a nickname. Akky.' Drake shrugged. 'Could be anything.'

'Actually, that might tie into something I got from the comedians over at Magnolia Quays.' Kelly rummaged through the stack of folders she was holding. 'Mr Car Attack came up with a list of National Insurance numbers.' She handed him a photocopy. 'I cross-checked those names with the other documents they provided, thinking I might find an anomaly. And, guess what?'

Drake took the second photocopy she handed him. It showed a copy of a driving licence.

'What am I looking at?'

'They needed someone to drive a van one day to pick up something and our friend "Wally" volunteered. Only it wasn't Waleed. The van hire company took a copy of his licence. Could this be Waleed's mysterious friend?'

'Duwayne Jones?' Drake stared at the photograph. 'What makes you think he's the one?'

'I did some digging.' Kelly placed another photocopy on the table. 'Duwayne Jones is small time. B & E, carjacking, and a history of mental issues.'

'Waleed said he met him in the Maudsley.'

'Jones did a stint there four years ago. Also, he converted to Islam during a spell in Wandsworth. Nowadays he calls himself Akbar Hakim.' Kelly lifted her hands. 'Akky?'

'Could be. Well done.' Drake nodded towards the MIU. 'Did you give this to them?'

'Thought I'd wait to see how you felt about that.'

'Well, no point in getting their hopes up if it's nothing.'

'That's what I figured you'd say,' said Kelly.

'I thought we were supposed to be a team?' Milo asked. He saw the looks on Drake and Kelly's faces and threw up his hands. 'Forget I said anything.'

'No chance of an address, I take it?' Drake asked Kelly.

'Not so far.'

'Well, I may have a lead on that.'

As Drake and Kelly headed out, Pryce appeared in the doorway of the conference room. They locked eyes for a second.

'A word, DS Drake.'

'We were just on our way to conduct an interview.'

'This won't take long.' Pryce planted himself in their path, hands in his pockets. He was a bigger man than Drake. Taller and heavier. 'I take it Superintendent Wheeler has explained why I had to set up the MIU?'

'You've decided it's too important to be left to the likes of us.'

Pryce sighed. 'I know we've had our differences in the past, but this is not the time for that.'

'Meaning there is a time for it?'

Pryce took a long look at Drake. 'Meaning, I outrank you.

If you're not happy with the situation, I suggest you put in a complaint, and we'll take it from there.'

'I was just seeking to clarify.'

'I think the situation is clear enough. You report to me now. Is that understood?'

'You're the boss. Sir.'

On the stairs, Kelly turned to him. 'What is it between you two?'

'What makes you think there's anything?'

'I don't know, maybe it's the daggers coming out of both of your eyes.'

'You're wasted in this job, Kelly. You ought to be a clairvoyant.'

'I think you mean a mind reader. A clairvoyant can see the future. Which if I was I would have been able to predict the arrival of Catwoman.'

Drake followed Kelly's eye to the front desk where Crane was waiting.

'Ah, Doctor Crane, right on time.' Drake flashed her a smile. 'You can tell us more about this kidnapping on the way.'

Crane looked to Kelly for an explanation.

'Don't ask me,' said Kelly. 'Some days he's just the life and soul.'

CHAPTER 29

Kelly drove while Drake went through the photographs. Finally, he tossed the envelope back to Ray.

'It's not here.'

'What isn't?'

'The picture you showed me at your place. The high angle.'

'That doesn't make any sense.' Ray opened the envelope and sifted through the prints. 'So, it's not here. Someone forgot it.'

'Never assume anyone is incapable of fucking up.'

'The world according to Drake!' Kelly was shaking her head.

'You know you can just have my copy,' Ray said. 'That might be easier.'

Drake twisted round to look back at her. 'It's not the picture I'm concerned about. I just want to know why I never saw it until you showed it to me.'

Ray sat back in her seat and stared out of the window. 'There's a word for your condition, you know.'

'I don't doubt it,' said Drake.

'I think she's saying you need help,' said Kelly helpfully.

H oward Thwaite kept them waiting in a conference room on the first floor of a converted warehouse overlooking Chelsea Harbour. Ray stood by the window. Kelly wandered around, helping herself to the coffee and cream that had been brought in on a tray.

'Not bad, eh?' she opined, biting into a chocolate biscuit.

Through the glass wall Drake could see dozens of bright young things busily tapping away at computers and working at drawing boards. He wasn't exactly sure what they were doing but he had seen enough to know that they had operations going on in places across the globe.

The door opened and Thwaite walked in. He looked more tired than the first time Drake had seen him. As if the weight of what had happened had begun to take its toll. His skin looked grey against his black clothes. Behind him followed a tall woman wearing a short pencil skirt and oversized spectacles. She rearranged a handful of folders and a tablet in her arms.

'I'm sorry to keep you waiting. I'm afraid we're very busy these days, what with one thing and another.'

'Well, we appreciate you taking the time. I felt this couldn't really wait.'

The look on Thwaite's face told him he was less than impressed.

'I understood the case had been handed to a new officer.'

'Actually, it's really an expansion of the original team,' Drake said. Thwaite seemed satisfied with this. He sat down and folded his hands.

'If that means you are taking the matter more seriously, then I'm glad to hear it.'

'One of the reasons we wanted to see you today was to follow up on a matter that has just come to light.'

'What matter?'

Ray stepped up. 'Why did you not mention that your wife had been held hostage in Iraq?'

Thwaite turned to look at her. 'I'm sorry, who are you?'

'Doctor Crane is a forensic psychologist who is assisting us with this case.'

'I see,' said Thwaite, curtly. 'Well, the reason is simple; I didn't think it had any bearing. I still don't.'

'Your wife wasn't alone. Two other people were taken hostage with her. One of them died. The other was Tei Hideo, the same man who was killed with her at Magnolia Quays.'

'The same . . .?' Thwaite's face grew ashen. 'But I don't understand. How could that be, he was Chinese or something?'

'Japanese by origin. He was a French national working for the United Nations.'

'I don't know what to say. How can that be?'

'Well, we're trying to understand the motivation behind the murders,' said Drake. 'So, it would be helpful if perhaps you took us through the whole kidnap episode.'

'Of course.' Thwaite signalled to his assistant, who poured him a glass of water.

'At the time, Marsha wasn't actually your wife,' Drake continued. 'But you were . . . involved, weren't you?'

'Yes. I was married at the time, it's true. Marsha and I were, as you put it, involved.' He shook his head in disagreement with himself. 'It was more than that. I planned to leave my wife for her.'

'He makes it sound like waiting to catch a bus,' muttered Kelly behind Drake's back. Nobody else seemed to hear. Thwaite went on.

'We . . . Our relationship was not public knowledge then. We were both in Iraq for separate reasons, but it gave us a chance to be together.'

'Can you tell us what you were doing in Iraq at the time?' Drake asked.

'I was overseeing a project. A hospital that was being constructed in Tikrit. Marsha was there for a charity she was working for.'

'Could the kidnappers have been targeting you?' Ray asked.

'It's possible,' agreed Thwaite. 'If they had been watching me. I thought about that at the time.' He shook his head. 'It was terrible. Everything came out. The press, you know, eager for details. It ended my marriage.'

'They demanded a ransom,' said Drake.

'They wanted three million dollars. One million for each hostage.'

'Your wife's maiden name was Chaikin,' said Kelly. 'She was Jewish.'

Thwaite nodded. 'That complicated matters somewhat. She had family in Israel. Distant, but nevertheless, their security services wanted to get involved. I refused their help. I thought it would only make things worse.'

Drake perched himself against the window. 'UK government policy was not to negotiate with terrorists, and not to pay ransoms. How did you get the SAS in to release them?'

'It's true we couldn't get any government support. They wanted nothing to do with it. I had friends trying to pull strings in Whitehall, but to no avail. I don't think they cared.'

'That's a little harsh, isn't it, sir?' Kelly interjected.

Thwaite looked over at her as if he had forgotten she was there. 'In a way it serves their purpose. The more brutal the enemy, the more justified you are in waging war against them. That's the pragmatic view.' He faced towards Drake. 'I was given the name of a security firm that specialized in this type of thing.'

'You mean a private military contractor?'

'Hawkestone, I think was the name. I can give you the details. Anyway, they were supposed to go in and negotiate the release.'

'Only it didn't work out that way, did it?' Ray said.

'No, it didn't.' Thwaite's eyes fixed themselves on the table. 'In the end it all went wrong.'

'What happened exactly?' Drake asked.

'Two of the hostages were released. Marsha and the man from the UN. The one you mentioned.' Thwaite's eyes came up to meet Drake's. 'A third hostage was killed.'

'Janet Avery,' said Kelly.

'Yes, that was her name.' Thwaite's eyes were focused on the table in front of him as the memories came back. 'They bungled the whole operation. Their operatives went completely off script. They killed a number of people. I was so angry. I said I wouldn't foot the bill for their incompetence.'

'How did that go down?' Drake asked.

'We reached a compromise. I paid the costs.' Thwaite's eyes found Kelly, expecting some snarky comment that never came. 'I wanted to wash my hands of the whole business.'

'But you got your future wife back unharmed,' said Drake.

'Yes, I did.' Thwaite fell silent for a moment. 'Do you really think this has something to do with why she was killed?'

'It's possible,' said Drake. 'We need to look into every aspect.'

'That sounds like the perfect excuse not to do anything,' muttered Thwaite.

'It might help to speed things up if you were a little more cooperative.'

'I don't understand,' Thwaite spluttered. 'Why are you still in charge of this investigation?'

'Sheer good fortune, I guess.' Drake glanced at Ray, wondering what she was thinking. 'One last thing, I need to ask about your finances.'

'My finances?'

'Yes. Just how close to bankruptcy are you?'

'This is outrageous. Now you want to poke about in my business affairs?'

'We understand that your wife has been keeping you afloat.'

'I really don't see the relevance of this line of questioning.'

'Humour me. The Magnolia Quays project was behind schedule before this happened. Your backers are presumably not happy about this property being the scene of a murder. It's not exactly going to help sales. What happens if they decide to pull the plug?'

'The investment so far would be lost. That would be disastrous for the company, and for me personally.'

'That doesn't mean they wouldn't do it.'

'They would never do that.' Thwaite's fingers drummed impatiently on the table. 'I think I've proved that I am competent and as interested in success as they are.'

'Presumably you stand to inherit a fair amount from your wife,' said Drake.

'Okay, that's quite enough,' Thwaite struggled to get the words out.

The assistant stepped in.

'As Mr Thwaite's lawyer I'm afraid I'm going to have to ask you to leave.'

'Well, I hadn't actually finished,' said Drake.

'If you want more from my client you're going to have to request a formal interview.' Behind the spectacles her eyes were trained sharply on Drake. 'Or charge him.'

Outside, they stood around the car. The sun was shining for a change. The pleasure boats in the harbour rocked gently at anchor.

'Didn't see that coming,' said Kelly. 'I didn't realize she was his lawyer.'

'Me neither,' said Drake. 'He was expecting trouble, even before we told him what it was about.'

'You think that means he is worried this is connected to his finances?' Ray asked.

'I think that's a reasonable assumption. Thwaite's backers

add up to a stack of oddballs.' Drake listed a couple of the bigger names. A Kuwaiti holding company, offshore firms, Russians registered in Belarus. 'Then there are the Apostolis brothers, and the Ziyade family.'

'Dirty money?' asked Ray.

'As dirty as it comes.'

'So what's your hypothesis?'

'There's two ways this could go.' Drake folded his arms and leaned back against the side of the car. 'There's the link to Iraq. Someone connected to the kidnapping is the obvious one. A relative of one of the kidnappers or the victims.' He turned to Kelly. 'We need to get a list of everyone involved at all levels. If there's a connection there we need to find it.'

'I'll get on to that right away,' said Kelly.

'We also need to get in touch with these contractors, Hawkestone.'

'I have a few contacts,' said Ray.

'I'll bet you do,' said Drake.

'They're generally cagey, but I can reach out to them.'

'That would be helpful.'

'What was the other line you mentioned?' Kelly asked.

'It's always possible that at the root of it all is some kind of rivalry between backers. There's a lot of money involved in a project like this. Someone might be getting itchy fingers.'

'The thing about this is that the perpetrators were trying to make a point,' said Ray. 'This was meant to stir things up.'

'Which would make perfect sense if someone was trying to make a big splash in the media. If the point here is to take down Thwaite, then they have done a pretty good job of undermining confidence in the whole project.'

'Making it perfect for a takeover bid.'

'We need to stick to the facts,' said Drake. 'Whoever did this had help on the inside. That's where we need to start looking.'

CHAPTER 30

Back at Raven Hill, Kelly jumped out of the car to head up to the Murder Room. Drake hung back, and Crane, sensing that he wanted to talk, let go of the door handle and sat back.

'You should know that I am officially no longer in charge of this case.'

'So they gave it to Pryce?'

Cal rocked his head from side to side. 'I had my chance. I blew it.'

'Why are you telling me this?'

He stared at her for a moment. 'I just thought you should know.'

'I can't pick sides in this fight. Wheeler brought me in to advise on the case.'

'Sure, I get that.'

'If Pryce is in charge, I have to answer to him.' Crane paused. 'You still think you can win this, don't you? I mean, solve the case, bring in the killer and save the day?'

'You think I'm making this personal.'

'Of course it's personal. I get that. When the Malevich case went down you took the fall and Pryce came out smelling of roses.'

Drake tapped a beat on the steering wheel but said nothing.

'You don't trust him,' Crane went on. Drake shook his head. 'That's why you need to win this case.'

'This is the last chance I get,' Cal said. 'They would have pushed me back to traffic control if Wheeler hadn't stepped in. He got me transferred.'

'You're saying you owe it to him?'

'I don't owe anyone anything. If I can't get back to where I was then I'm not sure I see a future for me here.'

'You're up against a system, Cal. People like Pryce know how to use it. Either you learn that, or you're always going to wind up holding the short end of the stick.'

'People like Pryce have been trying to take things from me for as long as I can remember.'

'That's good,' she said, cracking open the door. 'Hang on to that. You're going to need it.' She leaned in as she made to go. 'If you're asking if you can still count on me, the answer is yes. I've run into a few Pryces of my own.'

He watched her walk away, climb onto the Triumph and race off. Catwoman indeed. In her dark leather jacket and helmet she looked like some demon angel escaped from the underworld.

Drake sat there for a time, before leaning forwards to punch the ignition. He suspected that if he showed his face in the Murder Room, Pryce would assign him to some hopeless task. The best strategy right now was to stay out of his way. The only strategy.

All quiet on the reservation. The Freetown estate felt like the calm before the storm. For whatever reason, Pryce appeared to have pulled his men back. The van full of sleeping riot-squad officers was nowhere to be seen. Daylight was fading fast. Already the distant

206 • PARKER BILAL

glow of streetlights rose over the city. A siren moaned and blue lights reflected back off windows high up. A couple of kids seemed to recognize Drake's car. They waved him by with the familiar cry of 'Five-oh' as he passed the corner where they sat astride their bicycles. A couple of scooters revved up and flitted away. A black Mercedes with aluminium wheels and an airfoil on the back slid slowly by, heavy bass reverberating through closed windows.

The middle of the square had once had grass on it, but it had long since been covered over with cement that was now cracked and pitted with weeds. On one side there was a stand with a rising row of steps. Drake sat himself down in the middle of one of these. It wasn't long before he heard the whirr of bicycle chains. Four kids on bikes. One spun past him, did a sharp turn and skidded to a halt.

'Looks a bit of a mess.' The kid nodded at the driver's door where a faint pink cloud marked where the graffiti had been. He'd had a go at removing the paint from the side but hadn't been entirely successful.

'It's not easy to get the stuff off.'

The kid was watching Drake as if he didn't know what to make of him. He was about twelve. Buck teeth and bushy wild hair that looked knotty and unkempt. He wore a sweatshirt with a character wearing green armour that carried the words Jango Fett, Bounty Hunter.

'I used to live here,' said Drake. The kid drew to a halt.

'You a Fed, int ya?'

'Waste of paint if I wasn't.' Drake nodded at the others. 'Is that your crew?'

He got a shrug in reply.

'Is Chalkie still running the estate?'

'Chalkie?' Jango Fett was curious now. 'Chalkie died.'

'Then who, one of his boys?'

'Wynstan.'

Drake remembered Wynstan as a skinny youth back in the day. He had to be in his fifties by now. 'They used to call him Crazy Wynstan. Had a temper on him.'

Jango waited for more.

'I watched him throw a kid off that walkway up there.'

Trying to look unimpressed the kid stamped on the pedals and spun a few turns. Behind him, his posse circled like sharks. They were all mixed race. A smattering of Asian, African and Arab features.

'So why you 'ere then?'

'I'm looking for someone. A man named Akbar Hakim.'

'You come here lookin' for a snitch, innit?' The kid was shaking his head. 'Forget it, bro.' Drake watched him pedal away.

The interior of the Alamo resembled a sunken wreck. None of the chairs and tables matched. The bar counter listed to one side. In its lifetime, the tartan carpet had probably soaked up enough beer to sink a frigate. The tables were scarred and the upholstery looked like a pack of ravenous cats had been let loose on it.

Shabby furniture aside, what had really changed since the old days was the number of screens they had acquired. There seemed to be one whichever way you cared to look. They were overshadowed by one enormous television that took up most of one wall, no doubt to bring in the Saturday football crowds. Right now it was tuned to the local news. There was a murmur of excitement as the Birch Lane mosque came up. The blackened doorway was still cordoned off with crime-scene tape. Drake saw a woman with hair the colour of rhubarb backed by a crowd carrying white crosses and union jacks. Alongside her was the man he'd seen in the pub last time he was here, Stephen Moss. The placards read things like, TAKING BACK OUR COUNTRY, and STOP ISLAMIZATION.

'Hard to know whether to laugh or cry,' said a voice behind him. Drake turned to find Doc Wyatt standing behind the bar. 'So what murder and mayhem brings you around here this time?'

'You know how it is, a little of this, a little of that.'

Doc looked as if he didn't believe a word, or didn't care, both of which could be true. Finally, he rolled his shoulders in a gesture of reconciliation.

'You still drinking rum or what?'

Without waiting for a reply, Doc found a bottle and two glasses and poured them each a large shot. Drake looked down into the dark liquid. Drinking always summoned up the image of his mother, crouched forwards in the armchair that had been ripped to shreds by a succession of cats over the years. Her face lit by the glow from the electric fire, her voice a low, smoky purr.

'You're no better than me,' she used to whisper. 'You've got it too. One day you'll realize that, and then it will be too late.' She would dissolve into harsh, hacking laughter.

The news had switched to a demonstration outside Westminster, where protesters stamped their feet against the cold. Mostly men. All white. In shell suits and bargain-basement jeans, they had the look about them of the long-term dispossessed. Placards bore slogans like, BRINGING BRITAIN TO HER SENSES, and NO SHARIA. Along the bottom of the screen, the lead line was, MAGNOLIA QUAYS: PROTEST AGAINST RITUAL KILLINGS.

'You've seen this?' Doc asked. 'They're saying it was some kind of sharia thing.'

'You put ideas into people's heads and they'll say anything.'

'Same old story, right? All of this stuff is just a distraction.'

Drake had to smile. 'You haven't given up on your conspiracy theories, then?'

'Laugh, but you know it's true. I don't expect you to agree. Hell, you're a part of it.'

'Because I'm a copper?'

'Whatever,' shrugged Doc. 'Never understood why you did that.'

'That's funny, I always thought you of all people would get it.'

'Maybe I'm too thick.'

'You always used to say that if we don't try to fix things we can't expect nobody else to.'

'That's what you're doing, fixing the system?' Doc refilled their glasses. 'How's that working out for you?'

'It's like everything else,' said Drake. 'There are good days and bad.'

Doc nodded. At least he seemed to be thinking about it.

'So, what are people saying?' asked Drake.

'About the killings? Yeah, people round here are more concerned about what's going to happen to the estate.'

'How's that then?'

'Well, all of this development that's going on. Rumour has it that they're planning to flatten the place, turn it into some kind of luxury complex, shopping, high-end living spaces.' Doc nodded his head. 'Remember the old swimming baths? They're already drawing up plans to turn it into a mall. Can you imagine? Money, money, money. It's all about getting us to spend what we don't have, then we all in debt.'

'I hear another conspiracy lecture coming up.'

'Go ahead, laugh, man. I'm telling you, it's going to happen real fast.'

As Doc slid along the bar to serve another customer, Drake turned to survey the room. He had never thought of Freetown as a prime piece of property, but of course it was. They were sitting in the middle of a gold mine. A gold mine that could only be accessed by people with money. Investors. Property developers. People like Howard Thwaite.

What was it that he wasn't seeing? Something told him there was a connection between this place and Magnolia Quays. On the map he had drawn a short line between the site and Freetown. They still had no idea of how the killer or killers had got away from the crime scene, but the most likely explanation was that he had been working there. And that led him back to Akbar Hakim, Waleed's friend.

'Let me ask you something else,' Drake said when Doc returned.

'That's what I'm here for, man.' Doc made a show for the old timers down the other end of the bar. 'Cooperate with the long arm of the law!'

'Akbar Hakim.'

'Yeah, you asked me about him already. What can I say?'

'The name doesn't ring a bell? He used to be Duwayne Jones.'

Doc shook his head. 'Can't say it does. What did he do?'

'He was friends with Waleed, the imam's son from the mosque.'

'Ohh, him I know.' Doc rolled his eyes. 'Now that's one mixed-up kid. You catch my drift? He's madder than a sackful of hatters. Ya aks me it comes from all that religion.' He was shaking his head. 'The parents give the boy a complex. Tell him he no good, that he have to pray to stay on the good side of the Almighty. No drinking and no pussy. But what's a boy to do? It's all around him.' Doc stretched out a hand to demonstrate. 'All his friends are getting busy. He wants the same, but he knows that brings damnation. Mark my words, religion don mess up his head. You know what I'm talking about.'

Outside, Drake leaned on the car and took a long look around him. A helicopter hovered overhead, the single eye of its searchlight playing a jagged pattern over the rooftops. He watched it for a time, feeling the tension drain from his heart as the beam moved off and the buzzing sank into the distance. Then Drake's eye caught something and he wandered over towards the north end of the square. There was a large, elegant red-brick building on the corner. The old Victorian swimming baths. It had been closed down years ago, but nothing could be done to the place. It had fallen into disrepair. He could remember swimming there as a kid.

Now he noticed an advertising hoarding had been put up. It showed a computer-simulated image of some kind of commercial centre, all glass and smiles. Beautiful people who had just landed from Planet Perfect. THE FUTURE IS NOW read the tagline.

CHAPTER 31

Ray worked up a light sweat on the heavy bag. Over the years she had trained in a number of martial arts. As in so many other aspects of life, she wasn't orthodox or loyal in her tastes. How do you find a method that is perfectly suited to you? The answer is, you don't; it hasn't been invented, yet. So she switched and mixed. Taekwondo, Wado Ryu, Wing Chun, Muay Thai. She trained hard, learned new techniques, gained a degree of proficiency and then moved on. What emerged in the end was a kind of personal mix, and that was what she was most content with.

Now she threw a flurry of kicks, punches, elbow and knee jabs, circling the bag with light, fluid footwork. She practised barefoot, in a singlet and sweatpants, her hair tied back in a pony tail. She paused to drink water from a bottle and to towel herself down, then she went at it again.

An hour later she was showered and dressed and back at her desk.

She picked up the folder containing the crime-scene photos

along with a map of London. She circled Magnolia Quays. The question of whether the killer was trying to make some kind of statement intrigued her. If her interpretation of the high-angle photograph was correct then these killings could be seen as an attack on the city. Meaning what? The corrupting power of capital? Western civilization?

Ray had the sense that she was working in the dark. She felt she had the formal support of Wheeler and, to some extent at least, Cal Drake. Beyond that she was on her own. Not that this bothered her too much. Ray had spent most of her life pursuing unlikely interests. Her whole upbringing had, in that sense, been a mixed bag of influences and experiences.

It went back to her parents, this history of striking out into unknown territory. Her mother, Golnar, had grown up in Tehran dreaming of a glamorous, bohemian life in Paris and yet wound up in London with a man who was her diametric opposite. Where she was light and open, he was dark and secretive. Where she talked, he brooded in silence. Ray imagined they had connected in some reckless moment where they saw in the other a promise of freedom from the limitations of their separate upbringings. Edmund Crane had separated from his family because he wanted none of their entitlement: money, land, property. He went as far as he could in the opposite direction, bringing home a Muslim bride knowing they would disown him, which they did.

With a sigh, Ray brought herself back to the present. It felt as if things were moving swiftly, which in turn made her worry that she was missing something. That was the danger, that your own fascination took you further away from the facts, leading you along a deceptive path. It might feel right, but unless you were careful you would be sucked in by your own ambition, blind to other possibilities.

Trying to get into the mind of a killer was like trying to make sense of a kaleidoscope. The colours and shapes tumbled and changed.

It transformed itself from one moment to the next. It was all about the angle, the intensity of the signal, the light and colour. Every killer left a trace of what drove them. Little clues that could not be picked up by a forensic officer. Hints that came through decisions, the strategies employed. Every choice told you something.

Often it was about not losing sight of the fact that there was a stable centre, a spider at the centre of the web. That was her job, to identify the pattern, register the form, create a relationship between pursuer and the pursuit. To see where, in the slow spin of the wheel, the investigator might get lost. Turning the viewfinder until all the pieces fell into place. It was about understanding that each one was different, each had their own characteristics. Sometimes the difficult bit was holding on, believing that there was an end in sight, that it would all eventually make sense.

If Ray had an area of specialization then this was it. She had spent years studying the myriad shapes into which the human mind can twist itself to believe its own madness. Evil is not an absolute. It is everywhere. In some people it took root, became a means to an end, a way of life. It clung to the landscape, grew like weeds in the cracks. A person could become trapped in one moment of time. Some part of them that grows in abnormal proportion to everyone else. Evil creates its own nature.

Placing the high-angle picture at the centre, she spread the others around it, and stood up to get a better look. There was something different about it, to do with the light. She checked the time as she reached for her phone. She was in luck, Milo answered straight away.

'I wasn't sure I'd catch you.'

He was in fact on his way home. In the background she could hear the garbled squawk of a train announcement.

'I didn't realize this was your personal number.'

'It's no problem.' He didn't seem to mind her calling after hours. In fact, he seemed quite happy to hear from her.

'Milo, it's about one of the pictures you gave me.'

'Oh, yes. DS Drake mentioned it.' His voice sounded a note of dismay.

'Exactly, the one he couldn't find.' She lifted it from the desk in front of her. 'The thing is,' she went on, 'I've been trying to pinpoint what it is that makes it different. At first I thought it was just the angle, but then I realized that the light is also not quite the same. Did you notice that?'

'I did actually. I sent the copy you mailed me to forensics to try and find out which of the technicians took the picture, but they haven't managed to pin it down yet.' Milo was silent for a moment. 'Do you really think this is important?'

'I'm not sure what it means, but there is something.'

'The odd thing is that yours is the only copy of that picture we have. It wasn't in the original set that I had, or in the second set that I requested.'

'How do you explain that?'

'That's just the thing,' he said. 'I can't.'

Ray put down her phone and spread the photographs in a pattern in front of her. The light and the angle were distinct. It was almost as if the picture had been taken on another day, by someone else. Finally, with a feeling of frustration she gathered up the rest of the prints and replaced them in the folder, leaving that picture on top.

Her eye fell on the file Stewart Mason had given her on Goran Malevich. Leader of a former Serbian militia, the White Knights, who were officially disbanded in 1995 when the war in the Balkans ended. He resurfaced in London nearly ten years later. Malevich and his men moved into the local crime scene, taking over large chunks using the kind of techniques they had perfected in the war: intimidation, kidnapping, extortion, rape. There was still a question mark hanging over Drake, even though in her heart she felt it was hard to reconcile him with a person like Malevich.

On her laptop she clicked open Drake's Special Branch file, also provided by Mason. She was already familiar with its contents, but still she went over it again. Drake's parents had met at art college in Camberwell. Both had dropped out around the time Cal was born. Drake's father had been an exchange student. They split. Mother and son moved around a lot. No fixed address. Trouble with social security over benefits. The father overstayed his visa but eventually gained British nationality. Those were the days. Drake's mother had struggled with substance problems. Cal was in and out of care on a regular basis. By the time he was in his teens he had begun to make a mark on police records. Minor crimes and misdemeanours. Destruction of property. Breaking and entering. Possession of drugs with intent to sell.

At that point his life seemed to take a sharp turn. The juvenile criminal activity faded away overnight. The next series of reports were redacted documents that charted Drake's involvement with radical Islam. His attendance at Finsbury Park Mosque, meetings run by organizations like Hizb ut-Tahrir, and lectures by key figures identified as imams promoting hate.

By sixteen Drake was attending meetings of Al-Muhajiroun, a salafist group that was later banned in the UK after they began praising the 9/11 hijackers. Then a sudden about turn. In late 2005 he joined the army. In early 2006 he was posted to Basra with the Royal Anglian Regiment. He was wounded when a helicopter he was in crashed. He was awarded the Distinguished Service Cross for his actions. After that he retrained for work with the Royal Military Police in the Special Investigation Branch. On his return he was fast tracked through Hendon training college into the police. He was everything the Met were looking for to fill their diversity quota. Wheeler brought him into the organized-crime task force, which was jointly headed by Drake and Pryce; that was the beginning of their problems.

Ray sat back. Drake had taken himself from a bad set of circumstances, broken home, substance-abusing mother, absent father, through a distinguished army career and to the rank of detective inspector in less than ten years. Then he hit a wall. Had he lost faith in the system, or had he simply succumbed to temptation? She recalled her conversation with Wheeler.

'Cal is a good officer,' Wheeler had told her. 'One of the best detectives I've ever seen. He has his downsides. He had trust issues, and he's not the best communicator. I've told him time and again that he really needs to work on his personal skills.'

'What about the rumours of corruption?'

'He can rub people up the wrong way.' Wheeler sighed. 'Cal can be his own worst enemy.'

CHAPTER 32

Fenton's Used Motors was tucked down a gloomy, damp side street behind the Tube station. High brick arches flanked it on one side and a row of houses on the other. The entrance was a wide double-sided gate in a high chain-link fence topped with razor wire. A veritable fortress for clapped-out old bangers. Faded signs warned of security services and guard dogs, although there didn't seem to be much evidence of either.

Drake managed to back into an alleyway on the opposite side of the street. Lights flashed by from the trains clattering overhead. Either side of him were lock-ups or private garages where local residents kept their cars, their fight dogs and their stolen domestic appliances. It was quiet for the most part and he made himself comfortable. He'd even managed to rake up a couple of sandwiches and a half bottle of Dominican rum from a late-night supermarket along the way. He tossed all into the back seat for later. He wasn't hungry. For the moment he was nursing a tea and a bar of chocolate to restore some sense of balance.

Through his binoculars Drake surveyed the cars parked behind the high chain-link fence. Rundown, clapped-out and rusted heaps of junk with prices hastily scrawled across windscreens like cries for help. Akbar Hakim could have been sleeping in any one of them.

Kelly wasn't answering her phone. Understandable. She was off duty and, of course, some people had lives. Never mind. He was glad of the solitude. Being alone meant he didn't have to make conversation, or deal with somebody else's. He could think, or try to at least.

He found his mind turning to Ray. He wondered if she was involved with anyone. Hard to imagine what sort of a man she would go for. Smart, obviously. Rich, probably. She struck him as the kind of woman who didn't really have any particular need for a relationship. If something came along, then fine, but she wasn't going to spend time looking for it. As for casual hook-ups, he imagined she would have no trouble there. Probably spent half her time fending off men, and women. He wondered if that was her thing. It wasn't the vibe he got off her, but he'd been wrong about that before.

A wave of restlessness sent him reaching into the back for the rum. He cracked the seal and savoured the aroma rising up from the neck of the bottle before lifting it to his mouth.

The rum restored a certain clarity to his thoughts. He went back over his conversation with Waleed. Right now it felt as if he was putting all his money on one bet: that Akbar Hakim was the nexus around which everything turned. Was that anything more than wishful thinking? He tried to stack up the pieces. Hakim had been working at Magnolia Quays. Waleed had arranged for him to take his place at the building site. Waleed had also provided a place for Hakim to stay: the front room at his father's mosque. Drake had nothing to prove that it was Hakim who had stored the Thermite in the mosque, but he was confident that the picture would clear once he had his hands on the man. More important was the question of where the Thermite had come from and what they were planning to do with it. Drake hoped that Hakim would lead him further, to the man Waleed called Hakim's murshid, or guide. So far there was nothing to indicate who this third person might be.

The Thermite had been ignited by coincidence. That seemed clear. Hakim had the material in the small room and when some bright spark had chucked a homemade Molotov cocktail through the doorway it had set it off.

All of which brought Drake back to the present. He needed Hakim to get anywhere with this, and he needed to get his hands on him quickly. Settling back into his seat, Drake leaned against the headrest and studied the forecourt on the other side of the street.

Fenton's Used Cars looked as if it belonged in another age. Towards the rear, down an aisle between rows of rusty vehicles, stood a narrow house with a wooden door helpfully marked Office. High-powered security lights along the old railway arches cast a cold white glow over the rows of vehicles. Nothing moved. Drake trained the small set of binoculars on the house at the back of the compound. A brick building with a rundown billboard over it that read Bargains for All! He went from window to window, looking for any signs of life.

Setting the glasses down, Drake reached for the rum again and took another swig. He screwed the cap back on carefully. He didn't want to overdo it. This was going to be a long night.

Before he converted, Hakim had been plain old Duwayne Jones, a small-time criminal with a record going back to his days as a juvenile offender. Hakim was an unknown quantity. The name change, the sudden embrace of Islam, along with the stay at the Maudsley confirmed a record of mental-health issues. He and Waleed must have made a fine pair.

Drake reached for his phone. It was late, but what the hell. He listened to the ring tone. On the fifth ring he began to lose his nerve. It was close to midnight. He was about to click off when she answered.

'Cal, is that you?'

'Sorry about the late hour.'

'Not a problem,' said Ray. 'I was working.'

'Yeah, same here.' There was a long silence. Drake shifted in his chair. 'I was thinking about Thermite. I was trying to remember if there was a specific sharia punishment involving fire?'

'Not that I know of. If anything, it's the opposite. Burning is generally perceived as a punishment reserved for Allah's use only.'

'That's what I thought. Jehenem, hellfire.'

'There are instances of fire being used as a punishment, but those are exceptions. Where are you?'

'Fulham.' Drake rubbed his eyes and explained about Hakim.

'You think this is connected to the fire at the mosque?' asked Ray.

'It's just a feeling. Maybe it wasn't an accident. Maybe they wanted the Thermite to detonate.'

'You mean, they were trying to burn down the mosque. But why?'

'Tell me if I'm wrong,' said Drake, reaching for the bottle of rum and unscrewing the cap. 'Isn't there a gate in hell reserved for those who have betrayed the faith?'

'The seventh gate, according to some hadiths. Speaking of hell, don't you have people to do things like stakeouts?'

'You would think so,' Drake sighed. 'How about you?'

'I'm home, thinking about going to bed.'

'Sounds nice.'

'Don't go getting any ideas, DS Drake.'

'Me? Wouldn't dream of it.'

Still, he was smiling long after the line had gone dead. It had felt nice, just to be able to talk to her. The enigmatic Doctor Crane was turning out to be all right, after all. Drake reached over into the back seat for something to eat. As soon as he peeled back the wrapper he could smell something wasn't right. He held the package up to the light and read the sell-by date. Then he cursed and tossed the offending item back where he had found it. It was going to be a long night.

CHAPTER 33

A knock at the window jerked Drake from his sleep. He opened his eyes to see Kelly holding up two cups of coffee. It was still just about dark. Daylight was a purple scar over rooftops slick with rain. He struggled up in his seat as Kelly went round and got in.

'Christ, man, let some air in here before you fumigate yourself.'

Drake took her point. He ran the windows down and turned the blower on at the same time.

She stared aghast.

'You do realize that you're just blowing hot air into the atmosphere?'

'Do me a favour, Kelly, it's too early for witty banter.' He took the coffee gratefully, the aroma reviving him even before he'd managed to get any of it into his mouth.

'You didn't bring anything to eat, did you?'

'As a matter of fact, I did.' She reached into the pocket of her coat to produce a paper bag with grease stains on it. Inside were two croissants.

'You deserve a promotion, DC Marsh.'

'From your lips to God's ear. So, how long were you out?'

Drake glanced at the dashboard clock which read 6.04.

'I don't know, maybe an hour or so.'

Kelly sniffed. 'Smells suspiciously like a distillery in here.'

'I didn't expect to see you so early,' said Drake. 'I was planning to take it to the car wash.'

'Well, couldn't leave you out here all alone in the cold. So, any action?'

'Apart from an endless stream of drunken louts looking for somewhere to relieve themselves, you mean? No, nothing.'

'Great.' Kelly was drinking her coffee. 'I can't believe you stayed here all night without telling anyone. You could have had support.'

'You mean from Pryce? Pull the other one. If I tried going to him with a tip-off from a certified nut job he would laugh me out of the office and you know it.'

'Why do I get the feeling this has become personal?'

'It's always personal.' Drake hunched his shoulders and bit into his croissant. Normally, he wasn't keen on them, but at this particular instant he wasn't feeling fussy.

'Okay.' Kelly took a deep breath. 'Let me just say, I'm not even sure I should be out here with you. Pryce has made it clear that he wants us to run everything by him.'

'I understand,' said Drake, taking a slurp of coffee to clear his head. 'Maybe you should leave this to me. No point in getting yourself into hot water.'

'Will you let me finish?'

'Sorry, go ahead.'

'Okay, so if I have this straight, your theory is that this Hakim was working at Magnolia Quays using Wally's name. He disappeared the day the bodies were discovered. He was also staying at the mosque when it went up in flames. How am I doing?'

'So far, not so shabby.'

'It's the next bit that bothers me. What's the connection between the murder of two people who we now know were kidnapped in Iraq ten years ago, and a little local mosque?'

'That's what I'm hoping Akbar Hakim will be able to help us with.'

'Amen to that.' Kelly wrinkled her nose. 'What is that smell?'

'I'm thinking of bottling it. I'll call it, Natural Charm.'

'Natural Harm, more like.'

Drake cracked open the door and climbed out, his body stiff from sitting in the same position for so many hours.

Across the street a heavily built man was approaching the entrance to Fenton's Used Motors, fishing a heavy ring of keys from the pocket of his grubby old waxed jacket. He was trailed by a very old and somewhat lame Alsatian.

'Even the guard dog is geriatric,' muttered Kelly as they crossed the street.

'Mr Fenton?'

'Who wants to know?' The man squinted at the badge Drake was holding up. A knotty figure in his sixties. Underneath the flat cap sprouted a bushy, unkempt beard stained yellow with nicotine. His small eyes blinked as if in pain. 'What's the trouble now?'

'We're looking for someone we believe might be staying on your property.'

'I don't trust you people further than I can throw you. Got a search warrant, 'ave you?'

'We're not searching your premises, Mr Fenton, we're looking for a suspect in a murder investigation.'

'Same thing in my book.'

'Have you any idea what the fine is for harbouring a fugitive?' Kelly asked brightly.

'Who said anything about harbouring anyone? What kind of fine?'

The idea that this might cost him something struck Fenton with distaste. 'Who are you looking for, anyway?'

'Akbar Hakim,' said Drake.

'Never heard of him.' Fenton fiddled with more keys and chains.

'You probably know him better as Duwayne Jones.'

'Duwayne?' Fenton paused to look round. 'That loser? Haven't seen him in years.' The chains rattled off and he swung the gate open. 'Hang on a minute. What makes you think you'll find him here?'

'Is it possible he might be sleeping on the property?'

'No chance.' Fenton held up the chains. 'Not unless he's Harry fucking Houdini.'

Kelly and Drake exchanged a glance. While Drake engaged Fenton, Kelly moved in the direction of the far building.

'Isn't it possible he could still have a key?'

'He used to lock up for me, it's true, but he gave back the keys when I let him go.'

'He could have made copies.'

'Ah,' grunted Fenton dismissively. He hobbled towards a little hut by the front gate. A large sign over the door read, Sales. Not that it looked as though he was overrun with customers. Across the window were pound signs and exclamation marks. Bargains Galore! Everyone's a Winner!

'Get a lot of business round here nowadays, do you?' Drake asked.

'Nowadays? There's nobody around nowadays. Cheeky Somali monkeys wanting something for nothing. No offence, mind, but I can't do business with pirates.'

'Right.' Drake jerked a thumb over his shoulder. 'What's in the building back there?'

'Storerooms, offices. It's where I keep my accounts. And there's a garage for repairs.'

'What about upstairs?'

'Junk. Spare parts. Things that should have been thrown out ages ago. You never know in this game when something is going to come in useful.'

'Mind if we take a look?'

'Like I said,' Fenton wheezed. 'Come back with a warrant and you can do what you like.'

'Sure about that?' Drake squinted at him. 'You make me fetch a warrant and I'll bring the Inland Revenue, health and safety and anyone else I can round up. I'm sure they'd love to take the place apart.'

Fenton rocked back on his heels. 'Well, I suppose there's no harm,' he sniffed.

'That's more like it.'

He wagged a finger in Drake's face. 'But don't try planting anything incriminating. I've got my eye on you.' Then he led the way along towards the front of the building, jangling his keys. They might as well have brought along a brass band, Drake thought. If anyone was inside there they would have had time to pack and call a taxi. When Fenton opened the door, Drake pushed him to one side.

'Better stay here for the moment, sir.' He nodded to Kelly. 'Watch it. We don't know what state of mind he's in.'

'Don't worry. Not taking any chances, me.' She pulled an extendable steel baton from her waist and snapped it open. Drake had seen her use it to bring down and cuff a two-hundred-pound drunk and disorderly without breaking a sweat.

There was a musty smell of oil and damp earth in the old brickwork. No sound came from above. Either there was nobody there or they had heard Drake and Kelly coming in. If Hakim was here he was either asleep, or waiting to see what they would do. The rumble of a Tube train going by rattled the windows. As the brakes began to squeal, Drake nodded to Kelly and they started up the stairs. By the time they reached the top stair the sound of the train had faded. Silence of a sort returned. A car hooted in the distance, another replied. A motorcycle engine revved.

Then came the unmistakable squeak of a floorboard.

The hallway stretched back through the building from the staircase. It was gloomy and lit only by a faint glow that came from a window that had been papered over at the far end.

A shadow broke across the hallway.

'Police!' Drake called out. 'Akbar Hakim, if you're in here, we only want to talk.'

He motioned to Kelly. They edged down on either side of the hallway. Drake talked as they moved, keeping his voice low and steady.

'I know it wasn't your idea.' Drake tried to sound calm and reassuring. It felt like they were closing in on a dangerous creature, and cornered animals did strange things. 'Talk to me, brother.'

'I'm not your bruvva, man.' The voice rumbled out of the darkness. 'You don't know me.'

'That's why I'm here, okay? I'm here to listen, right?'

Drake motioned for Kelly to hold back. It occurred to him that Hakim might well be armed. The right procedure at this moment was to pull back and wait for support. But Drake sensed Hakim's doubt, could almost hear him breathing, could feel him shifting back there in the shadows, trying to evaluate the threat.

'You know what I think?' Drake paused, listening. 'I think you got yourself into something that was bigger than you expected.' The sound of his voice covered his footsteps. 'You panicked when you found out what you were into. Am I right?'

Silence. Drake glanced back at Kelly who was standing at the top of the stairs.

'Who asked you to store that stuff at the mosque?'

No reply.

Drake took another step forwards, hearing the creak of the floor too late.

Out of the corner of his eye he caught movement as a shadow peeled away from the wall. He turned to face it as Hakim crashed into him, knocking him aside and rushing towards the stairs. 'Hakim, hold it!' Kelly yelled.

He didn't slow or stop, but crashed straight into her. Drake saw them bump into each other, then heard Kelly cry as she spun away. Then Hakim was past her and down the stairs. Drake was already moving, fumbling for his radio as he ran. He already knew there was something wrong from the way Kelly had gone down. He knelt beside her. She was half sitting, half lying against the bannisters, one hand to her side.

'Fuck, that hurts!'

Drake put a hand to her right side and felt the wetness that he knew was blood. The knife had gone in under the tactical vest she wore. He ripped one of the velcro straps aside.

'He stabbed you.'

'How bad is it?' she groaned.

'I can't tell. It doesn't look too bad.' Drake studied the wound for signs of bubbles that would indicate a lung had been punctured. He couldn't be sure.

'Don't worry about me,' she gasped.

'Stop talking.' He pulled the straps tighter in the hope that it would at least slow the bleeding. His hands were already slippery with blood.

'Always wanted to be the mysterious scarred woman,' Kelly groaned.

'I can see how that might appeal to you.'

'Just get the bastard.'

Drake called for an ambulance as he went down the stairs two at a time. He came out of the door and barrelled into Fenton.

'What the hell's going on?'

'An ambulance is coming. Stand by the road to wave them in.'

'What?'

'Just do it!'

The sky was lightening. Ahead of him, Drake could see Hakim climbing onto a scooter and kicking it off its stand. The rear wheel slid about on the rain-slick cement as he started up. He gained speed, shooting straight out through the gate into the traffic without hesitation. It could have ended there, but by some miracle he wasn't hit. Cars hooted and tyres squealed. Hakim almost tipped over, losing control of the scooter. Drake watched him haul the bike upright and twist the throttle before shooting off again. Drake reached his car and threw himself inside. It started first time, something of a miracle in itself. He pushed the gearstick into place and floored the accelerator, skidding into the road and fishtailing as he swung left, calling out directions over the radio as he steered.

'Parsons Green Lane heading north. Suspect is on a silver Yamaha scooter.'

Drake turned the responses over in his head as he concentrated on not hitting anything. The scooter was weaving about the road ahead of him. Hakim was tall and made an awkward figure perched on the small machine, turning to look over his shoulder at Drake.

The road was narrow and Drake was forced to pull in time and again to make way for oncoming traffic. He had flashing lights on the front of the car but even then and with the siren on he knew it was reckless. A double-decker bus careered towards him and he just managed to swerve out of its way, feeling the rear wheel hit the kerb of a traffic island and hearing what sounded like a hub cap coming off. He changed gear and put his foot down again. The engine gave a high-pitched whine as he rushed straight into the junction without stopping. There were horns and shouts, the sound of brakes. He caught a glimpse of a startled man jumping out of the way as he spun the wheel. The scooter was racing away along the Fulham Road.

There was a jolt as the side of the car hit a lamp post. He bumped off the kerb.

There were calls coming in for more directions and he was yelling into the radio as he stamped on the brakes. A woman with a pushchair had stepped blithely out onto a zebra crossing. She glared at him, apparently oblivious to the fact that he had blue lights flashing on his car front and a siren going. By the time Drake got around her the scooter had vanished.

Slowing down, Drake cut the siren as he cruised along, scanning every side street. Realizing he'd gone too far he did a U-turn and started back trying to think the way Hakim would think. Get off the main road. How well did Hakim know the area?

Turning again, Drake decided to take the plunge. He sped down one street and then back up another. Racing across intersections, he cut straight through, glancing left and right before jamming the brakes and hitting reverse. Down a street to his left Hakim had tipped over and was trying to right the bike. Spinning the wheel and braking, Drake managed to both stall the car and ride up onto the corner with a crash of his tail light shattering. He twisted the ignition key. Once. Twice.

'Come on!'

It started on the third attempt. He heard the whine of the scooter as he struggled with the gearstick. He shot forward realizing, too late, that someone was coming in from the left. The collision shook him but his offside wing took the brunt of it, then he jolted away. Right, left and then right again. The scooter went straight across the North End Road without stopping. Hakim was either under the illusion that he had divine protection or was set on getting himself killed. Narrowly missing being broadsided by a black cab, Drake aimed the BMW down the street ahead of him. They raced between rows of parked cars. He was finally gaining on the scooter, when Hakim's luck ran out. A white van reversing out of a driveway slammed straight into him. Drake felt his wheels lock and heard rubber squeal as he came to a halt. Hakim had just gone flying, somersaulting over the bonnet of a parked car. Drake climbed out and rushed over. Scrambling over the wrecked scooter he saw Hakim hobbling up the road.

'Shit!'

Drake took off after him, trying to remember where this road led and what it was called. He passed a sign and called it in while gasping for air. 'Seagrave Road heading north.'

He heard a squawk from the handheld radio but was too busy running to listen. When he reached the corner Hakim was already halfway across the railway bridge on Lillie Road. Drake ran on as Hakim disappeared into the entrance of West Brompton station. Drake barged into the crowd gathered around the ticket barrier and waved his badge for them to let him through.

'Which way?'

The station master was an elderly man with an impassive face that might have been carved from ebony. Maybe he had a thing about the police. Maybe he didn't believe the badge was real. Either way, he took his sweet time before pointing a gnarled finger. Drake took the stairs three at a time to arrive on the overground platform just as a train pulled in. The doors opened releasing a swarm of passengers onto the platform. Drake pushed through, moving up and down, peering into carriages, scanning the people heading for the stairs, thinking Hakim might try to double back. He debated whether to get on the train and finally decided not to. The doors slid closed and the train moved out. Another train pulled in on the other side. Drake moved along the platform, wondering if it was possible for Hakim to have dropped down and crossed the tracks to the opposite side.

It wasn't until he reached the last carriage that his eye fell on a man inside standing with his back to him. He heard the warning buzzer as the doors closed. The man remained standing there, not moving. There was something about him and Drake knew. Then, just as the train began to pull out, the man turned and glanced over his shoulder.

Hakim.

CHAPTER 34

By the time Drake got back to Fenton's the place was overrun with emergency vehicles. Police cars, a couple of forensics vans and an ambulance. Kelly had already been taken away in another one. Wheeler was waiting for him and he wasn't happy.

'Ah, look who we have here, our very own Steve McQueen. Have you any idea how much your little escapade is going to cost us? The preliminary reports alone are enough to turn your hair white.'

'DC Marsh had just been stabbed.'

'We don't undertake the pursuit of suspects if there is a danger to the general public. You know that. I understand that you were upset, but that's precisely why you shouldn't have gone after him.'

'Any news on Kelly's condition?'

Wheeler shook his head. 'They think her lung's been punctured. The good news is that she's stable. That's all they would tell me. What the hell did you think you were playing at, Cal? Why did you go in there without support?'

'It was a long shot. I really wasn't sure it would lead to anything.'

'It was reckless. You put the life of a fellow officer in danger.'

Drake sank back against the chain fence. 'I wanted to be sure.'

'I warned you about this, Cal, going off on your own like that. This maverick act always ends badly. It's what got you demoted in the Malevich case, as if you need reminding. You can't spirit key witnesses away without going through the proper channels and procedures. You were wrong then and you're wrong now.' Wheeler leaned closer. 'People don't trust you, Cal, because you're secretive. You play your cards too close to your chest. Then when it blows up in your face you're surprised that nobody comes to your defence.'

It was a sermon Drake had heard before. He listened without saying a word.

'You're out on a limb here, Cal. Pryce wants your balls nailed to the wall, and you're handing them to him on a silver platter.' Wheeler levelled a finger. 'You're lucky that girl was not seriously wounded, let alone killed, heaven forbid.'

Wheeler was called away and Drake walked back up through the rows of parked cars to the house. He stopped at the top of the stairs beside what looked like a lot of blood. Fast Eddie, the senior Scene of Crime Officer, was up there with his assistant. A tall, willowy figure of a woman who looked like a ghost as she floated silently down the corridor in her pale blue jumpsuit.

'Heard you were with her when it happened.'

Drake nodded. 'He was going for the stairs. She got in his way.'

'Lost a lot of blood,' Fast Eddie nodded at the congealing pool.

'Yeah, I need to get to the hospital to see how she's doing.'

'Right.' Fast Eddie waved Drake to follow. 'After the Thermite at the mosque we decided not to take any chances, so we've been walking on eggshells.'

'And?'

'Nothing of any great value.' The forensics officer indicated a row of clear plastic bags lined up along the hallway. Drake sifted through, lifting each plastic bag up to examine the contents. A cheap digital watch, disposable lighter, a biro with a chewed end and a simple reporter's notebook opened to display a page of doodles, images of what looked like demons with hooked fangs and scaly heads.

'Twisted minds, eh?' Fast Eddie leaned over his shoulder.

'Yeah, right.'

He took a look inside the storage room where Hakim had been sleeping. The floor was littered with a stained mattress, pizza boxes, scattered wrappers.

'No weapons of any kind?'

'Apart from what he took with him, nothing.'

Drake lifted the notebook. 'Can I take this?'

'Sure, just make a note in the logbook.' Fast Eddie waved his assistant forward. 'Celia.'

Drake managed to get away without running into Wheeler again. He called the hospital from the car. They told him Kelly was in surgery. At Raven Hill, he found Milo in a state of shock.

'He stabbed her?'

'She's going to be fine, Milo. You can go and visit her later. Take her some flowers.'

'Maybe chocolates is better. Flowers can be interpreted as a romantic gesture.'

'A what?' Drake stared at him.

'Maybe not so good?'

'Chocolate is fine.'

'But if it's a stomach wound she can't eat anything, so chocolate's not good.'

'Milo, listen to me, chocolates will be fine. Where are you going?'

He was getting to his feet, tidying up his desk. He nodded over at the conference room where people were gathering.

'Briefing. You should be there too.'

Drake edged into the back of the crowded conference room. Pryce spotted him as he made his way to the front.

'Ah, DS Drake, glad you could join us. Bad luck with DC Marsh. How's she doing?'

'Too early to say. She's in surgery.'

'Right, well, I'm sure she's in good hands.'

When he reached the end of the room, Pryce turned to address everyone.

'Now, as you know, we were brought in to take command of the Magnolia Quays investigation. Now, despite the fact that one of our own has been hurt, I don't want this to deflect from our purpose. The suspect is Duwayne Jones, a.k.a. Akbar Hakim.' Pryce pressed the remote he was holding and an image appeared on the screen behind him. It was a mugshot from Hakim's time at Wandsworth. He was barely recognizable as the bearded man Drake had pursued that morning. Younger and leaner, the only thing that was familiar about him was the deranged look in his eye.

'Jones/Hakim is a small-time drug dealer with a history of Islamic radicalization. He's to be considered armed and dangerous. We think he's gone to ground in the Freetown estate.'

Drake cleared his throat.

'You're missing the point.'

Everyone in the room turned to look. Pryce cocked his head to one side. 'DS Drake, you have something to share with us?'

'Hakim is tied in to Magnolia Quays.'

'I'm sorry,' Pryce frowned. 'Do you have evidence to back this up? Something I haven't seen?' There was a murmur in the room. 'For those of you unfamiliar with DS Drake,' Pryce smiled as he went on, 'his methods can seem a little unconventional.'

'Hakim was working at the site,' said Drake.

'His name is not on the list of workers.'

'That's because he was using another name.'

'This is the first I've heard of any of this.' Pryce folded his arms.

'I was trying to bring Hakim in for questioning.'

'Yes, and as a result of that DC Marsh is now in hospital with a punctured lung.' Pryce exhaled heavily. 'I don't want to tell you how to do your job, DS Drake, but this is a Murder Investigation Unit. We work as a team. Do you have a problem with that?'

'No problem.' Drake raised his hands in surrender.

'Good, then that's settled.' Pryce turned to address the room. 'Okay, so, back to work. Bear in mind that Hakim has already attacked one officer. Let's make sure that doesn't happen again.'

As the team turned to file out of the room, Pryce signalled for Cal to stay behind.

'A word please, DS Drake.' Pryce waited until they were alone. 'Carry on trying to disrupt my authority and I will have you dropped from the team. I am leading this unit and your job is to assist in any way you can.'

'Got it,' said Drake, turning to leave. Pryce stepped up and put a hand out to hold the door.

'I'm not finished. What happened to DC Marsh was avoidable. If you had followed procedure and informed me what you were planning we could have gone in there with a team. We would have detained Hakim and DC Marsh would not be lying in hospital.'

'Perhaps.' Drake sighed. 'Look, Pryce, neither of us wants this but we're stuck with working together until this is over.'

'I'm ranking senior officer here, in case you hadn't noticed. You forget, Cal, I know you better than most.'

'What's that supposed to mean?'

Pryce leaned closer. 'It means that if I had my way you wouldn't be anywhere near this case. I don't trust you. You always seem to get away with it. Wheeler may fall for your charm, but I don't. One thing I can't stand is a dirty copper.'

Drake shook his head. 'There was an investigation, remember? And no charges were brought.'

'You and I both know that those investigations have one purpose and that's to give the Met a clean bill of health.' Pryce sneered. 'Public opinion, that's all those things count for.'

Drake stepped closer to him. 'If you've got something to prove your case then bring it on, but otherwise, you go back to what you are good at, fucking things up.'

'Wake up, Cal. Wheeler isn't going to be able to protect you for ever.'

Milo was waiting as Drake walked back out into the Murder Room.

'What was all that about?' he asked.

'DCI Pryce was just filling me in on my career prospects.'

'Things not looking bright, then?'

'Understatement of the year. So, where are we?'

'I don't know,' Milo said. He looked tired. 'I just don't see where to go from here.'

'If you're worried about Kelly, don't be. She's tougher than most men I know.'

'If the blade had gone in half an inch to the left it would have gone through her heart.'

'Yeah, but it didn't.' Drake patted Milo's shoulder. 'Let's find this bastard and make him pay. What's all this?' Drake leaned forward over the pile of documents on his desk.

'That's all about Thwaite's interests in Iraq. Kelly was working on that before . . .'

'Yeah, okay.'

Drake sifted through the folder slowly. A hospital building in the town of Tikrit. A ministry in Baghdad. He looked at the price tags. These were big contracts. Howard Thwaite had made a nice piece of cash out of the war.

'The other folder is on the kidnapping.'

Drake leafed through the second folder. He found Tei Hideo's CV which pointed out that in 2008 he was doing something for the UN. Looking at the impact of the war on bird populations. Well, somebody had to.

A series of newspaper cuttings from the time outlined the case further. Drake sifted through them slowly. Three UN scientific advisors taken hostage and held for ransom. Hideo, an American seismologist named Janet Avery, and an English art historian who was concerned about stolen Iraqi artefacts. He studied the photograph. A grainy blow-up from a newspaper article. Her hair was longer and darker, but it was clearly her.

'Marsha Thwaite.'

'Marsha Chaikin, as she was then,' said Milo. 'She and Thwaite had travelled out separately. He was still on his first marriage and had to keep up appearances.'

'Nice set-up.' Drake looked at the picture again. It was an amateur photograph taken in bad light that showed a young woman who had just been through a harrowing experience. Milo shrugged.

'When the government started to back out, Thwaite stepped in. He made contact with the kidnappers and got his firm to put up the ransom money. The kidnappers asked for three million dollars.'

Drake gave a low whistle. 'That's a lot of donuts. Do we know exactly what happened to the third hostage, the one that didn't make it?'

'Janet Avery. Yeah, it was nasty.'

'Break it down for me.'

'Okay, so the Hawkestone team were to go in, pay the ransom and collect the hostages.'

'It didn't go down like that.'

Milo was shaking his head. 'It all went sideways. People were killed.'

'Apart from Avery, who was killed?'

'Avery was already dead when they got there, according to reports. There were other deaths. Civilians. The rest is unclear.'

'Was there an investigation?'

'No, these guys were private contractors paid for by a private citizen. So, officially, it had nothing to do with the UK government. The rules of engagement in these situations were something of a grey area.'

Drake remembered the contacts he'd had with private contractors in Iraq. More than once as an RMP he had come up against them. They were arrogant, and often thought of themselves as being a law unto themselves. Unaccountable to anyone, certainly not to a British redcap.

'Try to get more details on the whole episode. There must have been reporters over there and someone must have filed the story.'

'Maybe a local paper, I can try Reporters without Borders.'

'Good thinking.'

'Oh, one other thing. I got something back on the security guy you asked about.' Milo scrabbled through the chaos on his desk to find a slip of paper. 'Flinders?'

'What about him?' Drake was on his feet heading for the door. He stared at the map that Kelly had pinned to the board. A knife could do a lot of damage. Vital organs. Nerves.

'No record of a Matthew Flinders with the Light Brigade in Iraq.'

Drake looked round. 'You're sure?'

'I checked twice. Came up empty.'

'Maybe he changed his name,' said Cal, 'the way people seem to do these days.'

'I'll look into it.'

'Check mother's maiden name. Things like that. Try to run down his birth certificate, Milo. He had a tattoo.'

'Is this priority?'

'Just when you have a moment. How about the camera footage, any breaks there?' Milo shook his head. 'I want everything we can get about the kidnapping. What was the name of the outfit they worked for?'

'Hawkestone.'

'Get on to them and try to find someone who was there ten years ago.'

'Okay, chief.' Milo was tapping his pen against his teeth.

'What is it?'

'I'm just thinking, maybe this could wait till I get back from the hospital?'

'Sure it can,' Drake nodded. 'Get over there now. I'll look in later.'

'You think DCI Pryce won't mind?'

'I think DCI Pryce can go fuck a duck.'

CHAPTER 35

Heather was talking about her mother who had apparently broken up with her boyfriend. She had moved in to get over the break-up and it was proving difficult.

'It's as if she's the daughter and I'm the parent. Everything is about her. I don't have a life.'

'Uh huh.'

Ray listened with half an ear. An unease had begun to make itself felt over the last couple of days and it would not go away. She couldn't really describe where this feeling came from, but it was real and she knew that until she dealt with it she would have no peace of mind. She had drafted Heather in for some overtime which, she was learning, brought its own drawbacks.

'So, what exactly are we looking for?' Heather's face was flushed. She pushed a damp strand of hair back from her brow with an irritated movement.

'Anything out of the ordinary.'

'That helps.'

'Sorry. It's difficult to explain.' Ray waved a hand vaguely at the pile of folders now spread across the floor of her office. 'I'll know when I see it.' She knew this wasn't an adequate answer, that Heather was uncomfortable with intangibles. She needed things to be spelled out.

'Just to be clear,' Heather said slowly. 'You think that this case might be connected to a former patient of yours?'

'There's something here that rings a bell, I'm just not sure which one.'

Heather counted off on her fingers. 'So, we don't have more than a rough time-frame. We don't have a name. What do we have?'

Ray sat cross-legged on the floor. She extended one leg and bent down, stretching her hamstrings, holding the bottom of her foot and pulling.

'I did work for the MoD, treating servicemen and women with stress-related disorders.'

'And you think one of them might be connected to this case?'

Ray leaned back, resting her weight on her hands.

'What we're looking for is a patient who showed symptoms of acute paranoia. A resentment towards the establishment, society, and an affinity with Islam.'

'Not asking for the moon, then?' Heather muttered.

They resumed their work, interspersed with the occasional break when they drank tea and snacked on biscuits that Heather produced from her bottomless stash. Three hours went by and they still had not turned up what they were looking for. Ray decided she really couldn't justify keeping Heather any longer and sent her home, despite her protests.

'I'm really not in that much of a hurry to get back to the old bat.'

'You've done more than enough today. Go home, get some rest and we'll take another swing at it tomorrow.'

Once she was alone, Ray felt her thoughts beginning to clear.

Perhaps it wasn't an old patient, but a relative of one of them that she was thinking of. That would mean that her initial impulse to separate male from female patients no longer applied. With a sigh, she set about bundling the files together and starting again.

Over the years she had seen hundreds of patients. Some lasted weeks or months, some just kept coming. Some she saw once and then never again. Others became regulars. In addition, she had done group-session work for a time, in hospitals and in prisons. All of that added up to a lot of possibilities.

After another hour Ray needed to get out. She left her office and went downstairs where she put on her boots and threw on her leather jacket. Outside, the air was cold enough to tell her that it was probably going to freeze tonight. The moon was full and clear, sailing through wisps of cloud backlit by the city's orange glow. She walked aimlessly, turning one way and then the other. Before long she was hit by the harsh white glare of Queensway. Music blared from kebab shops, call centres and trashy supermarkets, alongside a tide of tourist crap; the model red phone boxes, pillar boxes, policeman's helmets. A miniature parody of that distant country that once was England. Cheap suitcases stacked like dominoes, gold and silver exchanges, currency booths and newsagents where nobody spoke English. The street was an enclave of the world at large, the Middle East and beyond. The people jostling by her chattered to one another in Farsi, Arabic and Turkish, three languages she spoke confidently. She allowed herself to drift along, picking up scraps and titbits, like a crow scavenging on other people's lives.

This place felt familiar to her, not just because of the fact that she had travelled extensively, that she had visited many parts of the world that were represented here, but also because this anonymity was her home. The only place she truly belonged. It belonged to everyone and nobody at the same time. She understood that some people didn't like that. They preferred to cling to the fragments of the past, to close their eyes to what they didn't like, or didn't understand. To turn back the clocks, to whisk themselves back into another age, a safer one, one in which everyone looked like you and spoke the same language. Well, good luck with that. Like it or not, this was how things were now, and this was the way they were going to stay.

It was this uncertainty, she realized as she walked on, that made the city an unknown territory, a borderland where everyone could dream. This was the intersection where jihadis and far-right extremists mingled, each trying to tap into the chaos, to harness the energy here and turn it from light to dark.

Crane came to a sudden halt. People bumped into her, swore as they pushed past. The line of her thinking had brought her back to the sense of unease that had sent her out of the house in the first place. She wasn't sure where it came from. All her instincts were trying to tell her something. She spun on her heels and began retracing her steps back to the house. She felt a very real sense of imminent danger. She needed to find the connection as soon as possible.

CHAPTER 36

Kelly was sitting up in bed when Drake arrived, still hooked up to monitors that beeped and a drip intended to keep her sedated. Despite all of this she was flicking the wall-mounted television impatiently from channel to channel with growing irritation before throwing aside the remote.

'It's so long since I've watched any telly. I forgot how bad it is.'

'Aren't you supposed to be resting?' he asked.

'Milo came by.' She pointed to the basket of fruit on the bedside table. 'How come nobody gives you chocolate any more? Is that some sort of hint? Should I be worried about my weight?'

'I'm sure he meant well.' Cal held up the bottle of cava he had brought.

'Not sure I'm allowed to get pissed.'

'It's motivation. I thought, better than a Get Well card.'

'Right,' she nodded. 'Sweet.'

Kelly was weak and pale. Her hair stuck damply to the side of her face. She wheezed when she spoke. The punctured lung had taken its toll.

'The doctors say you were lucky.'

'That's me,' Kelly quipped brightly. 'Always the lucky one. It's true. Apparently the blade missed several major organs and nerves. Which I'm really happy about,' she concluded, lifting an arm. 'I have a little loss of feeling in my hand, but they say that should come back.' Kelly slumped back into the pillows, exhaustion mixed with disappointment on her face.

'I heard you racked up a fair old bill there in damaged vehicles and potential law suits.'

'You had to be there to appreciate it. Wheeler, needless to say, is not happy.'

'Now there's a surprise.' Kelly's eyes flickered shut for a moment. 'How about Chief Inspector Prat?'

'He's doing what he does best.'

'Ouch!' Kelly winced. 'Sounds nasty.'

'It is.' As the smiles faded, there was an awkward silence. Drake studied the floor. 'So, the thing is, I wanted to apologize for abandoning you there.'

'Aha, so that's what the bubbly is for, to buy forgiveness. Sorry, chief, but I'd have done the same thing in your place.'

'I'm glad to hear it.' Drake felt relieved to hear her say it.

'There was nothing you could have done for me. The ambulance was on the way. I just had to deal with that creepy old man stroking my hand.' She rolled her eyes. 'Which I have a feeling he really enjoyed.'

'Isn't that what it's all about, making people happy?'

'Statistically, you realize it'll be your turn next. I'll leave you with the creepy perv.'

'We'll cross that bridge when we get to it.'

'Spoken like a man, always avoiding the issue.' Kelly tried to change her position and winced as pain shot through her.

'You all right? Shall I call someone?'

'I'm fine. No sweat. Just help me back up.'

Drake leaned over and put his arm around her to help her.

'And don't go getting any ideas.'

'Wouldn't have dreamt of it,' he muttered. 'Until you mentioned it.'

She thumped his arm as he backed away to lean against the window sill.

'So where are we?' she asked.

Drake tried to summarize his thoughts.

'Pryce is pissed off that I didn't inform him about Hakim.'

'Which you didn't.'

'True.'

'But you're still convinced this is all connected to the mosque fire?'

'Is this you sounding a note of doubt?'

Kelly tried to shrug and winced instead. 'I just get the feeling you connect with this guy somehow.'

'It's hard to explain, but once upon a time I could have followed that same path.'

'But you didn't, right? Isn't that the point?'

'Probably.' This wasn't a subject Cal felt comfortable talking about. There were too many questions, and answers he suspected he didn't have. He looked around the room.

'So, how long are they going to keep you?'

'You miss me. That's sweet.'

'Actually, I'm worried about Milo. He's worried about you. Takes his mind off the job.'

'You're all heart, chief.' Kelly yawned. 'I'm kind of getting used to it, people taking care of you. No cooking or cleaning involved. Not that I spend a lot of time on those pursuits.'

'Well, don't get too comfortable. We need you back on the team.'

'Speaking of which, how's it going with Catwoman?'

Drake arched his eyebrows. 'You're talking about Doctor Crane, I assume.'

'Not sure I like the sound of this,' said Kelly frowning. 'You're bonding with her.'

'She's all right when you get to know her.'

'Steady on, I'm supposed to be the one suffering from delirium, remember?'

'I'll bear that in mind.'

'Oh, and one other thing,' Kelly said, as Drake turned to leave. 'Do me a favour and run that bastard Hakim into the ground when you find him.'

'Consider it done.'

CHAPTER 37

The storage space measured two by three metres. The glass-walled corridor offered a bird's-eye view over the Chiswick flyover and Gunnersbury Park. In contrast the room itself was as narrow as a tomb. Sheet-metal panelling and a brightly painted door to add fake cheer. Inside were all Crane's worldly possessions, stacked up in cardboard cartons. Even the padlock on the door was ordinary, chosen not to draw attention to itself. If somebody really wanted to break into this place they could do it with a tin opener.

Ray had been mobile, as she liked to think of it, since she was a teenager. She had moved around a lot, storing stuff in friends' basements, attics, barns. Over the years, she had progressed to lock-ups. Renting a garage on an estate somewhere. She had stored motorcycles and books, and in time there was a gradual accumulation of objects that she didn't want to lose, but had nowhere to keep. Time moved on, and the world, in a way, began to catch up with her. Now there were lots of people who wanted the same thing.

An anonymous place with a simple key. Your own space at an affordable price, available 24/7. In theory, of course, she no longer needed this. She had more than enough space now, especially since Julius had passed away. But old habits die hard and there was a part of her that would always feel the need for this escape hatch. A secret place she could fall back on when it all went sideways.

Now she gazed at the stacks of cardboard packing cases. They were sealed and covered in a series of markings that corresponded, in some weirdly archaeological fashion, to different periods of her life. This was how she best remembered the contents, by the time in her life when she first packed them. There were boxes that were connected to relationships, to her time at university, to different jobs, to living at home. It was, in short, a sort of blueprint of her life.

Ray was fine with that. She wasn't particularly interested in the past. The present occupied her too much for that. Every time she came here she would automatically begin rearranging the boxes, sifting them into piles, restructuring the order of her life. It was a necessary process. The idea was that it would make it easier to find things. It never worked that way. It was almost as if every time she entered this room she saw with clarity what needed to be done. What she often found strange was this encounter with her younger self. How organized that person was, or so it felt. It frightened her, in a way, how focused she had been, and that made her wonder if she had lost her edge.

Ray had brought a box cutter and a thick roll of duct tape with her. She took these out of her pockets and placed them on the floor. The labels on the boxes became more erratic and unreliable as the years went by. It was as though the focus and sense of purpose she had had in her twenties was gradually filtered out as life became something you lived through, rather than a project you were planning for. She cut open one box after another, reacquainting herself with its contents before sealing it up again and scrawling a few words on the outside with a marker pen.

She paused for a break, sitting on a couple of boxes in the corridor watching the headlights flashing by on the overpass down below. She was surprised to find herself thinking about her parents. A childhood memory of driving through the Sierra Nevada, en route to Marrakesh. Sitting in the back of the car, an old Jaguar her father had inherited from an uncle. Whatever happened to that? The novelty of it made it stand out. What she remembered most were the arguments. The embarrassment of sitting down in the front entrance of the hotel where they were staying and knowing that everyone could hear the shouting from upstairs. The looks of sympathy from the receptionist. She hated that.

Two men walked by along the corridor. Both looked West African. They were speaking what she thought might be Wolof. They wore tracksuit pants and T-shirts. One of them carried a towel slung over his shoulder. She wondered if there were people living in these storage units. It wouldn't surprise her, but then not much about this city did any more. How much could you get renting out sleeping units in here? She went back to work and soon found what she was looking for.

Ray's contact with Stewart Mason had begun back in 2008. Before he invited her to work for him at the Vesta Institute, Mason had been with British Military Intelligence – keeping track of Mason's movements was something of a challenge. He asked her to go to Iraq on a confidential mission.

'There have been incidents.'

'What kind of incidents?'

'Violence. Soldiers stepping over the line, abusing civilians.' A hotel receptionist in Falluja had been tortured and killed. 'It's the one thing we didn't factor in, cultural difference.'

Ray's first impulse had been to laugh. 'Oh, wait, you mean there are people out there who don't think the same way as us?'

'This is serious.'

'I don't disagree. What do you want me to do?'

Mason was a little pissed off at her attitude. He took his job seriously. Also, he took himself too seriously to enjoy being the object of ridicule. Understandable really, but unavoidable.

'We want to tackle the issue head on. The idea comes from inside the MoD. We want to debrief the troublemakers, talk to them, try to find out how to prepare soldiers in future.'

'Why not just teach them to show a little respect for people who don't look like them?'

'It's not as simple as that.'

'I'll bet it isn't.'

'Don't make me regret asking you in on this.'

It was a job. It paid well and she was curious herself to hear what they had to say for themselves.

Ray had vivid memories of the trip out there. A regular airline flight to Amman in Jordan and from there a military transport C130 to Baghdad. She was outfitted with flak jacket and helmet, standard-issue military clothing so that she didn't stand out. Right. It was like painting a target on your back. She spoke Arabic and her appearance meant she could pass for a local. Now she knew what it was like to look and feel like one of the enemy.

The first round of interviews took place on a military base. An office was set up for her and she was given a list of the men and women who had been involved in what were termed 'incidents'. They had been taken off active duty. They should have been shipped home, but nobody wanted to do that until they knew what they were dealing with. Her brief was to prepare profiles, to try to create a framework into which these people fitted, and to extrapolate from that where and why they had deviated. And how they could be expected to behave in the future.

It wasn't easy. Time was a factor. There were security restrictions and logistical constraints that didn't help. A number of the servicemen and women she saw were referred to further counselling for PTSD. That wasn't her problem. Her job was to understand where the impulse came to breach the rules of engagement.

Overall, and despite the limitations imposed on her, Ray found herself gravitating towards the conclusion that what these men, and the vast majority were men, actually suffered from was a crisis of faith. Understandable. They had shipped out to Iraq believing they were part of a noble project. There to bring liberation, peace and stability to the country. It came as a shock to discover that a sizeable portion of the local population viewed them less as saviours and more as foreign invaders.

She lifted her gaze to the lights coming on over West London. Remembering that time now made her think of Drake and what his experience must have been like. She wondered if it was doubts about his mission, or about his role, that had made him opt for the military police. Perhaps that was a way of compensating for feelings of guilt.

On her return home, Ray continued to see some of those servicemen as patients. They formed group sessions and she would come and listen. In time, many fell away. Now, with the connection made to Iraq, she felt she needed to go back to that time, to revisit those cases. If only to try to understand if there was something she had missed.

Ray loaded the boxes onto a trolley, locked up the unit again and dragged the trolley to the lift. When she got downstairs she loaded them into the car. Julius's old Audi still had its uses. As she drove back across town she tuned the radio into a phone-in where, once again, they were discussing the murders. Magnolia Quays had become a talking point. It was on everybody's mind. One caller was ranting about a cover-up, another waffled on about stoning people in Saudi Arabia and why one prince or another was always over there smiling and shaking hands with them, and now they wanted to do it here. It was the usual blend of fear and ignorance wrapped in a layer of outrage. Ray reached over and snapped the radio off. She'd heard enough.

CHAPTER 38

Wheeler's call came in as Drake sat down with Lenny Bryson. An investigative journalist. Old school. He'd made his name running in-depth stories on defence issues; Trident missiles, fishy arms deals and politicians who thought they were above the law. He had contacts in some very dark nooks and crannies in Whitehall. Staring at his phone, Drake debated whether to answer and decided there was no point in further aggravating Wheeler.

'I'd better take this,' he said, getting to his feet. 'Sir?'

'Do you mind telling me why you insist on making my life difficult? I've just had a call from the commissioner who in turn was chewed out by Howard Thwaite.'

'Is that a problem, sir?'

A long whistle sounded down the line that Drake realized was an exasperated sigh. 'The problem, Cal, is that Thwaite is not happy with the manner in which he is being treated. He is convinced that he is being victimized by an officer of the law who has some kind of personal grudge against him.'

'I have no idea where he might have got that idea from.'

'I told you to go easy on him. What exactly did you say to him?'

'We were there on Mr Thwaite's invitation. We were enquiring about the details of his wife's abduction in Iraq.'

'Then why is he saying that you are sticking your nose into his business affairs?'

'Interesting,' said Drake. 'I asked about his backers.'

'What does that have to do with his wife being murdered?'

'I'm not sure. The point is that we're looking for motive. We can't rule out the fact that this bizarre, theatrical set-up was some kind of distraction. Thwaite's company is a fairly hefty enterprise but on rocky ground financially speaking.' Cal glanced over at Lenny, who was making his way back from the bar.

'Where are you exactly? Sounds like a pub.'

'Victoria. It's busy.'

'Well, we shouldn't be discussing these things in public. Come into my office tomorrow.'

'Right, sir.'

There was a long pause. 'I don't have to tell you that you are not in a good position right now, Cal. You don't have a lot of rope to play with. Am I clear?'

'Perfectly, sir.'

'I don't want to hear anything more about this and next time you see Mr Thwaite you might consider an apology.'

'I'll work on it, sir.'

'You do that. And the same applies to DCI Pryce.'

'An apology?'

'Whatever your opinion of the man, there are protocols. You might have been equals in the past, but that's no longer the case. You have to show him the respect his rank deserves. It's bad for morale.'

'I . . .'

'No, Cal, not another word.'

Wheeler rang off and Drake returned to his seat as Lenny sat down. A large man with a perfectly round and mostly bald head, Bryson looked the part of the overworked, dishevelled reporter. His shirt was crumpled and had sweat marks under the armpits. Cal had explained the situation to Lenny over the telephone earlier.

Now Lenny took a long draught from his beer and licked his lips. 'So you're thinking what, some kind of revenge on Thwaite?'

'Could be,' conceded Drake. 'Could be something else entirely.'

'Meaning?'

'Meaning we don't know, and neither do you, by the way, until I give the word.'

'No worries there.' Cal had known Lenny for years and knew he could be trusted. 'But what possible motive could there be to kill them now?'

'No idea.'

Bryson shrugged. 'He could have read about it in the paper.'

'True. But why now?'

'There are two possibilities. Thwaite is pretty high profile, so it's possible someone simply saw his name somewhere and made the connection. Or else, this was planned as a way of taking Thwaite down.'

'Right,' nodded Bryson. 'A business rival.'

'He's the head of a pretty big enterprise. I tried looking into his backers, but it's not easy.'

'Nothing is nowadays,' said Lenny. 'Shell companies, fronts. Deregulation is another word for obfuscation.'

'The operation to free the hostages went wrong.'

'Yeah, that's what you said.' Lenny scratched his bald pate. 'I thought it rang a bell. I did some digging.'

The pub behind Horseferry Road was one of Bryson's usual haunts. He was cautious about where he went, and more than a little paranoid about being overheard. Understandable, perhaps, considering the amount of time he spent in the company of spooks and hacks. He had taken up residence in a corner, far from the doors and the bar. Two phones sat on the table in front of him alongside a crumpled copy of the day's *Racing Post*, now forgotten.

'Okay, so, Iraq 2008. By then the politics had gone out of the fight. The Iraqis were dealing with the economic fallout that came in the wake of Saddam's downfall. The middle class was badly hit. People who had been living well suddenly found it difficult to feed their families. There was a lot of resentment.' Lenny spoke from memory. 'Paul Bremmer, remember him? He was head of the Coalition Provisional Authority. Guess what he's doing today?'

Drake reached for his glass. When Lenny got going you just had to step aside and let him get on with it. He loved the details.

'He's a ski instructor. Probably where he should have stayed. Anyway, it was his bright idea to fire everyone in the army who was a member of the Baath party. Which immediately alienated most of the officer class in the Iraqi armed forces. Created a lot of bad feeling. Later on, it created ISIS. But hey, what are you going to do when your salary has just been taken from you by some jumped-up ski instructor?'

Drake took a long sip of beer. 'Tell me about the kidnapping.'

'It wouldn't have got that much attention, but the fact that renowned property developer Howard Thwaite was involved brought out all the gossip merchants. Still, even though he had a lot of pull in Whitehall, the fact that he was screwing one of the hostages wasn't enough to bend the rules. No negotiating with terrorists, no matter who your mistress is.' Bryson checked his phones and sat back.

'Thwaite went private, paid for the rescue operation himself. I tried to get in touch with the team that went in, but no luck. The company changed their name from Hawkestone to DRS.'

'Which means what exactly?'

'Deorum Risk Strategies.' Lenny sniffed. 'Where do they get these names? Deorum sounds like something you stick under your armpits. They always assume we're all morons and didn't do Latin at school.'

'Speak for yourself.'

Lenny set down his beer with a sigh. 'Deorum. It means the gods or divinities. Make something sound classical and that automatically makes you classy.' Lenny tapped his fingers on the table. His glass was empty.

'Tell me something I don't know.'

Drake got to his feet and went to fetch another round. The place had been quiet when he had arrived, but it was beginning to fill up as people congregated at the end of the day. He fought his way to the bar and then back out again. When he returned, Lenny snatched up his glass, thirsty and eager to talk.

'There was a case, brought by a human-rights group. It was later dropped. Somebody got hurt on that raid. Hawkestone, as they were then, went further than they should have done.'

'There was a third hostage,' said Drake. 'Janet Avery. Apparently she didn't make it.'

'Yes, well, that's where it starts to get funny.'

'Funny, as in you can't find any details?'

'I'm working on finding someone who was there at the time, but I have to say, so far it's slim pickings.' Lenny set down his glass. 'While we're at it, let me ask you a question for a change.'

'Fire away.'

'Your Greek friend, Donny Apostolis.'

'I'd hardly call us friends.'

'Like it or not, Cal, it's what happens. It's common knowledge that he holds a hand over you. You're protected. Word is that you did him a favour by handing him Goran Malevich on a plate.'

'So far I haven't heard a question.'

'Well, it's the one everyone's been asking since Malevich was liquidated. Did you do it?'

'There was an enquiry.'

'Sure, the DPS report concluded that you'd been irresponsible, going off script, running a witness on your own, not following procedure.' Lenny paused to take a drink. 'They concluded that you were promoted too fast, which was a nice way of saying that the Met had overdone it on the positive-discrimination score.'

'Well, it all worked out very nicely for them,' said Drake.

'Sure,' Lenny smiled. 'You get downgraded and that's the end of it. Everyone's happy and the scandal goes away. Only thing is, nobody ever really got to the bottom of what happened to Goran Malevich.'

'Why the sudden interest?'

'Nothing sudden about it. I've been asking you the same question for three years.'

'And you're still not happy.'

'I live in hope,' nodded Lenny. 'Maybe one day I'll get to the bottom of it.'

Drake peered into his glass. 'Sometimes I think I'll never get out from under this thing.'

'You were the golden boy, for a time. You got a second chance.'

'So what do I do with it?'

'Well, it's obvious, innit?' Lenny stared at Drake. 'You have to take Donny down. Fancy another one?'

CHAPTER 39

Stewart Mason wasn't happy. It might have been the weather, the rain coming down in waves, hitting the surface of the Thames, stirring up a dark frenzy. They stood sheltering under a tree on the Southbank. Mason wasn't even sharing his umbrella, which Ray didn't mind. She would have taken icy rain over close proximity any day of the week.

'You're telling me what, exactly?'

'Hey, don't shoot me, I'm just the messenger, remember?' She held up her hands. 'All I'm saying is that the investigation has taken a turn.'

'A turn? It's a little more than that, wouldn't you say? You said they're looking into your work in Iraq.'

'That's not what I'm saying. Not yet at least.' She paused to look out at the river again. A barge floated by, sitting low in the water, like an old memory. 'I'm saying it's just a matter of time.'

Mason swore loudly, causing a woman who was walking her dog to jump. She sidestepped and moved swiftly away.

'I just don't see where all this came from.'

'Marsha Thwaite was kidnapped ten years ago, held for ransom. She wasn't his wife then, but Thwaite paid a private firm to secure the release of all the hostages. An outfit called Hawkestone.'

Mason stamped his feet, whether out of irritation or cold it wasn't clear.

'Why didn't we know this?'

'Well, I'm guessing somebody did know. Either they didn't connect the dots, or they decided not to inform you.'

'That somebody's head is going to roll.'

'Do what you have to do, but that's not going to change this situation.'

Something about the tone of her voice caused Mason to turn on her. 'I don't see why you're so fucking cheerful about this.'

She angled her head. 'What makes you think I'm cheerful?'

'If this comes back on us you'll be caught in the blast too.'

'That's why we're having this conversation, remember? That was my research. I knew there were anomalies, borderline cases where it was impossible to predict how they would develop.'

Mason reached into the pocket of his cashmere coat for an electronic cigarette and vaped away nervously for a few seconds.

'Your work out there is classified. You debriefed those men because they showed signs of severe psychological trauma as a result of their experiences. Nobody has access to those files.'

'I'm not asking that.'

'What are you asking, then?'

'I want to know if there's anything you're not telling me; is it possible for one of those men to have gone off the rails?'

Mason stared at her, but said nothing.

'Come on, Stewart! There has to be a link. Two victims were held hostage in Iraq. You think that's just coincidence?'

'It might be a million things.' Mason was scrabbling in the dark.

'Where are we with your detective?'

Crane pushed a hand through her hair, discovering that it was soaked all the way through. She hadn't even noticed.

'Drake is no longer in charge. DCI Pryce has taken over.'

'And where does that leave you?'

'I thought I was getting somewhere with Drake. Pryce is a company boy.'

Mason snorted. 'What does that mean?'

'It means he comes up with the kind of answers they want to hear.'

'You're not turning into some kind of anarchist rebel, I hope, because you can't really afford to be alienating people at this stage in your career.'

Crane could feel her hackles rising. 'I don't work for you any more, Stewart. Either you start treating me like an equal or we're done.'

'We're never going to be equals, but I take your point.' Mason stamped his feet again. 'You trust this man, Drake? I thought you said he had a chequered past?'

'He's trying to get out from under this thing with Goran Malevich. He needs a win.'

'Sounds like you both need a win. Motivation is one thing. It doesn't make him innocent.'

Crane turned to look out over the river. As far as she was concerned the jury was still out on Drake, but listening now she could see what he was up against. Drake had betrayed the trust placed in him. To people like Mason, the fact that he was black only made this worse.

'Drake thinks this is personal. It's about revenge.'

'The tabloids would disagree with you. I thought you were in favour of this sharia narrative?'

'I was. There's just something that doesn't quite add up.'

'That's why you wanted to see me?'

Crane looked at him. 'What if there's a connection between this and the work I did?'

'Look, you've got nothing to worry about. You did nothing wrong. You provided psychological support for a group of soldiers. That's the end of it.'

She tried to read his face. 'Is it, really?'

'You have nothing to worry about,' Mason repeated, attempting a smile.

The question of how far she could trust Mason was a factor in all of Ray's dealings with the man. The word loyalty wasn't in his vocabulary. Part of the reason she had asked for this meeting was to sound him out, to find out where she stood. So far, all she heard confirmed her feeling that Mason would throw her under the bus in a heartbeat if he thought it was in the best interests of the country, or more importantly, himself.

'Did you keep track of them?'

Mason lifted the shoulders of his expensive coat. 'I'm telling you, it's fine.'

She pushed her hands into the pockets of her leather jacket. 'I went through my case files.'

'Did you now?' She could hear the bristle in his voice. He was growing impatient.

'I came up with a list of men who might fit the bill. All of them were interviewed. Seven of them I managed to locate. All are settled with families. Two died; one of them by his own hand. One of them is in prison. That leaves five unaccounted for.'

'I'm impressed.' Mason let out a low whistle. 'You have been thorough.'

'Of the three, one stands out, a soldier who was drummed out of the Light Brigade for getting carried away. He was vicious, had a violent streak.'

'He was a soldier. They are trained to be violent.'

'They're also trained to be stable professionals. This one wasn't. He liked to hurt people.'

'So why do you need me?'

'Because I'm trying to find out what happened to him.'

'What makes you think I can help?'

'Come on, Stewart. You're the inside man. You can pull some strings, make some calls.'

'What do you want to know?'

'I want to know what happened to Brian Hicks. He was drummed out of the military on the basis of my assessment. I want to know where he went.'

'You're worried that he's coming after you?' Mason's brow furrowed. 'Come on, none of this has been aimed at you.'

'Maybe he's just getting warmed up.'

'Believe me, if he comes after you, he'll be making a mistake.'

'That's easy for you to say.'

'You're taking all of this far too seriously.' Mason smiled. 'Let me buy you a drink.'

'Some other time, maybe. When all of this blows over.'

'Suit yourself,' said Mason grumpily.

'So, you'll make some calls?'

'Ahh.' It wasn't clear from Mason's response whether this was a yes or a no. As she watched him walk away, Ray wondered if she was wasting her time.

CHAPTER 40

At the Ithaka Café Eleni had made pastitsio. As he sat down, Drake realized he hadn't eaten all day. He closed his eyes and rested his head against the wall behind him.

'No ouzo?' Kostas asked from behind the counter. 'The way you look, I think you need it.'

'You may have a point.'

'No maybe.' Kostas wagged a finger. 'Ouzo is for the health. The secret to life is to drink a little, not too much. My grandmother lived to be a hundred and ten. Every day she took an ouzo.'

It sounded like a useful alibi, but Drake's mind was elsewhere as he watched Kostas setting two glasses on the counter and reaching for the bottle.

'So, are you winning or losing?'

'Come again?'

'The fight against evil.' Kostas raised his glass. 'Did the bad guys win or did you?'

'Right now, I think you can say the bad guys are ahead.' Drake picked at the bowl of olives Kostas had set on the table.

'There are days when the devil has to win, otherwise he gets too mad.'

'Right.'

Maybe that's what it was, placating the devil. He didn't want to think about how close Hakim had come to killing Kelly. It wasn't a good feeling. She would be out of action for a couple of months at least.

Kostas left him to it and Drake sipped his drink and stared at the screen behind the bar. The sound was turned down. A reporter was standing in front of the entrance to West Brompton station. Drake watched as the camera panned round to show the tracks heading north, where Hakim had vanished. They cut back to the press conference where Pryce was sitting on stage with his uniform buttoned up. Behind him was the mugshot of Hakim. He looked crazy enough, but nothing like the way he looked now.

'You shouldn't be watching this, you know?' Eleni said as she put down his food. 'It's not good for the soul.'

'That's what this is for, right?' Drake lifted his glass.

'That's only what that old fool says,' she nodded towards Kostas who was fiddling around behind the counter. She took away Drake's ouzo and replaced it with a glass of wine. 'Goes better with the food,' she assured him.

On the screen the woman with the dyed rhubarb hair was addressing a crowd. The tape underneath identified her as Jayden Delaine, leader of the Hope and Glory party. A group of unhappy, greying men stood behind her waving the St George's flag. Among them, Drake spotted the now familiar face of Stephen Moss, the neo-Nazi he had seen at the Alamo.

For a change, the Ithaka was not empty this evening. Drake sat back against the rear wall at his usual table. There was a family in the centre of the room. They looked like tourists who had lost their way. Adventurous Scandinavians by the look of them. Long-haired kids looking around the place nervously and parents whispering to them to finish their food. The Airbnb Experience. Spend a few days in the urban jungle. Catch a glimpse of the unknown before racing home and bolting the doors.

Drake was thinking back to his conversation with Waleed. Not the most reliable source perhaps, but he had sounded sincere. There was someone else. The murshid. Someone who was guiding the operation. Up until now, Drake had assumed that Hakim would lead him to this ideas man. The guide. Now that Hakim had slipped out of their grasp, they needed another strategy.

The only other customers in the place were a couple. Kostas had put them over in the corner, by the window, away from Drake and the family. He'd turned the lights down low on that side and even managed to find a candle. Old romantic that he was. The woman looked over at him and Drake realized he had been staring. She was pretty, with long dark hair that hung over her shoulders. It gleamed in the candlelight. Drake picked up his phone for something to do and flicked through the messages. One from Wheeler claimed that Pryce had spoken to him about excluding Drake from the investigation. There was to be a meeting early the following morning. Not exactly good news, but not unexpected either.

'No dessert?' Eleni asked as she cleared the plates away.

'No, thank you, that was delicious.'

Kostas appeared with a bottle of Metaxa. 'One for the road?'

'Some other time. I need to sleep.'

Drake managed to make it through the door without looking at the woman in the corner, but as he climbed the stairs the loneliness hit him and he found himself leaning his head against the door of the flat below his. He was still trying to decide whether to knock when the door opened by itself.

'I wondered where that heavy breathing was coming from.'

Maritza was wearing her baggy overalls, covered in paint stains. In her left hand she held a glass of red wine.

'Want some?'

He didn't really, but he said yes anyway as he followed her through to the living room. The walls were covered in paintings, most of them in the middle of some process of change that he had difficulty following. The room was cluttered with painting materials, glass jars filled with brushes, rolls of canvas, empty frames stacked against one wall, covered ones against another.

'You were working?'

'Just fiddling around, adding a few touches.' She smiled back at him. 'I'm celebrating.' She waved the bottle and refilled their glasses even though Drake had hardly touched his. 'I sold one today.'

When she smiled her whole face lit up. Wrinkles appeared in the corners of her eyes which made him think that once upon a time, long ago, she must have smiled a lot more.

'Congratulations.'

'On days like this, I think perhaps it's possible to survive.'

'There will be more days like this,' he said.

'Yes.' Their eyes met over the rims of their glasses. 'I hope so.'

She took his hand and led the way down the hallway to the bedroom. They passed a door with a stuffed gorilla stuck to it.

'Where's Joe?'

She turned to smile back at him. 'He's with his father tonight.'

He wondered if that was a coincidence. On the wall of the bedroom there was a picture of Frida Kahlo in an antique wooden frame. Maritza had told him once that it was a picture she'd had since she was sixteen and living in Mexico with a painter twice her age. It showed water stains, what might have been blood or wine, and pressed between the glass were dried flowers, which might once have been bright colours, jacaranda, hibsicus, all faded to the same brown. She had explained this picture to him the first time they had spent the night together in here.

He turned to see her set down her glass on the bedside table. There were candles on the dresser. She smiled as she put both hands to the opening of her jumpsuit and pulled gently. He heard the snap fasteners pop one by one as they came apart. She slipped her shoulders free and let her jumpsuit drop to the ground. She was naked underneath.

Making love with Maritza was always an almost spiritual experience. She gave herself to the moment completely. Drake found himself drawn in, feeling her move in his arms as she brought herself and then him to climax. Afterwards, he lay there gasping for breath. She rolled over on her side.

'I'm not sure how much longer I can keep doing this,' she said quietly.

He lifted a hand to stroke her back. 'How do you mean?'

'I mean you, me. I don't know what all of this means to you.'

'Does it have to mean something?'

She turned to look at him. 'Is this all you want, a warm body at night?'

Drake rolled onto his back and stared at the ceiling.

'I understand, it's difficult for you. Your childhood. It can't have been easy. But this could be a new beginning, for both of us.'

Her words echoed in his head long after she had fallen asleep. In the early hours, he slipped out of bed and took his clothes out into the hall where he dressed quietly. Then he let himself out.

It was cold and dark on the stairs. The light had gone out and he had to feel his way up. Inside his flat there was enough glow from outside for him to move around without switching on any lights. Drake lay down on the sofa fully clothed and slept for all of three hours. He woke in the middle of the night needing to take a leak.

His mouth was dry and he was sweating all over. He stripped off his clothes on the way to the bathroom. Then he stood in the darkened kitchen in his boxer shorts and drank a glass of water. Through the window the lights on the skyline resembled gas flares on the surface of an alien planet.

What did he want? What did anybody want? A place to hide? A million dollars? A penthouse apartment? He used to care about this city. Perhaps he no longer understood it. Who lived here, what did they do? What did they dream? Everyone wanted a pathway up to the stars, a tower like in the fairy tales, where nobody and nothing could touch you. Where you could look down at the little people moving around far below, as insignificant as ants. Somewhere away from it all. He lay back down and closed his eyes. Somewhere in the building there was music playing. The steady throb of a bass line that vibrated faintly through the walls. A moment later, or so it felt, the phone rang. It was Milo.

'They've found Hakim,' he said.

CHAPTER 41

It was raining when Drake arrived at St Mary's Cemetery. A thick layer of icy mist hung in the air, taking away his breath. A young uniformed officer stood off to one side, bent over at the waist, retching. Milo stood next to him holding a handkerchief.

Akbar Hakim was lying up against a stark tree, bare of leaves, that leaned over to one side, bent like a lightning bolt arcing towards the ground. The body was strapped to the tree trunk with baling wire that had dug into the flesh drawing lines of blood across the bare torso. A loop of the same material around the neck held the head back and offered a possible cause of death.

Drake's eye followed the length of the arms to where they came to rest in Hakim's lap. He swore under his breath. Both hands had been cut off at the wrist.

'Ever see anything like that?' Milo asked.

'Can't say I have.' Drake glanced over at the uniform. 'How's he doing?'

Milo looked back. 'He'll survive.' He nodded at Hakim. 'What does this mean?'

'The hands?' Drake shook his head. 'Generally it's for stealing.'

'That'll put a stop to it.'

Drake wondered where this deadpan version of Milo had come from. Maybe it had always been there, but was usually overshadowed by Kelly. Maybe he just missed her.

'You need to get out of the office more often.'

'Sorry?' Milo frowned.

'Forget it.'

Drake bent down towards the body again as something caught his eye.

'What is that?'

Before anyone could answer a fat raven dropped from the sky and settled on the man's shoulder, causing everyone to leap back. All except Drake. Fixing a beady black eye on him, the bird jerked forward and dug its beak hard into the man's cheek. Celia, Fast Eddie's second, let out a cry, as if it had pecked her, and immediately stepped forwards, shooing it away.

'Go! Go on, get lost!'

The large bird flapped its wings but did not budge. An urban bird, indifferent to humans. Another landed next to it, perching itself on Hakim's head. This one went for an eye. The woman screamed again, prompting a couple of uniforms to leap forwards, instinct overcoming protocol, ignoring the fact they were trampling over evidence to shoo the birds away.

'Great!' muttered Drake, stepping out of the way. 'Could we all please back up a little?'

He waited for them to clear before squatting down again in front of the body. He leaned forward to get a better look. As he did so, something wriggled out of Hakim's nostril and fell into his lap.

'What the hell?' As he rose back up in a hurry, Drake bumped into Archie as the coroner came up behind him.

'Ah, interesting.'

'He's got worms coming out of him.'

'Fascinating.' Archie had the happy smile of a man who loved his work.

'Did nobody hear anything?'

The uniform standing nearby shook his head, amused by this lack of common sense.

'Even if somebody had heard screaming they wouldn't come out to take a look.'

'So, who found him?'

'Local man, on his way to work. A Mr E . . .' The uniform squinted at a notebook he held in the palm of his hand. 'E K . . . Wednesday?'

'Tell me he at least speaks English?'

'Better than I do.'

Drake shot him a wary look and the officer shrugged defensively.

Mr Ekwensi was a concert pianist, on his way to the Albert Hall for a rehearsal. Under his coat he wore a tweed suit and a burgundy bow tie..

'We're doing Rachmaninov, with Dudamel?'

'Right, and what is that again?' Drake didn't have a clue what he meant.

Ekwensi was in his forties. Shaved head and eyes as sharp as cue balls behind horn-rimmed spectacles. His flat expression showing how little he expected from a police officer.

'Dudamel is a conductor,' he breathed slowly. 'From Venezuela.'

'I'll take your word for it. Tell me again what you saw.'

'I already told the other policeman.'

'I'm sure you did, sir, but I need you to tell me again, if you don't mind.'

'Look, I'm late as it is . . .'

'I appreciate that, and I suppose our friend over there can wait.'

The man sighed. 'Point taken, officer.'

'Just tell me what you saw.'

'I understand.' Mr Ekwensi let the air out of his lungs slowly. 'Corroboration.'

'I couldn't have put it better myself. Now, what exactly did you see?'

'Nothing. It was raining heavily. I thought it might turn to snow, which would be nice.'

'Just the pertinent details, if you don't mind.'

'Sorry, yes, of course. I know this area well, this spot. I could recognize it with my eyes closed. That's how I knew.'

'Knew what?'

'When I saw the tree. I knew something was wrong. Just from the shape of it.'

'You didn't see anyone? You didn't hear anything?'

'No sir, I saw a shape that didn't belong. Even in the fog, I knew. I realized it was a body. I was shocked. I've never seen anything like it. I mean, why? Why would anyone do something so . . . cruel?'

'Why indeed?'

The two men gazed at the macabre picture for a moment. Drake didn't feel much sympathy for Hakim, but this was a nasty way for anyone to go.

'Thank you, Mr Ekwensi, that will be all. Give the officer your details, in case we need to contact you again.'

'Of course.' The pianist's Adam's apple bobbed. 'Can I just ask, is this gang related?'

'It's too early to say. Thanks for your cooperation.'

'Not a problem. I hope you catch whoever did this.'

'So do I,' said Drake. The quizzical look he got back told him that this was probably not the most diplomatic thing to say under the circumstances.

Forensics were setting up a shield around the body. The publicity had panicked someone. And they had decided Hakim was a liability, better out of the way. Here was evidence of the man who had planned Magnolia Quays. He had chosen to rid himself of a problem, and then decided to capitalize on it and turn it into another spectacle. A public place, a macabre end. Drake found himself wishing Crane was here. He would have liked to have heard her thoughts.

As he was reaching for his phone he spotted Fast Eddie waving him over.

'There he is, the elusive caped crusader. Where've you been?'

'You missed me.'

'Steady on. I wouldn't go that far. I did have something for you, though.' Fast Eddie was struggling into his Teletubby outfit. 'Thermite.'

'What about it?'

'We think we may have traced where it came from.'

'Is that possible?'

'Actually, it wasn't all that difficult. Thermite consists of a combination of ferric and aluminium oxides. The percentage varies, both from manufacturers and when it was made. There have been changes over time, you see.'

'Cut to the chase, Eddie.'

'Right, well, we know where it was made and when. A military ordnance manufacturer in Wales. We contacted them, asked them to check their supply lists. Turns out that particular combination is no longer used. The last batch was sent out to Afghanistan three years ago.'

'So where did this come from?'

'Well, that's the thing.' Fast Eddie glanced over his shoulder. 'I started poking around. Thermite is not something you come across every day. I had to go back eight years to find a record of it coming up. That was in a raid on a Kosovo Albanian gang in Brentwood.

God knows how they got hold of it, or what they wanted to do with it.' Eddie paused. 'The point being that it was recorded as being destroyed.'

'Wait a second. You're telling me that this stuff was on our records as being destroyed?'

'Weird, right?' Eddie held up his face mask. 'All of this is above and beyond the call of duty. I hope you appreciate that.'

'Thanks, Eddie.'

'Just don't mention it.' Eddie pulled up his mask and walked over to the body.

Drake waved Milo over.

'Seen Doctor Crane?'

'I thought she was off the case, boss? Actually, I thought you were off the case. I wasn't even sure it was right to call you.' Milo fidgeted, as he always did when he was away from his desk. The real world made him uncomfortable in a way that cyberspace never did.

'You did the right thing,' Drake sniffed. 'How's it going with Pryce?'

'I'm persona non grata.' Milo studied the mud under his shoes. 'I don't mean officially, of course, they just ignore me. He doesn't seem to trust me for some reason, so I'm out in the cold. Do you want me to call Doctor Crane?'

'No, don't worry, I'll do it. Did you manage to get anywhere with the text messages?'

Milo shook his head. 'I had to drop everything to get here.'

'Where is Pryce, by the way? Why isn't he here?'

'Some high-level anti-terror meeting, as I understand it.' Milo was not happy. 'It's unfair. I mean, we do all the hard work, Kelly gets stabbed in the line of duty and now Pryce and his team sweep in to take over? It's not right.'

'Did nobody ever tell you that life is never fair?'

Milo nodded over Drake's shoulder. 'I think he's arrived.'

Drake spotted a pair of SUVs rolling up. 'Okay, so, I'm guessing that he's going to want me off the crime scene double quick, which means he's going to give me some bullshit task to take me elsewhere.'

'Sounds about right,' nodded Milo glumly. 'Oh, by the way, that name you gave me, the security guy?'

'Flinders?'

'Do you have any idea how many middle names people in this country have? What is that all about?'

'Insecurity. People want to cover all the bases, that and a fanatical devotion to football.'

'Okay, M. Flinders. No first name, thank you very much.' Milo was flipping through his notebook. Out of the corner of his eye, Drake saw that Pryce had noticed him. He was already leaning over to the WPC next to him, who then looked directly at Drake.

'Better get a move on, Milo.'

'Tattoo of a panther on back of right hand corresponds to insignia of the Light Brigade. Nobody by the name of Flinders was registered as serving with them in Iraq. To check middle names I had to request birth certificates.' Milo glanced up to see if Drake understood what a mammoth task this was.

'Superlative work so far, but you really need to speed it up.'

Out of the corner of his eye Drake could see the WPC marching with determined strides towards them.

'I remembered Kelly joking that people get tattoos all the time.' Milo smiled. 'So, I was thinking this could be pointless.'

'But it wasn't?'

'DS Drake?'

Drake ignored her. 'What was the name, Milo?'

'I found one birth certificate where the name Flinders appeared as maternal surname. A Brian Patrick Hicks.'

'Well done, Milo.'

'Detective Seargant Drake, I have to ask you to leave the crime scene immediately.'

Close up, the WPC was younger than she had appeared. He recognized the look of determination on her face. The conviction of the inexperienced. Milo glanced at her before finishing what he had to say.

'There's only one problem.'

'He's dead,' said Drake.

Milo's face fell. 'You knew? How could you know that?' It was hard to tell if Milo was impressed, or annoyed. The WPC stepped closer.

'I have to insist. DCI Pryce wants me to let you know that this is an MIU crime scene and you have no right to be here.'

Drake held his hands up in surrender. 'It's fine, I'm leaving. Look, here I go.' He turned to Milo as he left. 'I take it you checked all records for Hicks.'

Milo confirmed. 'I checked everything, including international databases. He was reported dead in Syria five years ago. Nothing anywhere since then.'

'Well done, Milo. Leave this one with me, okay?'

'If you say so, boss.'

Back in the car, Drake sat and watched Pryce. He seemed to be in a hurry. He was talking on the phone and issuing orders as he walked about. Busy man. Cal felt annoyed with himself for having lost charge of the case. It was a reminder that the problems between him and Pryce were not about to be resolved any time soon.

Instead he tried to turn his mind to the scene before him. This was the closest he felt they had come to the guide Waleed had mentioned. He had to be the person behind this. There was a hint of panic about this murder. The speed for one thing. No time for planning. So he had improvised. Cutting Hakim's hands off at the wrist was meant to tie it in to the sharia theme established at Magnolia Quays. This should have been proof that Hakim was connected to the previous murders. Somehow he suspected that wouldn't be enough to convince Pryce to give Cal another chance. Probably the opposite. Now he would want to solve the whole thing himself.

Drake reached for his phone. Through the windscreen, he watched Archie, standing off to one side, begin to go through his pockets.

'Can you speak?'

'Ah, our elusive scapegoat.' Archie rocked back on his heels.

'I'm guessing Pryce asked you not to speak to me.'

'That would be correct.'

'I need to know about the insects.'

'Yes, curious feature that.'

'Hakim went missing yesterday. Am I right in thinking that that leaves barely enough gestation time for those worms?'

'Ah, so not everything I've said over the years has fallen on deaf ears.'

Despite the loss of Hakim, Drake felt elated. He was sure that this was the break they had needed. The killer was beginning to reveal himself. Through the window Drake could see Pryce walking towards the coroner.

'You have company. Perhaps I could drop by later?'

'Late being the operative word,' Archie said before snapping off his phone and turning to address Pryce.

CHAPTER 42

When she got the call she had been waiting for, Crane had no idea what to expect. The caller tersely relayed a time and place before hanging up. The degree of cloak and dagger tactics struck her as being mildly ridiculous. On the other hand, what choice did she have? She wanted answers and for that she was willing to play along. Still, she would happily have owned up to feeling a little jumpy when she arrived at the deserted car park in Greenwich. It was empty but for a dark saloon that she was sure she had seen earlier in the day. Nerves, or had the driver been tailing her for a time before agreeing where to meet? You never knew with these military types. And this was one of Mason's contacts, which meant you could expect anything.

The figure who stepped out of the Audi had all the hallmarks of a military man. Tall, straight backed, head shaven so that his scalp glinted in the low sunlight. He wore a pea coat that he buttoned as he came towards her.

'Doctor Crane? Doctor Rayhana Crane?'

'Who wants to know?'

The smile suggested he was bemused by the fact that she answered his question with one of her own. He gave a roll of his shoulders, as if the coat wasn't sitting right and nodded to his left.

'Let's walk, shall we?'

He led off, walking up the incline without hesitation. Crane followed. He moved at a good pace and didn't speak or even look up until they had reached the top of the hill. There he paused to draw breath as he surveyed the view of the city, emitting a little grunt of satisfaction.

'Always loved the view from up here. Been coming here since I was a boy.'

The view from Greenwich Hill was, she had to concede, remarkable, but she wasn't in the mood for sightseeing or small talk.

'I don't want to appear rude, but I didn't come here for the view.'

'Of course not.' There was no trace of warmth in his smile. 'Stewart said you weren't one to beat about the bush.' He glanced back the way they had come, as if the mention of the man made him suddenly question his surroundings. 'The list you sent me was an interesting one.'

'I'm glad you feel that way.'

'I am not really sure how this connects to the investigation.'

'That's not clear yet, but it's possible there is a link between the murders and a kidnapping that happened ten years ago.'

'You think the killer is motivated by some desire for revenge?'

'I'm trying to get my head around the possibilities.'

'Then what?'

'Then I go to the police and present my case. Whether they act on it or not is another matter entirely.'

'I see.' The man seemed to weigh this up and come down on her side. 'Okay, well, from the list you sent me there is one that stands out: Brian Hicks.'

'Is he one of yours?'

'One of ours?'

'I mean, with Hawkestone?'

The man's eyes narrowed. 'We no longer operate under that name.'

'So I heard. Can I ask, why the change of name?'

'Moving with the times.' He gave another shrug, this time non-committal. 'It's a marketing thing.'

'Right, so not trying to keep ahead of the scandal?'

'What scandal would that be?' He nodded towards a coffee van parked further along. 'Do you mind?'

She followed along and waited for him to order a double espresso. She watched him pouring sugar in and stirring. The smell of the coffee cleared her head. She wasn't tempted to ask for one herself. Her throat was dry and there was an air of death about this man, in the blank sheen of his eyes. She needed to keep her focus.

'It's inevitable, I suppose. Every now and then you get a bad apple.' He sipped his coffee, staring off at the horizon. 'Maybe that's unfair. I don't think people set out to go bad. Whatever our opinion of the war, a lot of brave men and women found the courage to join the fight.'

'We can agree on that,' said Ray, sticking her hands into the pockets of her jacket. 'Even though I'm sure we wouldn't see eye to eye on the war itself.'

The man gave a little snort. 'Sure, I hear you. The point I'm trying to make is that there are things in here,' he tapped the side of his head, 'that defy all logic.'

'I've seen his medical record.'

'Course you have.' He glanced away briefly. 'You treated him for PTSD.'

'We were researching the way in which servicemen and women went off script. That was basically the remit.'

'Interesting.' He sipped his coffee like a connoisseur. 'What did you find?'

'That some people are wholly unsuited to the task of having an automatic weapon put in their hands and being sent off to a foreign country with a licence to kill.'

That brought the smile back. 'And that's what you concluded on Hicks?'

'He overstepped the line. He beat and tortured a number of civilians. They drummed him out for that. So he went into the private sector, where they are not so picky. He joined Hawkestone.'

'So you say.'

'That's why you're here, isn't it?'

He rocked back on his heels and tilted his head back to look at the sky. 'With some people the problems always come back around.'

'And so they did in his case. What went wrong?'

'Bad business, for everyone.' Hawkestone Man, as she now thought of him, fell silent.

'Are you going to tell me what happened?'

There was a long pause. He finished his coffee, crushed the cup and dropped it into a bin.

'June fifteenth, 2008. We were hired by Howard Thwaite. The money was no guarantee of safe release. These guys, the kidnappers, were unpredictable. Angry and resentful towards Westerners. They saw us all as part of the occupying forces who had taken their country from them. We were hired to go in and get the hostages out. Hicks and his unit located them just south of Tikrit. A typical local house built around a central yard. The kidnappers weren't worried about being caught. They had the authorities in their pocket. Military. Police. Local government. They were all family and friends. Tribal allegiance is big in that part of the world. So most were sympathetic or expected to get a good kickback.' He drew in a deep breath. 'The third hostage was a young American woman named Janet Avery. Twenty-seven years old. A volunteer with one of the aid organizations. They found her stripped, tied to a bed and covered in encrusted blood, semen and her own waste and bodily fluids. They'd been at her for ten days. It's understandable that the men were shocked.'

'I thought they were trained to be professional.'

'You know how it goes. The best training in the world doesn't prepare you for something like that.'

'Sounds like you think they were justified.'

'Two of our men, Hicks and Reese, lost it. They took one look at Avery and turned on her captors, two young men and their father, a former guard from one of Saddam's prisons. They mutilated them all, made the father watch as they tortured his sons. I have never seen so much blood. Sliced their faces, cut off their hands, and let them bleed. They cut off their heads.'

'How did Janet Avery die?'

'A stray bullet. One of ours.' Hawkestone Man took a deep breath. 'We ask men to do terrible things, and then we are surprised by what they are capable of. I'm not passing judgement.'

'They were trained. Disciplined.'

'No amount of training can prepare you for some things.'

'You were there at the time.'

Hawkestone Man nodded. 'We were standing by in case they needed support. We came in on helicopters to clean up the mess. It was horrible.'

'When you debriefed them afterwards, what did they say?'

'Reese blamed Hicks. Said he was the ringleader. Said he just went along. Reese was more scared of Hicks than anything else.'

'What happened to Reese?'

'He killed himself a year after he came home.'

'How long have you known all of this?'

'I knew the details of the raid and what had gone wrong.'

It was starting to rain again, soft light drizzle that pushed them in under the trees where they could hear it hissing through the leaves.

'Hawkestone was never prosecuted,' said Crane. 'It was all hushed up. The government knew public opinion was against military involvement, so they were keen on farming the work out to private contractors. Best to avoid a scandal and military contractors are private citizens and so not liable under military law.'

'It wasn't the proudest moment of my career,' he said, turning to gaze out over the landscape. 'But when you sign on to a firm like this you can't pick and choose. You're all in. The killing spree was kept quiet. They demolished the house in a controlled explosion to cover up the evidence. The whole thing vanished, as if it had never happened.'

'Hicks was guilt-stricken. I think he wanted to be punished.'

'You were treating him.'

Crane nodded. 'He was part of a group I was charged with debriefing.'

'As far as I can tell he kind of went to pieces,' said Hawkestone Man. 'After your call I made some enquiries. He was drinking heavily after he came back, and developed an addiction to painkillers.'

'He murdered those people.'

'He was being paid to fight for a country that didn't want him there, against fanatics who made up for their lack of training with religious devotion. Soldiers are trained to obey orders without question. Not to start asking existentialist questions. That's where the problems start.'

'We're too sensitive?' Ray lifted a quizzical eyebrow.

'If you want to put it like that, then yes.'

'I get the feeling you don't entirely blame Hicks for what he did.'

'It's a war. The lines get blurred.'

'What happened to Hicks in the end?' Crane asked. The rain was getting more intense. Hard, stinging darts against her face.

'Six years ago he went out to Syria on his own initiative. Joined the resistance, the fight against ISIS. Managed to get himself killed.' Hawkestone Man thrust his hands deep into his coat pockets. 'For what it's worth, I think he was trying to make amends. Maybe he thought that going back there would make things right.'

This, Crane realized, was the reason he had agreed to meet her. Not because Stewart Mason had pulled some strings, but because he wanted to put the record straight.

'Do your bosses know that you're here, talking to me?'

He didn't need to answer. 'Hicks was a good soldier. Shrewd, strong, resourceful. He was destined for great things. It's a shame to see a man like that go off the rails.'

'Hicks was a consequence, not an anomaly. There's nothing noble about killing women and children.'

Crane saw the anger flare up in him, but that didn't stop her.

'I have one last question for you. Is it possible that Hicks didn't die in Syria? Could he have survived and come home with a grudge?'

But Hawkestone Man had clearly had enough. He was rocking back and forth on the balls of his feet, eager to be on his way, eyes darting left, already picking the shortest line of escape. To his credit, he did answer her question, or try to.

'I'd like to tell you that's impossible. I can't tell you how much we want to put all of this behind us. The truth is that we don't know. Things out there are chaotic. One report contradicts another. All I can say is we've never been able to confirm his burial site.'

Crane stood there long after he had gone, oblivious to the steadily increasing density of the rain falling around her, the damp seeping into her skin. The details of what Hicks and Reese had done filled her with revulsion. She felt physically sick, replaying the details in her head. Of course, what had happened to Janet Avery was horrendous, but there had to be a way of dealing with evil that didn't turn us all into monsters. Surely, there had to be?

As she walked back down the hill, her mind replayed the conversation. There was no clear evidence that Hicks had indeed died in Syria. Did that mean that he was back in this country, alive and well and exacting his own vengeance on a society that had not cared about the sacrifice he and his mates had made? Did he want them to feel the physical and mental suffering he had known?

The only way to find out was to find the killer.

CHAPTER 43

Drake was surprised to find it was still there. The spot where he had chipped his name into the burred concrete all those years ago. It was tucked into one of the bends in the staircase running up the side of the building. The tips of his fingers traced the uneven letters: C-A-L.

On the third floor he moved along the catwalk, pausing here and there to look over the side. The square was quiet. In the distance a car revved its engine noisily. As it died away the snick of bicycle chains could be heard from somewhere out of sight below.

The last time he had stood outside number 227, the front door and windows had been boarded over. A thick streak of black soot stretched up around the door and along the underside of the gallery above. He remembered standing here in his uniform staring at it. The rain drizzling down just out of reach. It looked like ink spreading across water.

The door in front of him opened without warning and a girl of about seven stood there, her hair tied in ringlets.

'Whatyouwant?'

'I, er . . .' Cal tried to think of something to say. He managed a smile, but that only made the frown on her face deepen.

'We don't want it,' she said brightly. 'Whatever you selling.' With that she turned and addressed someone inside the house. A large woman brushed past her, fixing a coloured wrap around her head. She dragged the girl behind her.

'Get inside, I tell you!'

The little girl remained where she was, staring wide eyed at Drake from behind the woman's ample hips as the door swung closed in his face.

'Lost your way, Holmes?'

At first he didn't see where the voice was coming from, then the shadows parted and he saw the kid wearing a hoodie, his Jango Fett shirt still visible underneath.

Drake sighed. 'Trip down memory lane.'

The kid held out a cigarette, which Drake took as a peace offering. They leaned their elbows on the wall and looked down over the square.

'So, what is it, like, you miss the place?'

'I haven't thought about it for years. Too busy trying to get away.'

'Is that how you got into all this, the feds?'

'Yeah, 'spose it is.' Drake looked round. 'I joined the army. The only way I could see out.'

'Heavy. I could never do that.'

'You'd be surprised,' Cal said, looking over. 'Sometimes it's about knowing what you're afraid of.'

'Yeah, the army? Uniforms and salutin and all that? No way, man.'

'It's hard to explain, but I wanted to prove that I could do the worst they asked of me.'

'Right,' Jango shook his head. 'You still go out an die for them, innit?'

'I didn't go out there for anyone but myself.'

The kid studied him for a moment but said nothing. 'You think you made a difference?'

'Some days,' Drake said. 'One thing for sure. You sit back and it'll go round on repeat.'

'Yeah, well, true dat.'

Drake broke off the conversation to answer his phone.

'I thought it might be helpful to compare notes,' said Crane.

'Sounds like an idea.'

'Where are you?' she asked.

Drake suggested they meet at his next port of call.

'I can be there in fifteen minutes,' she said before hanging up.

'Gotta go,' said Drake, heading for the stairs.

'Say, Holmes?' The kid looked up from his own phone, his face illuminated by the glow.

Cal turned. 'What?'

'You serious about that, making a difference?'

'I wouldn't be here if I wasn't.'

Jango chewed that one over for a while, then he leaned over the side and whistled. When Drake reached the square he found it magically deserted. No sign of any of the kids who'd been there earlier.

Drake arrived at Magnolia Quays to find Crane was ahead of him. How she did it, he didn't know, but she seemed to move around the city with remarkable ease. She climbed off the Triumph as he parked and came round to climb into the passenger seat.

'Sorry, I stopped off for coffee,' he said, handing her a cup. 'I didn't think you'd be so fast. Black, right?' He didn't know, but somehow he guessed she wasn't the type to fuss around with milk, skimmed or otherwise.

'That's fine, thanks. So, why here?'

Drake peered through the windscreen at the fence and the advertising hoarding that announced Magnolia Quays.

'Ahh, I've got this feeling about one of the security guards. A man by the name of Flinders. Ring any bells?'

'Sorry.' Ray shook her head. 'Why not go to the firm?'

There had been a question mark hanging over Flinders ever since Drake had first run into him that night at Magnolia Quays. The service tattoo, pretending to be a fellow serviceman. People got tattoos to impress. Happens all the time. Only this had a feel to it.

'I'd like to have another look at him without tipping him off.'

'So, what, you're just going to wait here until he shows up?'

'That was the plan,' nodded Drake. He detected a note of scepticism in her voice. 'You don't approve?'

'No, it's not that.' She looked up and down the deserted street. 'Just doesn't seem like the most efficient use of your time.'

'Yeah, well, with Pryce in charge I have to take my chances.' Drake filled her in on developments at Raven Hill.

'Can he do that, just cut you out of the loop?'

'It's the Met, he can do what he likes.'

'What does Wheeler say?'

'Wheeler says, Don't rock the boat.'

'Sounds about right.' It pretty much summed up her view of the superintendent. 'I hear you found Hakim.'

'It would be more accurate to say that we found most of him.' Drake tilted his head against the side window. 'Double amputation of the hands. What does that tell you?'

'Both hands is unusual.' She gave Drake a long look. 'Like he doesn't know what he's doing.'

'Making it up as he goes along.'

'Doesn't mean anything, of course.'

'Right,' he agreed. 'Could be just improvising, looking for maximum shock effect.'

'Something like that.'

They were both silent for a moment, turning over the possibilities in their heads. Then Drake turned to her again.

'So, where are you?'

'Okay, well. Remember I told you I had done some work for the military?'

'The hush-hush stuff you aren't supposed to talk about.'

'Yep.' Crane turned to sit with her back to the door and one knee raised. The kind of person who could do yoga in a coffin. 'Well, it seems there may be a connection.'

'I'm all ears.'

'Okay, well the military wanted research done to try and deal with PTSD. Specifically, with actions related to soldiers going off script.'

'The ones who cracked under pressure.'

Crane winced. 'That's putting it bluntly.'

'Blunt is my middle name.'

'The point is that the experience of trauma is compounded in some cases by feelings of guilt, the sense that one has failed one's mission.'

'You were drafted in to deal with that.'

'We were trying to find a way to deal with it. I took a sample group and interviewed them before they shipped out and again when they returned from active duty.' Ray sipped her coffee. 'At some point things became more urgent. There were questions being asked about whether we were doing enough by our servicemen and women. Public opinion was hardening against the conflict.'

'They wanted answers, all tied up in a neat little bow.'

'Exactly. And as everyone knows, it doesn't work like that.'

'It never does.' He caught her look as he spoke. 'And don't even think about analysing me.'

'I can offer you competitive rates.'

He laughed it off.

'Stick with the story, Doctor Crane. I take it all of what you're telling me is classified. The Official Secrets Act and so on?'

'Absolutely. I called on an old contact. He has a thing for me.'

Drake sniffed. 'Do I need details?'

'Nothing to tell. He's never going to get what he wants.'

'Right, and in the meantime, he's ready to play fetch.'

Ray smiled. 'Sounds like you know what you're talking about.'

'Men, underneath that veneer of sophistication, we're all the same. We have trouble thinking clearly when there are women in the picture.'

'You'll have to enlighten me some time.'

'Meanwhile, are you going to tell me where this is all leading?'

'Okay, so the men who worked on freeing the hostages were an outfit called Hawkestone. Or they used to be.'

'Deorum sanctum or some such Latin bullshit.'

Ray was impressed. 'So you did get somewhere.'

'I hit a wall. You managed to get over the other side.'

'Two operatives, Reese and Hicks, went amok when they discovered that one of the hostages had been raped and tortured. They started killing civilians. It was all hushed up.'

'Hicks? Brian Patrick Hicks?'

'Does the name mean anything to you?'

'Milo found a link between Flinders, our security guard, and this guy Hicks.' Drake was checking the mirror for any sight of the Kronnos Security guard. 'There's only one problem. Hicks is dead.'

'He went out to Syria to try and win the war against ISIS singlehandedly. There was no confirmation of his death.'

'But there's nothing after that. Milo found no record of Hicks after his reported death in Syria.'

Ray sat back and closed her eyes. 'Which means we have nothing.'

'There has to be a connection. It's too much to be pure coincidence.'

'That's my thinking too,' nodded Ray.

Cal shifted in his seat. 'Can I ask you something?'

She glanced over. 'Is this personal?'

'It might be.'

Ray considered the idea for a moment before nodding. 'Okay, shoot.'

'Your career hit a bump in the road.'

She pushed the plastic cap back on her coffee cup before setting it on the dashboard. 'I was sued for malpractice. I lost my research post, my job, a good job. A job I liked.'

'What happened exactly?'

Ray settled herself back in the seat and stared up at the night sky. 'One of the people I was treating turned up in the middle of Manchester strapped inside a suicide vest.'

Drake gave a low whistle.

'I was trying to convince the powers-that-be that I was making a difference, that fanatics coming back from Syria could be turned into valuable assets.'

'You couldn't have prevented him from doing what he did.'

'That's the thing I ask myself all the time.' Ray was motionless in her seat. 'Maybe I could. I was so intent on trying to make a success of myself. Perhaps I missed something.'

'It's always easier with hindsight.'

'What about you, any regrets?'

Cal straightened up in his seat. 'More than I care to admit.'

There was a long silence before Ray finally broke it. 'I keep thinking back to those group sessions that I did.'

'Hicks attended?'

'This was just before he went to Syria, I think.' Ray had been trying to remember. Reading through her notes from the time.

'I went back over it all. I used to tape the sessions. I had forgotten all about that time.'

'Is there anything in particular that you recall?'

'That's the thing. He was upset, deeply affected by what he had seen, and what he had done. He knew the war had screwed him up, sent him into a spiral of alcohol and sedatives, but he didn't blame the people who sent him there.'

'You're saying he wasn't political?'

'He blamed himself. He wanted to die. He never expressed a desire to wreak vengeance on society, or on the people whose war he fought.'

'Then he takes himself off to Syria and gets himself killed.'

'Which leaves the question, who are we dealing with now?'

It was a good question, and one that Drake couldn't answer.

CHAPTER 44

Crane took herself off and Drake decided that she was probably right. He was wasting time sitting around. He decided to pay a call on Archie Narayan. The lights were on when he arrived at the coroner's office. In the downstairs reception area a worried-looking woman in a green raincoat sat on one of the sofas. She was in her fifties, heavily built. Next to her a younger, slimmer woman wearing glasses watched a man in his twenties strolling restlessly up and down.

'Hakim's family,' Archie explained when Drake found him in the basement. 'They insist that he be released for burial. Something about him having to be buried quickly.'

'I didn't know the family was Muslim.'

'Apparently it's just the brother.' Archie's tone echoed his usual scepticism on the subject. 'He's got a bee in his bonnet about religious rites. Makes you weary, all this kowtowing to deities that sprang from some fertile part of the human imagination.'

'One of these days somebody is going to nail your ass to the wall for incitement.'

'And I shall go to my death happy to pay for my convictions.'

'Ever the diva. Before you martyr yourself for free speech, how about telling me what you've got?' Drake nodded at the examination table where Hakim lay covered in a white sheet.

'Ah, yes, the worms? Well, as you know, we're no strangers to insects around here, but I have to say, this is a first.'

'Hard to believe.'

'Sarcasm?' Archie peered at Drake over the rim of his glasses. 'Strictly speaking, I'm not supposed to share anything with you. Pryce explicitly mentioned you by name.'

'Pryce can go fuck himself.'

'And I'm the heathen who will be burned at the stake,' Archie tutted, shaking his head before turning serious. 'You need to watch out for that one, Cal. He really doesn't like you.'

'Please, doc, tell me something I don't know.'

'He won't be happy until you're suspended, or worse.'

'Worse is probably right,' Drake admitted. He let Archie's words sink in as the white sheet was whipped away to reveal the remains of Akbar Hakim.

The body was slim, bony and dark, the skin broken here and there by lines of what looked like bites or scratches. Drake leaned in for a closer look. Archie pushed him gently out of the way.

'Try not to get too intimate, will you?'

'What are all these?' Drake indicated the tracks on the skin. 'Looks like he's been bitten.'

'Patience, dear boy.'

The autopsy had not really begun. The body had been subjected to low temperatures to kill anything that might be lurking. As a result there was a cockroach lodged in Hakim's left nostril. It looked as though it had expired while making a valiant bid to escape.

'Alas, poor Yorick! The one that got away.' Archie used a set of steel tweezers to remove the offending body which he dropped into a steel tray. 'Almost.'

'Why do I get the feeling you're enjoying this?'

Archie spoke without looking up. 'You're watching a professional at work. Live and learn.'

'Okay, tell me what we've got here.' Drake gestured at the tray. He had a bad feeling about this.

'A wide variety of fauna, I think you could say. Centipedes, scorpions, spiders, cockroaches, slugs, leeches, worms, adders. A veritable feast, almost all home grown or easily available. Nothing too exotic yet.' Archie set the tweezers on the examination table and stared down at the body. 'If you ask me, he was tortured.'

'Tortured?'

'To what end, I can't say, obviously.' Archie turned away to reach for his glass of single malt. Drake waved the offer away. He was feeling queasy. A steel bowl on the instrument trolley contained more cockroaches and grey worms the size of fingers, glistening black slugs.

'You found all of that inside him? Where would you even get that many insects?'

'Insects reproduce in a matter of days. It doesn't take long. Just the right temperature.'

'A little odd for this time of year.'

'It wouldn't take much. A boiler room for example. Plenty of those around. Introduce our friends here and away you go.' Archie took another sip of whisky.

'Could it be some form of religious ritual?'

'Seriously?'

'Just a thought,' shrugged Drake.

'Sometimes I wonder about you, DS Drake. All I can say is, if it is, I've never heard of it.' Archie lifted his eyebrows. 'Of course, putting people into coffins with live insects is nothing new.'

Drake could tell from the coroner's tone that he had more to say. 'Enlighten me.'

'Are you familiar with the techniques developed by the CIA under their SERE programme: Survival, Evasion, Resistance & Escape?'

'I've heard about it, nothing more than that.'

'I thought as much.' Archie heaved a heavy sigh. 'They used it to prepare their pilots for if they ever came down behind enemy lines. Later it was used as an enhanced interrogation technique, in Central America in the 1970s, and later in Afghanistan.'

Drake looked up from the body. 'You're not telling me he was tortured by the CIA?'

'Good lord, no. Well, I don't think that's likely.'

'Let's back up here. You're saying this man was locked in with live insects? How?'

'A confined space like a box. The feet and arms, what's left of them, show abrasions and contusions that might be consistent with someone trying to get out of a confined space. The fragments I have recovered suggest fresh pine.' Archie indicated a specimen tray with what looked like bloody splinters in it.

'The fauna would have been introduced and left to their own devices. In the right conditions they can reproduce in less than twenty-four hours.'

'So, he was kept alive, in a coffin, with all those insects?'

Archie reached for his glass. 'I can't think of a more hideous way to go, and I've seen a few in my time.'

'Why?'

'That's the kind of philosophical question the Met pays you for, or maybe they don't.' Archie frowned. 'Which reminds me, were you not suspended?'

'I mean, why torture him? Hakim was working with the killer.'

Archie held his hands up. 'That's your end of things. Maybe he was a liability.'

'Unless this was always the plan.' Drake looked down at Hakim. 'He's trying to tell us something.'

'You mean, it's the method used that is the point?'

'Hakim was a nobody. Confused. Our killer has been using him, convincing him he was part of some jihadist scheme. After that, the only purpose he served was to send another message.'

'What kind of message?'

'Well, first off there are the hands. Having both hands cut off is extreme, even by sharia-law standards.'

'But it does tie him to Magnolia Quays.'

'Yes, but why torture him?'

Archie gazed down at the body. 'I know this man wounded your colleague, but nobody deserves to die this way.'

'Maybe that's his point,' Drake said, thinking aloud. 'Guilt by complicity.'

'Of course.' Archie took a renewed look at the body. 'We are all guilty by association. Torture of this kind was committed in our name. You think that's his point?'

Drake seemed not to hear him. 'What was the cause of death?'

'I'd have to complete my autopsy, but preliminary examination suggests the most likely cause of death was heart failure.'

'So he was literally scared to death?'

'You think that's significant?'

'Right now everything is significant.'

'Given the right amount of stress you can kill anyone. I'll know better when I get a proper look at the heart muscle. Could be wrong, but there you go. Being locked into a chest with hundreds of creepy crawlies might do that to you.'

'Well, you can't say he didn't deserve it.'

'So much for compassion.'

Drake looked over at Archie. 'He stabbed Kelly. It takes more than a few cockroaches to row back from that.'

'Fair enough, but I wouldn't wish that death on anyone.' Archie poured himself another drink as Drake headed for the door. 'By the way, what exactly is your status, I mean, if Pryce asks me if you were here?'

'I think AWOL is the best description, and I was never here.'

Upstairs in the reception area Drake approached Hakim's mother, or tried to. He was intercepted by the agitated young man he had noticed on his way in.

'When are they going to let us bury my brother?' He was tall and aggressive, his nostrils flaring as he leaned into Drake's face.

'There are a number of formalities, legal and technical,' Drake said calmly. 'There's no point in staying here. Go home and we'll contact you when...' He didn't get a chance to finish his sentence.

'We're not going anywhere.'

Drake saw the flat, bullish expression and turned to the mother. 'Mrs Jones, there is nothing you can do by staying here.'

She was dabbing at the tear tracks on her face with a lace handkerchief. 'My boy,' she whimpered. She glanced anxiously at her other son.

'Why do they need to keep my brother anyway?'

Drake turned back to face him again. 'We're trying to find the man who killed him. Isn't that what you want?'

'I don't believe you. I think you's all incompetent.' He stepped closer, crowding Drake. 'This is about respect. Our tradition.'

'I understand that.'

The younger woman who was consoling the mother said, 'Lay off him, Jameel, he's a copper.' The news had the opposite effect of that she intended. It made him more aggressive. His look turned contemptuous.

'That's it, innit? It's cos he was Muslim, right?'

Drake glanced at the mother but she seemed so stricken with grief she barely registered what was going on around her.

'We believe Duwayne was killed by some people he was involved with.'

'That's bullshit!' Spittle flecked the brother's lower lip. 'And his name was Akbar Hakim.'

'His name was Duwayne!' the mother exploded onto her feet. 'You hear me? Duwayne. That's what we named him.' But it was too much for her and she collapsed sobbing in a heap. The boy folded. He watched his mother bury her face in her handkerchief, then he went and sat beside her, quietly putting an arm around her. Drake led the sister aside.

'Take them both home. It won't do any good to your mother if your brother gets himself locked up for assaulting a police officer.'

'I understand.' She glanced back. 'He's just such a child sometimes. Can't control himself.'

'Were they very close?'

'Daryl looked up to Duwayne something terrible. Even converted to Islam because of him. Now we have to call him Jameel.' She rolled her eyes before examining Drake more closely. 'I hope that doesn't sound offensive.'

'No worries. It would help to know a bit more about Duwayne's movements these last few months. Where he worked, who his friends were, who he hung out with? He was staying at the mosque for a time, is that correct?'

She rolled her eyes again. 'That was at the end. He'd been getting crazier and crazier over the last few months. Nobody understood what got into him. Mum was beside herself. She finally threw him out.'

'So, before that he was doing okay?'

'Well, okay . . . I mean, he was managing. He had his things, you know, his campaign against the war. He printed pamphlets, stood out on the high street bothering people. Outside the Tube station. Everyone knew him. I used to cross the street to avoid him. It was just too embarrassing.'

'When did all of this change, then?'

'About four months ago, something like that. He just went quiet. He got weird and dropped out, disappeared, really.'

'Do you know where he was working?'

'All over the place. Couldn't keep a job down. Always thought he was too good for them. I don't know where he got that from.'

'There was a used-car place in Putney.'

'That was years ago,' she nodded. 'He messed that one up too. It was one thing after another. He'd last a month and then not turn up, or he'd get into a fight.'

She glanced over at her brother, then scrabbled about in her purse for a tissue. 'Duwayne had mental-health issues. He kept saying he was going to make us all proud. At some point I stopped listening.' She looked up at him. 'You just wonder, don't you, if you could have done more?'

Drake had just reached the car when his phone started ringing. It was Wheeler.

'Where are you?'

'What's up, sir?' It was unusual for him to call so late.

'Get yourself over to Freetown. DCI Pryce seems to have got himself into a spot of bother.'

CHAPTER 45

The main square was already cordoned off. People stood along the line, their faces warmed by the glow of fires. Drake spotted three cars ablaze in the access road. Two riot vans were on the main square, illuminated by the flames. They had their shields down and were trying to advance on a small group of youths wearing balaclavas and hoodies. Some had their faces covered with scarves. A flicker of flame arched up into the darkening sky to land on one of the police vans. It burst alive as it smashed, spreading a sheet of fire over the vehicle.

'It's like the fucking West Bank!' yelled an officer on the perimeter when Drake flashed his badge and asked for DCI Pryce. He was directed to a command vehicle on the east end of the square. To get there Drake had to push his way through a crowd of terrified onlookers, residents and photographers who were busy snapping away, their faces illuminated by the flickering glow.

The command post was a high, box-shaped vehicle. Inside, Pryce resembled a conductor who'd lost control of his orchestra. Wearing a rather silly headset, he yelled at a bank of monitors.

'What happened?' Drake asked a dazed-looking uniform standing by the door.

'One of the police vehicles knocked someone down.'

'Knocked who down?'

'I don't know, some kid.'

'Where is he now?'

'He was taken to hospital.' The uniform shook his head. 'Looks bad.'

On the monitors Drake could see masked youths hurling Molotov cocktails and charging one of the riot vans that was trapped in the middle.

'Get them out of there!' Pryce was screaming. Catching sight of Drake he waved him over. 'I need you to get out there and make yourself useful.'

'How exactly do you want me to do that?'

'You're our liaison officer, right? So talk to them.'

Drake laughed in disbelief. 'You want me to go out and parlay with the Indians?'

'Just do as you're told, Drake!'

Judging by the Hitler Youth haircuts, it looked as though Moss and his mates had turned out in force. To counter this the local kids had been joined by some hardcore anti-fascist groups who had definitely come prepared. Some wore crash helmets, knee pads and body armour. Others were more lightweight, in balaclavas and hoodies, bandannas across their faces, Jesse James style. They tossed Molotov cocktails and swung sledgehammers. Setting cars alight seemed to be the new thing, as they raced along streets, kindling one after the other. The police for the most part were huddled together for safety. So much for law and order.

On the north side of the square Drake spotted a small van edging along the perimeter. It was hard to see through the moving body of people, but he knew what it was. He edged around until he could be certain. Not so much the van as the red electrocardiogram stripe along the side. The crowd surged and it vanished from sight as he was forced the other way.

Through the chaos, Drake spotted Jango hanging at the corner of the side street behind the Alamo with a posse of his mates. They too were in battle dress. Lopsided woollen hats taped on with duct tape, what looked like a WWI steel helmet, batting gloves, baseball bats and bicycle chains.

'What's going on?'

'They set their dogs on us, innit?' Jango pointed to the group of men clutching flags behind the more aggressive youth.

'They're just a bunch of losers.'

'Your lot killed Nemo!' The boy thrust his face toward Drake's. 'They've been fucking building up to this for weeks. Now they've taken one of us out, we're going to teach them a lesson.'

He pulled his bandanna up to cover his face and stepped out as the boys launched another assault. They were well organized, coming in on the enemy from two sides, effectively catching them in a pincer movement. Drake could do little but stand out of the way and watch.

Molotov cocktails were being ferried forwards from some hidden factory stationed in one of the side streets. Bottles filled with petrol with rags stuffed into the necks. They flew in slow lazy arcs across the battlefield. One landed in front of a Transit van lancing a ball of flame into the air. The vehicle lumbered backwards over the uneven ground now strewn with bits of masonry and debris, before it slew to one side and lurched off the kerb with a screech of tyres. Drake could see the other mob advancing. They wore masks covering the lower half of their faces. Behind them the crowd cheered their fighters on. With their flags and DIY-painted wooden crosses they looked like crusaders on social security.

'We need back-up, and fast!' a driver was screaming, his voice coming through Drake's hand-held radio. The radio responded with a burst of incoherent static. The local kids were dragging wheelie bins out to block the entrances to the estate. Drake saw them pouring petrol over a couple of them and setting them alight. The retreating vehicle struck one of the bins with the side of the van. Luckily they hadn't had time to weigh them down and they bounced out of the way.

A helicopter stuttered overhead, its searchlight washing over the scene. A kid with a catapult turned to fire up at it. It was pure anarchy. Half a dozen vehicles were in sight. Ahead of them a crowd had gathered. Up on the runways there was more movement. Drake could see kids in hoodies racing along the second floor. A lighted fuse dropped from one to explode on the ground like a star bursting. They were prepared. The sirens wailed, the rioters, men and women screamed and whooped. Dogs were barking.

To these kids this was an opportunity. They had the world's attention. This was their chance. And that was the tragedy of places like the Freetown estate; nobody paid any attention until they were going up in flames.

Drake worked his way around the periphery heading towards the Alamo. It was closed, the wooden doors shut. Drake hammered on the door until it opened to reveal Doc Wyatt. He looked both ways before hauling Drake in and shutting the door behind him again.

'You picked a bad time to pay a visit.'

The lights were off and a handful of people sat in the dark. When his eyes had adjusted to the gloom, Drake could make out a woman in her fifties, a regular whose name he used to know.

'I don't care what anyone says,' she muttered, to no one in particular. 'There's something special about this place. It's not the greatest place on earth, right? But it's special. And it's going. It's a fucking tragedy.'

'You have to get these people out of here,' said Drake.

'Look, man,' Doc shook his head as he bowed over the counter, his beads brushing the stained wood. 'People round here just trying to get by. That's all what it is. It's not complicated. It's them people across the river, politicians, money men, know what I mean?'

The fires outside sent a wavy pattern of light and shadow across the walls.

'You're not making a lot of sense,' said Drake.

'That's because it's late. I had a couple of drinks. Look, your mother . . .'

'Don't bring my mother into this.'

'Hey, mate. I knew her, remember? Sorry to say this, but I was still here to help her home when she collapsed on the stairs, or put her head down on one of the tables over there. Your mother, in her last years, was a part of this. She lived here. She had her problems, but everybody knew her. Some of us tried to look out for her. She earned that.' He set his fist down gently. 'You should have been here is all ah'm saying.'

'Nice. That's grand of you.'

'Oh, fuck off. I don't know why I bother.'

'How did this happen, then?' Drake jerked a thumb over his shoulder.

'Fucked if I know. Stephen Moss and his merry band of wankers.'

'The Hope and Glory mob?'

'Hope and glory my arse.' Wyatt wagged his dreads. 'Most of them are middle-aged losers. Failed at everything else in life and now they've found a cause. Fighting for England.'

'Is there anyone who they'll listen to?'

'Our lot?' Wyatt looked at Drake for a long time. 'You're serious, aren't you?'

'Why wouldn't I be serious?'

'Because they don't pay you enough.' He looked at Drake as if weighing him up. 'Okay, why not?' He turned and led the way across the darkened room to a gloomy corner. The opaque windows swam with clouds of light from the fires outside.

Three men sat around a bottle of Appleton Special set in the middle of a round table. The man in the corner was the darkest skinned of them all. In his late fifties and wearing a pencil-thin moustache and a tan leather jacket with 1970s-style flap pockets and epaulettes on the shoulders. His eyes lifted as they approached.

'Wynstan, you remember Cal?'

The eyes were small and steady, like two obsidian beads shining in the darkness.

'Yeah, man.' He spoke with a slow Jamaican lilt. 'Ain't seen you roun here for a while.'

Drake remembered 'Crazy' Wynstan from the old days when his dad, Chalkie, used to run the estate. Old-time Jamaican Yardies.

'You two used to be like peas in a pod.'

Wynstan's long fingers splayed out. 'Sit,' he said.

Drake waited while the two companions shuffled about and got to their feet to make space, then he slid onto the seat.

'You drink rum?' Wynstan gestured at the bottle. A glass was found. Wynstan poured. 'What's this I hear about you bein Babylon? That got to be a lie, I say when I hear.'

'Just trying to do the right thing.'

'Right. They never gwan let you be anything but lickle Indian, whadyacallim?'

'Tonto?'

'That him. Dey always de Lone Ranger.' Wynstan studied Drake. 'Not the same as when we as kids, nah? My old man would roll in him grave if he could see the state a tings. Ya feel me?'

'It's a brave new world.'

'No, man, nuttin new here. This old, old world. This stone age.'

He tilted his head. 'Dem ediats with dem flags and all? We seen worse, right?' He looked around his companions, soliciting nods from them. 'Remember Brixton? I'm talkin bout the uprising in eighty-one? Toxteth? Social unrest them call it. Irie. Babylon was burning in dem days.' There were murmurs of agreement.

'You know this mob?'

'Seen dem roun'about.' Wynstan sucked his teeth. 'Most of them dey bus dem in from Coventry or somewhere.'

'Who bussed them in?'

'Who knows?' Wynstan chuckled as he refilled their glasses. 'Rent-a-clown or some shit like dat.' There was a trickle of laughter from his two companions.

'You know what they want?'

'What they always wan, to push we black arse off dem streets.' Wynstan leaned over the table. 'Only dis time it all change. They dreamin of old times when Britannia rule de waves, nah? Nowadays we got de damn United Nations roun here, places I never hear of. An we don't have them clever dicks what speak in ya ear, man. I mean, you got to be a damn Rubik's cube to understand all dem tongue.'

Drake didn't get the reference, but the gist of what he was saying was clear.

'You think you can pull your boys back?'

'You get you Babylon boys to uproot Moss and him hoodlum from out my square and it done.' Wynstan held Drake's gaze steadily. 'Can ya do dat?'

'It's done.' Drake got to his feet and raised his glass in salute before draining it. As he made to leave he heard Wynstan calling him back.

'Hey, Kemosabe, watch out they dón' deport y'rass, nah?'

The laughter followed Drake out into the street.

He had to push his way through a scrum of journalists and

cameras to reach the command vehicle. Pryce looked round as Drake appeared.

'Ah, glad you could join us.'

Drake leaned over him to tap one of the monitors which showed Wynstan's two companions coming out of the door of the Alamo.

'They're going to pull their side back, but we need to do the same.'

'What does that mean? We don't have a side here, Drake.'

'You sure about that?' Drake looked at Pryce. Every officer in the room was watching them. 'Get Moss and his hoodlums out. Tell them we can no longer guarantee their safety.'

'Sounds like you're giving me orders.'

'Relax, I'm just trying to do my job,' smiled Drake.

'Have you been drinking, DS Drake?'

But he was already gone.

Outside, the helicopter chattered its way overhead. Already, the police vehicles were pulling back, corralling Moss's mob into the southwest corner of the square to lead them out. Things were calming down. The kids were getting ready to celebrate a victory. He even caught sight of a couple of them high-fiving it across the square.

Drake turned his head, looking for the Kronnos Security van again, but it was gone. He stopped in the middle of the street and stared at the building the van had been parked outside. It was set back from the square. The old Victorian swimming baths. A new hoarding had been fixed to the brick wall. It showed a bright picture of a smiling family and the logo, YDH DEVELOPMENTS – YOUR FUTURE IS NOW.

In the corner of the hoarding was another, smaller sign that read Kronnos Security. Drake ran his eye up over the building. He thought he glimpsed a wisp of white smoke coming from the flue of one of the old chimneys. The sky above was diesel black with an orange sodium lining. A deluge about to break. The helicopter had stopped moving. It hovered directly overhead, the down draught making the world flutter and shake, as if it was about to come apart at the seams.

CHAPTER 46

Dawn was breaking as Crane twisted the throttle grip and felt the power of the Triumph engine vibrating through her body, propelling her forward along the A4. The cold air was a deep leaden blue. Listening to the steady growl of the engine beneath her, she let her mind go back over the sequence of events that had led her here. After meeting Drake she had sped home and spent most of the rest of the night going back over her notes of the case. Everything she had on Magnolia Quays, about Marsha Thwaite and Tei Hideo. She went back through the boxes of old files from her time in Iraq. Much of that material was classified and Ray had copies of intelligence and military documents that she probably wasn't supposed to have. She constructed a timeline to connect then with now.

Somewhere around midnight she had risen from the table and stretched her arms to try to loosen up her neck. She went through to the bathroom and began to draw a bath. Returning to her desk she cleared away the material about Hicks and carried it down to the kitchen where she prepared herself a cup of ginger tea. On the long wooden table she spread out the material on the Magnolia Quays killings. A large map of the site. Photographs of the crime scene. Others of the two bodies. Close-up details of the victims. It was disturbing. She found herself recreating in her mind Marsha Thwaite's last moments. She would have been conscious. From the tortured expression and open mouth it was clear that she must have realized that she was being buried alive. She was screaming; a last cry that nobody ever heard. The sheer brute force of the stone had ripped away the hood and the gag, battering her face and head in the process. According to the coroner's report she had not been killed by the stonefall. Instead, she had suffocated slowly, her chest and lungs constricted by the stone casing she was set in. She died painfully and in utter terror.

After studying the layout of the construction site and her own sketch of the positioning of the bodies, Ray sat back. What was the killer thinking? If the aim was merely to murder the victims why go to so much trouble? Again, she had to conclude that he was trying to make a point. She returned to the prints of the murder scene. The grey figures rising out of the mound of stone. It could have been a display in a particularly bizarre art show. The figures could have been carved from the same limestone rock they had been buried in. A living sculpture. It sent her to her bookcase, looking for a volume on the despotic architecture of Saddam Hussein. The image triggered a memory of some of the more eccentric roadside statues built in Baghdad: arms rising out of the ground brandishing giant swords, nets full of helmets of dead Iranian soldiers. Macabre. And this too appeared to be in the killer's mind. A staged performance. The killer wants us to look, she thought, but what are we meant to be seeing? Two adulterers wrapped together as they receive their punishment? They had found no evidence that the victims were engaged in an affair – with one another. Ten years ago Marsha had been having an affair with the man who later became her husband, Howard Thwaite. So, was this some kind of moral message?

The other question mark was Hakim. How did his death relate to the Magnolia Quays victims? Clearly the killer intended there to be an ongoing progression. A deepening of his mission statement. So, how exactly? One was a stoning, and the other a double amputation. Where was the connection? Adultery and stealing. Was this just a list of sins? Both were punishments proscribed by the strict tenets of sharia law. She was lying in the bath when it hit her what tied the scene at Magnolia Quays to Hakim.

Betrayal.

Just outside Bristol she leaned the Triumph north and headed across the River Severn and up along the Wye Valley. The ride now became more pleasant as the motorway fell behind and she found herself winding along leafy country roads, passing small towns and villages. On the outskirts of one of these she paused and checked her GPS tracker before turning onto a small, muddy track.

The farmhouse looked as though it had seen better days. Once upon a time. Now an air of disuse hung over the place. A rusty tractor and trailer stood off to one side. Dogs were barking inside a fenced enclosure. She kicked the stand out and parked the bike on a piece of flat ground, posting her helmet over the side mirror. As she approached the house, the front door opened and a woman appeared.

'Mrs Hicks?'

'Who wants to know?' She was in her fifties, hair going grey, wearing grubby jeans and a long, shapeless cardigan that she held tightly against her with folded arms.

'I'm Doctor Crane. We spoke on the phone?'

'Doctor, is it?' Mrs Hicks ran an eye over her, sucking deeply on her cigarette. Her hair hung in ragged bunches about her face. 'You look young for a doctor.'

Crane turned to gaze out over the landscape that dropped away down into the valley where the glint of water could be seen winking through the trees.

'Lovely place you have here.'

'It's all right,' Mrs Hicks conceded. 'You sure you're not a journalist?'

'I'm a psychologist.' Crane produced a card from her inside pocket and walked up to hand it over. Mrs Hicks scrutinized both sides of the card.

'I don't understand. I thought all that business was over and done with.'

'What business would that be?'

'All that stuff about Iraq.'

'This is just background research.' Ray smiled.

'I've had it with all that, the snooping around. Why don't you just let him rest in peace?'

'Believe me, I'd love to do just that. I know how you must feel, but understanding what happened to your son is important. It could help others like him in the future.'

'It's not right.' Mrs Hicks stared firmly off into the distance. 'You never know, do you, what's going on in their heads?'

Crane nodded agreement. 'That's why I'm here. We need to learn from this.'

Mrs Hicks looked at her but said nothing.

'Did you see him often when he came home?'

'In the early days, but later . . .' She unfolded one arm to point. 'When he was here, he kept to himself. Locked himself away in there. It was scary. As if he had become another person. You can see he was obsessed, simply obsessed with the whole business.'

Crane followed her gaze towards a white caravan tucked around the side of the barn.

'He was proud of what he did, being a soldier, like. Fighting for queen and country.' Her eyes were hard and cold, as if to imply this was something Ray would not be able to grasp.

'Do you think I might take a look?'

There was a moment's hesitation. 'Aye, I suppose it's all right. Let me fetch the keys.'

She disappeared inside. A man pulled aside the lace curtain to peer out through the window. An older man with receding hair. He glared at her before disappearing from view. Mrs Hicks returned bearing a string of keys in one hand and a fresh cigarette in the other. She had also exchanged her slippers for a pair of wellington boots. The ground was churned up and muddy and Ray gave up trying to keep her boots dry. The caravan was an old one. The tyres were flat and it was propped up on railway sleepers to prevent it sliding away down the hill. Mrs Hicks fiddled with the key.

'He used to love this thing. Can't think why. Damp in the winter. Too hot in the summer.'

'Maybe it held special memories for him?'

'Aye, well. We used to go on holiday in it, when he was small and his father was still alive.'

'You lived in London then?'

'That's right. Moved out here. Couldn't stand it any longer. The noise, people, crime.'

The door squeaked open and she stepped aside to let Ray in. She remained outside, smoking her cigarette.

'I'd like to get my hands on the people who sent him out there.'

Ray turned on the steps. 'You blame the army, the government?'

A hand circled smoke in the air. 'All of them. The ones who did it to him.'

Inside the caravan the air was damp and reeked of mould. The windows had been pasted over with newspaper instead of curtains. It took a moment for Ray's eyes to adjust. Facing the door was a small kitchenette with a washbasin and electric hotplate. The sliding cupboards stood half open. A bag of sugar and a jar of instant coffee. There was no word from Mrs Hicks, so Ray moved further inside. The bedroom was darker than the living room. Again the windows were covered. Between alarming headlines topless girls pouted at her from sheets of yellowed tabloid pages. A purple sleeping bag lay on the unmade bed. A mattress of raw yellow foam poked through a torn tartan cover. The air was thick and heavy. It took her a moment to realize that the newspaper didn't just cover the narrow window at the far end, but continued all around the walls. From floor to ceiling sheets of newspaper had been taped roughly into place. As she leaned over to take a closer look she glimpsed through a tear the man she had seen in the kitchen window. Coming out of the house he began striding down towards the caravan. Crane guessed her time here was limited.

'He lived here for a time, between jobs, like.' Outside, Mrs Hicks was still rambling on. 'He was never right, not after he came back. Then, one day he just took off again, said he was going back to the war. Well, you can imagine . . .'

Her voice droned on in the background. Crane listened with half an ear as she studied the sheets of newspaper stuck to the wall. She noticed that some carried the same stories. The same pages repeated around the walls. Not randomly chosen, but selected. The garish headlines and models were a diversion from the stories about the rescue operation in Iraq and its aftermath. *Free at Last! Daring Raid Pays Off! Hostages Flown Home!* There were pictures of a young Marsha Thwaite, or Chaikin as she was then, walking down the steps of an aircraft. The story continued onto the next wall. *Army Heroes Face Enquiry. Military Contractors to Be Held Accountable. Hawkestone on Trial.* Underneath a picture of David Reese was the caption: *Soldier Takes His Own Life.* Crane was distracted by the voices outside.

'I'm telling you she's up to something.' The man whispering urgently.

'She's not a journalist.' Mrs Hicks sounded irritated.

'How do you know?'

'I asked her.'

'Oh, for fuck's sake, woman! You don't expect her to tell you.'

Through the thin walls, Crane could hear them arguing. Ignoring them, she pulled out her phone and started taking pictures of the walls. She forgot to turn off the flash.

'What did I say? She's taking pictures.'

The man stuck his head through the doorway. When she turned towards him he disappeared.

'Mark my words, all of this is going to be in tomorrow's papers. They'll dredge the whole thing up again. You'll see.'

When she appeared in the doorway the couple looked up.

Crane looked the man in the eye. 'I don't work for a newspaper. The pictures are for my own personal record. I hope you don't mind?' Ignoring him, she addressed herself to Mrs Hicks, who simply tossed her head as if it didn't matter to her either way.

As she took one last look round, Crane's eye fell on an old photograph, the colours fading, that had been taped to the wall next to the door. When she touched it, it came away in her hand, yellowed strands of Sellotape trailing from it.

'Who is this?' She held it up to Mrs Hicks who smiled.

'Who? Well, that's Brian and 'is brother, Luke, when they were small.'

Ray studied the picture. They were around ten or eleven years old. They had the same blond hair. One of them was slighter in build, the other had a more rounded face.

'Luke was a year and a half younger. He always looked up to his brother, followed him around like a lost puppy. Tried to do everything Brian could, but of course he failed miserably.' She took a long, thoughtful drag on her cigarette. 'Pathetic really, when you think about it.'

'Where is he now, Luke?'

'I don't know.' A blank look came over her, as if reminded of something she didn't want to remember. 'I haven't heard from him for a couple of years. Not since Brian . . .'

Her voice tailed off. By now the man had had enough.

'You have to leave now,' he insisted. 'You can't just come around here upsetting people.'

Crane faced him with a smile. 'I wasn't aware that I was upsetting anyone.'

He took a step towards her. 'If you don't leave, I shall have to throw you out.'

'I wouldn't try that if I were you.'

The man seemed to realize his mistake. He took Mrs Hicks by the arm and led her, rather forcefully, away. Ray trailed behind as the couple made their way back towards the house.

'Did Brian seek pyschological help when he got back? Did he see a doctor?'

'I can't deal with this any more,' Mrs Hicks moaned. 'I just can't!'

'You heard her,' spat the man. 'Go on. Clear off!'

Crane stood and watched the two of them disappear up the front steps and into the house. At the final moment, Mrs Hicks broke free and strode back down towards her. Ray stood her ground, preparing to defend herself. Mrs Hicks came to a halt and brushed her hair out of her face. She looked off into the distance for a moment before addressing Ray.

'You have no right to judge us. I don't agree with what they did out there. I don't care how bad things are. I don't know what he was accused of, and I don't want to know. However bad it was, Brian paid for what he did.' She was shaking her head as if in disagreement with herself. 'He went back there to try and make things right. He didn't have to do that, and he paid for it with his life.'

'I understand, Mrs Hicks, and I want to thank you.'

'I don't want your thanks!' She was almost in tears by now. 'Don't you see? I just want to forget.'

'I wish I could just walk away, but I can't. I need to ask one last question. How do I find Luke? Just tell me that and I'll be gone.'

Mrs Hicks clutched a hand wordlessly to her mouth and Ray thought she had lost her. Then she looked up.

'You promise?'

'You have my word.'

Mrs Hicks sniffed loudly. 'I've lost him too. He'll never come back here. Too many memories. The last I heard he was working in London. One of those men who stand outside nightclubs. What do you call them?'

'A bouncer? Do you know where?'

'No. We couldn't talk in the end. He turned his back on us.'

'How do I find him? Do you have an address?'

The woman shook her head. 'No, he doesn't want anything more to do with this family.'

'What does that mean?'

'He says we all betrayed Brian. It's not true. We stood by him. There was nothing we could do.'

She began to sob. Ray left her to it.

CHAPTER 47

The sound of a driver leaning on his car horn shook Drake from an uneasy sleep. He had a nasty crick in his neck and his back hurt. He rubbed his eyes and looked at the dashboard. Not even seven o'clock. Crane had been right, he had wasted his time. No sign of Kronnos or Flinders. He climbed out of the car and checked his phone as he walked around in a circle, limping slightly. He had a feeling there was a nerve trapped. His left leg felt numb.

Outside the gates to Magnolia Quays, the van driver had climbed down from his cab to walk up to the gates and peer through. Drake walked over and flashed his badge.

'Can I ask what you're doing here?'

'It's my job, innit?' The man spoke with a heavy European accent that Drake couldn't place. 'All the locks got to be changed.'

'The site is closed. There's a police investigation.'

'Police? No kiddin?' He reached into his leather jacket for a phone. Drake listened while he checked with his office. He didn't understand a word. Well, two words: magnolia, and Apostolis.

'You work for Donny Apostolis?'

The man shrugged. 'He's guvnor now.'

'You mean, he's running this project?'

'Like I say, he the boss.' The man turned away as his phone rang again.

Drake needed breakfast and remembered a café van parked down by the river behind the site. He said a silent prayer and it was answered when he spied the old Commer van sitting there. The man tying on an apron was a sprightly and bearded sixty-year-old.

'Any chance of a coffee? Large, black, no sugar.'

'Machine's just heating up, mate.'

'I'll wait.'

'Something to eat with that?'

'What have you got?' Drake followed the man's finger towards a chalkboard menu. He picked the first thing that caught his eye. 'Fried egg sandwich.'

'Bacon?'

'No, thanks.'

'Coming up.'

Drake moved over towards the river's edge. The gulls were whipping around overhead in that early-morning frenzy of looking for something to eat.

It looked like Donny had taken over the Magnolia Quays project from Thwaite. Cal doubted there was any way of proving that Donny had been involved in the murders, though it wasn't hard to see how that might have worked to his advantage. It would have been relatively easy for Donny to gain access to information about crushed rock suppliers like Dobson Creek.

More immediately Drake was concerned about why Flinders had not shown. There might have been an innocent explanation. On the other hand, he may have decided that returning to the site was too risky. Drake walked back to the van.

'Can you wrap that up for me?'

In the car, he managed to juggle coffee, sandwich and gearstick without causing injury to himself or anyone else. The choice of a fried egg sandwich was not the most practical, he realized, as yolk dribbled onto his trousers. Once he got onto the A4 he put his foot down and punched the coordinates for Kronnos Security into his GPS. It was somewhere out near Heathrow, on an industrial estate in Feltham.

The forecourt was separated from the road by high wire fencing but the gates were open. A line of vans was parked up against the front of a grey two-storey building. A row of windows ran below a strip of dark blue metal sheeting. The same dark blue colour as the vans. Yellow letters with black borders spelled out the name of the company: Kronnos Security Services, along with the familiar zig-zagging yellow line. A huge Emirates jet blotted out the sky as he got out of the car, screeching overhead so low he could taste burning aviation fuel.

Inside the front office a woman was busy behind the high counter. She was stapling sheets of paper together with the concentration of a brain surgeon. Seeing Drake standing there seemed to stress her more. She came over, still holding the stapler. Drake showed her his badge.

'You have an operative by the name of Flinders.'

'Matt Flinders?'

'That's the one. Any chance I could have a word?'

'Has he done something wrong?'

Before Drake could answer, she put a hand to the headset that sat lopsidedly around her neck. Lifting it into place, she said, 'Kronnos Security. How can I help you?'

Drake was impressed by how she had modulated her voice to sound gentler and more inviting. He used the interlude to look around the office. There wasn't much to see. A few large posters advertising their services which included cybersecurity as well as the real thing. A map explained how they were part of a world-wide network of similar firms.

'Sorry about that,' she said when she had finished with her caller.

'I was asking about Matt Flinders.'

The woman tapped her headpiece. 'Could have saved yourself a trip.'

'How so?'

'Well, he's not here. Nobody's seen him for days.'

'Do you have any information about him, home address, that sort of thing?'

'Well, I don't know.' She fingered her headset nervously. 'What's he done?'

'I can't really say.' Drake looked around. 'Is there someone I could talk to?'

'You mean, apart from me? Well, there's Mr Khan, but he's not going to be much help. He's the boss, technically, but you know.' She leaned forward, lowering her voice. 'He doesn't have much contact with the day-to-day running of things.'

'Then who does?'

'Me.' The smile wavered. A hand fluttered to the corner of her mouth. 'Is that egg?' She held up a box of pink tissues. Drake wiped his face.

'It could be a great help if you would let me look at his file.'

'This is something serious, isn't it?'

'Look, I can't tell you anything more right now, but I do need to speak to him urgently, and I don't want him to know I'm looking for him.'

'Gotcha,' nodded the woman. She was watching him closely, trying to decide whether to trust him or not. 'We're not supposed to give out personal details of our operatives.'

'This is a police matter,' he reminded her.

'I know, but people have rights, you know?'

'Course they do.'

'I could show you his file, I suppose, but it wouldn't help.'

'Why not?'

'Because the address he gave doesn't exist.'

Drake was intrigued. 'And you know this how?'

'Just routine. I needed to send him some documentation, for the insurance coverage. I looked it up. Didn't exist.'

'And what did he say to that?' There was no doubt in his mind that she would have confronted Flinders with the facts.

'He said he was between places, staying with friends.'

'Is that not a problem, employees not having a fixed address?'

She smiled. 'It's the way of things, isn't it? Nowadays, I mean, you get all sorts. We had one feller who was living in a caravan. Another had one of those shipping containers.'

'Right. So, you haven't seen him for . . .'

'Three days. Mr Khan is furious. Clients were upset. And he took the van.' She was fidgeting with her headset again. 'Actually, I was supposed to report it.'

'But you didn't?'

'Well, I thought, he's probably just in a spot of bother. He'll sort it out.'

'Bit of a charmer is he?'

'Well, I wouldn't say that.'

'But you were covering for him.'

Her face grew flushed. 'I try to help people. He had a hard time finding work. Why make life difficult for people when you can help them? Live and let live is what I say.'

One of life's homespun philosophers, ready to give the world the benefit of her insight.

'Telephone number?' Cal ventured.

'You're welcome to it, but I've been trying for days with no joy.'

330 • PARKER BILAL

She lifted a Post-it note from her side of the counter and handed it over. Drake copied the number onto his phone. He thanked her while he dialled.

Outside he leaned against the BMW and listened to the disconnected tone. The downside was that he was running out of options here. On the positive side he was more convinced than ever that he was on the right track. As he climbed in behind the wheel he called Crane.

CHAPTER 48

Crane woke early and went straight up to her office to get to work. She rearranged the material she had and began sifting systematically through it again. Not so much looking for what she had missed as trying to get an overall view of what she was dealing with.

What she had learned so far was that Brian Hicks had a brother called Luke. Eighteen months younger than Brian, Luke had never joined the military, never seen action in Iraq. He was, by the look of the material she had gathered on him, a bit of a waster, couldn't really stick to anything. He attended a business college in Wolverhampton for a couple of years, during which he managed to get himself arrested for intent to supply class-A drugs before he dropped out. The case was botched due to the contamination of evidence by the investigating officer. He caught a lucky break. After that he wandered around. Odd jobs here and there, none of which indicated a particular direction. Then he moved to London and started working in nightclubs and bars. Officially he was employed by Belovuk Clubs Ltd. The name, Heather had discovered, meant 'white wolf' in Serbian. That took her back to Stewart's files where she discovered that Belovuk had belonged to one Goran Malevich. Coincidence, or something more?

When Goran died, the company folded and Luke Hicks disappeared again. Now she was hoping to fill in the blanks. She wondered if Drake had been on to something with his interest in the security guard. Could Hicks have started working at Kronnos Security Services under the name Flinders? Someone with access to the security systems could access the building site as well as getting hold of manifests and tracking information.

It might come to nothing, but Ray had the feeling that if she had any luck she would be able to locate Luke Hicks, or someone connected to him. It still felt a little sketchy, which was why she was planning to wait until she had something more substantial before mentioning it to Cal.

She sat back in her chair. What effect might it have to see your brother go to pieces, so much so that he heads back into a war zone with a deathwish? Luke and Brian must have been close. Luke would have felt Brian's pain. Perhaps he grew tired of living in his brother's shadow. Luke had achieved little in life, while Brian had joined the army. He went off to Iraq, got himself into a little trouble and then started earning money as a private contractor. When that went bad he came home, only that didn't bring peace either.

The door opened and Heather stuck her head round.

'Got a moment?'

'Sure, what's up?'

'I just made some nettle tea and wondered if you'd like a cup?'

Ray winced. 'Coffee please, if there's some going.'

'No problem.' Heather made as if to go and then changed her mind, stepping inside the office and closing the door. 'Oh, I forgot. He's here again,' she whispered.

'Who is?'

'The man who won't take no for an answer. Richard Haynes.'

Crane slumped back in her chair. She'd forgotten about Haynes. She recalled him only as a stubborn problem, not even a proper patient, that would not go away. 'I thought I'd made it clear.'

'I know, I know.'

'And you gave him the recommendation to Doctor Marsden?'

'Just as you said, yes. But . . .' Heather lifted her shoulders.

'Well, leave him be and I'll be out in a minute to speak with him.'

'Okay, fine.' Heather gave an exaggerated sigh of relief. 'I'll get you that coffee.'

The door closed. It opened again ten minutes later to reveal Heather holding a tray.

'More biscuits? I warned you about that, Heather.'

'Well, these are special. I made them myself. They have coconut in them. Very healthy.'

'Thanks, anyway.'

'In my humble opinion you worry too much about your waistline. Oh and problem solved.' Heather pointed out towards reception. 'He left.'

'One less problem to deal with,' said Crane. She reached for her coffee as she went back to her papers, acknowledging that, whatever you said about Heather, she did make good coffee.

Brian Hicks was never prosecuted. He came home and went to pieces. How had it been for his brother to witness that? The older brother he had idolized. By all accounts Brian had suffered a breakdown. He was wandering the streets, sleeping rough. Heather had turned up a classified ad from this time (how exactly she did this, Ray didn't know, but it was one of the best reasons she knew for keeping her on). The ad was taken out by Luke in a number of national papers, looking for information about his brother.

How much would Luke have learned of his brother's history? Was he angry, disappointed? He had probably looked up to his older brother. Brian had done everything right. Turned himself into a hero. Gone abroad to fight for queen and country while Luke stayed home.

When Brian returned he was changed. Almost immediately he had gone off again, to fight for the Kurds against Islamic State, one of the most vicious militias the world had ever seen.

Ray knew that the reason this case was so important to her was because Brian had been one of her patients. She had failed him, failed all of them. Was that what she was hoping to find here, some redemption of her own?

The door opened and Crane looked up to see Heather backing into the room. She was moving in a strange, stiff way. Something fell from her hand, spilling its contents on the wooden floor. The shaker containing fish food.

'Heather?' Ray was already on her feet, coming around the desk. 'What is it?'

Heather turned towards her, one hand clapped over her mouth, her eyes wide with horror. Ray grabbed hold of her shoulders.

'What? What is it?'

Heather couldn't bring herself to speak. Wordlessly, she raised a trembling finger and pointed. Leaving her there, Crane stepped out of the office into the reception area. It was silent and deserted. She couldn't see anything out of place. To the right was Heather's desk. The brown leather sofa against the wall for visitors. The coffee table covered in magazines. Between the sofa and the window stood the fish tank with a little heap of fish food in front of it. Crane moved instinctively towards it.

She was almost there when she realized that something was wrong. The fish swam through the brightly lit water, their colours bright, silvery blue, orange, red and yellow.

There was something in the tank. Something that shouldn't have been there.

Ray stepped closer. It was dark and heavy and lay on the little layer of small stones on the bottom. It wasn't one of the rocks they had put in there for decoration, it was a hand. A human hand. The fish were nibbling at it.

Crane could hear Heather sobbing to herself in the office. She moved across the room without taking her eyes off the tank, and reached for the phone on the reception desk. She lifted the receiver to her ear and started to press the buttons when she realized the line was dead. She turned to go back to her office for her own phone, only to find him blocking her path.

'Haynes?'

'Hello, Doctor Crane.' He was smiling.

Crane started to move. She saw the Taser in his hand as it flashed. The wires shot out to pin themselves to her chest. She looked down as the charge jolted through her, then she felt herself begin to fall. Somewhere far off she heard a scream that might or might not have been her.

CHAPTER 49

Drake circled back to Raven Hill. He had tried everything he could think of to put a track on Flinders, but without luck. He'd tried contacting Crane, but it went through to voicemail every time. No doubt she had more important things to do than talk to him. He found Milo in a despondent mood.

'You missed the debriefing. Pryce was asking about you.'

'Don't tell me: he wanted to praise me for my help last night?'

Milo winced. 'I didn't get that impression. Did you sleep in your car again?'

'Why do you ask?'

'You're wearing the same clothes as yesterday and you've got a Bounty wrapper stuck to your sleeve.'

Drake removed the offending item. 'One of these days you're going to make a fine detective.'

'So, where were you?'

'Camped out at Magnolia Quays, hoping to catch sight of our security operative.'

'Right. But if he's the one, do you think it's likely that he'll show up pretending everything is fine?'

'Human beings are creatures of habit, Milo, and besides, he thinks he's cleverer than the rest of us.' Drake tried unsuccessfully to stifle a yawn. 'Did we get anything more on Hakim?'

'That's a negative, boss. Forensics are working on hair and fibre samples but it's slim pickings.'

'And no sign of the missing limbs?'

'Nothing.' Milo tapped a pencil against the desk. Drake was just about to ask him to stop when he looked up brightly. 'I did look into that name you gave me. Hicks.'

'You found his military record?'

'It all checks out. He was in the Light Brigade and he disappeared in 2013, probably in Syria.'

'Right.'

'You knew that?'

'I had a chat with Doctor Crane. She has a source inside the MoD.'

'Might have saved me some time if you'd shared that, boss.'

'You're right,' Drake sighed, hauling himself to his feet. 'I need coffee.'

'There is one other thing,' said Milo. 'Hicks had a brother. Younger than him, never served. Luke.'

Drake stopped halfway across the room. 'A brother? She didn't mention a brother.'

Milo looked pleased. 'Ah, well, maybe the good Doctor Crane is not infallible.'

'Maybe. Is there any way you can get a photograph of this Luke?'

'I can try. Where are you going?'

'I just had an idea.'

'Care to share?'

'I'll let you know if it pans out.'

'And there's everyone saying how secretive you are.'

'Don't believe a word of it. And if Pryce asks . . .'

'I haven't seen you.'

'Attaboy.'

Drake found himself heading towards Paddington. It felt like he had exhausted all the possibilities. For some reason that made him wonder how Crane was doing. The fact that he hadn't been able to reach her on the phone was beginning to bother him.

By the time he reached the mews behind Westbourne Terrace, the sun had slipped across the rooftops to the west and the sunken street was deep in shadow. He rolled to a halt and switched off the engine. The house looked quiet. There was a light on in the upstairs room that was her office. Drake walked over and leaned on the doorbell. He heard the buzz faintly upstairs. A bus rumbled by on the main road. He stepped back and reached for his phone to try once more. This time he heard a phone ringing.

The sound was coming from his left, behind the garage door, the living area. Drake moved over to take a look. There was no sign of light in the glass at the top of the double doors, but when he put his hand to it, the door slid sideways. He stepped inside. There was a low white light coming from the kitchen. The gentle hum of the refrigerator. The punch bag hung motionless in the air before him. The Triumph was parked off to one side where it had been the last time he'd been here. Now he could feel that something was wrong.

Ray's phone was lying at the bottom of the stairs. He climbed cautiously to the first floor. The reception area was dark but for the white light in the top of the aquarium over on the far side. The door to Ray's office stood ajar. As Drake walked towards it, his boots trod on something. He knelt down to take a look and found the thin electric wires that he knew came from a Taser.

Pushing open the door to Ray's office he found it empty. The desk light was on but there was nobody in the room.

Drake returned to the reception area. He moved over towards the window and tried to picture what had happened here. Whoever had done this had been let in. There were no signs of forced entry. They had come in through the front door, walked upstairs, like any client. A client who had then turned a Taser on Ray and taken her out of here.

The hum of the water pump drew Drake's eye to the aquarium to his right. The fish were swimming about as if nothing had changed. Well, not all of them. Several fish were grouped together in one corner of the tank. The light flashed off their flanks, silver and blue. They seemed to be busy with something. When he realized what it was, Drake swore out loud.

'Fuck!'

He was looking around for something to fish the hand out of the water when he heard a thumping noise coming from somewhere further back. Someone was kicking a door. Thump thump.

There was a small bathroom in the corner of the little kitchenette area where they had a kettle and one of those espresso machines that feed on capsules. He pushed open the door and saw Crane's assistant lying on the floor. She had a gag in her mouth and her hands were tied behind her back with a plastic strip.

CHAPTER 50

Drake didn't wait for the cavalry. Heather had no information on the assailant, apart from his name, Richard Haynes, which meant nothing to him. It came to him then, as he was standing there looking at the hand at the bottom of the fish tank, that he knew where to go.

It was some kind of instinct that sent him back to where it all began: Freetown. In the wake of the previous night's clash there was a sense of caution in the air. People hung back in the shadows waiting to see what would happen. Boys in hoodies melted round corners.

Outside the swimming baths there was no sign of the Kronnos Security van where he had seen it the previous night. The high old iron gates were locked with a heavy chain. It was completely dark now and the Klieg security lights on the perimeter fence illuminated the side of the building with cold white light. Nothing moved. He drove to the end of the block and parked the car. Then he sat back in the dark and waited. The palms of his hands felt sweaty. A part

of him would have killed for a drink. Another part of him knew he
didn't want it. Not really.

There was a tap at the window. He looked up to see Jango turning
in circles on one wheel. Drake wound down the window.

'You spying on someone?' the kid asked.

'It's my job, remember, keeping the peace?'

'Right . . .' Jango nodded slowly.

'What's your excuse?'

'Same thing, innit?'

Drake nodded. He jerked a thumb over his shoulder. 'You ever
see anyone going in here?'

'You mean, for a laugh?'

'I mean regular like.'

Jango spun to look up at the brooding, dark building.

'Serious?'

'Serious.'

'Werewolves.'

'Werewolves?'

'Yeah, like crackheads and oddballs. There was a whole family in
there a while back. Runaways. From the war?'

'What war?'

'Fuck do I know? Always a war somewhere, right?'

'So a lot of traffic.'

'Right. Traffic. You being the feds an all.' Jango chuckled at his
own humour. 'That's all done now. They put up the fence. Security.
Cameras and all.'

'Yeah?'

'Yeah. Man comes by. Alarms, Holmes.' He did another twirl.
'You have to know where.'

'You can get me in?' Drake had a feeling this was going to cost
him. He reached into his pocket. 'Show me.'

'Serious?'

'How serious is this?' He held out a twenty. Jango looked at it with disdain.

'That's just sad.'

'Fair play. Same again when I get out.'

Jango considered the offer, then nodded and sped to the corner where he waited for Drake to catch up. He pointed to a gap at the bottom of the chain-link fence.

'You expect me to crawl through there?'

'Nah, man. Just use your bat cape an' fly over, innit.' The sound of the kid's laughter echoed down the street behind him.

Drake shook his head, staring at the tear in the fence.

'Well, it's not going to get any easier,' he said to himself. Then he got down on his knees, rolled onto his back and dragged himself through. Something caught and he felt stitches tearing on his coat, but he was through. He dusted himself down, for all the good that might do, and started towards the house, trying to ignore the smell of dog shit that had now attached itself to him.

The windows were boarded up. Drake's flashlight picked out the sheets of plywood that covered the entrance, now spray painted with tags and graffiti that meant nothing to him. The screws had been removed on one side. Drake pulled the wood out far enough to slip through.

It took a moment for his eyes to adjust to the light. He saw a set of stairs leading up through an archway to a reception area on the first floor. He remembered the place now. A lot of the chequered floor tiles were cracked and missing. Debris was scattered about and there was makeshift scaffolding along one wall.

Feeling his way along, Drake came to another set of steps that led down to the left. There was a faint hum vibrating through his feet. It grew stronger as he moved down and along a small corridor to a door that was ajar.

The boiler room was hot and humid. A row of perspex cases ran along the scarred brick wall. An overhead strip light revealed their contents. At first he thought they contained some kind of smoke. The sides were black and somehow moving. Then he realized what it was: insects. It was so warm in there it could have been tropical. Flies, cockroaches, worms, thousands of them, they skittered over one another, crawling and flapping to try and get out.

Retracing his steps to the entry hall, Drake crossed to the other side and through an archway. Signs built into the wall announced Changing Rooms, Men and Women. At the far end another set of steps led up to the main pool area.

As he came out into the open space, Drake stood for a moment to admire the layout of the interior. It had class even though it was run down. The walls had been defaced with graffiti, slick tags that added their own nonsensical comment to the chaos, obscene diagrams that summed up the contempt with which this city viewed its own history. The tiled walls and wrought-iron suspension beams gave it the look of a seaside pier. It felt like stepping into the past.

Drake's memories of coming here as a child were vague. It could have been in another lifetime. The hoarding outside announced it as a new commercial venture, another shopping centre or mall. The beginning of a makeover that he suspected would wipe the estate off the map. You want people to come in here and spend money, not fear for their lives. This was the shape of the future; take from the poor to feed the rich.

A spiral set of iron stairs led up to a gallery that ran the length of the pool. The upper floor was strewn with rubble, broken bricks, piles of junk left behind by temporary residents. Cartons of food, pizza boxes, crushed soft drink and beer cans, along with winking needles and scorched strips of aluminium foil. Against the wall, a foam mattress, sheets of cardboard. Rat droppings.

Drake's eye was drawn to a flickering light at the far end. It was coming from something just out of sight, hidden behind a wall that extended from the right. The pulsations reflected on the wall, changing colour, suggesting a television screen. He walked slowly forwards.

The television was an old one, battered and grey, resting on a trolley. It was plugged into a laptop that was playing some kind of video. The images, Drake guessed, came from Iraq or Syria. Guerilla fighters in the back of pick-ups, the black flag of ISIS waving as they swept by. The music playing was a stirring war chant. Something ancient and mesmerizing about it. Drake saw children being pulled from rubble, babies, clearly dead, laid out in rows on the ground.

All of this was secondary.

Facing the television set was a hooded figure dressed in an orange jumpsuit. Seated upright in a chair. Whoever it was, they weren't moving. Drake's instinct was to rush forward, but he remained where he was. He listened until he was sure nothing was moving before going round the side of the chair. Crane was bound and gagged. Her head lolled forward to reveal a deep gash behind her left ear. It was a heavy old school chair with a folding desk panel across the front. Her arms were stretched out and held in place with duct tape. As he loosened her gag and crouched down beside her, her head came up and her eyes opened.

'You took your time,' she said, spitting out the gag.

'Good to see you too. You were ahead of me.'

'He was seeing me as a patient.' Crane was trying to catch her breath, impatient to be free. 'How did you get here?'

'Flinders, or Hicks, whatever his name is. I was looking for him.'

'I knew him as Richard Haynes. His real name is Luke Hicks. Is Heather all right?'

'She's fine. Where is he now?'

But Crane was looking past him, towards the television where another scene was unfolding. Drake followed her gaze.

On the screen a man in an orange jumpsuit was being forced to kneel in the sand. Another stood behind him. He reached to his waist and pulled out a large combat knife. He pulled the man's head back, placed the knife to his throat and began to saw away. Drake closed his eyes.

'Get me out of here, Cal.' Crane squirmed, suddenly frantic.

There was a tool box in the corner. Going over, Drake dropped to his knees only to find that it was locked. He scrabbled about to find something to lever it open. A screwdriver lay on the ground. Picking it up he began trying to jam it in under the side of the plastic lid. At the back of his mind, he registered that Ray was mumbling something. Also that the sound coming from the television had turned to martial music. Jihadis singing of the glory of martyrdom. The volume was louder than it had been. Perhaps if he hadn't been distracted, he might have realized that something was wrong, that Crane was speaking through a gag that he had just removed. The delay was only a matter of seconds, but it was enough. As he turned he felt the blow hit the back of his head.

CHAPTER 51

It came back slowly. A bad dream that just kept getting worse. He tried to roll over and found he was unable to. He could smell water. A heavy dampness that made his skin crawl. Then his feet started to lift off the ground. Rising, rising, followed by his legs and hips. His weight tilting, the blood rushing into his upper body. Drake had a bad feeling about this. His feet were bound together at the ankles and attached to a rope that ran up into the air.

'How do you feel about heights?'

As his vision cleared Drake found himself facing the man he knew as Matthew Flinders, the bearded security guard from Magnolia Quays. Luke Hicks. He was holding Drake's telephone. With a snort of bemusement he tossed it casually over the railings. There was a delay before Drake heard it crash to the bottom of the pool far below, splintering into pieces. There wasn't time to think as Hicks began hauling on the rope again. Drake was dragged along the floor, through the dust and debris, broken plaster.

'Me, I've never had a head for heights. Always gave me the willies.' Hicks had rigged up a pulley system between the iron railings. He was grinning as he carried on pulling the rope. 'Sounds like I have your attention now.'

'You don't need her, Luke. You've got me.'

'Course I do. You're a part of this, remember? You fought for this country. You believed in the cause, didn't you?'

Drake grunted as the rope dug itself more tightly into his ankles.

'She has nothing to do with this.'

'That's where you're wrong, I'm afraid. She is the final piece in the puzzle.'

The rope creaked, Drake felt himself lifted a few more inches into the air.

'Why? What's your point?'

The rope slackened slightly. 'My point? You're asking about my point?' Hicks stared at the floor, shaking his head. 'You know what it is. You were there. You saw the betrayal.'

'I have no idea what you're talking about.'

Hicks had the same vacant smile on his face. 'You know what I'm talking about. Don't pretend you don't.'

'None of this has anything to do with Ray. Just let her go and we can talk.'

'Talk? The time for talk is passed.' Hicks gave Drake a kick. The pain knifed through his ribs and he let out a groan. He swung back and forth, grazing along the floor. 'You're as much a traitor as anyone. You betrayed your religion, your people.' Hicks paused to wipe his brow on his sleeve. He squatted down. 'My brother was a good person. He fought to keep this country free of people like you. Sometimes being good isn't enough, right?'

Drake flexed his wrists, checking how tight the rope was.

'Your brother murdered civilians. That's why he was thrown out of the army.'

Hicks spun and pointed in a rage. 'My brother saw what we were up against. He knew. He understood the dangers we faced. I saw them too. I saw people like you. People with no moral fibre. Weak, foolish, corrupt. My brother gave his life in sacrifice.' He brought his face close to Drake's. 'This is not about you, or me.'

'What is it about, then?'

The boot swung again. A dull pain that echoed through his ribcage. Something had cracked. Drake ground his teeth together so as not to cry out. Hicks hauled angrily on the rope and he felt himself jolt upwards. He threw out his hands to steady himself as he was dragged along the floor, nails scraping through the dirt and rubble, on his back heading towards the edge of the gallery.

'No, really, I'd like to hear.'

Hicks let the rope sag. He wasn't finished. He had more to say. 'Don't you think it strange that our closest allies are the most barbaric of all? Isn't that hypocrisy? The Saudis decapitate. They stone people. Well, I'm going to bring that little truth home to people in this country.'

'Cutting off someone's head on television isn't going to change that.'

He twisted from side to side as the ground opened up beneath him.

'Television?' Hicks echoed. 'Try live feed, the internet. The world is going to be watching.'

'Help me to understand.' Drake was clutching at straws. Like a man drowning in air, weightless, swaying from side to side. Talking was his only option. 'Why kill Hakim?'

'Isn't that obvious?' Hicks rolled his eyes. 'You're supposed to be a detective, remember? Hakim is part of the hypocrisy. Whatever happened to integrity? I mean, I get it. The old world has gone. Left and right don't mean anything. We're waging a war on terror and our so-called friends are knee deep in spreading the hatred we're sacrificing our servicemen and women for.'

There was a moment's silence. Drake wondered if he had pushed him too far. Hicks seemed to have tipped over the edge.

'Hakim bought into the whole Salafist dream. He thought we were going back to some purity from the early days of Islam. He didn't get it.'

'So you decided to kill him.'

Hicks paused again. 'I thought he best served our purpose that way. It was the sacrifice he had always wanted to make.' A broad grin broke on his face. 'He got what he wanted.'

'You gave him the Thermite.'

'Yeah, he managed to fuck that one up too.'

'It wasn't his fault the mosque was attacked.'

'No, that was Stephen Moss and his boys. They went in too soon. What can you expect, right? Moronic thugs looking for an excuse to break something.' Hicks knelt close to Drake's head. 'That's what I'm trying to explain. Give me one battalion of men truly devoted to their cause, and I could change the world.' He clenched his fist tightly, lost for a moment in his own failed ambitions, then he straightened up and stepped back. Drake twisted from side to side as the ground opened up beneath him.

'We're wasting time,' said Hicks.

He gave Drake a final kick that sent him over the edge.

CHAPTER 52

Crane heard Drake cry out and then there was silence. She assumed that he was dead, or at the very least unconscious. Hicks was coming back. He paused in front of her.

'Well, Doctor Crane, what do you have to say for yourself? Oh, I forgot.' He pulled the gag away from her mouth. 'You didn't have time to listen to me. I'm sure you've got plenty to say now.'

Ray worked to loosen her jaw. 'I don't think I have anything to offer,' she said finally.

'Oh, come on. Don't be so modest. Just because you failed my brother doesn't disqualify you completely.'

Crane was silent. She sensed that he was trying to provoke her, that he needed her to justify his anger.

'Your brother knew he had done something wrong. He lost control, and he blamed himself for that.'

'Ah, interesting. And so, you were unable to save him from himself, is that your theory? Convenient, don't you think? Like everyone else in this world, all you care about is absolving yourself of blame.' He drew his face close to hers. 'Well, all that ends here and now. You see that camera?' he pointed. 'In a short while the world is going to watch you having your head sliced off, as it happens.'

'You're playing into their hands.'

'Oh, political advice? Is that it now?'

'You're trying to create a war. Hatred, that's what you want?'

Hicks smiled. 'So simplistic. I mean for a woman of your education, your analysis seems a little crude. I don't want war. Think about it. In order to wake people up there has to be violence. People don't understand anything else.'

'You won't solve anything like this.'

Hicks grinned. 'Hello! Some of us don't want to be cured, doctor.' He moved over towards the wall and began busying himself with his equipment.

'That's what this is about, isn't it?' Crane began to laugh. 'It's so simple. You're right, I'm a little slow. Your mother even said so.'

Hicks had ceased what he was doing. He was staring at her.

'My mother?'

'Your brother was the achiever. The popular one. The success. You envied him.'

'You spoke to my mother?'

He was standing in front of her now. Crane looked up at him. She nodded.

The blow was expected. Still, it was sudden and more violent than she had imagined. She felt blood in her mouth.

'What did she say?'

Crane lifted her head, tried to move her jaw from side to side to check if it was broken.

'I think the word she used was pathetic.'

This time he grabbed a handful of her hair and pulled her neck back. 'Liar!' Then he let go and stepped back. The smile was returning. 'I get it. I get it.' He was nodding to himself. 'You're a

part of all this. A part of what I'm up against. Your kind despise me.'
He tapped his forehead. 'I get it. It's all around, all over the world.
We're despised for who we are.'

'The world has moved on, and you can't accept that.'

'You're wrong. I understand better than you think. That's what
I'm going to change. When people see what's happening, where this
is leading, then they'll know.'

'Your faith in humanity is touching.'

'Laugh all you like, but that doesn't change the facts. This whole
country is on edge. They just need the right spark, just a little nudge.'

'Dream on. It's not going to happen.'

'Really? You think you understand human nature because you
have a degree?' Hicks chuckled. 'Look at Tunisia, at Egypt. People
stood up and created chaos. The same thing can happen here.'

'Those people suffered for decades. They had nothing to lose.'

Talking was a way of distracting him, except that Hicks seemed
capable of talking and working at the same time. Nothing seemed
to deflect him.

'We're sleepwalking towards our own annihilation.'

'Who is we?'

He stared at her. 'We've forgotten what made us special.'

She had to laugh. 'Oh, this I have to hear.'

Hicks hung his head, trying to compose himself. When he looked
up the sly confidence had gone and Ray found herself looking into
the face of pure malevolence.

'Brian died because his country betrayed him. They sent good
men off to die. He lived with the guilt of what he'd done, every day
of his life. He was tortured by it. That's what made him go back out
there, that's what killed him.'

'You're confused, Luke. Maybe you need to rethink your
grand scheme.'

'You think so?' Hicks began to laugh. He freed Crane from the chair and pulled her to her feet. He held her upright, then he let go and hit her, a full backhanded slap. She collapsed to the ground. 'My brother deserved a medal for what he did, fighting for our values, our way of life. Instead they threw him under the bus. You were supposed to help him. You failed.' Hicks gave a snort of disgust. 'Why am I wasting my breath? You'll never understand.'

Ray spat blood on the ground. She was struck by the realization that Hicks was beyond reason. He was working within the parameters of his own logic.

'I've got news for you,' she said finally. 'Nobody understands your kind.'

'Keep going. You won't be laughing for much longer.'

As she struggled upright, he turned and walked away.

CHAPTER 53

Drake felt himself falling freely. The walls tilted over him, the ground rushing up from below. Then the rope tightened and he jerked to a sudden halt. The impact snapped through his spine and he swung out like a pendulum into mid-air.

Upside down, he swayed back and forth, wildly at first, before starting to slow. His eyes stayed on the rope above him, listened to the creak of it, wondering if it would hold. Below him was a sheer drop, around six metres down from the gallery, then maybe another four to the bottom of the pool which was empty but for a slick of rusty water gathered in the bottom. Spinning round, Cal felt the rope fastened to his ankles biting hard into his skin. His hands were still bound in front of him. His heart began to settle down, realizing that he wasn't going to die, not just yet at least. The swinging grew less pronounced. He came to a halt over the centre of the empty pool. The rope ran through the iron roof arches and down to the broken railings where it was fixed. He hoped Hicks at least knew how to tie a knot.

A fall from this height would probably kill him. The thing about death was that you never quite accepted it. He remembered that from Iraq. Even when it was staring you in the face. Survival instinct took over, told you there just might be a way out of this. The moment you resigned yourself to your fate you were dead. He'd seen that too.

His eye was caught by something moving, at the bottom of the pool, something with a long tail scurrying around the edge. Another reason not to wind up down there. He craned his neck to look back at the gallery. The television had been switched off and Hicks appeared to be setting the stage for his next performance.

Drake could hear Crane trying to reason with Hicks. He heard the sound of a chair being dragged across the floor. Drake just hung there, wondering what was coming next. He heard footsteps clicking down the stairs. There was silence. He looked across at the rope that ran down from the ceiling towards the railings where it was tied. If he could just swing back across, perhaps he could free himself. It was a long shot, but it was all he had.

He began to swing his body, bending at the waist to gain speed. He wasn't sure what he was doing really, he just knew that he had to do something. Increasing his speed and arc with each pass he began to gain momentum.

Then disaster struck. He lost momentum and began to gyrate in circles. He threw out a hand to stop himself and went spinning round and round until he was dizzy.

'Fuck!' he swore, forcing himself to wait until he slowed and could start again. He closed his eyes and tried to focus on exactly how to move. He was trying to fight the feeling that it was a hopeless plan. Then he opened his eyes, sure he had heard something. He saw a shadow moving up the staircase towards the gallery. Jango waved to him.

'Holmes? What you doin', man?'

'You alone?' The boy nodded. 'Listen, go and get help.'

Jango was still assessing the situation. 'Damn, Holmes! You in for a nasty fall.'

'Just do what I say.'

'No doubt. Chill, man.' Jango rushed up the last steps to the gallery and leaned on the railings. From his pocket he produced a folding knife. The blade jumped into his hand at the press of a button. 'I got it covered.'

'No! Wait!'

'What?' Jango stopped what he was doing.

'If you cut the rope now this is going to end badly.'

'Yeah, right . . .' Jango peered down into the bottom of the pool. 'So, what you reckon?'

'Can you lower me? Slowly. The rope's probably not long enough, but if I swing, I can reach the side there. Can you do that?'

With a shrug, Jango set the knife down and began struggling with the knot. It took forever.

'Look, forget it. Just get out! Now!'

'I've got it!' Jango jerked back as the rope suddenly came free.

Drake plummeted, coming to an abrupt halt as the braking device blocked.

'Whoa!'

'Sorry!' Jango grabbed the rope and started pulling. Drake was grateful Hicks had taken the time to set up a pulley system. The boy would never have been able to hold his weight otherwise.

'Lock it off.'

'Chill, Holmes. It's taken care of.'

Whatever that meant, Jango disappeared from sight, which had to be a good thing.

By now Drake was level with the side of the pool. He was still a couple of metres away. He began to swing again. As he gained momentum, his outstretched fingertips brushed the edge of the pool before he swung away again. Almost!

As he swung back out over the pool he felt the air whistling past his ears. He reached the end of the swing and began to come back across. He was almost there when the tension in the rope went – whatever Jango's skills were, they didn't lie in tying knots. He found himself flying outwards, missing the edge of the pool by a hair's breadth. An inch lower and it would have cracked his skull, maybe even broken his neck. He skidded across the tiles to slam into the wall. The air went out of his lungs and he lay for a moment to catch his breath and assess the damage.

He had landed hard, his ankle striking the edge of the pool with a snap that told him some damage had been done. He struggled to sit upright. His foot stuck out at an awkward angle. He worked to untie his feet. His hands were still bound together. But there was something that bothered him more than any of this, and that was the silence. Where was the boy?

Drake stayed close to the wall, dragging himself along the floor towards the stairs. He had just reached them when he heard Hicks.

'Where are you?' he called. A flashlight beam played over the walls. 'How far do you think you'll get?'

Drake rolled over, sliding back against the wall.

'This doesn't change anything. Nothing at all.' There was a little chuckle of laughter. 'I already told you, this is bigger than you and me. It's bigger than all of us.'

Hicks didn't know where he was. The rope had slid through the roof girder and dropped into the bottom of the pool. He wasn't going to look for Drake. He had other things to do. After a time, Drake heard Hicks move away. There came the sound of the television playing again.

Drake hauled himself up the first step. It was easier than he had imagined. Using his knees and one hand he could pull himself up, one step at a time. The old iron stairs creaked and Drake stopped, wondering if Hicks had heard anything, but the noise of the television was loud enough to drown other sounds out. When he reached the top, Drake poked his head out cautiously and looked to his left. He could see the flicker of blue light from the television that was just out of sight.

Drake discovered Jango lying on the ground. A lifeless form, his head twisted to one side, his eyes open. Hicks had slit his throat with his own knife, which lay beside the boy's body, covered in blood. Cal's head dropped and he closed his eyes. Clenching his fists helplessly, he had to bite his tongue to keep from yelling out. It was a long time since he had felt such rage.

He could hear Hicks moving around but he'd disappeared from sight. He seemed to be trying to string a black banner on to the wall. Drake couldn't see Ray. He estimated she was just off to the right. The banner carried the familiar ISIS symbol, the white ring around a handwritten declaration of faith. As in his previous murders, Hicks seemed to have thought all of this up for maximum visual impact.

Drake crawled forward, sliding as quietly as he could over the floor, the stickiness of Jango's blood on his hands. He reached the wall and peered round. Hicks had set up a camera and lights. Everything was prepared, as if for a film shoot. Crane was on her knees, her eyes covered by a blindfold. She was awake though. What surprised him was how calm she was. Not screaming. Not hysterical.

He pulled himself back as Hicks stepped into view. Hicks disappeared then reappeared, pulling a balaclava down over his face before pressing a remote he held in his hand and addressing the camera.

'Know that none of you will be spared. You cannot hide from Allah's justice.' He pulled a large knife from a scabbard at his waist and grabbed a handful of Crane's hair. Drake stopped breathing as Hicks jerked her head back to expose her neck.

'For too long you have lived a life free of consequence.' Hicks held up a large hunting knife. The blade glinted in the light. 'You attack the House of Islam and now you will understand the price you must pay.'

Drake had Jango's knife in his hand. It was covered in blood and slippery in his hand. If he could get himself upright, then he could launch himself at Hicks. He would only have one chance.

'Fuck!'

Something wasn't working. Hicks put his knife down and began to check the connection between camera and computer. There was some kind of technical glitch. Drake crawled further along the wall to the other side. The pain in his ankle told him he probably would not be able to stand on that foot. Hicks was showing signs of impatience. Agitatedly, he went back and forth between camera and the laptop that sat on the tool box, trying to get them to synchronize. Then he disappeared from sight.

Drake edged along the wall. He wondered if there was a chance of reaching Crane while Hicks was occupied. He reached the end and peered round. Hicks and Ray had disappeared. He was hauling himself to his feet when Hicks stamped on his knee. The pain arched through him. He cried out, then felt himself being twisted over onto his back. Hicks had the big hunting knife again, and from this angle it looked bigger than before.

'Where is she? Where's your little girlfriend?'

For a moment Drake didn't understand, then he did; Jango must somehow have managed to almost free Crane's hands before he was killed. She'd finished the job herself.

'It's over, Luke. Give up now, before you make it worse.'

'You're right, it is over, but not for me.'

Hicks grinned. Then he stepped back and kicked. Drake felt the boot digging deep into his right kidney. A series of kicks followed. Drake tried to protect himself, crawling backwards but Hicks kept at it, his boots thudding into his ribs over and over. Finally, it stopped. Hicks leaned over him, trying to catch his breath.

'This is bigger than you or me.'

Drake wriggled away, rolling onto his side. As Hicks grabbed his shoulder, he spun back and managed to land a hard punch to the throat. It felt good. Hicks staggered back and Drake managed to get up on to his hands and knees. Then Hicks roared back. Another blow in the stomach flipped Drake over onto his back.

'You're going down, Drake, down where you belong, with all the other misfits.'

Over his shoulder, Drake spotted Crane. She hadn't gone for help. Or maybe she had; either way she was back, and Drake was glad to see her.

She was holding Drake's extendable steel baton. She pressed the button and it jumped open. Hicks heard the sound. He turned in time to meet the first blow. Ray brought it down on his collarbone. She knew what she was doing. Hicks dropped the knife. The second blow was to the solar plexus. Hicks bent forward and charged.

Drake wanted to tell her to make a run for it, but somehow he had the idea he didn't need to worry. Crane sidestepped neatly and kicked Hicks's left knee, knocking his leg out from under him. He swore as he went down heavily.

'Bitch!'

Hicks got back up again slowly. Again, she waited for him to lunge. This time she hit him twice in quick succession: the baton to the ribs and then an elbow to the back of his neck. Hicks fell to lie winded in the dust for a moment before pulling himself up using the railings. As he was leaning against them, getting his breath back, Hicks turned away from Crane, and Drake saw his hand going inside his jumpsuit, saw the glint of metal and knew it was a gun. He managed to take one step on his bad leg before launching himself with all his weight. His shoulder struck Hicks low down, lifting him so that his hips struck against the top of the railings.

As he was going backward, Hicks clutched onto Drake, pulling him over the railings. Drake felt his balance tipping. As they went, Hicks loosened his grasp and the two men came apart. Drake heard him scream as he fell. There was a long pause followed by a sickening crunch as Hicks struck the bottom of the pool.

Drake was hanging by his fingers. Luckily it was his good hand, but his other hand was useless and he wasn't going to be able to hold on for much longer. He glanced down and saw the twisted figure lying splayed on the white tiles far below, a tear of blood spreading slowly from his head. Drake felt his fingertips uncurling. When he looked up he saw Crane reaching down towards him, a smile on her face.

'Looks like you could use a hand there.'

CHAPTER 54

Together they limped down the stairs and out into the open air with Ray supporting Drake.

'You know, maybe you should consider doing this full time.'

She looked surprised. 'Is this your way of telling me I'm a lousy therapist?'

'No, I'm telling you . . . Ouch!' Drake winced as she helped him to sit down on the kerb. 'I'm saying that you would make a good detective.'

'How would that work?'

'I don't have a clue. I was just thinking aloud.'

'The private sector? Surveillance, retrieval, missing persons. This is you thinking of a career change?' She sat down next to him.

'Maybe it's time.' Drake leaned back and looked up at the sky. Orange sodium lights blotting out the stars. In the distance he could hear the sound of sirens drawing closer. In a few minutes they were surrounded by flashing lights as ambulances and squad cars pulled to a screeching halt around them and boots clattered to the ground.

'Armed police!'

Cal held up his badge to identify himself. 'Detective Sergeant Drake.'

An excitable officer in full body armour crouched over him.

'I need to know who's inside the building. How many are armed?'

'Two dead males. One adult and one child.'

'Any possibility of explosive devices?'

'I didn't see any, but I would proceed with caution. He was a tricky bastard.'

The man frowned at him, then stepped back and issued orders. As the SO19 team raced inside, Milo came running up.

'You all right, chief?'

'Fine, Milo. Just a few scratches.'

Milo looked sceptical. 'So you got him?'

'We got him, Milo. Couldn't have done this without your help.' Over his shoulder, Drake saw Pryce leaping out of an unmarked black SUV wearing a tactical vest. He didn't waste time but came marching over.

'So which part of keeping me informed do you not understand?'

'Ah, DCI Pryce. Better late than never, I suppose.' Drake looked up at him.

'What did you say?'

'Clear the way!' The ambulance crew came down the steps carrying a stretcher with Jango's body on it. Drake wondered where the kid's parents were. If there was anyone to mourn him. At the far corner, he could see a collection of kids on bikes gathered to watch. One of them lifted Jango's bicycle and pushed it reverently away.

'Consider yourself suspended, Drake. Active immediately, pending an inquiry.' Pryce leaned closer. 'This time you won't get away with it. I shall personally make sure we make it permanent this time.'

'Knock yourself out,' said Drake. Pryce shook his head in disgust, then signalled to his men and headed inside the building.

'What were you saying about going private?' Crane cocked her head.

'Here comes the super,' said Milo.

Wheeler was striding through the crowd. Behind him news vans were pulling up.

'Just in time, as usual,' said Drake. 'Help me up, will you?'

'Well done, Cal,' said Wheeler, grasping his hand. 'Doctor Crane, are you all right?'

'A few scratches, nothing serious.'

'That's good to hear.' Wheeler waved a paramedic crew over. 'Please take care of Doctor Crane, will you?'

They led her over to one of the ambulances parked along the street. Drake watched her go.

'I think she may have saved my life.'

'Outstanding. I told you she was a good 'un, Cal.'

'Yes, sir, that you did.'

They were silent as Hicks's body was wheeled past them.

'What makes a man do something like that?' asked Wheeler.

'You'd be better off asking Doctor Crane,' said Drake, suddenly exhausted. He couldn't claim to understand Hicks's motivation. There was a lot about him that would probably never be explained.

'The point is that you've done an excellent job.' Wheeler was glancing nervously over his shoulder at the line of press, where cameras were being set up.

'Well, you might have to take that up with DCI Pryce.'

'You only have yourself to blame there, Cal. I warned you, and besides, it's not exactly a secret that Pryce had it in for you.' Wheeler was slapping his gloves into the palm of his hand. 'I know you were trying to set the record straight. Wanting to go it alone, put yourself back in the race. Getting out from underneath that business with

Malevich. But this is not the way. Pryce was in charge and there are procedures, protocols. I warned you.'

'I understand.'

'I'll do what I can, but you went behind Pryce's back, which put yourself and others in danger.'

'It's okay, chief. I get it. It doesn't matter anyway.'

'What does that mean?' Wheeler's gloves came to rest.

'It means I'm no longer sure this is what I want.'

Wheeler was aghast. 'You're in shock, Cal. I understand. After what you've been through, the pressure and what with DC Marsh being wounded. You need to take some time.'

'I don't need time.' Drake looked over at Crane. She had finished with the paramedic and had her hands taped up. He longed more than anything to be free of all this. He turned back to Wheeler. 'I feel clear-headed for the first time in years.'

'You're a good cop, Cal. You have instincts.'

'That's what I used to think too.'

'If this is about Pryce . . .'

'It's about all the Pryces.' Drake looked up. 'I can't beat them all. Not in the long run.'

'That's just exhaustion talking, man. We may not get it right all the time, but at the end of the day, it's fair, and it's all we've got.'

'Perhaps that depends on your point of view.'

A row of onlookers had gathered up on the galleries across the square. To Drake it felt like Freetown was judging him.

'Are you serious? Cal, this is all you've got.'

'Maybe that's the problem. Maybe it's not enough any more.'

'At least sleep on it. You're a copper, Cal. It's in your blood. We need people like you.'

'The thing is, I'm no longer sure you do.'

Wheeler's assistant was trying to get his attention.

'The press, sir. They're asking for a statement...'

'I'll be right there.' Wheeler turned to Drake. 'Don't make any rash decisions until we've talked this over properly,' he said, before walking away.

Drake eased himself back down to sitting on the kerb. Crane came over to sit next to him. Together they watched Wheeler step into the spotlights as the cameras came on.

'Just think,' said Ray. 'In a few years that could be you.'

'Somehow, I don't really see it.'

A paramedic was standing over them. 'Should get that foot looked at, sir.'

'Yes, just give me a second will you? Thanks.'

'So, are you serious about quitting?'

'I think it might be time,' nodded Cal.

'Sounds like you've thought this over.'

'It's been a while coming, but I'm sure.' He was surprised that she didn't even try to talk him out of it. 'Once you've lost the faith, it's time to move on.'

'Who's going to catch the bad guys?'

'There are more ways than one to skin a cat.'

'Spoken like a true skinner of cats.' Crane stood up and held out her hand. 'We should talk.'

'Yeah.'

As Drake watched her walk away, he had a feeling it would be sooner rather than later. Then he tilted his head back and looked up at the sky. He wasn't sure, but he fancied he could almost catch a glimpse of the stars, way out there beyond the electric glow.

ACKNOWLEDGMENTS

ACKNOWLEDGEMENTS

Starting a new series is never easy. There are a lot of moving parts that require patience and perseverance. Thanks go out to Euan Thorneycroft for taking the time to read through one version after another. In the end we got there! Also to everyone else at A.M.Heath for their sterling work.

This book also marks the beginning of a new relationship with The Indigo Press. Thanks to everyone at Indigo, including Susie Nicklin, Alex Spears, Michael Salu, Vimbai Shire, and above all to the ever-inspirational Ellah Wakatama Allfrey; thanks for having so much faith in me.